Vivien Ferrars is the pseudonym of a doctor who has spent 40 years promoting healthy consciousness development at two Harvard Medical School hospitals as well as in private practice until she retired to devote herself to full-time writing.

This book is for

Alexander McCall Smith

who tempers lucidity with
kindliness, wit and grace

Of Human Vice and Valour

Vol. 2

Ten Miles and Worlds Apart

by

Vivien Ferrars

AUSTIN MACAULEY PUBLISHERS™

LONDON • CAMBRIDGE • NEW YORK • SHARJAH

A CIP catalogue record for this title is available from the British Library.

ISBN 9781528981996 (Paperback)
ISBN 9781528982009 (Hardback)
ISBN 9781528982016 (ePub e-book)

www.austinmacauley.com

First Published (2021)
Austin Macauley Publishers Ltd
25 Canada Square
Canary Wharf
London
E14 5LQ

The first idea for what was to become *Of Human Vice and Valour* arose from childhood memories of musical gatherings in my parents' home, on the one hand and, on the other, from memories of brief encounters during summer holidays in the Alps and in the Turin countryside. I only wish that I could thank all the real-life people who inspired the totally fictional characters in this novel. But almost a century having gone by, the best I can do is remember the impressions their realities left in me and dedicate my fiction to their vague and elusive memory.

A further inspiration came from Emily Carle's autobiography, *Une Soupe aux Herbes Sauvages,* which provided the idea for the character of Maté. I must also acknowledge Thomas Hardy, Balzac, Verga, Roger Martin du Gard, Galsworthy, Bertold Brecht and Thomas Mann as literary precursors.

More immediately, I want to thank all the people who helped me through the long process of incubation, gestation and final bringing to life of story and characters alike. Among them, I include Vera Bertolini, Raffaello Emaldi and Patrizia Chiesa of *Noste Reis,* who introduced me to the mysteries of Piemontèis orthography and grammar; my dear friend and fellow poet and horseman Bott Ikeler for uncomplainingly reading the endless first draft and suggesting a more prominent role in the novel for the political climate of the time; my piano teacher who advised me on musical details; fellow writer Jennifer Bresnick for supplying moral support and computer literacy where mine failed; long-term friend and fellow scholar Gillian Gill for commenting on the first draft; Roger Vande Wiele for capturing the spirit of the novel in his book cover, and Greta Smagghe for her friendly and unfailing technical assistance.

Last, in terms of process sequence but certainly not for their much-valued contribution, I thank the editorial and production staff at Austin Macauley for actually bringing the novel into the light of day.

To all and all, my heartfelt thanks.

Table of Contents

Epigraph

Give me peace, my harsh thoughts:
is it not enough that Love, Fortune and Death
all war around me, even at my very door,
without me finding other warriors within me?

And you, my heart, are you still as pure as you once were?
Disloyal to me alone, that you go search out
fierce escorts, and become the ally
of my enemies – all too swift and nimble.

In you Love spells out its secret messages,
in you Fortune flaunts its every splendour
and Death replays the memory of that blow

that might break what's left of me;
in you every graceful thought becomes entrenched in error:
and I blame *you alone* for my every pain.

Francesco Petrarca

Chapter One

Pier

On that Sunday in the winter of 1925, the borough church of Santa Rita, on the outskirts of Turin, was full despite the numbing cold. High mass always brought out the best attendance of the week, perhaps because, starting at ten in the morning, it allowed the faithful to sleep in on their one day of rest. Or perhaps it was because its choir, Don Carlo's own creation and joy, lightened the burden of the Sunday obligation.

Stepping aside from the altar for the sung *Kyrie,* Don Carlo scanned his flock. The congregation settled back in the seats with the usual shuffling and nose blowing. In the front pews sat the *Asilo* nuns, for once not in charge of snotty pre-schoolers. Next came knots of devout black-scarved women, heads bowed over praying hands, and after them came the *Figlie di Maria* with their light blue sashes; and behind them family groups, distracted by fidgeting offsprings. And at the very back, the men, hats in hand, crowded together against the portals, as though reluctant to admit their presence in the house of God.

Don Carlo folded his hands in front of him, closed his eyes and waited.

In the choir section, a tenor voice rose in a solo, and the congregation went quiet. Old women wiped away tears. Girls craned their necks for a better look at the handsome singer. Even the men poised by the door seemed, for a moment, to forget the cafés awaiting them just across the square.

The voice was young, now and then a bit tentative on the high notes, but the Latin vowels gave it scope and it quickly gained in confidence. The high notes now soared with the thrilling clarity of a boy soprano, but the lower register had a virile amplitude that was almost shocking.

Handsome blond head thrown back, blue-grey eyes raised to the vaulted ceiling, the singer seemed to offer his listeners a glimpse of heaven. Throughout the *Gloria*, the *Sanctus* and the *Agnus Dei,* the clear, resonant voice rose again and again in a reverent silence.

As soon as the celebrant disappeared through the dark cotton *portières* at the end of the service, the harmonium wheezed to a halt, and the men and boys of the choir gathered up their scores, preparing to file out into the vestry in their turn. Just beyond the portières, they came upon Don Carlo, on the lookout for the singer he wanted.

"Pier," he said, when the young tenor appeared, "come to my office before you leave. I need to talk to you."

None of the choristers spoke, but the ripple of tension showed in the glares that followed the lanky, scruffy youth. Pier shuffled by Don Carlo with a bare nod, shoulders hunched, ears blazing, hurrying to his place at the back of the choir's narrow dressing area. *What can I have done wrong*? he wondered, yanking his surplice over his head. His mind ran through the *Sanctus,* lingering on the spots where he'd stumbled in the past. He couldn't spot anything wrong. Around him, cassocks were hung on pegs, surplices folded and thrust onto shelves as the singers piled into street clothes – coats, scarves, hats and galoshes – all the while keeping up a steady flow of chatter. "The price of wood's up again…"

"Taking advantage of this bitter weather."

"If it were just the price of wood! Everything's going up."

"These days money doesn't buy what it used to."

"Can't make soccer practice this afternoon, I have a *pensum* due tomorrow and Father Giacomo will skin me alive if I don't get it in." The usual after-mass patter; but today the room bristled with a new tension.

"What do you make of the mess in Rome?"

"Ach, the king will stop him."

"He hasn't though, has he? He swore in the *Milizia*, like Mussolini wanted."

"Yes, he did. But he refused to sign the Duce's dissolution of the Chamber."

"Just you wait, the communists will rise. Look what's going on in Emilia-Romagna. They'll take to the streets again."

"Yeah, and be shot to shreds…"

In the bustle, one of the men, struggling into his overcoat, bumped into Pier. "Watch what you're doing, you clod," he snarled.

Pier flattened himself against the wall bench, making himself small, but his fists clenched, his ears burned red hot with an urge to smash his hobnailed boots into the man's gleaming shoes.

Finally, Pier was alone in the vestry. He stretched his old corduroy jacket over his home-spun sweater, fussing with the buttons, putting off the moment when he would have to face Don Carlo, getting more anxious as minutes ticked by, feeling that keeping Don Carlo waiting would only make things worse. Then word would get back to San Dalmass that he had messed up in church, Don Michel would tell his ma, and her lips would pinch into their thin grey line. And his father would sneer, and brother Clot would snigger and gloat.

At length, Pier forced himself out into the vestry and there ran into Battista, the sacristan, trundling in through the cotton portières, busily rubbing his brass candlesnuffer with a checked rag. Catching sight of Pier, the old man jerked his head toward Don Carlo's door, urging Pier on. Resenting his prompting, Pier shuffled to the open office door and stopped.

"There you are, Pier," Don Carlo, still in his vestments, called out eagerly. "Come in and shut the door." He leaned back in his chair waiting for Pier to get to the desk. "Do you remember," he asked, "the visitors we had last Advent?" Pier looked blank. "The older priest," he prompted over his glasses. "*That,*" Don Carlo stressed, cocking his head to one side and expecting Pier to be impressed, "was Don Marco Veronese, the music master at *San Giovanni Battista.*" Pier still looked blank.

"The *duomo,* Pier," the priest cried. "Turin's cathedral!"

Pier blinked, searching his memory: he did remember the long hours of rehearsal last December, and the midnight mass that followed it, the brilliance of the candle-lit church, the heady scent of incense, hot wax and unseasonable flowers. He could still hear the glorious tide of sound as it surged and wove and ebbed and surged again. And he could still feel the thrill of his own voice weaving through it all, now and then soaring above it. Then he did recall the small knot of men, mostly priests, at one of the rehearsals. But what did that have to do with him? Had he done something stupid that evening, offended someone in some way?

Seeing that Pier had remembered, Don Carlo went on, "Don Marco tells me he has a vacancy coming up in his tenor section. What would you say to trying out for it, see if you can suit?"

Pier stared: the priest was smiling. Not scolding. Not blaming. Not angry.

Don Carlo added, "It *could* mean you singing the Easter mass *at the duomo.*" Pier's mouth fell open. Don Carlo smiled, enjoying his *protegé*'s dawning comprehension. "What do you think Don Michel would say to that, eh?"

Don Michel, the *parco* of San Dalmass, Pier's native country parish, the law his ma lived and breathed by, as did most of the womenfolk of *Cioché 'd bòsch.* Pier owed it to him that he was here now, that he'd ever had a chance to sing. Somehow, the old priest had managed to talk his pa into letting him off, grudgingly, the Thursday afternoon farm chores so he could take part in the first communion choir practice. How old had he been then, six, seven? And two years ago, when his pa'd decided it was time for Pier to earn his bread at the new FIAT factory, Don Michel had sent him to Don Carlo so he could continue to sing.

"Well?" Don Carlo asked, snapping his fingers. Pier heard the edge in his voice and muttered, "You mean…" He got no further. Don Carlo laughed, "Yes, you knuckle head! Don Marco wants you to try out for the *duomo*'s choir."

"Me!? But…but…" Pier stumbled, "what about…here?"

"You can always sing here, of course. Don Marco may well *not* take you on." Pier shuffled his feet, twisted his hands in the hem of his sweater. Don Carlo snatched his glasses off his nose and threw them down on his papers. "Don Marco," he explained, "is a graduate of *Santa Cecilia,* the best *conservatorio* in Italy. He can do far more for your voice than I can. Don't you understand? It's the opportunity of a lifetime." He locked eyes with Pier, willing him to grasp what was being offered to him, watched the first gleam of comprehension appear, then gradually grow hot in the lad's eyes. He smiled: he had him now, he could see desire burn in those grey-blue eyes that never looked straight at you. The lad was far too prickly for his own good, but he was hooked now.

Pier stood taut as a spring in front of the desk. He felt his throat going dry, his eyes misting over, a fine tremor shake his limbs. He swallowed hard, angrily: he hated wanting anything this much! But *yes*, he *did want it*! He *would* try for it!

Instantly, his pa's voice sneered in his head, *Go to it boy, make a fool of yourself!* His excitement dissolved. Even here at Santa Rita's, he knew he was not good enough for 'those people'. Oh, they wanted him to sing all right, and when he sang they listened, they even paid him to sing at their weddings and funerals, but he was never one of them, and they made sure that he knew it. And knowing it made him angry and ashamed of his shortcomings. He could read and

17

write all right, his ma had seen to that. But at *La Speransa,* farm work came first. He'd *started* third grade, had learned to add and subtract, but that was it.

"What's worrying you?" Don Carlo inquired gently. He got no response. "You've done so well here in just two years. Look how easily you read a score now. Your voice is a God-given gift. You've got a duty to nurture it. Set aside your fears."

Pier bit his lip, shuffled his feet, had to swallow twice before he could speak, but in the end he nodded: yes, he wanted to try. "But…" he still stammered, "what if I make a fool of myself?"

"How could you make a fool of yourself?"

"I don't know, make some stupid mistake." Don Carlo shrugged.

"If you make a mistake, you practice some more, till you get it right; just like we did with the Sanctus."

"But…" Pier still shuffled, pulled at his shirt collar, "I can't talk to those people! They don't like me, I never know what to say to them."

Don Carlo sighed: *those people.* He knew just what the lad meant: the lad had a wonderful voice, but he was a peasant. He didn't know how to handle social situations. He was awkward, self-conscious with his fellow singers and with the parishioners who hired him to sing at their functions. For all his talent and his good looks, people admired him but kept him at arm's length, like a prized animal in a zoo. Pier sensed their diffidence and it made him angry. This anger made people leery of him and their admiration soon dwindled into… Into what? Don Carlo struggled to name what he sensed, but knew it was there all right. That initial 'not one of us' feel quickly slid into condescension then into contempt. *He doesn't play by the rules,* Don Carlo thought. *He doesn't* know *the rules.*

He stood up and went to stand next to Pier. "It's just because…*all this* is…still too new to you," he said, putting his affectionate arm around the lad's shoulders. "It takes time. But you'll soon learn, living in town, mixing with the right people…" Don Carlo bit his tongue, startled at what he had just said: there it was again, *the right people!* Uncomfortable, he rushed on, "Look how fast you've picked up reading a score, and playing the harmonium. Give yourself a chance…"

"But I don't even know where the *duomo* is!" Pier cried in dismay.

Don Carlo almost laughed with relief. "That's easy to fix," he said, leading Pier to the old map of Turin hanging on the office wall. "Piazza Castello you already know," he said, pointing to the map's centre. Pier shook his head. Don Carlo stared, taken aback: the lad had been in Turin two years and hadn't yet found his way to the centre of town. He pondered for a moment. Then he tapped another spot on the map. "Look," he said, "this is *la* FIAT, where you go to work every day. So you know how to get that far." Pier moved closer and studied the map. Don Carlo tapped a second spot, a clear space with a large blue cross in the centre on which converged a number of roads. "This is Santa Rita's. This is where we are." Pier looked closer, fascinated. Don Carlo traced a finger along one of the roads to a short distance from the church. "And here," he said, tapping the spot, "is Corso Sebastopoli*,* Nina's *Lavanderia,* where you live." He watched Pier taking it all in, then traced the route Pier took each day to go to work. "And this is how you get to *la FIAT.*"

Pier continued to peer closely at the map. He'd never used one before. He'd seen this one on Don Carlo's wall, but he'd thought it just another picture, like all the others on the walls.

Don Carlo went on, tracing yet another route on the map. "The rest is easy, a straight run from here to here." He tapped emphatically on another bold blue cross. "The *duomo,*" he announced, "is right here, just behind *Palazzo Reale.* You go and find it."

Pier continued to peer at the map, nodding, beginning to get excited. "Yes," he said at last, "yes, I'll go."

"Good!" Don Carlo cried with relief. "I'll let Don Marco know to expect you."

"No, don't!" Pier screamed out. Don Carlo stared at him. "Please!" Pier pleaded, shrinking his lanky frame, hands making frightened 'slow-down' motions in front of him, "Not yet, not yet. Just let me… Let me go look around first."

"As you wish," Don Carlo sighed, "but you'll do it soon?" Pier's head bobbed up and down, promising, ears blazing against his light hair.

"It's only three months to Easter," Don Carlo stressed. "If you're taken on, there'll be a lot to learn, new things to get used to, new pieces to practice…" Pier's head bobbed eagerly, eyes on the floor. "So be it then," Don Carlo acquiesced. He sketched a valedictory sign of the cross in the air, walked back to his desk, sat down and resettled his reading glasses on his nose.

Pier bolted out of the room, and ran all the way to the bicycle rack outside the vestry's door.

At home with Nina

Pier straddled his bicycle and pedalled furiously towards home, the bights of his scarf streaming behind him in the wind, his mind spinning with excitement and unanswered questions. Singing at the *duomo* by Easter! Would the music be things he already knew? How different was the *duomo* from Santa Rita's? As different as Santa Rita's had been from San Dalmass? And who else was in the choir, how good were they? Would they think him good enough? One of the men in Don Carlo's choir kept on about all the years he had studied voice at the *Conservatorio*, whatever that was. And *he,* Pier, had never even seen a score before he came to Don Carlo. Would Don Marco still think his singing good enough? But singing at the *duomo* by Easter! The thought was overwhelming. He couldn't wait to tell Nina his news – Nina, the married sister with whom he lived in town.

Then an unpleasant thought sprung up: Lorèns would be there, wanting his Sunday dinner. Pier's pedalling lost its zest. He couldn't tell Nina with her husband there. Lorèns would be sure to say something mean, make fun of it. Pier couldn't go home now, excited, with him there.

With a quick look over his shoulder for oncoming traffic, he struck across the *controviale* and headed towards the wide-open military parade grounds nearby. In the pale winter sun, bare plane trees cast skeletal shadows on the dingy snow.

Dispirited, Pier rode aimlessly along the quiet Sunday streets until well past suppertime. When he at last returned to Nina's place, he found it dark, his sister gone to bed. His pressing need to tell his news would have to wait. Tomorrow, he told himself, after supper maybe, when Lorèns had gone off to his café.

On Monday night, after his workday at FIAT and his usual practice session with Don Carlo, Pier rode home eager to tell his news. The portals to Nina's tenement were already locked, but the pass-through door in one of the panels was still on the latch. He threaded his bike through into the covered carriageway and latched the door behind him. At the sound of the door closing, a curtain was yanked back from the half-glassed door of the *portineria* and a wizened face peered out at him. Pier raised his chin in a silent greeting, but the concierge dropped her curtain without acknowledging him.

He wheeled his bike into the well-like, cobbled courtyard. High above it, a rectangle of night sky glimmered faintly, framed by the four-storied walls. Here and there, dim squares of light from curtained half-glassed doors punctuated the dark. Somewhere unseen, a dog barked, hoarse and miserable. Pier stopped to chain his bike next to Nina's *retro* door, the kitchen-cum-day-room behind her laundry store. Through the thin cotton curtain, he could see familiar shapes. Lorèns at the supper table; on his left, a small, wriggling mass in her high chair, and Nina, shuttling back and forth between table and stove. A child's scream of protest broke the evening quiet, answered by a taunting laugh. It triggered Pier into motion. He unlatched the door and stepped in.

"Why must you always tease her?" Nina snapped at her husband, slapping the bread board down on the table. She turned to Pier, scolding, "Where have *you* been all this time? Practice must have been over ages ago. You know I worry when you're out on your bike at night."

"Don Carlo wanted to talk to me," Pier answered.

"Oh, about what?"

Pier unwound his muffler, threw it down onto a chair with his cap and jacket, sat down opposite baby Anna. Nina set a bowl of soup down in front of him, then sidled onto her chair, her swollen belly keeping her away from the table. She started to spoon food into Anna's mouth. Lorèns slurped up some soup.

"*Minestrina* again," he grumbled, "third time this week." Pier took his first spoonful. "It's good," he said. Nina passed him a bowl of grated cheese. He shook some into his soup and gave it back.

"I can't see why she can't make a proper soup once in a while," Lorèns muttered. Nina snapped back, "I haven't had time."

Pier glanced at the shelves that lined the back wall: he had built those for his sister when he'd first come to live with her, fall before last. Tonight they sagged under the weight of bundles of starched and ironed linens. A bell tinkled in the shop. Nina got up and went to serve her late customer. Lorèns poured himself a glass of wine, drank it down, eyeing his brother-in-law.

"So, what did Don Carlo want with you?" he asked. Pier shrugged, eating his soup. "You in trouble?"

The door from the shop swung open, saving him from having to answer. Nina bustled in, climbed a three-step stool, lifted down a stack of ironed sheets and tablecloths and went back into the shop.

Lorèns poured himself another glass of wine. Anna was gnawing at a crust of bread. Nina came back, paused to enter some figures on a clipboard hung on the airing shelves. "Two still to come," she muttered, glancing at the wall clock. Eight forty: another late closing. She sat down and started to eat her soup.

21

"This soup is cold," Lorèns said, pushing his bowl towards Nina. She got up, dumped the rejected soup back into its pot, added hers and set the pot back on the stove to reheat. "Can't even have supper in peace," Lorèns grumbled, sipping his wine. "Why can't you close at eight like all decent shopkeepers?" Nina didn't answer. She leaned sideways, one hand on the back of her hip, to put another log in the stove. Lorèns glanced at Anna, who had fallen asleep in her high chair. "She sleeps now, she'll keep us up all night," he predicted.

"Oh, let her be," Nina answered tiredly. But Lorèns' knife was already beating an irritable rat-tat-tat on the tray of Anna's high chair, rattling her tin cup and plate and startling her awake.

Lorèns laughed at her frightened howl. "Better now than when *I* want to sleep," he said. Nina picked up the frightened child to soothe her.

On the stove, the reheating soup boiled over, filling the room with a burnt smell. "See what you've done now!" Lorèns snarled. "Can't even reheat a pot of soup." Nina, the child perched on her shoulder, grabbed the pot's handle and dumped most of the soup into Lorèns' bowl, pouring the bit that was left into her own. She sat down, stirring her soup to cool it. Lorèns brought the first spoonful to his mouth and cursed. "It's scalding," he growled. He grabbed the wine bottle and dumped a big slug of wine into his bowl, stirring the new mixture. Pier watched the soup change to a swirling, half-digested purple. On Nina's shoulder, Anna stopped crying. Thumb in mouth, she watched her mama's spoon stir the soup in her bowl. She stretched her hand toward the soup.

"Mmmmm," she cooed.

"Want some?" Nina asked.

"Mmmmmm," Anna repeated, hand reaching. Nina part-filled her spoon, raised it to her own mouth to check the temperature.

"MMMMM!" Anna screeched.

"Here you are," Nina feed the waiting mouth. Anna took in the spoonful, broth dribbling down her chin. Lorèns slurped in his purple-coloured soup. Nina gathered another quarter-spoon of soup, cooing to her child. "Ksksksks…open up, little bird." Eyes glued on her papa, Anna opened up. She took the soup into her mouth, held a moment, then pushed it out with her tongue, splattering around.

Lorèns jerked back. "You think that's funny," he scolded. "Here, have some of mine." He filled his cheeks with the wine-tainted soup and spewed it out between rattling lips. The foul mixture scattered across the table, staining Nina's clean tablecloth. With a taunting laugh, Lorèns refilled his mouth, splattered out soup again, bits of it landing on Pier's cheek, grains of pasta dropping into his glass. Pier sprung to his feet, fist drawn back, his chair clattering to the floor, a deep flush rushing up his neck, face and ears. Nina froze, watching Lorèns fill his mouth for a third sally, dreading a fight. Then the shop bell tinkled. Nina groaned, looked down at her starched white apron now splattered with purple stains. On her shoulder, Anna was again howling.

"I'll go," Pier said, wiping off his cheek. He stormed into the shop.

While he was taking care of the first customer, the bell tinkled again and a second woman walked in; the last customer expected to pick up her laundry today. It was some fifteen minutes before Pier got back to the kitchen to find Nina rocking Anna in her arms. Her shoulders sagged, her face looked haggard. Lorèns was gone. The kitchen was a mess.

"Here," Pier said softly, "Let me take Anna." Nina passed the sleeping child over to him. In her sleep, Anna snuggled deeper into Pier's shoulder, her thumb seeking her mouth. Nina got up and started to clean her kitchen. Neither of them spoke. Pier's news would again have to wait.

First foray downtown

During the days that followed his talk with Don Carlo, Pier went through the motions of his usual routine – ten hours in the shattering machine noise of the joinery department at FIAT, morning and nights, the half hour ride to and from work, then the tense evenings in Nina's *retro;* the practice sessions at Santa Rita's his only relief.

All through that week, he was distracted, hardly knew what he was doing. He struggled to keep from lashing out at mundane irritants in his daily life, the noise of the factory, the men's crude banter, much of it at his expense, the foreman's throwing his weight around, even the *carabiniere* on his beat in Via Nizza; they all triggered his angers, his longings and fears. He wanted to strike out and obliterate all these intrusions, but his talk with Don Carlo held him back. He had to find his way to the duomo and check it out. The task scared him and he hated himself for being afraid. Still, he would go check it out, he promised himself; soon. Next Saturday, after work.

The map on Don Carlo's wall was seared in his brain. Now he traced it once again in his mind: a straight run up Via Nizza, around Porta Nuova, then up Via Roma to Piazza Castello, then left onto Via Garibaldi, right onto Via XX Settembre and there, across the last square, he'd find the duomo.

But everything beyond FIAT was unknown. When he'd come to the city, two years ago, he'd brought with him from his country home an inchoate sense of danger, of lurking evil that had kept him from venturing beyond home and work. He just put in the long days at FIAT, milling the oval frames that, in some other department of the factory, would become rear windows. Ten hours a day, he stooped over his lathe, keeping his mind on his sessions with Don Carlo to numb himself to the soul-killing labour.

On that Saturday morning, he woke up in Nina's kitchen feeling taut, his skin prickly, a fine tremor making his hands unsteady. He picked up his *cafelàit* to drink it and it spilled. At work, he spent his ten hours keeping a tight rein on himself, head down, ignoring the bullying and taunting. He could not afford to be side-tracked, to be caught short on his quota at six o'clock, to give the foreman an excuse to hold him back to make up the slack.

At last, the six o'clock siren split the air. Pier shut off his lathe and started out. "You're *not* walking out on *that* mess!" the foreman yelled after him. "Get back here and clean up that sawdust." Pier gritted his teeth, set his empty lunch pail on the floor and went for a broom and dustpan.

When he at last got out in the open, it was twenty past six. Drifting fog shrouded the January evening. He shivered in the damp cold without noticing it, elbowing his way through the tangle of workers collecting their bikes from the racks, and extracted his. He forced himself to lead his bike as far as the gates, as regulations required. All around him, goodnights were called out, men flung taunts at the women workers, everybody bustling homeward. On Via Nizza, the flood of bikes rumbled westward, while Pier headed in the opposite direction, pedalling towards the city centre. He rode past the long FIAT factory wall, past the railroad's shunting yards, until he arrived at Turin's central station, Porta Nuova. He had never before ventured this far into the city and the sheer magnitude of the scene left him gaping. On his left rose the station's steel and glass building, fronting on one of the city's main boulevards, Corso Vittorio. Here, the bustle was tremendous, all kind of vehicles travelled back and forth on four separate lanes – horse-drawn cabs and drays, trams, lorries, motorcars. Between the central roadway and the outer lanes, a broad, tree-lined promenade was dedicated to trams and pedestrians. On the tracks, trams lined bumper-to-bumper, metal screeching, sparks flying off overhead cables, shooting out from under steel wheels grinding on steel rails as one tram after another stopped, started, clanked its bell to clear itself a path across the constant stream of traffic and turn into a side street. Arcaded, four-storied palazzos lined the corso, housing a string of shops that displayed an unimaginable array of goods in brilliantly lit windows.

And the crowds! Pier had never seen so many people, all *kinds* of people, rushing everywhere, working men and women bundled up against the cold, running for trams. Under the arcades, men in tailored coats strode about their business, or strolled, chatting, in pairs or small clusters, brimmed felt hats and leather gloves keeping the winter cold at bay. Here and there, fur-wrapped women gazed, chatting, into a display window.

Suddenly, an angry metal clamour – a tram's clanking pedal bell – broke out behind Pier. Startled, he glanced over his shoulder: behind his windshield a tram's driver yelled inaudible curses, agitated shoulders jerked as his foot stamped on the bell's pedal, wide gestures waving Pier off the tracks. Hurriedly, Pier scuttled his bike off the track, and a *Via Nizza* tram turned onto Corso Vittorio. To get clear of traffic, he lifted his bike onto the concourse fronting the station. But here, too, he got in the way – this time of an elegant couple hurrying towards a waiting automobile. Their porter, loaded with their luggage, growled, at Pier "Do us a favour, bumpkin, get yourself out of the way." His head jerked toward a crowded bicycle rack next to a newspaper kiosk, and Pier hastily trotted over to it. There he stood gaping at the busy concourse.

On the right end of the station's façade, arriving passengers poured out of its glass and steel doors, suitcases or bundles in hand. On the left end, a similarly encumbered crowd jostled to enter the departures' hall, well-dressed passengers, attended by porters, doing their best to keep some space between themselves and the working-class horde.

Pier was tempted to follow the throng into the station, but somewhere a church bell struck seven. He must get a move on: churches closed at eight. Reluctantly, he wheeled his bike back to the curb. Somewhere out there must be the *duomo*. Drifting fog veiled everything in a dream-like vagueness, but the map in his head was clear. Watching out for traffic, he steered his bike into the carriageway at the right of the central gardens. Deep under the arcades, brightly lit shop windows winked as he rode by. From one of these came a burst of laughter. Pier glanced toward the sound, saw a group of men and women filing into what looked to be a café. *I must come back*, he thought, intrigued. He longed to see more of the life of this place.

Keeping an eye out for traffic, he forged ahead toward the vaguely visible end of the central gardens, where the two carriageways converged into a broad cobbled street, Via Roma, the heart of elegant Turin. Pier rode into it, hugging the right curb. Cars sped by, their wheels splattering his face with oily drizzle. Horse-drawn cabs plied their trade back and forth at a sedate trot. A few minutes later, he found himself in another arcaded piazza with, in the centre, a statue of a man on a high-stepping horse. Pier skirted the monument and picked up the second half of Via Roma. Soon he could guess, through the fog, yet another square and, facing him, an elaborate palace. The map in his head told him that was Piazza Castello. He was nearly there.

His pedalling slowed down, his attention drawn to the alluring shop windows under the arcades – dummies in ladies' and gentlemen's clothes, a bookstore, china and crystal, furs, jewellery and suitcases. In one of the windows, men and women lounged in plush chairs, sipped from stemmed glasses, laughing. Out of the night, a church bell struck the half hour: seven thirty. He had better hurry. He threaded his way across *Piazza Castello* into Via Garibaldi, a narrow street encased between dark buildings. After the many splendours he had just ridden through, Pier found it oppressive. He hunkered down on the handlebar and sped to the first crossroad, remembering that it was close to his destination. It soon opened up into a square and there on the right, atop a flight of stairs, loomed a massive church, wreathed in strands of fog. He had found the *duomo.*

Spellbound by the massive façade, Pier dismounted, led his bike to a nearby lamppost, chained it to it, hurried up the steps and pushed on the massive carved portals. They did not budge. Locked. His heart sank. He had left it too late. Then he heard the faint squeak of a hinge on his right. A pass-through door, of course. Two women emerged, the second stopped to hold the door open for him. Pier snatched his fog-soppy cap off his head and stepped in.

Inside, he stood frozen in awe, the holy smell of incense and hot wax enveloping him in a sense of sacredness. At its far end, the golden doors of the tabernacle gleamed in the light of tall wax candles. The silent nave stretched out in subdued splendour, flanked on each side by a series of chapels. He'd never seen so many: there were no side chapels at San Dalmass, just a long, plain room. Santa Rita's nave had two side chapels, just before the altar railing; they stretched out in the form of a cross. Here each chapel had its own altar, a wealth of paintings and sculptures, marble walls reflecting the discreet gleam of brass lanterns. Pier drew a deep breath. Was he really going to sing here?

He started forward along the nave, peering in at each chapel he passed. A scattering of women still kneeled in the pews, most wearing close-fitting hats, one sporting two pheasant tail feathers; only a few wearing black scarves.

As he ambled along the nave, one by one the women rose, genuflected and left. Pier approached the altar railing. Somewhere behind him he heard a hacking cough. Pier glanced over his shoulder: an old man was hobbling out of the nearest side chapel, he stopped at its railing to lower a brass lamp on its chain, licked his fingers before fiddling with a knob on the lamp's side. The flame subsided to a modest glowing spot.

Pier's eyes turned back to the main altar. Behind him the old man limped noisily to the centre aisle, skirting the first row of pews. At his clip clopping, Pier became aware that his hands clutched his cap in front of him. Hastily, he tucked it under his arm and hid his callused hands in his pockets. The man coughed again, this time right behind him, then a hoarse whisper said, "Time to close." Pier nodded but did not move. After some moments, he swung around and strode down the nave.

"Ahem!" The old man coughed pointedly. Pier glanced back at him: the old man was glowering at him, head jerking toward the altar.

Pier flushed scarlet: how could he have forgotten? He faced the altar again, dropped to one knee and crossed himself. The man nodded approval, showing bad teeth in an unexpected smile. He hobbled along with Pier down the nave, stood on the threshold, watched him start down the stairs, then called out after him, "Come again soon," before closing and bolting the door.

Pier hobnailed boots clattered down the steps. As he stooped to unchain his bike, a deep-voiced bell called eight times from the duomo's campanile. Pier stood transfixed, clutching his bike at his side, the booming sound reverberating in him, stirring him to his depths. Stunned, he gazed back at the *duomo*, filled with awe. And with fear. And with desire. He would be back, he promised himself. Soon. Meet with Don Marco. Tomorrow he'd tell Don Carlo he was ready to try.

Pier discovers opera

Navigating the Piazza Castello traffic towards the bright lights of Via Roma, Pier's mind flew back to scenes he'd noticed on his way in – brightly lit public rooms, gleaming with mirrors, brass, and chrome, elegant people lounging behind vast windows. Back home at *La Speransa,* the brightest light was the oil lamp on the table, corners always remained dark. Nobody lounged. Even after supper, when people came together in the animal warmth of the stable, it was to spin or knit or weave baskets, never to just sit. And the only public place in *Cioché ëd bòsch*, beside the church, was *l'òsto,* across the square from San Dalmass', God and the devil, his ma said, the tavern where men hung about when they should have been working, drinking, arm wrestling, or shouting themselves hoarse in endless games of *la mora.* And Lorèns' café in Santa Rita wasn't that different, just a hole in the wall and men drinking and swearing over cards. And women…well, he'd never seen women lounge, let alone in a public place. Even Nina, who owned her own shop, never lounged.

He sped down *Via Roma,* eager to get to the café he had glimpsed under the arcade of the prancing horse. Once in the square, he found that the bronze horseman's raised arm pointed him straight to the café. He drew up to the curb near the base of the nearest arch, leaned his bike against its pillar, then peered furtively around its granite edge. There they were, the revellers, seated at a window table. Pier's eyes rose to the brass legend above the café entrance: *ËL CAVAL ËD BRONZ*, the bronze horse.

Inside, a waiter in black pants and short white jacket approached the window table carrying a tray, set it down on a serving stand and presented a gold-necked bottle, cosily swaddled in a white napkin, to one of the men, who glanced at it and nodded approval. Fascinated, Pier watched a weird ritual unfold: the waiter's thumb pressed against the cork; a pop, a slight puff of vapour, then foam surged from the bottle's mouth; but, before any could spill, the bottle tipped over a glass, the foam half-filled it, fizzing, clearing. A quarter twist, a lift and a swift shift to the next glass. The pouring ritual, repeated glass after glass, etched itself in Pier's mind - the precise pouring, twisting and lifting. Behind his pillar, Pier watched, impressed by the neatness, as the white foam rushed to the brim, but never ran over. At his side, his hand mimicked, unbidden, the waiter's precise motions.

Then his attention shifted to the revellers. They, men and *women,* daintily grasped their glasses' stems, reached over the table to clink glass to glass, sipped, then nodded appreciatively to their host before taking the next sip. Pier gawked: that was *not* the way one drank wine, for wine it had to be. At *Ël Cioché ëd bòsch,* men drained their glass right off, then banged it on the table. And women…well, wine was never wasted on women.

By and by, the café's patrons began to leave, alone, in pairs, in small groups; they dispersed, still chatting, calling out greetings, promising to meet again soon.

Some disappeared down side streets, others boarded the few motorcars waiting by the curb, still others made for the line of horse-drawn cabs stationed at the square's corner. One small group, two couples, strolled past Pier on the way to the cabs, silk gowns rustling, a whiff of perfume teasing his nostrils as they passed him. He heard one of the men call out to the driver, *"Teatro Regio,"* as he climbed in. Horses strained, wheels rattled on cobblestones, inside the cab a woman's laugh tinkled in the night. The woman in grey furs, Pier thought.

He scrambled onto his bike and followed the cabs, keeping well back, hugging the curb. The cab drove up Via Roma, heading for Piazza Castello. There, it joined a queue leading up to a green and gold marquee. Pier hung back and watched. Under the marquee, big glass double doors stood wide open, despite the chill and the fog. A stream of people in evening clothes ambled in through them, crossed the glittering foyer and vanished through velvet portières. Outside, green and gold uniforms bustled to each arriving vehicle, opened doors. The cab he had followed was next. Pier watched as the two men emerged, white scarves against black cloaks. They turned to hand the women down. Again, the rustle of silk under fur wraps. Gloved hands. Rings; glitter on a wrist. Arm in arm, the two couples entered the theatre, greeted in the foyer by a portly man in a black suit who bowed and ushered them the velvet portières. Then there was a lull in the stream of theatregoers. Pier looked around, spotted the billboards by the entrance. From where he was, he could see pictures but could not read. He could read the elegant golden letters above the marquis: 'TEATRO REGIO, the Royal Theatre'.

Pier edged closer, keeping to the shadows, but his attention was soon diverted by the arrival of a long-nosed moto-car, yellow with black fenders. The portly little manager rushed out to greet the newcomers. Intrigued, Pier watched closer. Inside the car, four people could be dimly seen. Ushers sprung to open the car's doors, stood back deferentially, as a gentleman emerged and the manager rushed forward, hand outstretched in welcome, *"Professore!"* he cried, shaking the man's hand. A second man emerged. Beaming, the little manager exclaimed, *"Commendatore! Che piacere!"* He bobbed, smiled and pumped. A box of chocolates appeared in the open car door, then a cane, then opera glasses, one by one handed to the usher in attendance. *"Eccellenza!"* the little manager cooed, *"Che onore!"* He bowed, outstretched hands fluttered toward the other, stopping short of contact. The honoured guest responded with a tilt of the head and a brief smile, and then turned to hand out the car's last passenger. At her appearance, the theatre manager all but swooned in an ecstasy of excitement. *"Contessa!"* A gloved wrist rose out of the fur cape. The manager bowed over it to place a reverent kiss an inch above the crimson silk.

By and by, the tide of theatregoers dwindled, then stopped. Two ushers released the velvet portières and they swung closed. Heavy, padded doors were closed over them. Two more ushers walked the outside glass double doors closed, then stopped by them inside, on the watch for late arrivals. Inside the foyer, the portly little manager rubbed his hands to shake off the chill of the night.

Outside, Pier watched on. After several minutes, he caught a faint sound of music. Inside the glass entrance, the two uniforms left their post and joined the group of clustered mid foyer. With a quick glance right and left, Pier wheeled his bike to the nearest billboard. Photos, two glamorous women, three men, with names under them: Anna Boffo, Soprano and Antonio Cavalli, Tenore. Pier blinked: *he* sang the tenor part in the choir, and the baritone ones as well. He could sing either, though he sometimes still stumbled in the high range.

From inside, muted sounds swelled and fell. Pier strained to catch the sound of singing, but all he heard was music. He stood back to study the billboards. On a second billboard, he saw a group of people in strange clothing, standing in tortured postures with exaggerated gestures. Their open mouths made it clear they were singing. Was singing here at all like singing in church?

After a brief silence, the muted sound of music reached him again and then, tantalising, arose the sound of singing voices. Pier listened eagerly, wishing he could hear more clearly, catch the words.

He stepped out onto the square and scanned the theatre façade for a place where he might peek in. Nothing. He stepped back some more and looked again, right and left. Was that an alley he saw under that arch?

He wheeled his bike along into a narrow side street that flanked the theatre. But here, too, every opening was shuttered up tightly, the sound of music no clearer. He lingered on in the drifting fog, uncertain what to do. Then further down the narrow street, a swatch of light appeared for a moment across the wet cobblestones, and for a moment the singing voices came through clearer. Pier hurried toward the invisible door. As he bumped his bike along the cobblestones, a match flared up, followed by the red glow of a cigarette being lit, then a man coughed. Heart racing, Pier, still a few paces away, called out, *"Bon-a sèira."*

(Good evening.) He hurried closer, his heart battering his ribs, his throat going dry, making him cough.

The cigarette tip glowed once more, then, came the laconic response, "*Sèira.*"

Pier rushed into speech to engage the smoker. "Is this door to the theatre?" he asked awkwardly.

The man took a long drag at his smoke, broke into a bout of coughing, before answering, "The *stage* door, yeah."

Pier's chin jerked up, pretending he knew what the other meant. He stood in the dark, clutching his bike, trying to figure it out. He thought back to the billboards he'd just seen, those strange people on the second billboard: that must be what they did on stage. He nodded his new understanding. By the closed door, the cigarette glowed and dimmed. Pier cleared his dry throat and took a step closer. "I've never been in a theatre; what is it like?" he said. There was no response. He couldn't let it drop at that, he must say something more, draw the man out. And then, to his horror and shame, he heard his voice speak out loud the thought in his mind. "How much does it cost to go in?" A rush of heat swept through him like a flash from an opened furnace. His face flared up red, and the hair on his nape stiffened. By the closed door, the man scoffed, then cleared his throat and spat. In the dark, Pier felt his mocking gaze rake him up and down, from fog-soggy cap to gnarled hands, to cracked, hobnailed boots. The cigarette glowed one more, then came the scathing response.

"More than you make in a month." On the handlebars, Pier's hands clenched into fists, ready to strike. He loathed the man. Shaking with rage, he sucked in his breath, open-mouthed, struggling to control himself. Then, deliberately, he loosened his grip, expelled every last bit of air from his lungs and breathed from the diaphragm, the way Don Carlo had taught him to do when he got overwrought.

Just then, from inside the theatre came an exchange between two voices, a man and a woman's, a baritone and a soprano. "A baritone," Pier said out loud.

"And what would *you* know about baritones?" the voice in the dark scoffed. Pier's cheeks burned.

"I sing in the choir," he retorted. To his shame, his voice was shaking. *This man has no right*, he raged. But then he steadied his voice and added, "At Santa Rita's."

He had succeeded in getting the pleading whine out of his voice, but it still shook. He took another deep breath. "And, come spring," he continued, "I'll be singing at the *duomo.*" He stopped short, appalled at himself: that wasn't true. It might never come true. He hadn't even talked to…

He heard his own voice, now firm and clear, say, "Don Marco."

Against the dark wall, the cigarette glowed brighter. "At the *duomo,* eh?" The man puffed, squinting to get a look at him in the dark. "With Don Marco! Well, well…" Breathless, Pier nodded. "And you've never been in a theatre? Ever heard opera?" Pier shook his head in the dark, but the man got the message. "Come on then," he said, taking a last drag at his smoke and flicking the butt into the gutter, "but be quiet as a mouse." He pushed the door open and stood waiting. Stunned, Pier didn't move. "Well," the other snapped, "you want to come in or not?" Pier dumped his bike against the wall and scrambled up the steps. The door closed soundlessly behind them.

Inside, a fantastic tide of sound assailed him. The doorkeeper, a finger to pursed lips, grabbed Pier's sleeve and dragged him along twisting corridors to a spot from where he had a partial view of the stage and a bit of the orchestra pit. On stage, a bass was arguing with the contralto. Then the full orchestra took over.

Pier stood transfixed: he'd never heard such sound. At Santa Rita's, the harmonium got loud at times, but the voices always dominated. Spellbound, he listened and watched. When the music surged, his heart pounded, something caught at his throat, tears burned down his cheeks, time dissolved into ecstasy. When the tenor or the baritone sang, their parts seared themselves into his brain.

A sudden tug on his sleeve broke the spell. "Now you must go," the stage door man whispered, "before they come backstage." He hustled Pier back to the stage door and out of it. "Now," he said, mocking, "you've been inside a theatre." The door closed noiselessly.

Alone in the night, a dazed Pier retrieved his bike, straddled it and took off. He had travelled several blocks before he realised he did not know where he was going. He stopped, struggling to regain some semblance of reality. He ran his handkerchief over his face, surprised to find it wet with tears. He shook himself, panting, trying to call to mind the map on Don Carlo's wall, the route from FIAT to Piazza Castello. Next, he tried to regain his bearings, guess where he was in relation to the square with the bronze horse. He thought he'd travelled vaguely in that direction when he'd left the theatre and it had been a short ride. He should be able to sort himself out. Then a church bell struck the quarter hour and he thought he recognised its tone, the bell he'd heard on his way in earlier in the evening. He headed towards its fading tones.

Some fifteen minutes later, he was back in Porta Nuova's gardens. From there on, he was sure of his way. He pedalled fast down Via Nizza. Out of the night, another church bell struck twelve. *There'd be hell to pay with Nina*, Pier thought, for being out so late. But it was well worth it: he had discovered opera.

Chapter Two

Home is where they must always take you in.
Anonymous

Lena

Lena stuffed her week's wages into her skirt pocket and gave it an affectionate pat: twelve *sòld* more than last week. Her mama would be pleased. Lena smiled to herself: bringing her earnings home to her mama was one of her pleasure. The first time, she recalled fondly, she'd been just a tiny tot.

The smile faded. She recalled that her papa had been in a temper for weeks. He had stormed at all hours of day and night, in and out of their two rooms at the back of the decrepit farmyard that housed a half dozen families, a disused farm at the edge of town, the city had swallowed long before she was born. The fights were all about money. She understood that even then. Her papa wanted money. And when he came home drunk and there wasn't any, like on that awful night, he'd hit anyone within reach, Pinòt, Mama, even herself. And *that* was startling because usually she could sweeten his mood by being nice to him. But not that time. That time, she had not been able to calm him down, not for weeks. It had gone on and on and nothing she could do made any difference. Then Pinòt had run away.

That too had been about money. With Papa, it was always about money. Papa wanted the money Pinòt had earned that week at the butcher's, and Pinòt wouldn't give it, so his papa went after him with his belt and Pinòt knocked him down, and then got scared and ran away. So, her papa had laid into her mama. He had beaten her so badly that she'd just laid on the floor like she was dead. That scared her papa and he, too, ran away. After that, the courtyard women came around. Her mama had been taken to the *San Gioann* Hospital and had been there for a long time. And even after she came back, it was a long time before she was strong enough to work. And by then, her job at the paper mill had

34

gone to someone else. The yard women tried to help, even sharing their food. But they, too, never had much to spare. Then one afternoon, Lena overheard them talking in the courtyard as they sat at their needlework under the medlar tree.

"Poor Gioana," Lena heard one say, "and she thought she'd married well."

"She had," another affirmed, "Simon's family's well off. They own a wholesale wood and coal business. Even had their own home in *Madòna 'd Campagna*. And one day, it would all have been Simon's."

"That's how it goes with drink…"

"If you ask me," put in another, "Simon was never much for work."

"Yeah, can't blame his father for giving up on him."

"… And she with that little girl to care for…"

Lena blushed at the memory. The women's talk had turned her world upside down. She'd been shocked and hurt that they spoke of her as "that little girl". It still hurt now, years later. That was how she'd found out that things weren't as they should be with her papa. She'd always been scared of his temper, but she'd thought him just like the other men in the yard. They all got drunk, yelled at the kids and beat the women. She'd seen them bruised often enough. But that "Poor Gioana" and the women's pitying tone that afternoon changed everything. It even changed how she saw herself – now a useless burden on her poor mama, who was still too weak to be up all day, let alone go out to work.

The feeling of being useless had made Lena miserable. Day after day had she racked her brains for some way not to be a burden, and then one day she recalled the time, the previous summer, her mama had taken her along to the paper mill where she worked. It had been a long walk, out of Lingòt and across the fields, the heat shimmering above the road in the distance. She remembered a big white house they had passed, set back in its own gardens, a *biancospino* hedge in bloom all around it. They had stopped to watch the white geese float lazily on its pond. And then she'd remembered the lady she'd seen looking down at them from an upstairs window.

That scene now became the seed of a plan. One morning, she waited for her mama to go in for her necessary morning rest. At that time, she knew that the yard women would either be at work or busy indoors at their chores, so she could sneak out of the yard unseen. Once out on the road, she ran all the way to the big white house in the fields and stopped, breathless, by the gate in the *biancospino* hedge. It was closed and she had to stand on tiptoe to reach the bellpull. And

35

after an eternity, a lady had come to the door and looked down, surprised, at the tiny girl at her gate. "Yes? What do you want?"

At her workbench, Lena smiled, remembering how tall and forbidding the woman had seemed to her then. How old had she been, seven, eight? No, before that, before she'd caught *ël grip* and had been taken to the *San Gioann*. That had been just weeks after she'd started school, so she must have been six. She shuddered, remembering how scared she'd been in the hospital, away from her mama, alone in a quarantine ward full of sick strangers, and her mama not allowed to come to her. Once she'd seen her mama through the tiny glass pane in the locked ward door, waving to her. But they didn't let her come in.

Tears welled up in Lena's eyes. She swiped at them, without stopping work, with the back of her fingerless glove, and brought her mind back to the day, long ago, when she had got her first job. She'd stood on the road, feeling very small, and blurted out: "I want a job." And after a moment of surprise, the lady had come to let her in and led her to the kitchen to shell peas for the cook. At lunchtime, she'd been given bread and cheese and a bowl of black cherries. That afternoon, Lena had left with two *sòld* in her pinafore pocket and a job for the next day, helping the maid polish the brass. She'd run all the way home, clutching the outside of her pocket to be sure not to lose her two *sòld*.

At her workbench, Lena now patted the week's wages in the pocket under her apron, its small bulk already warm against her thigh, vastly reassuring. Things were so much better now that she and her mama were alone in their two rooms. At that time, long-ago, everything was frightening. The night she'd put her two *sòld* in her mama's hand, expecting her to be pleased; her mama had cried, then kissed her and hugged her until it hurt. That was the first time since her mama had gone to the hospital that they had milk and butter.

A smile played on Lena's lips. She wound the next three-inch-long wire into a neat little loop, the two bights parallel, and threw it into a tray on the bench. Next to her, a middle-aged woman picked up a handful from Lena's bin, capped each blunt end with a clasp, fastened it with a hand press, snapped the safety pin, closed and tossed it into the finished bin. All down the bench, women worked in pairs. Throughout the workshop, seated at different workbenches, women working in pairs made safety pins of different sizes.

Across from Lena a thin plain woman teased: "There she goes again, like a cat that's got at the cream. What is it this time, all those boys who winked at you last Sunday?"

Good natured, Lena answered: "No, I just feel like smiling."

"What? No reason?"

Lena shrugged: "I don't have to have a reason. I just feel like smiling."

Further along the bench, a finisher joined the banter: "And if you look like Lena, all that smiling pays off." Along the table girls tittered, drawing the attention of the overseer at a nearby workbench. He took in the nudging elbows, the suppressed guffaws, and Lena's face, bent low over her work, blushing. He ambled over.

"What's going on here?" he asked sternly.

Lena looked up at him and smiled. "Ach, nothing," she said. "They're just teasing me again."

The man smiled back at the bright brown eyes gazing up at him, lingering with pleasure next to the buxom eighteen-year-old.

From further down the bench, a middle-aged finisher called out: "There, you see? It's working right now!" The women snickered up and down the bench.

"You leave her alone," the foreman scolded. "Lena's a good girl. You work as hard as she does, maybe you'll have me smiling at you as well."

"That'll be the day!" the woman rebutted. "Not as long as I've got *this* on my face!" She wiggled the mole near the tip of her nose, its three dark hairs quivering inquisitively, like a mouse sniffing the air. The bench roared. The foreman waggled a warning finger at the women and strolled away to a nearby workbench.

Soon, the chatter at Lena's bench resumed. A girl down the bench leaned over and shot a loud whisper at Lena: "So, how much did you make this week?"

Lena's answer stirred up a disbelieving chorus: "What, that much!"

"Never!"

"Why, that's more than last week!"

"Not again! You'll get us all in trouble: you'll give the boss ideas and he'll raise our piece work quotas, and then we'll all have to scramble."

Lena just smiled: she did not scramble, her fingers just worked fast without her having to think about it, even in the cold.

The six o'clock whistle pierced the air. Saturday night: another week done. By the coat rack, the chatter continued. Lena listened, her mind on her own tomorrow, her beloved Sunday routine: sleeping in a bit, *cafelàit* in bed next to her mama. Then to the nine o'clock mass together. And then at midday, their pasta dinner, shells, like always on Sunday. She liked shells. She wondered what kind of sauce her mama would make this week. In the afternoon, they'd walk together, stop by the *Cinema Lingòt* and look at the next week's offerings – a new film each week and a farce, usually *Ridolini*. Tomorrow they wouldn't go in. They'd been the Sunday before last, and they didn't go to a film more than once a month. Maybe they'd stop and visit Cichin-a, Mama's friend around the corner, on *Via Passo Buole*. Lena smiled to herself. *A sa sta bin con mia mama,* she thought. Life was nice with her mama. No fights, no violence and no fear. They worked and shared what they earned. It was more than enough now with their two jobs. Lena patted the pay packet in her pocket once more, pleased to feel it there. She walked out into the wintry dusk a happy girl.

Pier goes back to the theatre

His first foray into downtown Turin left Pier tingling with excitement. He had caught a glimpse of an unimaginable world – a world of pleasures, of zest for life, the antithesis of his family's oppressive endurance. And all that time this world had been right *there*, on his doorstep. The fervid life of the city called loudly to him, lured him back. He longed to be part of it, to immerse himself in it. He craved to *belong* to it.

A plethora of images haunted him, glimpsed window displays glittering under deep arcades; the sparkle of nightlife in the cafés; the rustle of silk, the opulence of furs, and the lingering memory of a lady's scent. All these things, all leading at last to the Teatro Regio, crowded in and stirred him to a fever pitch of longing. He was itching to be back *there* again, inside the great opera house, bathed, drowned, dissolved in the tide of sound and light and *life* that was happening *there*, taking place right there on that stage. And beyond the stage, the footlights, the orchestra pit and the audience, sensed rather than seen. He envisioned the front of the house as a vast gilded cavern, an enrapt audience – the golden people he had watched filing in, fêted and revered, under the theatre's marquee. He knew he was not one of them, would never be. But he longed to be where they were, to be *near* them, breathe the same air, feel their aura and catch the scent of their life.

That first night, riding back to Santa Rita, excitement kept him taut, tingling. It kept him awake on his couch in Nina's dark, cold kitchen until just before dawn. And then, still sleepless, he'd suddenly sunk into deflation: he'd never be part of that golden world. He'd never belong, never fit in. Even at Santa Rita's he was…well, he was the stray dog that had snuck in with the sheep. He felt tolerated, but never included.

He had finally drifted into a restless sleep only when the rectangle of glass in the courtyard door had already begun to take on a bluish hue. And shortly thereafter, Nina, clambering into her kitchen with a bundle of firewood, woke him up. "What, still asleep?" she scolded, "You'll be late for mass." But then she took a look at him and grew concerned. "Are you ill?" she asked. "What time did you get back last night?"

Pier sat up on his couch, yawning. The kitchen's chill made him shiver. He drew his top blanket around himself like a shawl. At the stove, Nina removed the iron rings from one of the three cooking holes and rattled her poker between the bars of the grate to get rid of yesterday's ashes. Pier glanced at the kitchen clock: seven thirty: he did have to get going. Nina struck a match and held it under the kindling in the stove's grate. A modest flame flared up, casting flickering lights on the walls behind her. Listlessly, Pier got up, hanging on to the blanket tucked around him under his arms. His free hand scratched his tousled head.

"So, what time *did* you get back last night?" Nina asked again. "I waited up till after eleven and you still weren't here. Where did you go?"

"I checked out the duomo," Pier muttered, morose. "Like Don Carlo told me to."

"You did! And…? What happened?"

Pier shrugged: "I got lost."

"But in the end, you found it? What happened? What's the place like?"

"Big," Pier said with a shrug.

"Did you see Don…what's the name, the choir master?"

Pier shook his head. His sister handed him the water she'd heated for him and he poured it into a hand basin for the usual Sunday wash.

"I didn't go to see *him*. I just went to check out the duomo first."

"And…?"

Pier snorted into the water in his cupped hands: he hated water in his nose, ever since the day he'd almost drowned. Now the warm water soothed him. He lathered up the farm-made soap between his palms and scrubbed his face, neck and ears. Then he dropped his blanket to his waist, shed his undershirt and lathered his armpits. Eventually, the splashing stopped.

"So, when you're going back?" Nina asked, handing him the towel she'd warmed by the stove for him.

He shrugged, buried his head and neck in the towel. "Don Carlo will tell me when Don Marco wants to see me."

He got into the clean shirt Nina had set out for him on a chair. She poured him a bowl of hot *cafelàit*: he was not due for Communion this morning, so he could have his breakfast before mass.

On his way to Santa Rita's, Pier thought guiltily of Don Marco and the duomo. They had become a means to what really drew him to the city: the theatre and the nightlife.

The thought shocked him: up to two days ago he had hardly dared to hope that he might be taken on, become part of the exalted world of the cathedral, and now... He flushed, utterly confused, feeling two-faced, ashamed. At the same time, part of him hovered on the edge of elation: he *had* to get back to the theatre, to the city, to the magical world he had half-seen last night.

That noon, after the last mass, he stopped in at Don Carlo's sacristy and hovered in the open doorway, in his usual way, not stepping in until Don Carlo called him. Then he took one step into the room. "I've been," he said. "Now I can go see Don Marco."

"Good boy!" Don Carlo cried, getting up and walking around the desk. "Well done," he said, laying his hands on Pier's shoulders for a congratulatory shake. "I'll call him this afternoon. No time to waste: Easter is just weeks away."

Pier's audition was set up for seven thirty the following Tuesday after Pier's workday at FIAT. On Monday evening, Don Carlo coached Pier one last time on the selections for his audition, all familiar pieces Pier had sang many times at Santa Rita's functions. Pier went through the practice in a strange mood, at once eager and indifferent. So much so that, on parting, Don Carlo noted, with a valedictory pat on the back, "You seem less nervous about this than I am! Go and do your best. Make us proud."

And Pier did: right after the audition Don Marco scheduled Pier's first individual training session, stressing that Easter was only weeks away.

But Pier felt deceitful. He knew that he had put his heart and soul into his singing for a private reason: the duomo had become just a means to an end. And that very same night, right after the audition, he headed for the Regio's stage door.

Pier at *La Speransa*

Pier was already half awake when *Santa Rita's* bell struck five on Sunday morning. He had begged off singing this Sunday because his pa wanted him home to help with the winter copsing. The bell's last tone dissolved into silence. Pier became aware of the usual clip clop, clip clop of the kitchen faucet, dripping in the stone sink in the corner. Outside, all was quiet.

He lingered awhile, completely covered, reluctant to leave the warmth of the kitchen couch that, at night, served as his bed. But he knew time was a-wasting. His eyes then his nose peeked out tentatively from under his covers. A nipping cold made him duck back. He wished he could doze off again, wait for Nina to come down and light the stove, get breakfast ready. But Pa wouldn't take kindly to his getting there late.

The *retro* was still pitch dark. He was thirsty; hungry too. He craved his breakfast. But today was Sunday and Nina would not be down yet for a long time, not before seven. And he had to get going well before that, no later than six thirty, if he was to get to *La Speransa* by daylight. For a moment, the thought crossed him that he could get up now and light the wood stove so the kitchen would be warm for his sister when she came down. If he did, he could have some hot *cafelàit* before setting out, a definite incentive. But Lorèns would grumble at lighting the stove this early on a Sunday.

He peeked out of his covers again. The glass in the upper half of the courtyard door was still pitch black, with no hint of dawn. It would be hours before Nina came down. He curled up tighter in his warm cocoon, giving up any thought of making a fire or getting a warm drink. But sleep failed him: today his pa expected him to work in the woods with him and Clot – a cold and unrewarding prospect. Pier hated the cold; and copsing the *Parpaja* woods was his *Pa's* job; *he* got paid for it, and his ma saw precious little of any money ever paid to Pa. And Pa was a harsh taskmaster, nothing ever good enough for him, and hell to pay if he wasn't satisfied.

The clanking of a tram rolling to a stop reached him from out on the *corso*. The first run of the day: time was getting on. Pier reached overhead in the dark, feeling for the dangling string that switched on the kitchen light. With his legs lingering in the warmth of his bed, he grabbed the heavy flannel shirt draped across a nearby chair, pulled it on and topped it with a heavy wool sweater. A drink of tap water, a jacket stretched over his sweater, a muffler, cap and mitts and out he walked, quietly latching the door behind him, noticing dense ice

41

crystals on the glass pane: winter lace, his ma called it. He glanced up at the sky: the narrow rectangle defined by the courtyard's buildings was just beginning to pale. He had to get a move on.

Outside, the street was still deserted. Even Corso Sebastopoli, around the corner, the tram's terminal, was quiet this early on Sunday morning. Just three empty trams at the start of the line. No drivers or conductors in sight. *Probably in there,* Pier thought wistfully, glancing into the café where Lorèns spent his evenings, *getting their cafelàit.*

He straddled his bicycle and sped away along the broad boulevard that had once been a carriage road linking the city's royal palace to the royal hunting pavilion of *Stupinis*, some ten kilometres away. Soon, he was out of *Borgh Santa Rita*. A few more small clusters of houses, and the corso dove into open country. Two bridle paths, one on each side, flanked the roadway, sheltered by now bare plane trees. Beyond this, snow-covered fields stretched away into the distance, rambling lines of willows or mulberry trees marking the course of irrigation ditches, the usual boundaries between now dormant fields. Overhead, a crow called in flight, *"Caw, caw, caw,"* making its way through the lightening sky. Out of nowhere came the faint call of a bell, summoning the faithful to early morning mass. *It must be close to seven,* Pier thought, pedalling faster, his breath condensing to small white puffs as soon as it left his mouth.

The sprint warmed him up, but the cold hurt his face and hands. He tucked his nose into his muffler and slipped his left hand under his sweater, into the warmth of his waistband. He was now approaching the hunting pavilion. Two long stable buildings, one on each side, flanked the *corso*. On the bridle path across the road a string of eight horses walked out to morning exercise, their hooves spurting up snow and ground in dirt. Pier hurried on, soon leaving them behind. Straight ahead, inside the wrought iron palisade that enclosed the pavilion's inner grounds, the imitation Versailles palace spread out vast wings. On its roof, a bronze stag with a good rack of antlers proudly sniffed the air. Here the *corso* split into two lanes that circled the palisade and enclosed the castle in two arcs of majestic plane trees. Beyond the palace, on the far side of the enclosed park, the two lanes converged to form a broad country road, a long pale ribbon flanked by woods, that narrowed with distance until the woods on either side closed upon it in an unbroken horizon.

Pier travelled some distance up the road on the right side, and then picked up a shortcut through the forest, a rough track deep in snow. He walked, pushing his bike against the drag of deep snow. It would still take a good half hour to get to *La Speransa*. Around him, the winter woods lay silent, with now and then a soft scurrying under the snow, or a flutter of wings among skeletal branches. Pier trudged on. He had just reached *Parpaja,* the ancient castle-like manor house that guarded this quadrant of the king's playground, when a loud flutter broke out on his left: he had startled a flock of pheasants; one long-tailed male and five females, crashed their way out of cover and took to the air. He stood watching their flight, wondering if Pa's shotgun was stashed in its usual hideaway.

He walked on, leaving *Parpaja* behind. Today they would be working somewhere in its domain, wherever Pa hadn't got to yet. He scanned the woods around him, looking for signs of copsing done. From the East, a low sun found its way through the bare trees and dazzled his eyes. Pier hastened his pace: he was nearly home, but it was getting late.

The first ray of sun found *La Speransa*'s stable door propped open with a bucket of fresh-drawn water. Chicken strayed out into the sunshine, cautious heads checking right and left, hesitant, a foot in the air, clucking. Inside, a cow screamed a full-throated protest. A barrow loaded with soiled straw bedding filled the doorway, its wheel biting into frozen gravel. Behind it, Maté's bloated face, purple with effort, squinted into the morning sun. Morning stables was well under way. Below the kitchen window, Vigin-a worked the pump handle until water plashed into the bucket under its iron spout.

Maté glanced at her as he passed on his way to the manure pit. "Get a move on," he barked, "Can't you hear Gioia's getting wild? Get in there and help your sister finish the milking."

"I'm getting breakfast," Vigin-a whined, pumping.

"That's your ma's job. You get in there and do as you're told."

Maté walked on, pushing his barrow toward the pit in the far-right corner of the yard, beyond Maria's kitchen garden. Vigin-a shot his back a baleful look and trudged her full bucket into the kitchen. From the stable came another of Gioia's grating screams.

In the kitchen, Maria glanced up from the breakfast *polenta* bubbling on the wood stove at the noise of Vigin-a coming in through the yard door. "Gioia needs milking," she said. "You'd better go help Tilde."

Vigin-a rolled her eyes: Ma couldn't stand Pa, but always took his side. She yanked open the door into the stable and clattered down the two stone steps. At the far end, Clot was pitching a last forkful of cow manure into an almost full barrow. Tilde, Vigin-a's younger sister, had just set down a one-legged milking stool next to Gioia, preparing to milk her. She heard the clatter of wooden clogs and glanced over her shoulder. "Bela's done," she said, washing the cow's udder before milking. "Can you start on Stèila?"

Vigin-a kicked another one-legged stool toward the third cow. It startled her and she kicked out, wheeling her read quarters in the stall's mucked-out floor. Scolding her, Vigin-a perched on her stood and started to wash the udder. Behind her, Clot was now cleaning out the first pigsty, emitting a strident whistle between his lower teeth. The tuneless, high-pitched noise drove Vigin-a wild. She glanced balefully at him but knew better than to provoke a squabble. The stiffness around her discoloured left eye reminded her of an argument with him that had led to her pa's latest blow. She glowered, on the brink of yelling at her brother. But just then, her pa walked by the stable door, wheeling his empty barrow toward the tool shed. She clenched her teeth, shoved her thumb into Stèila's tit and yanked down. Stèila gave a sharp kick and flailed Vigin-a's head with her tail. Vigin-a slapped the cow's flank and hissed, "You, stupid cow!" She yanked hard on the tit, and milk squirted into the pail.

Once more, clogs clattered on the kitchen steps. Maria came down with a bucket of pig slop and made for the sties. Eager snouts, snorting and grunting crowded around her. Maté's bulk loomed in the doorway, blocking out the sunlight. "Here comes *tò preivòt,*" he sneered, jerking his head over his shoulder towards the farm's gate.

Maria's lips tightened into a thin grey line. She heard the scorn in Maté's taunt, "*tò preivòt,*" (your little priest.) It infuriated her, but she would not let him bait her. She peered through the barred window: Pier was just then wheeling his bike through the gate. He stopped to latch it behind him. Even across the farmyard she could see that his face was dark with cold. "Just in time for breakfast," Maté added, taunting. She watched Pier stoop down to pat the watchdog, Taboj, who, belly to the ground, whined, yanking at his chain to get closer. Maria scooped up her bucket and hurried to the kitchen to get breakfast on the table. A pot of milk sat on the side of the stove. She moved it to the centre to bring it to a quick boil, and watched a thin skin form on the milk, then crinkle, then swell into a dome. She lifted the pot off the stove before it spilled over and set it on a brick shelf nearby. The milk dome subsided, leaving a puckered skin on top. Maria lifted it off and set it aside in a saucer before spooning ground chicory into the boiled milk, then stirring to blend it in. Behind her, the yard door opened, and Pier stepped in, blowing on his hands to warm them.

"There you are," Maria said with a quick glance over her shoulder, "come warm yourself up."

Pier stepped up to the stove, fitted into the old fireplace, no longer in use since, the previous year, Minot, Maria's oldest living son, had brought his mother the stove. "*Coma a va?*" he asked (how is it going?).

Without answering, Maria handed him a bowl of the chicory brew which at *La Speransa* passed for *cafelàit*. Pier sat down on the hearth shelf, hands cupped around the bowl, enjoying the warmth. Maria bustled about, getting the breakfast to the table. Pier glanced at the saucer on the brick shelf. "Is nobody eating that?" he asked. Maria handed him the saucer. Two fingers picked up the cooling milk skin and threaded it into his mouth. One by one, the rest of the family filed in, the morning chores done.

"Did the fowls get their grain?" Maria asked, with a glance over her shoulder at the assembling family.

"I fed them," Tilde answered, approaching the stove. Maria handed her a board heavy with the steaming polenta.

Clot drifted over to the brick shelf by the stove and peered at the empty saucer. "Who's eaten my milk skin?" he whined, a baleful eye on Pier.

The family sat down to breakfast. Maria laid down two pitchers by Maté, one of cold milk, the other of chicory *cafelàit*. Maté spooned a big mound of polenta onto his plate and drowned it with milk. "Hurry up," he said digging in, "it's dark by four in the woods."

Pier glanced up at the clock above the hearth's head beam: it was still stopped at 3:20. Then the faint voice of San Dalmass' bell came over the winter fields, calling to the second mass of the day: it must be getting on for eight.

Right after breakfast, Maté, Clot and Pier headed out toward the section of the *Parpaja* woods they were to work that day. They walked in single file, each man's long tools bundled up on one shoulder, the short ones in a sack, bumping on their backs with each step. Pier walked last. He also carried the lunch sack his ma had handed him as they moved out, its top tied up into a knot. For some ten minutes they retraced Pier's morning route, then Maté veered off to the left. Another twenty minutes and they came to a wide bridle path. Here, Maté dropped his tools on the verge. He grabbed the lunch bag from Pier, fished out the bottle of wine packed in with their lunch. He uncorked it and took a long pull. "We'll start here," he said, sizing up the day's work as he re-corked the bottle. A few steps into the oak grove, he jerked his chin at Pier. "You get up there. That dead limb needs to come down." Pier dropped his tools at the foot of the oak. "And mind you don't injure the bark below," Maté lectured. "First cut under, second cut from above."

Pier nodded: he knew how to prune off a branch. His pa had set him to pruning by the time he was five, and up on tall trees by seven, because he claimed a light body worked best among the high branches.

Pier tied a generous length of rope to his pruning saw and shinned up the oak to the dead branch, then reeled up his pruning saw. Down below, Clot had started work on a second oak with Maté looking on. Pier eased his blade under the dead branch, close to the trunk, and started to shove and draw. The sawing noise drowned the voices below. He concentrated on his task – shove and draw, shove and draw. But his mind was on Teatro Regio, and soon, in his head, singing voices engaged in passionate arguments. Some three inches into the upward cut, he disengaged the blade from under the branch and eased it into place for the top cut, snug to the trunk, so the bark could heal the cut. Somewhere nearby another saw whined as it bit into wood – Clot, somewhere in his oak. He could hear no other tool at work. He scanned the woods below: Pa was gone.

Pier returned to his task and soon his mind began to replay the *Kyrie* from the Easter Mass he was to sing at the duomo. Every now and then companionable sounds of pruning nearby reached him – the rustle and crash of a small branch falling, the snapping of dead twigs breaking off as Clot moved to a new position in his tree. Pier's branch at last crashed to the ground and he climbed down from his oak. Clot was chopping down a broken alder that had fallen across the bridle path. Pa was still nowhere to be seen.

Pier moved on to his next task, trimming branches that the heavy snow cover had bowed too low over the bridle path to clear a mounted man's head. The winter sun was now at its highest and Pier could feel its pleasant touch on his shoulders as he plied his pruning pole. His stomach rumbled with a sound of sloshing water. It must be past lunchtime. He glanced up and down the path, scanned the surround woods for his pa. A squirrel sat up on a fallen tree, watching him. High in the canopy, a blackbird broke into a series of thrills and whistles. Pier spotted him, iridescent in the sunshine, high up in a nearby oak. Pa was nowhere to be seen. Clot called out to him. "Give a hand here." Pier walked over and took hold of one handle of a two-man saw.

"Know where Pa went off to this morning?" Pier asked his brother. Clot only shrugged, drawing sharply on the saw. For the next fifteen minutes, they plied the unwieldy blade back and forth through the stubborn hardwood, their own harsh breath and the screech of the saw absorbing them, becoming the whole of their world.

Then suddenly, the morning peace was shattered by a shotgun blast, then a second one, in quick succession. It exploded somewhere out of sight, bounced east, west, north, south, echoes confusing its tracks. From the undergrowth, birds broke cover and flew away screaming. Under the snow panicked rustles spoke of ground animals scrambling for deeper shelter. The woods held their breath, hearts pounding. Startled, the brothers froze in mid-pull, taut over their tree trunk, eyes locked in inquiry. Neither spoke. Then Clot lowered his eyes and hauled on his saw handle. Pier got the message: best not to inquire. He fell into the saw's rhythm.

It was another good twenty minutes before Maté reappeared. Blank faced, he stood on the path, inspecting his sons' morning's work. Without speaking, he shoved the now empty wine bottle at Pier. Pier did not move. "Go fill it at the Donkey's Nest," his pa ordered, naming a nearby spring. Then he stepped off the path and sat on a stack of logs. "We'll knock off for a bite."

Pier went off towards the spring, invisible in the woods. With a quick glance over his shoulder to make sure he was out of sight he drained the bottle of its last few drops of wine. The scarce draught fuelled old angers. His face flushed scarlet, his ears burned. Once more, he glanced back: he'd rather die than let his pa see that he could still get to him.

He found the spring and squatted on its verge to fill his bottle. Shaking with anger, he thrust the bottle into the icy water gurgling between snow-covered banks, and watched it fill. His mouth was parched, his throat tight. He brought the bottle to his mouth and drank deeply. The cold hurt his chest, but it also calmed him. His stomach sloshed again. He dipped the bottle into the spring again, watched it refill.

When he returned to the bridle path, Pa and Clot were sitting on the logs, munching on bread and cheese. From somewhere up the path, came the sound of hoof beats, approaching fast. Soon a horseman appeared cantering toward them: chestnut horse, brown corduroy jacket, peaked hat. Pier recognised the *Parpaja* game warden, responding to the gun shots. He rode scanning the woods right and left. He reined in his horse sharply in front of Clot and Pa.

He knows, Pier thought. His stride changed; he swung his bottle as he walked, trying to appear nonchalant.

"Oi, Maté," the warden barked out, restraining his prancing horse. Pier handed his pa the bottle. Munching, Maté lifted his chin in greeting to the mounted man. The horse danced sideways in the snow and was sharply reined in. "Seen anyone?" the warden asked.

The man's tone told Pier that he expected Maté to lie. Maté bit into his cheese and shook his head.

"But you heard the shots," the man insisted. Maté nodded, munching on. The mounted man looked hard at Maté, then shifted his scrutiny to Clot, then back to Maté. Clot kept his eyes down and his mouth full. The warden turned to Pier. "You? Seen anything?" Again, his tone disbelieved the answer.

Pier said, "Heard two shots."

Maté shoved bread and cheese at him. Pier bit into his bread.

"Did you *see* anyone?"

"No one as shouldn't be here."

"So, you did see something. What *did* you see?"

Mouth full, Pier mumbled, "Birds squawking, flying off."

The warden sat on his horse, glowering at the stolid faces ruminating stale bread and cheese on the stack of logs. The horse pranced again and the man pulled him up sharply, keeping his eyes pointedly on Maté, shook his crop at him and hissed, "You mark my words, Maté Venturi: I'll get the bastard one of these days." Maté nodded, munching. The man jabbed his spurs into the horse's flanks, and it shot down the path, spurting up soiled snow.

Pier watched him canter away. *He knows,* he thought again. From his perch on the logs, his pa took a long pull from the water bottle, his face stolid, his eyes on the departing horseman, watching him get smaller and smaller down the lane. But behind the stolid, blank face, Pier recognised the familiar smirk. His eyes fell to the ground, ashamed and helpless.

When they returned to *La Speransa,* the afternoon light had already faded to a purple dusk. The yard gate squealed, setting the guard dog barking and tugging at his chain. A feathery smoke rose from the snub brick chimney. Whiffs of mist hovered in patches over the frozen fields, like uncertain ghosts. Through the window above the pump, Pier saw the women moving about the dimly lit kitchen – Ma stooping over the stove, Tilde setting the table, Vigin-a placing a bottle by Pa's place. The three men stowed their tools in the shed, then Maté and Clot went through the stable and into the kitchen. Pier went back into the yard, to Taboj who was straining on his chain, whining and wagging his stump of a tail. Pier squatted down and tousled the dog's head, laid his cheek to its muzzle. The dog whimpered, his tongue flickered over Pier's face. The kitchen door flew open and Vigin-a yelled out, "You, out there! Hurry up, Pa's waiting."

Pier stood up with one parting scratch to the straw-coloured head and walked into the house.

"Sit down," Maria said over her shoulder, "supper's waiting." Pier found his place at the table.

"You'd better hurry," his ma said. "You've still got a two-hour ride back in the dark."

"It's not that bad," Pier answered, mulish. Ma always made it sound like Turin was at the world's end.

At the head of the table, a fresh batch of polenta steamed on a board, a pitcher of milk next to it. Maté helped himself then pushed the board towards Clot, on his right. One by one, the others helped themselves. Maté had started to eat. Maria was still busy at the stove. Nobody spoke. Slurping and the clatter of tin spoons against earthenware bowls filled the room. Maria came to the table carrying a shallow crockpot. She set it down by Maté, then went to her own chair at the foot of the table. Maté poured himself a third glass of wine and drank it down. He drew the crockpot closer and lifted its cover. An enticing aroma wafted down the table, bringing back to Pier's mind those morning's shots in the woods: what had Pa bagged? What would be hung up to season in the hidey-hole at the back of the hay loft? Would Ma get to cook it? He doubted it. Most likely Pa would sell it *a l'òsto* and disappear from *La Speransa* for as long as the money lasted. Eyes on his bowl, Pier dipped his spoon into his *polenta e làit.* From the end of the table his ma asked, "Have you seen Minot?"

Pier shook his head. His older brother worked in town as well, but he lived in *Niclin,* some half hour's ride from *Santa Rita.* The six days workweek didn't leave much time for visiting. Besides, Pier's duomo duties took a lot of time, and he spent as much time as he could at the theatre. But, he reminded himself, he'd better not mention the theatre around his ma. To her everything about the city was evil, and a theatre…well, *that* she was sure to think a den of sin.

But the *duomo*… He was eager to tell them about that and he still hadn't had a chance. *Them* meant his ma and his sister Tilde. He'd never tell anything to his pa, or to Clot, or even to Vigin-a: *she*'d want to hear all right, but there was no knowing what she would do with it.

A shark kick struck his ankle under the table. He looked up, caught Vigin-a's eye, her chin directing him to the head of the table before she hastily looked down again. Pier noticed the dark bruise on her cheek.

At the head of the table, Maté dipped the spoon into the crockpot, spreading its appetising smell. Pier's mouth filled with water. He watched his pa frown, lift the spoon above the pot, glower, then look up. "*Chi ch'a l'é mariasse ancheuj?*" (Who got married today?) he asked, glaring at the shut-down faces around the table.

Eyes down on her bowl, Vigin-a muttered under her breath, "*Un pò 'd sautissa a fà nen nòsse.*"(a bit of sausage doesn't make it a wedding feast.)

Next to her, Clot snickered, smelling trouble in the making. Head down, Pier shot a glance at his ma. She was sitting rigidly upright. Even in the dim light, he could see that her cheekbones burned red. Her eyes looked back at Maté, defiant, her mouth open for rebuttal. Next to him, Pier felt Tilde tremble. He felt her shift in her seat and guessed she had nudged her ma's knee under the table.

For a moment, his ma held his pa's glare, then her mouth snapped to a pinched grey line, her eyes still on Maté, no longer seeing him, staring straight past him. Then her shoulders sagged. When she spoke, her voice was faint, deflated. "You've earned a bit of meat today," she muttered.

Maté glared at her. The elusive smirk Pier had seen that morning as his pa had watched the game warden ride away, hovered for a moment on his face, then he taunted, "*E tò preivòt a l'é 'mbelessì.*" (and your little priest is with us.)

Pier froze in his seat, his knuckles turned white on his knife and fork. But there was nothing he could do. He mustn't start a row. *He* could leave, but his ma and sisters couldn't. Vigin-a's black eye spoke clearly of what would happen.

At the head of the table his pa answered her, "Aye, that *we* did. But then," he added, "there's no reason for *you women* to have any." His eyes ran over the stunned faces, daring them; then he dragged the crock pot up to his plate, and tauntingly dumped three more pieces of sausage onto the three he'd already taken.

After a moment, Clot reached for the pot, drew it up to his plate. He threw a sly glance at his pa's plate: six pieces. He could get away with three. He helped himself, then pushed the pot across the table to his brother.

Pier stirred about in the tomato sauce, counting the pieces left: four. His ma and his sisters still hadn't got any. He took one piece. At his left, Vigin-a hissed under her breath: "Take it, take it all. *He*'ll just get it later." His ma gave him a subtle nod, *Go ahead, take it*. He took another piece. Tilde, Vigin-a and his ma spooned sauce over their polenta. Two pieces of sausage remained unclaimed. Nobody spoke.

When Maté was done eating and had finished off the bottle of wine, he rose, belched and stretched, stepping over to the coat rack by the door. With deliberate, provoking slowness, he put on his cap and hunter's jacket and strolled out into the night. Clot clattered to the stable door and down the stone steps. The women bustled about, cleaning up after the meal.

"Hadn't you better get going?" Maria said to Pier. "It's a long ride in the dark."

Pier shrugged. "The moon will be out soon." He didn't want to leave yet. He wanted to sit in the warm stable and tell them his news, the changes about to happen in his life in the city. But Vigin-a was taking her time with the dishes and Ma was messing around in the pantry. Only Tilde, busily putting things away, was eager for a chat.

"And how is Nina doing?" she asked, wiping a dish dry.

"Don't you go calling her that," Maria scolded from the pantry, "her name is Catlinin." She came back into the kitchen, a notebook in her hand. While the girls finished the washing up, they asked about Nina's life in *Santa Rita*, about baby Anna, now almost two, and about Lorèns' salesman's job. When the kitchen was neat again, Vigin-a went out to the stable with an armful of un-spun wool. Maria sat down at the table to make an entry in the notebook where she kept track of the piecework done for *L'Asia*, the prosperous farm that had long been a source of income during the winter months.

"Can I help you, Ma?" Tilde asked before leaving the room.

Maria waved her off. "You go ahead. I'll come down by and by."

Tilde stepped down into the stable with Pier in tow, crossed the ten feet or so of brick-paved area, to the mound of clean straw at its far end. Beyond it, the mule and cows ruminated in their stalls. Right next to the kitchen steps, stood a carding machine. Vigin-a sat at it, powering it with her foot. With every swing of its upper jaw, the carder swished and squawked, releasing a cloud of wool dust. Vigin-a fed handful after handful of wool into its maw, coughing as the dust irritated her throat. A few feet beyond her, a spinning wheel sat idle, its spindle half-full. Maria would soon return to it, once her record keeping was done. Clot was nowhere in sight.

Pier walked past the swept area to the mound of clean straw, piled high for the night's last bedding check. He threw himself down on it with a sigh of relief, and one of his ma's sayings came to his mind: "More straw, less currying." He smiled. Ma had a saying for everything. He looked down the line of stalls along the back wall: Gioia and Stèila's hides were spotless, but Bela's rump already sported a large brown plaque, where she had laid down in her own manure. From the stool where she sat knitting, Tilde saw his smile and smiled back, then she scurried over to join him, bringing her knitting with her. At the clatter of her clogs on the bricks, guinea pigs and rabbits scurried out from under the straw, burrowed in the stall bedding. Hens sleeping on the stall partitions squawked briefly, then resettled. Tilde snuggled down with her knitting at Pier's feet. "Now," she whispered, leaning closer, *"conta, conta."*(Tell me, tell me.)

Pier glanced toward Vigin-a. The moan and tear of her carder roared in the quiet stable. Pier drew closer to Tilde. "You'll never believe what's happened to me," he begun.

"What, what?" Tilde urged eagerly, leaning closer still, "did you sing at another big wedding?"

Pier shook his head, dismissive: big weddings were no longer a big deal. He'd been to a *theatre;* he'd heard famous singers sing *opera*. He stopped short: he couldn't tell Tilde about opera. Ma would sure to be hear of it. One couldn't keep much from Ma. He must stick to the duomo.

And so, he told her about Don Carlo's introduction, about his first ride downtown; about his try-out with Don Marco. And, since then, his three nights a week of coaching at the duomo, after work; and his continuing practice at *Santa Rita's*. And, come next week, the rehearsals at the duomo for the solemn Easter Mass.

The kitchen door swung open. Maria stood on the top step. "In you go then," she said. Her black and white cat, tail erect, took her time down the three steps. Maria closed the door behind her and went to her spinning wheel. She glanced at Tilde and Pier on the straw. "You really need to get going," she told Pier. "Didn't you hear San Dalmass' strike nine?"

"I heard it," Pier said.

Tilde cried out, "Ma, Pier sings at the *duomo* of Turin. Easter Mass!"

"What's this?" Maria asked. "What about Santa Rita's and Don Carlo? After all he's done for you…"

Pier sat up, propped on his elbows, in the straw. He should have expected it; the more fool he. But he'd expected… No, he'd *hoped* that his ma would be pleased, proud even, maybe, that he was called to sing in the city's most important church. Maybe even happy for him. Instead she made him feel like he'd done something despicable.

"But Ma," Tilde protested, "it was Don Carlo who sent Pier to the *duomo!*" She glanced at her big brother with pride in her eyes. "Don Marco, he is the…the…" she snuck a glance at her big brother for reassurance before risking the new word, "the c-a-n-t-o-r of the duomo. He was in Santa Rita's last December, heard Pier sing, and asked Don Carlo to send him to him." Breathless, she stopped and looked at Pier: his was staring at his feet, crossed in front of him. Tilde's eyes filled with tears. There was no understanding Ma, she was that hard. She swallowed her tears and turned to her mother, a note of defiance in her usually mild voice: "Don Carlo showed Pier how to get to the duomo from Santa Rita's. He showed him on… on a…m-a-p" – again that quick glance at her brother, checking that she had said the new word correctly – "showed him out to go. Right to the duomo. Right behind the king's palace, in the centre of Turin…"

"In the centre of Turin," Maria muttered with distaste. She'd been *in Turin* only on a few desperate errands. She'd been to sell her wares to merchants. And once to …sell her soul. The dark cobbled streets still darkened her mind, filled it with dread and shame. And Turin had killed Catlinin's first husband, dear Bertin. Run over while doing his job, delivering Nandín's farm produce.

In those few echoed words, the centre of Turin, Pier heard what he was up against with his ma. He heard her fear, revulsion and mistrust. That was what he was up against. He didn't know why, but to his ma the city was sinful, evil, deadly.

Maria marched over to the pair, waved Tilde aside: she wanted to sit down on the stool near Pier. "What's this then?" she demanded.

Behind her, the clatter of the carder stopped, and Vigin-a called out, "What are you all whispering about?" Nobody answered her. She watched the threesome – Pier stretched out on the straw, her ma, leaning in towards him, Tilde at her elbow. Curious, she left her chair and approached. Pier told his story all over again, carefully omitting any mention of his ride to Piazza Castello or the Teatro Regio.

"So, you are still singing for Don Carlo," his ma quizzed him again when he'd finished.

"'Course, I am!" Pier assured her. He thought of the three nights a week at the duomo and qualified. "Don Carlo lets me practice at Santa Rita's between sessions with Don Marco."

"So, you don't sing *for* Don Carlo. Hmmm," Maria muttered, unconvinced. For some minutes, she studied Pier sideways in deep thought, then she concluded, "We'll see what Don Michel has to say to all this."

"But Ma," Tilde put in, "Don Michel's the one who sent Pier to Don Carlo…"

"We'll just have to see," Maria repeated. The subject was closed. She stood up. "Now you've got to go," she told Pier. "Tomorrow's a workday." She motioned him back to the kitchen. Tilde rose to follow, but a sharp snap of the fingers sent her back to her knitting. Vigin-a drifted back to her carder. They'd got the message: their ma wanted to be alone with her son.

Maria walked back to the kitchen with Pier and shut the door behind them. He stood by the yard door, putting on his cap and muffler. He knew his mother's farewell ritual: the wicker basket, a few eggs nestled in straw, the slab of fresh farm butter – a secret gift for Catlinin, for the daughter who'd given up the name her mother had given her, changed it to get by in the city, changed her God-given name from Catlinin to Nina. The secret gift for Catlinin, stranded in the city and pregnant again. For the daughter she'd not seen in three years, not since she had married this city man. And for Anna, the granddaughter she had never met.

Chapter Three

Lena's Sunday

Morning dawned, bright and clear, on Lena's beloved Sunday routine. By half past seven she sat in bed in the room. she now shared with her mother, alone. Outside the rear window patches of snow dotted the fields and glistened in the early sun. Sparrows chirped under the eaves. In the trees lining the irrigation ditches blackbirds whistled and shrilled.

Their *cafelàit* long finished, Lena still lounged in bed, hugging her folded knees, shoulder to shoulder with her mama. "Are we going to visit Cichin-a this afternoon?" she asked.

"Hmmm. What do you think?" her mama asked back. "We were with her last Sunday. Would you like to do something else? We could go window shopping. *"*

Lena gave a happy shrug. She enjoyed her cosy walks with her mama, no matter where they went. "Adelaide's thinking of going downtown," she said.

"Well then, why don't you go," her mama answered her. "It's a sunny day, warm enough for a walk *al Valentin*."

"But what are *you* going to do?" Her mama smiled. "What?" Lena nudged the shoulder, snuggling up closer.

"*I* used to walk *al Valentin*," her mama said, a dreamy look on her face, "when I was a girl. And in summer we'd go to the Junction. I learned to swim there."

"You learned to *swim*!" Lena exclaimed, surprised. She studied her mama's smiling face. She'd never thought that her mother was once a young girl. Now, looking at her, she could see how pretty she must have been. That came as no surprise: despite the fat, the wrinkles and the grey hair pulled-back into a tight bun, her mama was lovely to her. She had lovely soft eyes. She nudged the shoulder next to hers. "What're you smiling at?"

"About learning to swim," Gioana said. The smile faded and she added, "All that was a long time ago." She cast the covers aside and got out of bed and stretched out a hand to Lena. "Up you get, you slug-a-bed. At this rate, we'll be late for mass. You know what a time it takes to do your hair."

Lena took her mama's hand and gave it a sympathetic squeeze. What her mama had *not* said recalled troubled times. '*All that*' had been before she'd married. Gioana returned the squeeze. "Come sit by your mama," she urged, turning the room's only chair to face the window. Her foot dragged a low stool for Lena to sit by her knees.

Lena sat down, retrieved the wide-toothed comb from the windowsill, and leaned back. Gioana began her grooming by running her fingers up and down Lena's neck and nape, massaging, then raking down the length of her daughter's tangled hair. "Ouch," Lena protested.

"Hold still, child," Gioana said. "There's a nasty tangle back here. I'll take it slow. Hand me the comb."

Lena passed the comb back to her mother and leaned deeper against her knees. The wide-toothed comb explored the tangles along the full length of Lena's curls before getting to work from the bottom up, lifting one small lock at a time, gently working each tangle loose, her hand braced against Lena's skull to avoid yanking. Lena sighed with contentment, her eyes gazing unseeing at the late February patchwork of snow and soil outside the window. In the distance, the trees that marked field boundaries were beginning to exhuded a green haze.

Her eyes fell on the dirt road crossing the fields, now a mere depression in the tired snow. It was on that road that she, as a small child, had run breathlessly home from her first job. Lena smiled, remembering. Outside the kitchen came the courtyard's homey Sunday noises. A tram came to a stop on *Via Nizza*, its metal clatter muted by the distance. Lena sighed again, happy with her familiar comfort. Behind her, her mama began to sing.

> "*A l'Hotel ëd La Reusa Bianca*
> *A-i é na fija da maridé*
> *Da maridé, da maridé!*
> *A-i é soa mama ch'a la penten-na*
> *Con un pento d'òr e d'argent,*
> *D'òr e d'argent, d'òr e d'argent!*"

At the hotel called The White Rose
There is a daughter of marrying age.
Her mother combs her hair
With a comb of gold and silver

Lena smiled at her golden life with her mama. She reached around and stroked her mama's knee. Her mama came to the ballad's refrain and Lena joined in.

"*Mama mia dame sent lire*
Che 'n America mi veuj andé!
Mi veuj andé, mi veuj andé!"

Mother mine, give me a hundred lire,
For I want to go to America!

Gioana went on with the next stanza:

"*Fija mia, me bel tesòr,*
Cento lire te le darò,
Fija mia, me bel tesòr,
Ma in America no, no, no!
No, no, no! No, no, no!"

Daughter mine, my darling treasure,
I will give you the hundred lire
But don't go to America, no, no, no!
No, no, no!

Promptly, Lena came in with the insistent refrain:

"*Mama mia dame sent lire,*
Che in America mi veuj andé!
Mi veuj andé, mi veuj andé!"

Gioana was pecking away at a stubborn snarl and was slow to pick up the next line. And when she did her voice stammered as she pecked away at a resistant know:

> *"Vaje pura, fija maledeta!*
> *An fond al mar it dovras resté!*
> *E dovras resté, dovras resté!"*

> Go then, you cursed daughter!
> Rot your bones at the bottom of the sea!

Struck by that *fija maledeta,* Lena failed to pick up the refrain. She couldn't imagine anything that would ever make her mama curse her. Gioana tapped her shoulder with the comb. "Pass me those clips," she said, "I'll just put up your hair for you and we're done."

Lena handed the clips back, her mind still on the ballad. "Whatever did she want to go to America for?" she said, inspecting her hairdo in a hand mirror. Why would anyone want to go to such a faraway place? Everything that mattered to her was right here. "Anyway," she promised, "*I*'m never going to leave you."

Gioana heard the unspoken thought behind this promise: *Not like Papa and Pinòt.* Gioana laughed at her daughter's promise. Another thought flashed through Lena's mind, *Good riddance.* Instantly she felt guilt stricken.

Gioana gave her a quick peck on the cheek. "Anyway, not 'till you fall in love!" she said. "Come along now, get your prayer book and let's go."

Arm in arm, they walked to their church, on Via Nizza. They strolled past the row of old farmhouses just like theirs, peeking in at each gate, exchanging greetings. At the corner, they turned onto Via Passo Buole, where their friend, Cichin-a, lived in one of the four-storied casements recently built for workers.

On the corner of Via Nizza, they spotted the usual clutch of young men in front of the neighbourhood *Café-Bar.* Catching sight of Lena and Gioana, the youths nudged each other. "Well, Gioana," one of them called out, "when are you going to let me marry your daughter?"

Lena blushed, staring at the sidewalk in front of her. Gioana gave her hand a quick double squeeze. Without slowing down, she countered, "When you spend your Sunday mornings at mass and not at the café," she said, "Tòni Barel."

The young cock's friends laughed and teased. "That's told you, Tòni Barel!"

"Ask a fresh question!"

"Lena can do better than a *fagnan* like you!"

"Oh yeah? And when did you last set the world on fire?"

Gioana steered Lena across Via Nizza and they climbed to the church door, exchanging greetings. Outside the heavy portals, they stopped to put on their headscarves, then pushed a pass-through open. One behind the other, they filed in, genuflected in the aisle, and made for their usual pew at the back of the church.

Waiting for the mass to begin, they watched the faithful drift in; find their usual places on the pews, each one according to his or her standing in the community. The nuns from the *Asilo* and first grade school occupied the first two rows. Behind them sat the homeowners, *ij padron èd cà*, and the shopkeepers, *ij comerciant.* Next came the artisans and white-collar workers and then, in the rear pews, the factory workers and the servants from nearby middle-class quarters of the city. Every now and then a worker intruded on one of the forward pews, upsetting the usual order. Nobody protested, but elbows nudged, disapproving eyes glared at the upstart. The challenge made the congregation uncomfortable; with, here and there, vague stirrings of envy.

After mass, as usual, Gioana and Lena called in at the corner greengrocer, open for the after-mass trade. The grocer wrapped up their small purchase in a paper cone, cast a quick glance at his wife, who was serving another customer at the far end of the counter and, seeing her engaged, he walked around to hand Lena her package. On the way he grabbed a handful of dried figs, and slipped them into the cone's open top. "Something sweet for this sweet girl," he said winking at Gioana. Lena's mouth puckered into a perfect little OH, and her eyes flew to her mama's: was it all right, could she accept the gift?

"Go ahead, girl," Gioana said, with a smile at the grocer. "Take it." Behind them, the wife was scurrying over to check on the goings on. Gioana took her daughter's arm, their parcel safely between them, and, on their way out, called out a good day, "*Bondí",* to the shop at large.

On the way home, Gioana said, "I'm thinking of spending the afternoon with Teresina. She's too much alone these days, since her daughter's gone."

"Shall I come with you?" Lena offered.

"Perhaps best not, " Gioana answered, "don't you think?"

Lena nodded: she and Teresina's daughter had been close friends until she'd been killed in a hit and run on Via Nizza, a couple of months ago. "Then," she said, "I'll go downtown with Adelaide." And so it was settled.

Pier meets Matilde Agiati

As soon as his three-times-a-week practice at the cathedral began, right after his session with Don Marco, Pier regularly found his way to the Regio stage door. At first, he just stood on the dark street, waiting for the doorkeeper to appear for his nightly smoke. But before long the old man began to look out for Pier to let him in, and Pier quickly became a regular backstage feature. At first the stage crew resented the obstruction of the body in the wings, but soon began to look upon him as an additional pair of hands willing to fetch and carry. And a few members of the chorus began to acknowledge the presence of the star-struck opera fan.

The first one to actually speak to him was a middle-aged contralto, Matilde Agiati, struck as much by Pier's good looks as by his assiduousness. She began to smile as she passed him in the wings, sometimes exchanging a few words with him during intermissions. Over the course of the opera season, a sort of friendship established itself between them. She enjoyed his eagerness, and he liked that he could talk with her about his passion for opera in a way he couldn't do anywhere else. And she seemed interested. At first, he only told her about his work at the cathedral, but in time he dared to confess that he longed to sing opera. Matilde took a friendly interest in Pier's ecstasies and longings, in part because, through them, she relived her own youthful longings, now bitter-sweet dreams in the light of her stalled career, a voice among many in the chorus, and, on the side, a trainer of others.

One night, towards the end of the opera season, Matilde, rustled passed him in her costume as she exited the stage at the end of a scene. She smiled at him as usual, but Pier just turned away from her. This unusual reaction nagged at her through the rest of the performance: what was wrong with the lad? He *was* rather thin-skinned. She could not go after him right then, as she had to be back on stage shortly. But after the final curtain she sought him out backstage, and caught up with him just as he was yanking open the alley door to rush out. "Pier!" she called, taking hold of his sleeve. "Wait up. Is everything all right?" Pier threw himself against the wall, looking on the verge of tears. "What's wrong?" she asked with concern. He only shrugged, pulled away from her and turned to the door. "Wait!" she called after him. "Don't leave like that. Let's talk. Ten minutes while I change. All right?" Pier nodded, head down, morose.

Matilde hurried through her change and, nine minutes later, rushed to the stage door. Pier was nowhere to be seen. Her heart sank. She pulled the door open, almost afraid; and there she saw him, across the street, barely discernible in the dim light, one foot propped up against the wall behind him, hands thrust deep into his pockets. She hurried across the street. "I was afraid you hadn't waited." She threaded her arm through his. "Come; let's go sit down somewhere we can talk." She steered him the short distance to a quiet café in Via Po.

"Coffee?" she asked him, as a waiter approached, "Or maybe hot chocolate? Let's have hot chocolate. It'll cheer us up."

Pier barely nodded, morose. A few minutes later, a steaming cup between her hands, she tackled him. "Now then, what's upset you?"

Pier shrugged, staring into his cup, hands wrapped tight around it.

"Trouble at the *duomo?*" she asked, and got no answer. "At home, perhaps?" She waited. "A girlfriend," she added as an afterthought. Pier had never mentioned any girl.

He shook his head, chin tucked low. Matilde cocked her head to one side, coaxing. "We're friends, aren't we?" After a moment she added: "If you … tell me what's upset you, I might be able to help."

Pier dragged his eyes to her face, and she realised how close to tears he was. She reached a hand out and laid it on his arm. "Can't be as bad as that…" she said quietly. She waited, looking at him with affection. A tear rolled down Pier's cheek.

He jerked back in his seat, splashing chocolate on the checked tablecloth. Flustered, he set his cup down on the stain, picked it up again and took a token sip. "You've been kind to me," he mumbled. He stopped, coughed, swallowed.

Again, she cocked her head, half sisterly half coquettish. "We are friends…aren't we? And you are young, just starting, really, while I am… Well, I'm an old hand at this game. What good am I if I can't try to help you along? Come, let me try."

A rush of feeling swept over Pier. He grabbed her hand on the table between them and cried, "It's coming to an end!" His voice cracked, and tears rolled down his cheeks, shaming him. Angrily, he swiped at them with the back of his hand.

"What is?" she asked softly. But Pier had pulled back into himself. She stroked his hand, coaxing.

"All this…" he croaked, with an all-inclusive gesture. "The season!"

She was puzzled. "What about the season?" she asked.

"It's coming to an end!"

"You mean…the *opera* season!?" Matilde said, trying to disguise her surprise. Pier nodded, took a disconsolate sip at his chocolate. She patted his hand, a smile on her kind face. "So it is," she soothed, "But… there'll soon be another one, come fall."

"Yes, but I…" Pier started, and choked up again.

Matilde waited. After a while she gave his hand an encouraging squeeze. Pier heaved a deep sigh, and glanced at her, quickly lowering his eyes again. "And I've never even been up front," he whined, aggrieved.

"Up front? You mean…in the house?" she queried.

"Yes! And now it's all over," he mourned.

"But that's easy to fix," she said, "if it's that important to you..."

Pier squirmed, ashamed, but nodded: yes, it was. It was very important.

"No need to fret about it. We might be able to fix it. There are still two performances, next Saturday and Sunday. Let me see what I can do."

His feverish eyes now pinned themselves to hers, hovering between hope and disbelief. "Really?! You can?"

"I can try. But it'll be up in the gallery, 'standing room only'. We are sold out."

Pier's two hands grabbed hers and squeezed it with trembling gratitude. Then, suddenly, his fire went out: he released her hand and crawled back into his shell. *What now?* Matilde thought, beginning to lose patience. Still she waited. Pier slouched in his chair, eyes cast down, chin tucked into his chest.

"There's something else, isn't there," she said softly. A long pause. Then Pier nodded, reluctant, chin still down. Again, she waited. "It's the summer…" he mumbled at last, "the *whole summer*… and… no opera…"

"You can listen to records," Matilde said, smiling at his despair.

"And where would *I* get to listen to records?" Pier barked out.

"I can lend you some if you like," she offered.

"Yeah, but,… *Where* would I listen to them?"

Matilde grasped then the shocking limitations of Pier's life: a gramophone was beyond his reach. She felt sad, somehow guilty, wanting to make up for the lack, but somehow hesitant. She knew by now how hypersensitive Pier was about his rough edges, about the aura of country bumpkin that clung to him. It struck her now that he'd never spoken of his country home. He'd mentioned the sister with whom he lived in Borgo Santa Rita, but that was it. "Can't you use the gramophone at the duomo?" she suggested. Pier threw her a brief look of scorn: she wouldn't understand... "Or Santa Rita's, perhaps," she tried again. "I'm sure there's one at Santa Rita's. Choirmasters usually have one in their practice equipment. Can't you listen there?"

"I can, to *church* music..."

Matilde thought she was beginning to understand. "You're afraid," she said tentatively, "that the cantor won't approve of your interest in opera?"

Pier shrugged: how could *she* understand? She was a city person and an opera professional. She belonged to the theatre. How could he tell her that the theatre was the work of the devil, the city itself sinful, evil? And *he* didn't care if it was! Hell, or no hell, he *wanted* that world! And he was lying and cheating to get to it! Lying to Don Marco, lying to Don Carlo, lying to his ma!

Matilde waited, but he'd clammed up, in morose silence.

After a while she sighed and said, "Look, you could come and listen to records with me some afternoon."

"I can't," he muttered, unwilling to mention his job at FIAT. Then he added, "Afternoons."

"Well, perhaps some evening then," she said.

His eyes flew to hers, leery, eager, "Really? You mean it? But ... where?"

"Why, at my home. We can drink coffe, listen to records and talk opera." She saw him crawl back into himself. She guessed at his problem, and added, "My sister will be there; and at times my husband," she said. "They won't mind."

"They won't? They'd let me come to their home, evenings?"

Matilde laughed. "Not every evening, no. But now and then. Yes, of course you can come. I often have...musical people over."

"Really? I could!? When could we start?" he asked eagerly.

Chuckling, Matilde named the date for his first visit. What she didn't explain was the fact that, besides being a member of the *Regio* chorus, she was also the theatre's voice and diction coach. She would simply introduce Pier to her family as one of the students who came to her home for additional help.

Matilde's coaching

Pier's visits to Matilde's home began shortly after the end of the opera season. The first time Matilde received him in the living room, her sister Agnese poured the coffee, while Matilde put a first record on the gramophone, then settled down to her needlework. The husband didn't appear. The three listened quietly. To Agnese, recorded music was an ordinary feature of everyday life. She hardly paid attention. Matilde listened with a keen professional ear, listening for expressive and interpretive nuances. But Pier was soon totally absorbed, the music blotting out the middleclass living room that had been so intimidating when he'd first walked in. Week after week he came and listened, body and soul transported into the world of the opera – the Seville of Figaro, the Paris of Alfredo, the Egypt of Radames, the ducal palace where Rigoletto paved the way to his own undoing. The coffee grew cold in his cup as he listened, riveted, on the edge of his seat. Matilde watched him absorb the music. Soon she began to feel an amused tenderness she couldn't quite put into words, a peculiar almost-ache that made her need to help him. One night they listened to *I Pagliacci*. As the last notes died into silence, Pier rose to leave, as usual. But, still immersed in the lingering mood of the drama, he unexpectedly burst forth into Canio's cry of pain:

> *"Ridi Pagliaccio e ognuno applaudirà !*
> *Tramuta in lazzi lo spasmo ed il pianto;*
>
> *In una smorfia il singhiozzo e 'l dolor!*
> *Ridi, Pagliaccio, sul tuo amore infranto!*
> *Ridi del duol che t'avvelena il cor!"*

Laugh, clown, and people will applaud!
Turn your pain and tears into jokes,
Your sobs and sorrow into a grimace!
Laugh, clown, over your shattered love!
Laugh at the pain that's poisoning your heart.

Matilde stared at him: she had never yet heard him sing. At times he had hummed a bar or two when discussing some aria or other, a reminder rather than a rendition. But tonight his voice had burst out with the agony of Canio's pain and humiliation. Amazed, Matilde took Pier by the hand and drew him to her teaching room next door. She sat down at the piano and spread out the *Pagliacci* score. "Let's have the whole aria," she said.

"But I don't know it," Pier said, suddenly shy.

"You can sing from the score, can't you?"

Pier leaned over her shoulder for a few moments, and then began:

Recitar!

To act!

His voice broke and he coughed his throat clenched and dry.

"Deep breath," Matilde said, modelling her instructions, very much the teacher. "Stand like you do when you sing at the duomo. Now breathe deep and loosen up."

Pier obeyed: he straightened his spine and opened his chest. His head swivelled from side to side, to loosen his stiff neck. He breathed deep, from the diaphragm.

Matilde nodded approval. "Now try again," she said. Pier sang.

> *"Recitar! Mentre preso dal delirio*
> *Non so più quel che dico e quel*
> *Che faccio!*
> *Eppur e d'uopo! Sforzati...*
> *Bah! Sei tu forse un uom? Tu sei*
> *Pagliaccio!*
> *Vesti la giubba, e la faccia infarina.*
> *La gente paga e rider vuole qua."*

To act! While, a prey to delirium,

I no longer know what I'm saying or doing!

And yet I must! Force yourself...

Bah! You think yourself a man?

You're a clown!

Dress up in your doublet, powder your face.

People are paying and here they want to laugh.

Pier sang to the last, wrenching note. The piano fell silent. Matilde did not move. She had expected a trained voice from a cathedral soloist, but she had not expected the agonised passion. "You took my breath away," she said, turning to him, and again she was shocked: in front of her stood a beaten wreck of a man, a defeated clown whose reason for being had just betrayed him. Did that mean that the kid had interpretive and expressive talents as well? She took his hand. "Is *Pagliacci* your favourite opera?" she asked.

Pier shrugged. "Not really. It's just that bit."

"I see," she said. "What's your favourite opera?"

Again, Pier shrugged. "I don't know."

"Can you sing something else for me?"

"Opera?" he asked.

Matilde nodded.

"But I only know a few bits and pieces," he demurred, "from last season, you know, listening in the wings."

"Sing anything you like."

Tentatively, Pier hummed *Che gelida manina…*

"Ah, *La Bohème*!" Matilde searched through her stack of scores, opened one, and flattened it out on the piano. Pier studied the score over her shoulder, then began the aria, his notes clear and accurate. Matilde appreciated the voice, but cringed at the heavy dialect accent. She glanced at him: his presence didn't match the role. It wasn't Rodolfo's, the gay, expansive bohemian eager to fall in love. Pier sang:

> *"…in povertà mia lieta*
> *Scialo da gran signor*
> *Rime e inni d'amor.*
> *Per sogni e per chimere*
> *E per castelli in aria*
> *L'anima ho millionaria…"*

> …in my merry poverty
> I squander like a great lord
> Poems and hymns of love.
> When it comes to dreams and fantasies
> And castles in the air
> I have the soul of a millionaire…

Matilde averted her eyes: that was just what this young man did not have – a rich, free spirit. Or if he had ever had it, it had been crushed out of him. Suddenly

66

she recognised what had drawn her to him: he was like a stray dog, always on the lookout for the next kick. And yet, and yet… She studied Pier's presence: his features were fine, his build tall and wiry. But the way he carried himself spoilt the total effect.

Matilde stood up. "You have a beautiful voice," she said, "and a superb foundation. But opera is…well, different." She saw Pier's features crumble and rushed to explain. "You see," she said, "when one sings in church one cultivates *one* persona – reverent, dignified, and proper for singing in the house of God. *But* on the stage… Well, it's different. Opera is all… well, it's about people, about passion, *all passions;* the ugly as well as the beautiful ones. The characters are *all kinds* of people. So, it's not enough to sing beautifully. One has to *look the part,* to look like the character, to actually *behave like* the character one is singing, be it a hero or a villain. You have to convey to the audience…when, whatever kind of person your role calls for – a lover, a clown, or a nobleman. Do you see what I mean?"

Pier was nodding, listening eagerly. Matilde went on, "Look at the way you say *each word:* if you're a count…" she straightened her spine, raised her chin, and her hand swung out in an elegant gesture, "… you have to say it *like a count.*" "If you're a beggar…" – she slipped off her piano stool and hobbled around the room like a cripple – "…you have to speak *and move* like a beggar. Same words, but different characters, different attitudes and completely different sounds. You see? A world of difference."

Pier's eyes dropped to the floor. That phrase, a world of difference, had struck a deep chord. He knew first-hand that world of difference: in the Santa Rita's changing room, the man who had bumped into him and, instead of apologising, had snapped at him. *There* was your world of difference! It was like 'they' heard a language he didn't hear, something that told him he did not belong. At that thought, his shoulders hunched over, his hands clenched into fists, his chest closed in. Matilde watched his frame shrink, or rather contract in upon itself. For a moment she feared she'd triggered some deep flaw on the boy's make up. But then he spoke. "Do you think," he asked, shy but eager, "that I … could learn all that?"

She almost laughed with relief. "It'll take a lot of work," she said, "a lot of dedication. Not everybody has what it takes. But you… do have a marvellous voice, it'd be well worth a try."

"How?" he asked, shaking with eagerness, "How do I learn?"

"Well," Matilde answered cautiously, "we could…start with the basics, things like diction and body technique…"

"But who could teach me?" Pier asked eagerly; but then a second thought stopped him. "How much would it cost?" he asked.

Matilde shrugged: "Let's see what we've got to work on first. *And* whether you really *are* prepared to take on all that work. We could give it a couple of months. I won't have much time once rehearsals start again, next fall. But let's see how far we get between now and then."

Afternoon on the river

With the advent of spring, Lena's Sunday outings shifted from downtown window-shopping to walks in Turin's elegant riverside park, *ël Valentin* and, on hot days, to the upstream confluence of the Sangone into the Po, just outside the city limits. On a hot Saturday in mid-June, Lena walked home from work arm in arm with her best friend. "How about going to the Po tomorrow?" Adelaide said. "*Al Valentin?*" Lena queried. Adelaide's elbow nudged her ribs. "No, silly, to the Junction. You know who's likely to be there."

The Junction was the summer playground of *Lingòt's* dwellers. To the elegant up-town park they went for a glimpse of how the well-to-do lived. They went to watch the rich sip cool drinks at outdoor cafés, automobiles and horse drawn carriages cruise the winding carriageways, ladies and gentlemen in riding attire canter sleek mounts up and down the bridle paths. Or, walking on artfully landscaped river banks, they could watch slender sculls from the exclusive right bank clubs skim the placid current, nimble and silent as water spiders.

Adelaide shook her head. *Ël Valentin* was not where the action lay for the young of *Lingòt*. They went there like they went to the movies, as spectators, to gape at the life of a world not their own. *Their* playground was the Junction, a spit of land between two rivers. That was where families went for Sunday picnics and the young went to seek out romance. The scions of Turin's affluent classes, of *la gente bene,* went there as well. They went to look for working girls with whom they could flirt with a freedom forbidden in proper society. They rowed out from their right bank clubs, beached their crafts, swam and sunbathed, always keeping an eye out for possibilities.

Lena hesitated: she liked the Junction, and she liked going out with Adelaide, who was daring and great fun. But her mama might already have plans for tomorrow.

"Oh, come on," Adelaide nudged. "You know who'll be there!" She put on a posh downtown baritone and mimicked: *"Finalmente, il mio sole."* (At last, my sunshine!)

Lena blushed to a china pink. She resented her friend's parody of the beloved greeting. Eyes down, she grinned, but was uncomfortable. She did not answer. Adelaide elbowed her ribs. "Oh, come on! You know you like him!"

Indeed, Lena thought, she did like Ottavio a whole lot. But she did not like being teased about him. He was *her* friend from a two-man scull, a student from the *Universitá.* She shook her dark curls and pulled away from Adelaide. She would not walk arm in arm with her if she kept teasing.

"Oh, come now!" Adelaide coaxed, trotting after Lena to take her arm again. "Don't get all huffy. You know I'm just teasing." Lena shook her off, walked on by herself. But Adelaide persisted, trotting alongside. "Well? Will you come?"

"Might," Lena said, still standoffish, "If my mama doesn't have other plans."

Adelaide rolled her eyes: *Lena and her mama! Would she ever cut the apron strings?* "Tell you what," she said, taking Lena's arm again, "I'll come by after lunch, say two o'clock?" Lena didn't answer. "Then you'll come, yes?"

"Well, maybe," Lena said.

Adelaide pouted and Lena instantly felt guilty: she'd hurt her friend's feelings. Adelaide never meant any harm. Teasing was just her way of having fun. Lena felt the need to make peace but was still miffed. "All right," she conceded, "come by at two o'clock. Then we'll see."

The next morning dawned bright and clear on Lena's beloved Sunday routine. By seven thirty, she was sitting in bed, hugging her folded knees, her mama by her side, their empty breakfast bowls on the nightstands. Her eyes drifted to the window checking out the weather. Wheat fields rippled rusty gold in a gentle breeze. Swallows swooped, hunting for bugs. Under the eaves their nests greeted each return with hungry twittering. She asked, "Are we going to Cichina this afternoon?"

"Well, we were with her last Sunday," Gioana answered. "Wouldn't you rather do something else? A walk *al Valentin* maybe?"

Lena shrugged, thinking of the Junction. "Adelaide's asked me go to the Po," she said.

"Why don't you go?" Gioana encouraged her. "It's going to be a hot day."

Promptly at two o'clock, Adelaide knocked on Lena's door. "You ready," she called in. Then she spotted Gioana at the kitchen table and added: "Oh, Gioana, *bondì.*"

Lena called out from the bedroom, "I'll just be in a minute." And moments later she came through the door, a wide straw hat on her dark curls. Gioana handed her a bulging string bag in which she had squeezed a bottle of lemonade, wrapped in the beach towel. "Watch you don't get too much sun," she warned. Lena gave her a quick peck on the cheek. "I won't," she promised, and walked out.

Arm in arm, the two girls headed off across the courtyard, twittering. From her doorway, Gioana watched them until they disappeared through the courtyard gate. *Like me and Cichina thirty years ago,* she thought, wistfully. Ah, those Sunday afternoons at the Junction! The excitement, the thrill, the anticipation one Sunday to the next! She too, had been pretty girl then, very much like Lena, though she'd worn her hair was wound up about her ears. Gioana smiled fondly at the memory. Her friend, dear Alfredo, had liked to see it loose, down to her waist. She remembered his voice like it was yesterday. "Must leave down, dry it in the sun," he'd say, uncoiling her tresses after bathing in the river, "otherwise you'll catch cold." She saw him now, standing in front of her all serious and dignified in the wet bathing costume that covered him from shoulders to ankles. *A proper bedside manner,* she thought, with a smile, *like the doctor he was studying to be.* And then one afternoon he'd given her a boat ride on the Po. A day like today, a late June afternoon. They met at *ël Valentin.* He'd led her, hand in hand, down the steps of an *embarcadero,* given her an afternoon on the river. He rowed them up-stream for hours. She sat on the soft cushions under the fringed canopy, feeling a proper lady. And then he began to sing, a lovely song she didn't know. And she caught his eyes deep in hers, all the way from his rowing seat, and she knew he was singing what he couldn't tell her any other way. She paid attention to the words then and her heart leapt for joy:

> *"Quanto é bella! Quanto é cara!*
> *Più la vedo e più mi piace..."*

How beautiful she is! How dear!
The more I see her the more I like her...

And her heart sang out, "*Am veul bin, am veul bin!*" (He loves me, he loves me!) *Yes, a lovely late June day, just like today.* But then the university had closed down for the summer, and Alfredo had gone home somewhere far away. She'd waited for him in the fall, but he'd never come back. *Perhaps,* she thought, *if I'd been able to read, he might have written to me.* But she did not believe it.

Gioana drew the faded sun curtain across her open kitchen door and went inside for her Sunday nap.

At the courtyard gate, the two girls turned right and headed towards the fields at the far end of Strada delle Basse. There, a narrow lane, hip-deep in ripening wheat, led to the tram terminal near the city limits. Its square, surrounded by recent four-storied workmen's housing, jutted out into the farmland like a promontory into a golden sea. Across the square, the footpath again dove straight into fields.

Some fifteen minutes later, the girls approached the last of the irrigation ditches separating field from field, all the way to the Sangone. Beyond it, wheat gave way to grass, and at the far end the river winked silver between low-growing shrubs. The girls leapt across this last ditch. In the meadow ahead of them family parties lingered over picnic lunches in the shade of acacia trees. Women gathered the remains of their meals into baskets; children ran, shrieking, at their games, while men played *Taròch* or *bocce* on the grass. Ahead, the *Sangone* whispered softly over a nearside shallow, while a strong current scoured its opposite bank. Children paddled in the shallow water, with mothers keeping an eye on them from the bank. Some fifty yards away the *Sangone* merged with the Po. Its young, clear waters swirled and eddied into the placid older river. Along the right bank, pleasure crafts floated in a deep, dredged channel.

The place the two girls were heading for was a small sandy beach at the confluence of the two streams. On their left were the *Sangone* shallows to paddle in, and on the right…ah, the possibilities of the left!

Adelaide gave Lena's arm a quick squeeze. "There they are," she nudged excitedly. She had spotted two beached sculls and, few yards away, a party of young people lounging on beach towels – young men in rowing gear and girls in woollen bathing costumes – among them two rowers in green and white club stripes. "They are here," she whispered, and hurried across the sand. And just then the taller of the two rowers caught sight of them and jumped up to run and meet them.

"You've come!" he cried, taking Lena's beach bag from her. "I was beginning to lose hope,"

From one of the beach towel a baritone voice rumbled, "Yeah, at last. Now maybe you can stop fretting."

"Never mind them," Ottavio said to Lena, spreading her towel next to his own. "They like to tease."

"Yeah, don't listen to him," said another rower who was busy dribbling sand on the back of his girl's legs. "It's all envy." From her prone position, the girl gave him a good swat.

Lena settled down on her towel and uncorked her walnut oil.

"Shall I help you?" Ottavio offered, reaching for the bottle. Lena smiled, but shook her head. She would not go that far. Adelaide switched cheeks on her towel to look at Lena and gave her a wicked grin. *She* had no such scruples: she was enjoying the ministrations of her date, Giancarlo, whose oily fingers glided easily on the back of her legs, now and then straying above the hem of her costume. Lena ignored her.

"At least, let me do your face," Ottavio coaxed, "otherwise you might get oil in your eyes."

Lena passed him her bottle and watched while he carefully spread tanning oil on his fingertips, then she puckered up, eyes tightly shut, mouth a ripe rosebud.

"Ah, temptation!" someone moaned on one of the towels. Ottavio did not resist the temptation: he landed a playful kiss on Lena's lips.

"Hey!" Lena cried out, and slapped his hand none too hard. "You're playing with me."

He laughed. "That was too much to resist. But here, let me. I'll be good."

The afternoon drifted agreeably by. Lena lay in the sun next to Ottavio, half-dozing. At one point she was vaguely aware of Adelaide and Giancarlo strolling away towards the line of bushes. When she opened her eyes again, Ottavio's arm rested across her waist. She liked that, too. When she, at last, she sat up, the sun had lost its sting. Adelaide and Giancarlo were back. The river traffic now headed mostly downstream. Next to her, Ottavio sat up as well, resting his weight on his elbows, and looked about. His hand grazed Lena's thigh. She liked his hands, their neat, trimmed nails. She liked the feel of his smooth, soft skin. She liked *him*. She ran a finger on the strong middle sinew. Ottavio turned his hand over and closed it over hers. They sat in silence.

Sometime later, she said wistfully, "Soon you'll have to go."

With a sigh, Ottavio glanced up: the sun was low in the West. It cast long shadows on the ground. And the academic year was almost over. He nodded wistfully.

He turned to face her and said, "Come out with me tonight."

"Tonight? Where to?" Lena cried, taken by surprise.

"*Any*where. It doesn't matter. To a café, to the *Valentino,* to a film…"

Lena said: "We go al *Valentin* in the afternoon. I've never been at night."

Ottavio smiled. "It's very different at night."

On his towel, Giancarlo guffawed, "I'll say it is!" Adelaide and the other girl twittered, and her young man sang in a deliberately suggestive voice:

> *"Pei sentieri abbandonati,*
> *Van I cuori appassionati*
> *Degli amanti intrecciati…"*

> On the deserted walks,
> beat the passionate hearts
> of entwined lovers…

Giancarlo wiggled his eyebrows at Ottavio over Adelaide's back. "Regular lover's lane," he sniggered. He joined in his friend's song:

> *"…Tra i glicini e i pampini in fiore…*
> *…S'intreccian gli amanti,*
> *E bocche tremanti si parlan d'amor…"*

> Under the wisteria and jasmine in bloom,
> Lovers entwine,
> Trembling mouths speak of love…

"Never mind them," Ottavio said, reclaiming Lena's attention with two fingers under her chin gently turning Lena's face toward him, "Come out with me tonight. We can go dancing, if you like."

"Dancing!" Lena cried, wide-eyed.

"Yes, dancing under the stars," he teased gently, referring to a line in his friend's song.

"Is there a *festa*?" she asked.

Ottavio took her hand in his and shook his head. "No. It's just a garden," he said, describing a popular right bank dancing club, well beyond the fashionable districts. "There are lanterns in the trees and lots of stars, above. I'm sure you'll like it."

"Oh, I would!" Lena cried. "I love to dance! It's just that…"

"What?"

Lena squirmed, suddenly uncomfortable. When she'd been dancing in the evening, her mama had always accompanied her. Had Ottavio meant to include her mama? She didn't dare to inquire. But Ottavio didn't know her mama. They'd never met anywhere but at the Junction, and he'd always rowed back to his club at sundown, while she and Adelaide walked home. "I'll have to ask my mama." And suddenly she knew she'd not want her mama along.

"Well, then, it can't be tonight," Ottavio said, disappointed, but undaunted. "How about next Saturday?"

Lena hesitated. "I'd like to. I'll let you know on Sunday."

Ottavio smiled. "Sunday comes *after* Saturday. Let me know earlier this week."

"But I work until six," Lena said, alarmed.

"So? I can pick you up at your work place and walk you home."

"But you don't know where Fornara is!"

"You've just told me the name of the place. I'll find it," he said.

Lena bit her lip. Did she want Ottavio to walk her home to Le Basse? A flush of shame reddened her face. Guilt made her rephrase her thought: *Was it all right if he walked her home?* What would her mama say? She wished she could ask her.

Giancarlo's voice broke in on her thoughts. "Come on, Ottavio, we've got to get going. I've got an appointment in two hours."

"An appointment?!" Adelaide sat up.

"My aunt and uncle," Giancarlo lied, "the weekly family dinner." He gathered his towel and his sun lotion and headed for the beached scull.

"Must go," Ottavio said, gathering up his things. "I'll be there on Wednesday. At six on the dot." He grinned at her and joined his friend, already in their scull. With a last wave to her, he shoved off. Alone on the beach, Lena watched them go. Then Adelaide joined her. Over the widening distance, they heard Giancarlo's scold. They couldn't catch the words, but the tone told them he was quarrelling with Ottavio.

Chapter Four

Farm and Church conflict

The onset of the good season created more problems for Pier. It all began with the May haying: on Sundays Maté expected all his sons, jobs or no jobs, to be back at *La Speransa* for the big field works. Pier's new activities at the duomo made that impossible. The Annunciation, at the end of March, followed by Easter in early April, had kicked off a string of holy days the church celebrated with elaborate rituals in. Then May brought Pentecost and June the Ascension, and then the quick succession of the big saints' days, Saint John, Saint Peter and Saint Paul. Besides, May and June were the busiest wedding season. In demand at both Santa Rita's and at the duomo, Pier's earnings from weddings during the month of May had dwarfed his FIAT wages. But it all took time, and he got so tired that Don Marco had begun lecturing him about burning the candle at both ends. In fact, Pier had had no free Sunday in three months. Now that the big farm works were here, he worried about not doing his bit at *La Speransa*. He knew that if his pa did not get what he wanted, he made life hell for everyone around him, even Taboj, poor brute. But he couldn't be in two places at once.

A comforting thought: he had set aside quite a bit of money for his ma from his wedding earnings. It might soften the trouble he caused her by not being in the fields on Sundays. But now, with the wheat harvest under way, the biggest job of the season, he could not stay away. With the good weather there had been, most of the fields must already be cut. He *had* to show up next Sunday, if only for a few hours to help with what was left. But he had a Santa Rita's wedding with a *Messa cantata,* so he would not be able to head out until well after noon.

On Sunday, as soon as he was done with the wedding, he straddled his old bicycle and headed out to the farm. He got to the fields around one thirty. In the shade of the mulberry trees, Maté and his helpers were just beginning to stir from their after-lunch nap. The wheat cut the day before lay drying in long golden swathes. Pier walked his bike across the stubble toward the resting men. His sister Vigin-a was stowing the debris of their meal into a basket. Out in the field, Tilde was already tossing forkfuls of cut stalks into the air to speed up their drying. The empty wagon stood by the irrigation ditch, in the shade of polled mulberries, and the mule, neck up-stretched, nibbled at the tender leaves. At the click-clicking of the approaching bicycle, it turned its head, jaws working.

Passing it, Pier stroked the long, bay nose. Clot's voice rose from the nearby shade. "Well well, look who's here." Minot sat up and nodded to Pier, whom he had not seen in several months. Maté didn't move, but Pier was aware of the baleful eyes under the hat brim, tipped low against the glare.

"Hot day for a bike ride," Minot said, handing Pier an earthenware water jug.

"Just as hot for field work," Clot retorted.

Their pa sat up, yawning, one hand feeling behind him for the almost-empty wine bottle. He drained it and tossed it to Vigin-a to stow away. Wiping his mouth on the back of his hand, he grumbled at Pier, "You sure took your time."

Pier did not answer. From a blackberry patch along the ditch came the hum of bees. On the verge, by the brambles, Pier spotted a spare pitchfork. He scanned the field ahead: half of it still needed turning. He headed for the swathe next to Tilde's. The sun beat down and the air was still and heavy, sapping all energy. Tilde looked weary. Birds followed her, squabbling over dropped seed and stirred up insects. Midges hovered around her head in a dense fog. She tossed her head to escape them and caught sight of Pier, smiled and waved to him. Pier waved back. He glanced at the sky: clouds rolling in from the mountain. There should be time enough to get the wheat in before the rain.

He pitched his fork into the mounded stalks and tossed them a couple of feet into the air. Dust made him cough. Ahead of him, he heard Tilde cough. The rustle behind him told him Minot was starting on the swathe next to his.

It was well past sundown when the loaded wagon ground out of the stubble and onto the lane, heading for home under scudding clouds. In the driver's seat, Maté shook the reins on the mule's back, urging it on. Tilde, Clòt and Minòt trailed behind the wagon. Vigin-a had finished her row and gone home, leaving the others to load the wagon. Pier straddled his bike and sped ahead, feeling for the packet of money in his back pocket. He wanted a few minutes alone with his ma.

At *La Speransa* Taboj's bark announced the new arrival well before Pier came through the gate. The old dog leapt about on his chain, tail wagging, eager

77

to welcome. Vigin-a was at the pump, drawing water for her ma's vegetable patch. "So, you made it after all," she said.

It annoyed Pier: she knew perfectly well he had made it. She'd been in the field when he arrived, seen him work. "Where's our ma?" he asked, ignoring her taunt. Vigin-a jerked her head towards the kitchen window, then walked to the garden gate with two dripping buckets. He propped his bike against the wire fence and squatted to stroke Taboj's head. Through the fly-screened window, he saw his ma moving, getting supper ready. She caught sight of him and called out: "Long time no see."

Pier cringed: it *had* been a long time. He stopped by the pump, played the handle to wash the dust and sweat off. He splashed water on his face and neck, and then drank greedily from cupped hands. The house door squealed open and he looked up.

"Come in quick," his ma said. "Don't let the flies in."

Pier shook the water off his hands and hurried into the kitchen. "Hmmm," he said, sniffing, "*povronà.*"

His ma nodded. "With hard boiled eggs," she said and then asked, "*Tuti bin a ca?*" (Everybody all right at home?) Pier nodded. He knew her anxieties: Nina and her child, Lorèns and his doings.

"When's Catlinin due?" his ma asked, refusing to use Nina's shortened version of her given name.

"Couple of weeks, midwife says."

"Vigin-a will go help," Maria said.

Pier frowned: Nina and Vigin-a didn't get along. "Tilde might be better," he said.

"Tilde's too young," his ma dismissed him. "Anna's growing well?"

"She's doing fine."

"You?"

"I'm fine," he answered. He looked out of the window. No one was there. He reached into his pocket. "Ma," he said, slipping his bundle of notes into her hand. "I've done a lot of weddings this month…"

She fingered the wad and her eyes widened. "Does pa know?" she asked, quickly stowing the money into a pocket under her apron.

Pier shook his head. "He's mad at me for not being here more. But I just couldn't."

Maria nodded. "Don Michel tells me you're doing well."

The door slammed against the wall. Vigin-a bustled with in fresh water for the evening meal. She peered at the two figures standing close together, her ma's hand under her apron, Pier with his back to her. She heaved her buckets onto the sink and looked out into the yard. "What's taking them so long?" she grumbled. "My belly's dragging on the floor."

"It *is* late," Maria noted, glancing at the window. "It's getting dark, and you with that long ride back. You'd better eat now and get going. Vigin-a, cut the bread while I shell the eggs."

Grudgingly, Vigin-a obeyed and busied herself with the bread. But she couldn't resist muttering, "Pa won't like it,"

Dancing under the stars

Monday morning at work, Lena began to regret that she had agreed to Ottavio's picking her up at Fornara. She shouldn't have let him come. Last night she couldn't bring herself to tell her mama. That must mean there was something wrong with it. She had never before held anything back from her mama.

She threw the wire loop she had just wound into the receiving bin, picked up another wire, wound it and threw it into the bin. And yet, she thought, it was so lovely, on Sunday, lying there on the sand side by side. She remembered his bare shoulder grazing hers and shivered.

But seeing him away from the Junction, she thought, here, outside Fornara, that was… She couldn't put it into words, but the thought made her uneasy.

She glanced at the women working down the bench. They *would* ogle and tease. Out on a date, they'd say. They *would* call it a date. The girls were always talking about their dates, their *moròs,* what they wanted on their dates, what they *did*. Lena could hardly credit their stories, but the girls *bragged* about it. Half of the time she just tuned them out, refusing to hear.

They teased her about that as well, said she was turning a deaf ear because she was dying to know. And it was half true: she *was* curious about dates. But what the girls said…well, it was all hints, half words, smirks and rolling of the eyes, incomprehensible and, to her, most uncomfortable. And now, on Wednesday afternoon, Ottavio would be here for all to gawk at.

A new thought added to her discomfort: *Monsú* Andrea would see them together. He was a good boss, always nice to her. His good opinion mattered to her. What would he say now? She could almost hear him: "Stepping out with your young man, eh? And a very fine young gentleman he looks…" She blushed: she couldn't bear them all talking about him.

And yet… She did want him here, waiting for her across the street. She wanted very much to see him. She wanted everyone to see him. And Wednesday was such ages away…

Fed up with herself, she threw the latest loop into the receiving bin and grabbed another handful of wires. "Ouch!" she cried. One of the wires had stuck into the heel of her hand. She yanked it out and blood spurted, running down her wrist. The woman seated next to her scolded, "There now, you've gone and hurt yourself! What's the matter with you today, you're miles away."

Lena sucked at her wound. "It's nothing," she said, wadding her handkerchief against it.

"Nonsense!" the woman countered. "Go wash your hand. And put some iodine on it. You don't want to get gangrene."

A girl mocked from across the bench. "That'll slow her down."

Lena went off, upset at her own clumsiness. Her mind was still on her problem, her date with Ottavio. *She* was calling it a date now! It wasn't a date, was it? She'd wrestled with that question for days without daring to ask about it. Last night she'd finally mentioned it to her mama. They were in bed, the light already off, when, without meaning to, she found herself saying, "Tomorrow night, Tavio, wants to walk me home from Fornara." She noted she had deliberately dropped the initial O, to make his name sound more like the names common in *Lingòt*. Her mama's head had swivelled towards her in the dark: "Oh?"

Instantly, Lena felt guilty. "I won't let him come if you think it's not all right."

"Well, tomorrow is a work night."

Lena blushed. She hadn't given that any thought. "It's just that…" she stammered, "he's asked me to a dance on Sunday night and I told him I'd ask you and tell him on Wednesday."

"A dance on Sunday night? Where?"

"It's…in a garden. That's what he said, in a garden. With lanterns in the trees. It sounds ever so nice, Mama. Dancing under the stars."

Gioana was silent. Lena began to be afraid she'd say she couldn't go. Then she worried that her mama was hurt because she wasn't included. She said, "Maybe you could come too."

Her mama laughed. "Child, young men from the university don't go dancing with their girls' mamas in tow."

"Am I his girl, Mama?" Lena asked breathlessly.

Gioana found her daughter's hand on the sheet. "You like him a lot, your 'Tavio, don't you?" She felt her sweet girl nod on her pillow, sensed her blushing. "Nothing wrong with that, child," she said.

Lena gave her mama's hand a grateful squeeze. Side by side they lay for a while, silent in the night. Then her mother spoke again. "It's just that…well, you need to be careful. Students, you see…" she hesitated. "Well, their lives are not like ours. It's… different for them."

Lena waited: her mama would explain. After a while Gioana went on: "Your 'Tavio's from *Firenze,* you said. That's very far away. He'll go back to his family for the summer, won't he?"

Lena recalled his words last Sunday, and her throat tightened. "When the exams are over."

"He'll likely make his life where his family lives…"

Away from Turin. The thought shocked Lena. Her eyes misted over. "I could never live so far away from you," she whispered.

Her mama gave her hand another squeeze. "There you are," she said gently. "You want to be careful not to… Well, not to let your heart carry you away."

They had left it at that. Lena hadn't fallen asleep for a long time. Next to her, her mama sighed over and over again. At last the smooth breathing next to her told Lena that her mama was asleep. Still, Lena remained restless. She tossed and turned under their sheet. At last fell asleep and dreamt of Ottavio. He was on the back platform of a train pulling away from Porta Nuova, moving faster and faster. She was running on the tracks, after it, her hands reaching for him on the rear platform. He too, was reaching for her, leaning over the guardrail, his hands signing 'come on, come on'. But the train was pulling away faster and faster. She couldn't keep up with it. She stood on the tracks, watched it grow smaller and smaller, then disappear.

In the morning, over their *cafelàit* at the kitchen table, she told her dream to her mama.

"You would like to go to the dance, wouldn't you?" Gioana said, when her tale was over.

Blushing, Lena nodded. "I would, Mama."

"Well then, perhaps you should go," Gioana said. "Just be sure you come away early enough to catch the last tram."

Half laughing half crying, Lena reached across the table to give her mama a big hug. Gioana held her tight for a moment, then took hold of her hands, looked deep into her eyes and said: "Just don't do anything you wouldn't do if I *were* there to see it."

So, Lena thought, tonight she could tell Ottavio that she would go to the dance. But the thought of him walking her home to Le Basse still troubled her. Maybe she'd tell him to leave her at the tram stop in front of the Cinema Lingotto. Yes, that felt better. She'd tell him that.

That night, after they'd all gone to bed, a row broke out in the courtyard next door. The racket went on for hours – a man's drunken curses, children crying, crashes, the dull sounds of blows and a woman's screams. Through it all, Lena and her mama held each other tight in their bed until the slamming of a door, dying into silence, told them the man had left. Long after that, Lena, heart pounding and throat parched, could not fall asleep. And she was again startled awake before dawn, this time by a drunken woman singing the same snatch of ballad over and over again:

> "*S'i beivèissa nen tant ëd vin*
> *St'ora si mi saría già mòrta, òh,*
> *Trala – la – la – là!*"

> If I didn't drink so much wine
> By this time I'd already be dead, oh
> Trala – la – la – la!

The sound shocked and shamed Lena, unbearable. She was used to brutish, drunken men, but a *woman*...

What they'd heard earlier that night hurt her like a wound received in a nightmare from which she couldn't wake up. Her heart kept pounding: a *woman* drunk... She couldn't even talk to her mama about it; it was all too close, too painful. She just wanted to close her eyes and drift away forever, pretend that nightmare had never been part of her life.

Then a frightening thought flared up in her mind: what if Ottavio had been here tonight? What if he'd walked her home tonight and heard it all? She'd been right: she must end their walk at the cinema. And the same thing on Sunday. It would be natural to say goodnight at the tram stop where he'd come to pick her up.

All through the day, the distressing tune heard in the night hounded her, a disturbing background to her thoughts of Ottavio and Sunday's dance.

Time and again throughout the morning, she struggled to keep the awful tune from breaking through her lips. She even resorted to holding a wire length between her lips, the way a seamstress holds her pins. But after lunch the tune snuck by her guard and she hummed it. Before she could stop herself, the finisher next to her, began to sing it:

> "Dame mach un bicer ëd vin,
> Ch'i l'hai tanta mal a la testa, òh!
> Trala – la – la – la!"

> Oh, do give me a glass of wine,
> For I have an awful headache.
> Trala – la – la – la!

On the *trala-la-la-la*, the rest of the bench joined in, going on to the next stanza.

> "S'it bevèisse nen tant vin
> Mal la testa at passerìa, òh!
> Trala – la – la – la!"

> If you didn't drink so much wine,
> Your headache would go away!
> Trala – la – la – la!

Lena sat, lips pinched, furiously plying her wires through the whole ballad, mad at herself. She'd brought this upon herself. What if she did something like this on Sunday, what if she embarrassed herself like this with Ottavio? The thought was unbearable.

83

Then she recalled her mother's words. "Their life is different." Lena found comfort in that thought: Ottavio was from Florence, he didn't know *Piemontèis*. That ghastly tune would mean nothing to him. It would be all right.

All around her, the women kept singing, the whole workshop together:

> *"S'i beivèissa nen tant vin,*
> *St'ora sì i sarìa gia mòrta, òh.*
> *Trala -la-la-la."*

> If I didn't drink a lot of wine,
> By now I'd be dead, oh.
> Trala-la-la-la.

Suddenly, an immense sadness descended upon Lena, a desperate, overwhelming loneliness. She broke into a child-like, uncontainable howling.

Wednesday night came and went without incident. Ottavio came, walked her as far as the cinema and said goodbye there. On Thursday morning, she was greeted at Fornara by the expected teasing, but somehow it didn't hurt. Yesterday's emotional storm had come and gone, leaving only a hazy trace in Lena's memory. If anything, her desolate sobbing softened her friends' teasing, so Lena went on sunnier than ever, like a spring sky freshly scoured by a passing storm. Now all she could think about was next Sunday night, and dancing with Ottavio under the stars.

On Saturday afternoon, walking home arm in arm as usual, Adelaide asked: "So what you going to wear?"

Lena had already given this a good deal of thought: what did girls wear at his kind of dance? Her choices were limited: it would have to be either her church dress or the black skirt. She worried that it wouldn't be good enough. But then she thought of the silk blouse her mama had given her for her last birthday, the loveliest thing she'd ever had, silky, sweet, brilliant colours, with puffed sleeves and a *jabot* at the neckline. She answered without hesitation: "My birthday blouse."

"And your hair, what are you going to do with your hair?"

"My hair?" Lena cried, surprised. She had given no thought to her hair. People always said it was lovely. Now Adelaide's question started her worrying, so, on Saturday she and her mama washed it after work.

On Sunday night she went to meet her friend with a new bounce in her step. But she froze before she reached *Via Nizza*. What if Ottavio wasn't there yet? What if she got there first and had to wait? She looked around for anyone around watching her. Then she tried to reassure herself: if she got there first, she could pretend she was studying the cinema's posters. She started to turn the corner but then a new, awful thought struck her: what if he stood her up? She stepped back from the corner and flattened herself against the wall. She'd wait here, out of sight, watch for him to arrive. Then when she saw him, she would step out and walk to meet him, like she'd just got there.

Her anxiety stretched the next few minutes into eternity, but soon a tram stopped by the cinema. It looked empty. Her heart sank: he wasn't going to come! The tram chugged away, and she saw him, looking around for her. She ran out to meet him. He reached out and caught her hands. "You are here! I'm so glad."

"Me, too!" she cried, suddenly blissful.

"Come," he said, offering her his arm to walk across *Via Nizza.* "I have a surprise for you."

She beamed up at him, dazzled, relishing his gesture. *Just like in the movies,* she thought, taking his arm the way she'd seen film stars do in the films. He laid his hand over hers. Across the street they boarded an in-bound tram. Ottavio paid the fares and escorted her to a seat, sitting in the seat behind her and leaning forward toward her.

"So," she asked, turning in her seat to face him, "what's my surprise?"

"Wait till we get off," he urged.

A few stops later Ottavio got off the tram and turned around to hand her down. The gesture delighted her. "Where are we going?" she asked. "You'll see," he told her, taking her hand and leading her to the horse-drawn cabs lined up by the entrance of the local hospital. "*Ai Glicini, per favore,*" Ottavio called up to the driver before joining Lena in the cab. This was her surprise, Lena thought, excited, a ride in a cab. She'd never been in a cab before. He was taking her to the dance in grand style, like a lady. She gave him a blissful smile.

The cab rolled off at a sedate trot. Soon the horse's hooves rang hollow. They were crossing the river. Lena had never ventured beyond the bridge. The elegant buildings that lined the tree-lined riverside boulevard had always intimidated her.

Beyond it, tree-covered hills rose, gently at first, then more steeply, rising to a height of some five hundred meters. Here and there, fancy villas dotted the hillside, ensconced in terraced gardens. Lena glanced at the dark mass of the hills: a few lights flickered here and there. She wished she could come and see it in daylight.

The cab turned right onto the riverside boulevard. Ottavio sat close to her, holding her hand. "And now your surprise," he said, close to her ear.

"What? Another one?" she cried.

Ottavio laughed, delighted. He placed a little velvet box in her hand.

"For me?" she gasped, accepting the little box gingerly: she'd never received a present from anyone but her mama, and that only for Christmas and birthdays. Lena gazed at the box in her hands, hesitating to open it. The cab rolled along under the plane trees. Streetlights on tall poles cast intermittent swatches of light on the tarmac, for a few yards interrupting the darkness.

"Here, let me," Ottavio said, taking hold of the box and opening it.

"Oh!" Lena gasped. In the lighted stretch they were crossing she saw the pink and white cameo resting on velvet. "It's so beautiful!"

"See the delicate profile?" Ottavio said. "It made me think of you." He picked up the cameo and turned it, silver back uppermost. He pointed to an inscription. "It's in my own handwriting. A memento of our lovely summer."

She took the cameo from his hand and raised it close to her eyes. "I'm afraid…" she murmured, her voice thin and shaky. The cab rolled into a dark stretch. "I…can't…see."

Ottavio laughed. "How silly of me. You'll see it at the club." He leaned closer and whispered: "It says, *Per Lena, il mio sole.*" (For Lena, my sunshine.)

Lena felt his breath warm on her cheek. Thoughts racing, she hid her face into his shoulder: he loved her, he loved her! But she could not read. She could barely make out printed words. In the club he would know she couldn't read.

"Will you wear it for me tonight?" He laid his finger in the hollow between her collarbones. *"This little spot here is just made for it."*

Lena offered her throat to him. She was being silly: he'd told her what the words said. She could pretend she was reading them.

The dance club in a wisteria garden seemed like a dream to Lena. Song after song, she danced dreamily in his arms. She'd never been so close to anyone, bodies touching. She wished the night would never end. She wished she could go on dancing under the stars forever.

Then the music stopped. It was time to leave. They walked, closely entwined, towards the cab waiting for them under the trees. Above the dark ribbon of the river, stars blazed in a velvet sky. She remembered Giancarlo's song at the Junction – *"Firenze, stanotte sei bella in un manto di stelle."* This was Turin, not Florence, but it too was beautiful in a mantle of stars.

Firenze, she thought wistfully. That was where Ottavio's family lived. How faraway was it? Her finger rose to the cameo at her throat. Soon he would leave. She leaned her head against his shoulder. "I'm so happy," she whispered. Ottavio raised her hand to his lips.

In the cab they sat close together, swaying to the rhythm of the trot, Ottavio's arm around her shoulders, in silence.

By the time they crossed the river, the silence had become oppressive. "Something wrong?" she asked timidly.

"No, nothing," came the abrupt answer. A moment later, he added, "Yes, there's something's wrong. I'm leaving day after tomorrow."

Lena drew a sharp breath: her mama had told her. She knew it had to come. *"But not tonight,"* she pleaded silently, trying not to cry. "But," she asked in a small voice, "you'll be back next fall?" She felt the shake of his head.

"I'm afraid not. My studies are done. I've got to go home."

For a long time, the horse's clip-clop filled Lena's awareness. Last Monday night her mama had said: "He'll make his life where his family is…" Lena reeled with grief. Outside, the horse's trot lost its hollow sound: they were back on the *Lingòt* side, back to everyday reality, her dream stranded on the right bank. Lena sighed. Her head still on his shoulder, she asked softly: "Will you be going back to your family?"

Ottavio drew a sigh of relief: she wasn't going to make a scene. "I will. I am to join my father's law practice. I am to take over from him, eventually, like he did from his father, and he from *his* father before him. Always been meant to be a lawyer, since I was born. It's the family's legacy, you see."

"But…you don't want to?"

He shrugged. "I'm not saying that. I'm just… I'm sad to leave Turin."

"Yes…" she sighed.

In the cab silence reigned once more.

After a while Lena asked, "But…you're…not unhappy? About being a lawyer?"

"No, I'm not. The law suits me well enough. I'm lucky to have the family business handed to me… In due time, of course."

The family business, Lena thought. In *Lingòt* that meant a lot. People who had a family business were important. They sat in the front pews.

"Does everybody in your family work for your father?" she asked.

"The men, yes, they do."

"You have brothers?"

"No brothers, just two sisters. So, you see, I'm the heir. It's up to me to continue the family tradition."

Lena nodded, not seeing, not able to imagine what the words meant, but sensing the obligation. They sat in silence, holding hands. The horse trotted on. Her head on his shoulder rocked gently with the roll of the cab. Suddenly, Lena realised that they were in approaching the Cinema *Lingotto.* She wanted to be let off here.

"Please, stop the cab," she cried urgently.

"What, here? I can't let you off here at this time of night," he objected. "I'll drive you to your door."

"No," she said, "I'd rather we said goodbye here. It's only a minute or two."

"All the more reason," he insisted.

"No, please," she cried, suddenly panicked. "Stop, stop!" she called out.

The cabby pulled up and looked to Ottavio over his shoulder.

Ottavio waved him on, "Around the next corner, up the road."

"No," Lena pleaded, "please…"

Ottavio drew her in close. "Please don't spoil our enchanted evening," he whispered in her hair. "Let these last few minutes be as perfect as the rest."

She sagged against him. She could not fight him. She couldn't disappoint him. She fought back tears: she wouldn't make a fool of herself. She would say goodbye properly. Her hand found the cameo at her neck. She would remember their 'enchanted evening' under the stars forever.

The cab rolled up *Via Passo Buole,* turned left into Le Basse. Lena held her breath: all was quiet. "It's here," she said in front of her gate. "Thank you so much. It's been lovely. And my beautiful surprise. I'll love it, always."

And then, before he could answer, there it was, the drunken woman's song: *S'i beivèissa nen tant vin…* The slurred dialect words lingered in the soft June night. Ottavio sniffed the air like a beast sensing danger. The drunken voice pierced Lena like a dagger, like a badge of infamy. *St'ora sì i sarìa già mòrta, òh! Trala-la-la-la!*

Lena made to bolt off the cab, but Ottavio caught hold of her. "Wait," he cried, "let me." He hurried around the cab to hand her down. "I'll walk you to your door."

No, no, please no! Lena kept shaking her head. She wanted it all to go away. She wanted him to leave, to not to have heard.

"I'll feel better if you let me," he said with a strained smile. Head bowed, Lena pushed the gate open and stepped into the courtyard. He stood just inside the gate, watching until she closed the kitchen door behind her.

Back on Via Nizza, the cab trotted sedately towards Ottavio's rooms in Via Po. In its dark corner, he sat stunned. The drunken woman's song hounded him, the squalor behind that desolate voice unbearable. He pressed his handkerchief to his mouth. This was Lena's world! The image of his sisters came clearly into his mind: Onoria, proud, accomplished, engaged to the heir of the Piccoluomini; and his younger sister, a history and philosophy student at the University of Florence. How would dear little Lena fare with them? There could be no question of ever bringing her home. The family expectations left no room for a beautiful innocent who could not read, no matter how dear.

In the kitchen, Lena ran, sobbing, into her mother's arms. "Shsss, shsss," Gioana soothed, rocking her gently until the sobbing stopped. "What's upset you? What happened?"

"It's that Ester again!" Lena wailed. "Oh, Mama, *he heard* her!"

Gioana grasped the full extent of the disaster. "I'm so sorry, my treasure," she said. "So, so sorry. Come, come and sit here with your mama, calm down."

She led her to the table and poured out a glass of lemonade for her. "Take a sip. Catch your breath," she urged, stroking Lena's shoulders, giving her time to calm down. At last, Lena lifted her head, wiped her face dry. She saw her mother's anxiety and rushed to reassure.

"Oh, Mama," she cried, "he was lovely!" And there and then she told her mama all the details of her first date. By the time she was finished both were smiling through tears, holding each other's hands.

"Oh!" Lena exclaimed, remembering.

"What is it?" Gioana asked. Lena's hand flew up to her cameo.

"He wrote something on the back," she said, fumbling with the safety lock.

"Here, let me," Gioana offered, reaching over. She undid the catch and handed the cameo to her daughter. Lena received it reverently. She turned it over. She drew the candle closer and peered at the silver back.

"It's here," she said, pointing. "Look, Mama, it says, 'For Lena, my sunshine'. It's in his handwriting!" She could see the inscription clearly now, but she still could not read it. "It's for me to remember him by."

"Did he write his name?" her mama asked softly.

Lena looked closer: on the right, below the writing, she could make out a small circle. "O," she said, pondering. Then she got it: "It's an O! O for Ottavio!" Her hand closed over her precious souvenir and she pressed it to her heart.

Don Marco's upset

Pier's trying to help with the wheat harvest got him into trouble with Don Marco. After that Sunday in the wheat field, Pier began to cough – the dust perhaps, or inadequate rest. Whatever the reason, Pier's Tuesday session with Don Marco didn't go well. Don Marco was upset. Assuming that Pier had been partying over the weekend, or perhaps smoking, he scolded him bitterly. Pier promised he would stop "as soon as the wheat is in".

Don Marco stared. It hadn't occurred to him that the lad still did farm work. It was bad enough his making his living at FIAT's bodyworks. Wood dust and chemical fumes didn't make for good breathing. And Pier wasn't any too strong at the best of times, though his chest had improved with the chest expansion exercises he had added to his warm-up routine before each voice practice. "You must be careful of your health for your voice's sake," he scolded. "Gargle morning and night. And go to bed early. Start tonight."

Pier promised, but it failed to put Don Marco at ease. All evening, he brooded about it, and snapped at his housekeeper. When the hall clock struck ten, he growled and stomped to the phone. At the other end Don Carlo's voice said: "Santa Rita's parish."

"I know it's late," Don Marco barked without identifying himself.

"Good evening, Don Marco," answered Don Carlo, surprised at the unusual absence of civilities, but recognising the well-known voice. "Something wrong?"

"Something not right, at the very least," the duomo choirmaster snapped back. "I'm worried about our Pier. Do you know that he's still working in the fields with his people?"

"No, I didn't. But it doesn't surprise me. I hear the father is a real tartar. When is he doing that?"

"Apparently, he was out harvesting wheat two days ago. And how does he get there?"

"His bike, I'd guess."

"But that's…what…at least an hour each way? He can't do that. Tonight his voice was reedy. And he was coughing. As it is, I am concerned that his constitution may not stand up to professional training. But he's got a gift all right. It's our job to guard it for him, Don Carlo."

There was a brief silence, then, before Don Carlo could respond, Don Marco went on: "You don't think he is…playing around on us, do you?"

"I can't see when he'd find the time. He is here every evening he is not with you."

"Not smoking, is he?"

"Not that I know."

"And that sawdust, at FIAT, is no good. But at least on Sundays… He needs his rest. Fieldwork is too much for him. We must put a stop to it."

Easier said than done, Don Carlo thought, feeling chastised. But he kept silent. The lad had to make a living somehow. Santa Rita's didn't have the resources to provide for him. He'd hoped that, once Pier was at the cathedral, Don Marco, with his wide connections, might be able to fund Pier's training from the church's deep pockets. At the other end of the line Don Marco heard the long sigh.

"I can talk to Don Michele at San Dalmazzo," Don Carlo said, sounding skeptical, "ask him to talk to Pier's father. But from what I hear he is a difficult man."

Don Marco was content to leave it at that. He retired to his quarters at the duomo and went to sleep, relieved at having addressed the Pier problem. But in Santa Rita's, Don Carlo lay awake. He knew from Don Michel that Pier's father wanted no truck with the church, that he rebuffed any attempt to restrain him, and mocked his wife's devotion. Nina, Pier's sister, had told him of the man's heavy drinking and brutality. The *La Speransa* family lived in an atmosphere of constant fear and mutual mistrust.

All night Don Carlo tossed and turned, worrying. Finally, at dawn he tossed his covers aside. There was no telephone at San Dalmass. To have a talk with Don Michel he would have to take himself there on his bike in the heat.

Later that morning, in the San Dalmass' sacristy, Don Michel shook his head. "This isn't a good time," he said. "We'll get nowhere in the middle of the big farm works."

"The big works is why he has to be spoken to *now*," Don Carlo countered. "Pier is stretched too thin. Have you seen him lately? He's as thin as a rake."

Don Michel shook his head. "Hasn't been around lately."

"He was here on Sunday."

"Not here in church, he wasn't."

"Not in church, no. He was at Santa Rita's singing at a wedding till past twelve. Then," Don Carlo added, the sweat from his own bike ride making his cassock sticky, "instead of eating his lunch and having a rest, as he should have, he pedalled all the way here in that heat, and spent the afternoon working the wheat field with the rest of them."

Don Michel's shoulders shrank in a helpless gesture. "That's how it is *an campagna.*" Farming life was like that: you worked with the season, whether you were up to it or not.

"But Pier had already put in his sixty hours at FIAT!" Don Carlo flared out.

"So had his brother Minòt. That makes no difference to Maté. He'll have his sons do what he tells them."

Don Carlo shook his head in frustration. He stormed up and down the small country sacristy, smashing his fist into the opposite palm. "Pier's got something else going for him," he barked. "He doesn't have to do this! But at this rate…" He stopped abruptly. "Let's go talk to the man right now," he said, making for the door.

Don Michel slapped his thigh and cried, "*Sacré*, no! Maria and the girls won't thank you! You don't know the man. You tackle him before the family, he'll feel he'd lost face and he'll take it out on them."

"Well then, when can we get hold of him? He must be made to see reason!"

Don Michel reflected that Maté and reason didn't have much truck with each other. Now *he* was pacing his sacristy, slamming fist into palm.

"Don Marco will be very upset…" Don Carlo grumbled.

"Then let *him* come deal with the man," Don Michel snapped.

Don Carlo glared at him. "*The Church,* Don Michel," he articulated sternly, calling the country parson to order, "is asking *us* to bring this man to reason."

Don Michel shook his head in submission, only muttering, restive. He knew that *'us'* really meant *him*. "Maté and reason…" he said without finishing the sentence.

"When can we get hold of the man?" insisted Don Carlo.

Don Michel sighed, shoulders drooping. "We can have a go tonight. He's always there after supper," he added, his chin jerking towards the tavern across the church square. "Maybe if we catch him before he goes in…"

"I can't be here tonight. I have a parish council meeting," Don Carlo objected.

"Might be just as well," Don Michel mumbled, resigned. The church trying the intimidate by a show in numbers would only put Maté's back up.

Don Michel's misgivings proved all too justified. After a restless supper of bread and cheese, he strolled out in the fading daylight to and the spot where the lane from *La Speransa* joined the one from *L'Asia*. Here he took cover in a hazelnut bush that marked the junction and waited for Maté. When he saw him approach, dim in the dusk, he stepped out of cover and into the middle of the lane, as though returning from the neighbouring farm.

"Oi, there, Maté," he called out, "I'll be glad of a word with you." He waited for Maté to get alongside. "Lovely night," he said falling into step.

Maté spewed a stream of tobacco juice onto the path's verge. They walked a few yards in silence, then Don Michel forced himself to speak again. "Had a visitor today," he said. Maté ignored him, working on his chew.

"From Santa Rita's," Don Michel added, "It's about Pier…"

Maté walked on, chewing. After a few steps, Don Michel tried once more.

"Looks like the church has big plans for your son, Maté. Don Carlo, you know, from *Santa Rita's*… He was sent to…to see what we could do to…to help him along."

No response. Don Michel hadn't had high hopes, but the dead silence next to him disarmed him. They reached the church square and Maté made for the tavern. Don Michel grabbed his arm: "They are worried about him at the duomo," he urged, holding on to him. "He's wearing himself out, working all day at FIAT, practicing nights, singing at functions, and then coming home to work in the fields on Sundays. It's too much for him, Maté. His health can't take it. You need to let him off."

Hand on the tavern's doorknob, Maté stared pointedly at the hand on his arm, then, without a word, he knocked it off and spewed a streak of tobacco juice between the priest's boots. "They want him," he stated, "let them buy him off me." He shouldered the tavern door open and swaggered in.

The next day, Don Carlo and Don Michel stood at attention in Don Marco's study at the cathedral, reporting on the outcome of their San Dalmass' delegation. As Don Carlo spoke, Don Marco's face turned a darker and darker hue. Half a step behind Don Carlo, Don Michel kept very still. His hands fretted his biretta in front of him, turning it around and around. In the silence that followed the end of Don Carlo's report, Don Marco got up from his desk and strode to the window. He stood with his back to the two parish priests, staring at the cobbled square below. Minutes went by in rigid silence, Don Michel barely daring to breathe. Outside, a tram clanked by, blasphemous, and Don Michel jumped. Don Marco didn't notice it. Don Michel glanced at Don Carlo, next to him: he still stood just as he had at the end of his report.

Suddenly, the rigid back by the window rumbled. "How much?"

The two priests turned in unison to face Don Marco's back, black in the sun-flooded window.

"How much?" Don Marco repeated his voice icy. He turned to face them. "How much is a son's life worth to this father?"

The two parish priests looked at each other, helpless shoulders lifting, hands flying out: they couldn't say.

"Well?" Don Marco snapped. "What will the brute's price be?"

Don Michel shook his head, at a loss. He knew Maté's cussedness and greed. He knew what a farmhand got for a year's work in San Dalmass. But how did one reckon the price of a father's hold on his grown sons? He glanced up at Don Carlo. He too was at a loss.

"Well?" Don Marco snapped.

Don Carlo's hand grabbed his chin. It was not the first time the church had bought a soul it wanted. A subversive image flashed through his mind: renaissance *conservatori,* hordes of orphaned or discarded children in the church's care, trained to sing for the greater glory of God, poor little blighters castrated to retain their soprano range. He banned the thought from his mind. "How much is it worth to the…" He checked himself – he had almost said "to the church". He mumbled, "…to the choir?"

"That's not the point," Don Marco hissed.

Don Carlo turned to Don Michel, "How much does a farmhand get a day?"

"Couldn't say," Don Michel shrugged, "*an campagna* they don't hire by the day."

"Yes, yes, but labour gets hired and paid. What do they pay?"

Don Michel's shoulders climbed to his ears, apologetic: "Farm hands aren't hired by the day. They work by the year, or at least by the season."

"So, how much!?" Don Marco growled.

Don Michel mumbled a figure and Don Carlo picked it up: "So if we divide that by 365 day and multiply by the number of Sundays..." He named his estimate of the cost of getting Pier off farm work.

Don Michel stared at his feet, blushing and shaking his head: Maté would never go for that.

Don Carlo consulted Don Marco's face. It said, "Try again." Don Carlo tried again. This time he calculated based on FIAT wages, and named his figure. Anxiously, he checked Don Marco's face: the eyes were hard, but he was still listening. He looked and read "maybe" on his screwed-up face.

Don Marco harrumphed. "We'll think about this," he said, dismissing them. "We'll let you know."

What Don Marco *did* think about was how to teach the crusty old sinner a lesson while getting what *he*, Don Marco, wanted. And what he wanted was Pier. The two parsons had got nowhere with the old cuss, so there was no point sending one of them to negotiate how many pieces of silver. What Don Marco itched to do was thrash the ignorant bastard, reduce him to a pleading heap. But he knew a face-to-face confrontation would get him nowhere. So, he pondered, toying with various scenarios. The Church's prime weapon through the ages had been the fear of hell. But these days *that* wouldn't bring the old cuss to heel. Could he be cowed with the power and magnificence of the church? A pleasing image: a purple-robed prelate descending from a long-nosed automobile in the shabby farmyard... He quickly discarded the thought: any display of wealth would jack the price up. Have him picked up and delivered here, deal with him on Don Marco's own ground. But what if the man refused? He could hardly kidnap him. Or could he?

Finally, he settled on intimidation of a different kind: threaten him with the weight of the law. He'd send a lawyer, legal-looking documents threatening severe consequences if he did not release his son. Yes, that might work. Plus ransom money, if it couldn't be helped. He found himself cursing the greedy bastard to hell. A momentary twinge of conscience deplored his bloodthirstiness. But he shrugged it off: it had always been the church's privilege to blast sinners to hell.

Guido

Walking home from Fornara on a Saturday in July, Lena set eyes on Guido for the first time. She was alone, having bid good night to Adelaide a block earlier. Lena walked deep in thought, looking forward to tomorrow's *festa dël pais*, the Niclin fête celebrating the town's patron saint's name day. There would be the big tent with a band and a wooden dance floor, swings, a carousel, all kinds of booths, even a fortune-teller. Oblivious to the cluster of young men lounging at the corner *Café-Ba*r's outdoor tables, she stepped onto the sidewalk and was waylaid. "*Ohi, tí, bela cita, andoa it vade tant an pressa?*" (Hey, pretty girl, where are you off to in such a hurry?) Lena stepped back into the road and walked on. She hated it when strangers addressed her in the familiar *ti*. The young man yelled after her, "What's the matter with you? Stuck up or something?"

Lena kept walking. Behind her, the loungers guffawed and taunted the *fieul* she had snubbed. "You won't get far with Lena that way. And Toni, here, is sweet on her. You going to fight over her?"

"Oh yeah?" the snubbed young man swaggered. He was a newcomer to the neighbourhood. But nobody told Guido Delloria what he could or couldn't do.

Toni spoke up. "No call for me to fight him off. Her mama will see to that. Right tied to her mama's apron strings, is our Lena."

"Yeah, Gioana won't let you have her unless to go to mass on Sunday." The gang sniggered. Guido glared from one to the next, establishing the pecking order. "So what's wrong with mass on Sunday?" he drawled back, "or with her mama looking out for the girl?"

The waitress delivered the cool drink Guido had ordered. He took a long draught then laid his glass on the table and lit a cigarette, displaying his silver lighter. Nobody spoke. Guido inhaled then blew smoke circles. "So, you know her," he said casually. "Sure we do," one of the youths answered. "Lives around the corner."

"Yeah, on Le Basse," said another.

A third one sniggered. "With her mama."

Guido wondered what the private joke was. New to the neighbourhood, he was in the dark and hated it.

One of the gang's tried to kick-start the fun again. "Bet you Toni won't stand for it," he taunted. Guido took another long pull at his *gaseus*. He would engage the gang on his own terms. Ignoring the gang, he stared at the green grocer's shop across the street: he'd soon teach them not to tangle with him.

Still, the teasing rankled. All his life, he had to fight for the deference he felt was his due. At home he'd been shoved aside in favour of his older brother. Guido hated playing second fiddle to Giacu, who was a clod. But, being the first-born son, Giacu, was their father's heir. So, there it was. Besides, Guido was the family's black sheep. He had no feeling for a farmer's life, no interest in vineyards, not even in the winery his father was so proud of. He was drawn to engines – cars, airplane – and to fast-moving life of the city. His father would never forgive him his mechanical bend; nor would his mother, who wanted a priest and a doctor in the family. But Guido had known what he wanted early on, ever since that mechanic from Asti had delivered the farm's first tractor. And now here he was where he wanted to be, twenty-six, and working in a FIAT lab. But the fireworks, at fourteen, when the old man had found out that he had forged his signature to apprentice himself to the Asti mechanic.

Thinking back to that storm, Guido sneered: farm machinery didn't turn him on. He was after racing engines, automobiles, motorbikes, airplanes even. He saw himself on the FIAT racing team one day, gymkhanas, racetracks, cheering crowds.

Yes, he scowled, he had taken all the pushing around he was going to take. Brother Giacu, now thirty, was still bossed around by his father, forever second in command, and forever second-guessed. And Michelin, Mama's darling, was dutifully studying to be a priest. But not *he*. No, he, Guido, had picked his own way, and proud of it. And disappointed as well, he admitted to himself: the family would never acknowledge that this was a major achievement.

He pushed the disturbing thought aside: that was their loss. They just didn't get it. They had no sense of the future. They couldn't see that the future lay in industry, in the cities, in automation, not in vintage wines or cheese. Cars, trucks, tractors, airplanes: *that* was the future. His folks still went about in horse-drawn buggies, for heaven sake! But here *he* was, in *Turin*, at FIAT, working with the engineers to develop bigger and better engines.

And he wasn't going to stop there, not he! He was learning his way around big organisations, learning to use the hierarchy to his advantage, at FIAT and in the party. He had joined Fascist Party two years ago and here he was, already the head of the Lingotto Youth Corps. And that was just the beginning: with his education and family connections, he could easily work his way up the Party's ladder. He had a good eye for opportunity. Right now he was angling for an appointment on the membership committee of a good part of town. He'd be a big fart one day, a man of influence.

But for all that, he continued to feel the pull of *Colin-a Longa*. Time and again he went home expecting the family to cheer his town success, and time and again he left dispirited, feeling short-changed. His father waved his excitement aside like an irritating fly. His mother shook her head pityingly, bemoaning what he could have been but for his wrong-headedness. And she went on and on about Michelin and his seminary, about Giaco's engagement to the vineyard adjoining *Colin-a Longa,* gloating that the wife's-to-be property would make the Dellorias the biggest wine producers between Alba to Asti.

Yes, his home visits were upsetting, yet, somehow, he couldn't stay away. Like today, Saturday, the eve of *San Giaco*'s day. He resented the made fuss over his brother's name day, yet here he was, running home to celebrate with the family.

Out of resentment and rebellion, a different possibility coalesced in his head: what if he didn't go to *Colin-a Longa* tonight? He'd never marry a vineyard to extend his father's holdings. When the time came, he meant to please himself; he'd find himself a beautiful city wife. This thought evoked the image of Lena. He got up, stepped into the *Café-Bar* and approached the woman at the espresso machine for information on Lena.

Sunday morning found Guido in a sober suit and hat in the shadows of the church portico. A few minutes before the start of the ten o'clock mass he spotted Lena crossing Via Nizza, arm in arm with her mother. He drew back into the shadow, instinctively squaring his shoulders.

Lena and Gioana climbed the flight of stairs, pausing at the top to put on their scarves and exchange greetings. Guido watched them file in ahead of a knot of women and children. He waited until a couple of men entered the church then tagged along behind them, stopping just inside, as most men did, waiting on the hoof for the end of the obligatory Sunday mass. From there, he watched as the churchgoers found their places. He saw Lena and her mother file into the second pew from the last and clicked his tongue irritably. In their church, his family's pew was up front, among the notables. He wanted Lena's to be up front as well, or at least in the middle, among the artisans and shopkeepers. But no, there she was, right at the back, a mere nobody. He almost left the church, but the incoming tide kept him pinned where he was.

Lena sat in her pew, her mother next to her in the aisle seat. She sat sideways, facing the in-coming faithful, greeting friends and acquaintances. Guido saw her smile brighten when a man greeted her. He frowned: she had no business doing that. Was she here for mass or to make eyes?

Then he noticed the men: their eyes sought her out as soon as they entered, brightened when they saw her in her usual seat. He now looked upon her with a different interest: her smile wasn't flirtatious. It was simple and trusting, a friendly child's smile. Her appeal could be a valuable asset to a man of his ambition. Yes, quite an asset, if she could be trusted.

He sneered, thinking of Giacu with his loaf-faced wife and himself with Lena. For a moment he gloated, imagining himself at *Colin-a Longa*'s dining table with Lena at his side, her beauty a spit in his brother's eye. But it was no good: she was a nobody. That was too bad.

His attention returned to the men at the back of the church, their eyes resting on Lena. *Come mosche tirà a la merda,* he thought with contempt – flies drawn to excrement. But their being so drawn gave him a hot rush: what a scoop it would be to bag the beauty they all drooled after! Like driving a racing automobile. She might not be fit for a wife, but she was well worth a good chase.

Don Marco lays down the law

It was a good three weeks from the failure of his first San Dalmass delegation that Don Marco's legal envoy had last reported how his had fared with Maté.

"A hard nut," was the lawyer's assessment, and he added with an appreciative grin: "If he haggled with the devil, he'd soon own a piece of hell."

Not amused, Don Marco cut to the chase. "How much?"

The attorney named Maté's price. Don Marco scowled. But after a silence he asked: "And it's binding? He can't go back on it?"

The attorney assured him with a nod. "Before the law, human and divine. Of course, *I* can only speak for the first. But I made it absolutely clear to the old goat that, at any breach of contract we'll come down on him like a ton of bricks."

"And he bought it?" Don Marco squinted at him sideways, lips pursed.

The lawyer nodded, assured. "I took the trouble to find out a bit about his antecedents before I went," he grinned. "Turns out his real name's Mathieu Vallard. Up in Val di Susa, he was known as DesPrès, because he comes from the *Vallée des Près*, over the border, near Briançon. He kept a small sheep farm over there, as cover, or rather his family did – yes, he *did* have wife and children in France. But he was a smuggler by trade – livestock, tobacco, liquor, watches…anything he could lay his hands on. He was well known all the way down to Rivoli. He came out here years ago, to hide, when the border patrols of both France and Switzerland were after him."

Don Marco nodded, thoughtful.

"So, you see," the lawyer concluded, "We've got him: he steps out of line, we turn him over."

"Statute of limitations?" queried Don Marco.

"Applies to the smuggling," the lawyer conceded, "though I doubt very much he'd knows anything about that."

"He might surprise you," Don Marco countered.

"Ah, *but*… That little border scuffled I mentioned, it ended up in a chase over the *Mer de Glace* and one of the French guards got killed. So, you see, we've got him all right."

"So, with all that, why do we pay him, why not just have him arrested?"

The lawyer's shoulders rose to his ears. "There's the family, out at *La Speranza*. He's a lout, by all accounts, including the parish priest. But, now and then, he *does* do some work. There're jobs on a farm a woman and children can't handle. They need him."

Don Marco nodded assent, bitter though it was. At least Pier was now free. On Sundays, anyway, came the unwelcome afterthought. Pier still worked at FIAT. Don Marco worried about all that wood dust and fumes, six days a week. He wanted him out of FIAT as well. But he couldn't do anything about that just yet. Perhaps when he was surer of the lad. Time would tell. Meantime, he'd start with setting down new rules for Pier, see how he handled himself. He would tackle him tonight.

That evening, when Pier arrived for his session Don Marco called him into his study. "Sit down," he ordered from behind his ample desk. "We need to talk."

Pier stepped forward, reluctant. He hated being sat down in somebody's office, it made him feel…trapped. He took a deep breath and, mindful of

Matilde's instructions, squared his shoulders and raised his chin. *No reason to be afraid,* he told himself. He sat down. "Yes, Don Marco?" he said.

"You've come a long way since last February," the cantor started. "But lately you've been looking worn out. I've been worried about you." His eyes assessed Pier's reaction. Pier kept a blank face, with attentive eye contact. The priest reflected: three months ago, his eyes would have been on his boots. The lad was coming along.

Aloud, he continued, "Don Carlo tells me that the two nights a week you're not here, you practice at Santa Rita's."

Now how would he know that, Pier thought, bristling. His face remained unruffled.

Don Marco got up and paced the office. He fetched up by the window overlooking the square. A tram trundled by, filling the room with the usual screech and rumble of metal. Don Marco waited it out by the window, then turned to face Pier. He found him waiting, eyes riveted on his face. Don Marco suppressed a smile: he obviously had Pier's full attention.

"You need more rest," he decreed. "You need a proper schedule with specific times for work, for practice, *and* for *rest*." He stopped, assessing the lad's reaction. Pier lowered his head obediently. Don Marco continued, "I've been watching you, this spring. Since the good weather's started, you've been getting thinner, more drawn. I wondered what you were doing to yourself. Then you told me about the winter wheat." Don Marco shook his head sadly, scolding. Pier waited, attentive.

Don Marco resumed: "It's all very proper that you should want to help your family at *La Speranza…*" He caught Pier's start, his eyes narrowing in surprise that the cantor knew the name of the family's farm, a name he had pronounced in its Italian form. The lad's reaction pleased him. "Yes," he said, "we've heard…" He let the statement hang a moment before continuing: "As your voice teacher and your mentor, I see that you've simply been *doing too much.*" He laid stress on the last words, scolding, the concerned regret on his face reminding the culprit of earlier warnings. He leaned forward and scanned: "You're burning the candle at both ends."

For the first time, Pier's eyes wavered, and he looked down. Don Marco smiled to himself, satisfied, and went on: "Arrangements have been made so that you won't be expected to work on the farm anymore."

Pier's alarmed eyes flew to Don Marco's. "What arrangements?" he demanded. "What about my pa?"

Don Marco held a pontifical palm toward the lad, demanding calm and obedience. "Your father has agreed."

"My pa's agreed!? To what?"

"You needn't concern yourself," Don Marco cut him off. "You won't be expected in the fields anymore. No more needs to be said."

"But…my ma, my sisters?"

"They won't suffer from it," Don Marco assured him. That point was closed. He returned to his desk and sat down.

Pier was rocked by a storm of emotions: he resented the cantor's intrusion; was amazed that his pa had agreed to let him off; wondered what had made him agree; feared the fall-out at the farm; and was relieved at having sanctioned Sundays off from field work.

It took some time before he considered that Don Marco had taken a lot of trouble for his sake. He was unexpectedly touched. But then a second thought arose: it was his voice the priest cared about, not him.

Despite this second thought, he found himself blushing, ashamed of his deception about the theatre, ashamed that he was using the old priest.

Sitting back in his chair, forearms squarely on his desk, Don Marco watched the waves of emotions flow by across Pier's face, enjoying the lad's amazement, waiting for expressions of gratitude. None came. *That's still too much to expect,* he told himself: *the lad's still barely housebroken; it will come in time.*

"Now for your new rules," he resumed, "to take proper care of your voice. Exercise is good for your wind, but you must not overdo it, use care. Your bicycle…" He waggled his head. "No more bike rides in bad weather or late at night. If you sweat, you must change right away so you won't catch a chill. From now on you are to take a tram to come here after dark; or to go anywhere else. Is that clear?"

Pier nodded, not looking up. He was angry: the priest had no business telling him how to live his life. What he was asking was absurd. He came here straight from FIAT, for his session, seven to nine in the evening. If he had to take the tram to the duomo, his bike would be left back there, at FIAT. He'd only have to get back there to get it, and that would make his ride home even later at night. And his sessions with Signora Agiati, how was he to fit them in, without his bicycle? Yes, there were trams, but that would take forever.

"Any problem?" Don Marco broke in on his thoughts.

"It's just…" Pier started and got no further. Don Marco's silence pressured him to explain. But what could Pier say? He couldn't mention his opera lessons. He needed Don Marco, he owed him his new free Sundays; and part of him recognised that the irksome new rules were meant to protect…*my gift,* he scoffed to himself. He valued his voice as much as the priest did, but without his bicycle he'd lose his freedom. Having to use the trams chafed like a tether, a steel clamp and chain on his ankle.

He struggled to redirect his thinking and finally stammered out: "It will be…a big change. It'll … take time to get used to it."

"But you will," Don Marco affirmed

"Yes, I will. But it will take me longer to get here," Pier said, envisioning the six o'clock hordes pressing into already packed trams. "I might not be able to get here by seven…"

Don Marco smiled, benevolent and firm. "You'll find you will, if you leave FIAT by 6:15." Pier still demurred. "And if you don't," Don Marco dismissed the problem, "we'll revise your schedule. We'll make it 7:15."

Don Marco picked up a typed document, the interview over, and soon appeared engrossed in reading. Pier did not move. As he turned a page, Don Marco glanced up briefly. "Get your score ready in the practice room," he said. "Start your warm-up. I'll join you in fifteen minutes."

Pier stood up and headed for the door without a word. He was angry.

"Oh, and," Don Marco called after him, "this Thursday, take the tram. Then we will see how it works." He returned to his reading.

Pier grabbed the door handle.

"And one more thing," Don Marco's voice stopped him again. "You'll find you'll blend in better in town if you speak of your parents as mom and dad, instead of ma and pa."

Pier flushed and yanked the door open.

Later that night, after his session, Pier leapt on his bike and pedalled furiously up Via Venti Settembre. His anger, contained for the sake of his training, broke out now in that frantic dash over the cobblestones. Don Marco had yanked his chain: he was telling him how to live. He'd got him out from under his pa, but had put himself right in his place, telling him how to speak, how to breathe!

In the deepening summer gloaming, Pier struck out across the part of the city he had only recently discovered, on Signora Agiati's suggestion – the fashionable district of La Crocetta. Up Corso Re Umberto, he zipped around the leisurely evening traffic, and cursed when trams clanked their bells at him. It was only when he reached Piazza D'Armi that he realised that he was winded and drenched in sweat. Still fuming, he heard again Don Marco's voice, "If you sweat…don't catch a chill."

Cursing, he slowed down. He didn't want to catch a chill. It did mess up his voice for weeks. But then Don Marco's parting voice struck again. "You'll blend in better in town…" To hell with mom and dad! He'd always said ma and pa, everybody did!

Then he remembered the Santa Rita's schoolboys, shedding their chorister's garbs in the changing room: they *did* say mother and father. And the younger ones said *mama* and *papà*. And at the duomo, people spoke Italian more often than *Piemontèis*.

Then the image of his sessions with Signora *Agiati* came to his mind, the care she put into shaping the way he pronounced the words of the arias they were working on. With Don Carlo and Don Marco, the way he said his Italian words had never come into his lessons because he was singing in Latin.

Somehow, the thought of Matilde Agiati calmed him down. He was learning so much from her. He was learning to *act*, so that, one day, he'd have a chance to sing opera. He was learning a lot more: he was learning *how to be,* how to feel, how to carry himself so as to fit in better in the city.

Don Marco's words now echoed again in his mind: "…you'll blend in better." That was what he wanted more than anything, *to fit in,* to fit in *in the city*. He liked the way he felt when he moved and talked like the elegant men he'd been watching in Via Roma, at The Regio and at La Crocetta. He could see and *feel* the difference between them and the workers at FIAT; or the men that hung out with Lorèns' at the Santa Rita café. There was no question which he liked better, which he would rather be.

Suddenly, he found himself smiling, and discovered he wasn't angry any more. He now pedalled easily, rolling around in his mouth the uncustomed words - *madre, padre, mamma, papa* - trying to get the vowels right. And his wind was back to normal. He *would* learn to fit in in the city. Elated, he broke into full-throated song: *Libiamo, Libiamo, ne' lieti calici...* Then, abruptly, he stopped himself, concentrated on breathing through his nose: *Signora* Agiati had warned him not to sing outdoors in the night air. It was bad for his vocal cords.

Chapter Five

The citification of Pier

During the two months that followed the start of his training with Matilde Agiati, Pier lived and breathed for those two evenings a week when he would be with her. At all times, whether at home, at FIAT or at the cathedral, he shaped everything he did on the instructions Signora Agiati had given him. From week to week, she led him through 'acting like' the characters in the roles he sang. She always worked with him on leading roles, be it protagonist or antagonist, both tenor and baritone. Under her guidance, Rodolfo followed Alfredo, then came Figaro and the Count, then Radames and Andrea Chenier.

"I'll leave your voice training for better teachers than I," she told him, "but on stage you have to *act* as well as sing. On stage the audience sees this person *before* you ever sing a single note, and what they see prepares them for what they will believe; so you have to look the character you want them to believe in. The way you look must make them accept that you are…" she drew herself up into a haughty stance, chin in the air, "…a prince or…", abruptly she collapsed her posture and waggled her head, "…a pauper, a hero or a villain, whatever your role calls for."

One of the tasks she assigned him between sessions was to pick a character each morning and to *be* that character for the entire day. "You can't just *pretend,*" she drummed into him. "You must *be* that person, whatever you are doing – eating, drinking, talking, walking down the street."

Pier took her instructions to heart: at home, at work, on his way to the duomo, he practiced. At work, he remembered her recommendations to take what she had called 'body breaks' to offset the long hours of stooping at his lathe: recalling Signora Agiati's regal walk, he stretched his spine, squared his shoulders and raised his chin whenever he laid aside the piece of work he had just milled, and walked to fetch the next plank. Time and again, he mentally repeated her instruction: "Walk like you are the crown prince."

Now that he no longer worked at *La Speransa* on Sundays, he began to expand his forays into parts of the city Signora Agiati had mentioned as places where he might hear proper Italian spoken, the fashionable La Crocetta district, Via Pietro Micca, Piazza Solferino, the wide, shady avenues of aristocratic Turin where the villas of old courtiers now housed the city's upper class. Everywhere he went, he watched, noticed, remembered, and he fashioned himself on what he saw around him.

By late July, the women at FIAT began to nudge each other when he walked by. There was a female crew at the workstation next to his. The women began to walk past Pier's lathe giggling and nudging each other, trying to catch his eye. Pier went through the motions of his job oblivious to their antics, his mind engaged with images from elsewhere. From time to time, in the occasional lulls in the crushing machine noise, he could be heard singing *sottovoce* snatches of arias. More than once his *capo reparto* recalled him to his task with heavy sarcasm: "Keep your mind on your work, Caruso."

At this time, Pier was beginning to worry that the summer was going by so fast it would soon be fall, and Signora Agiati had said last spring that she wouldn't have time for his sessions once rehearsals for the new opera season started. The thought of a new opera season sent shivers down his spine: he would be able to go back to the Regio! But he'd lose…*all this*, he thought, fighting off despair. He'd lose his two evenings a week with his guide to that wondrous world, a world he couldn't have imagined six months ago. He had to get as much as he could from her while she had the time. She seemed pleased with his progress in body technique, but not so pleased with his diction. Time and again she shook her head at the way he said certain words. Twice last week she had got frustrated over vowel sounds she said were two broad or too tight or too flat; and he was having trouble with his sibilants, as she called them, his 's' and 'z'. Last week it had led to knuckle-wrapping. "Ts, ts, ts, Pier, *ts*, not ds! Try again*: distan – ts – a*." He had repeated the word till he got it right and she had smiled. But later he had trouble remembering in which words the 'z' was pronounced ts and in which ds. The word *menzogne* came to his mind: he was almost sure that it was pronounced dz, but it worried him that he was never sure. He just wasn't used to the Italian sounds, and it was easy to make mistakes.

Last Tuesday she had almost lost her patience with him. She'd wrapped her pencil sharply on the table, screaming: "No, no, no, And NO!" Her finger had rapped on her lips to nail his attention there as she repeated with exaggerated articulation the word he had bungled, insisting that he get the proper Florentine Italian pronunciation. "Now you try it," she had demanded. He had done his best to reproduce her sounds exactly. "Much better," she'd relented. But he could see that she was still not satisfied. "Part of the reason you are having so much trouble," she said, leading him to the apartment door, "is that you hear nothing but *Piemontèis* all day long. You must spend more time with people who speak good Italian."

He had nodded obediently, and said *"Buona notte"* in his best Italian. But as he clattered down her polished granite stairs, an angry voice in his head shouted at her, "And where would *I* find good Italian?"

The next day he was haunted by again her imperious voice saying, "Do it again!" All right! He'd done it again. He'd do it a million times if he had to, till he got it right.

Another thing she'd spoken to him about was his clothes. He had resented it, even though he knew she was right: he always felt out of place, except at FIAT where he didn't care to fit in. So, he again asked her for guidance. "A pair of city shoes," she prescribed. "No hobnailed workboots, except at work, if you must. Light gabardine slacks and a blazer for summer. A dark blue suit and white shirt for functions. With a silk tie, of course." He had followed her advice and it had cost him all his summer earnings from weddings and other private functions, but at last Signora Agiati had nodded her approval.

Pier enjoyed his new image: walking down the street or sipping an espresso in a Via Roma café, people now made eye contact with him, occasionally even acknowledged him with a nod or a smile, a fact that gave him inordinate pleasure. In his old clothes, strangers had looked right through him, like he wasn't there.

And Nina loved his new clothes. She took very good care of his white shirt, he thought with a smile. And his blue suit was always brushed and pressed to perfection. Yes, Nina took pride in her brother's progress; in his new look in his city clothes and new city manners. He saw pleasure and pride in her eyes. Then at times she scolded him because he was spending too much; and his pleasure was quickly obscured by the thought of the hardships in his sister's life.

The Niclin Fête

Guido began his Lena campaign that very morning. At the *Ite Missa est,* he shuffled out of the church with the other men clustered by the doors and took his observation spot in the shadow of the portico. In a few minutes, the mass ritual properly finished when the officiating priest left the altar, Lena and Gioana emerged from the church and paused to lower their scarves before starting down the steps. Guido tipped his hat forward, preparing to follow.

"Lena, wait up," a young voice ahead of him called out. Lena and Gioana waited, looking back at a sprightly girl trotting to catch up with them. "*Bondì,* Gioana," Adelaide greeted the older woman, then turned to Lena. "Could you meet me at the *filobus* this afternoon? I'm going with my mama, to see my sister's new baby, but I'll be there."

"All right," Lena agreed.

"Two thirty then. I'll join you right off my tram."

"Say hello to Marta for us," Gioana commissioned her.

The *filobus:* that suited Guido just fine. There was only one *filobus* in this neighbourhood, the trolley that extended public transport from the city terminal to Niclin, a good half an hour's run into the countryside. So, Lena and her friend were going to *festa dël pàis,* Niclin's annual celebration of its patron saint's day. He would follow them. There always was a *bal* at these fêtes, where strangers could dance with no need of introductions.

By a quarter past two, knots of young people began forming at the *filobus* terminal. Girls clustered together, excited at the outing, making eyes at the boys who stood in boisterous groups nearby, exchanging crude sallies of wit, bating the girls, who twittered and whispered.

Guido stood apart from both groups, watching for an opportunity to catch Lena's eye. He didn't find it easy: she was engrossed in her friends' chatter; or else she was being very coy. He began to suspect she was aware of him looking at her and was deliberately played hard to get. He got increasingly annoyed at 'her game'.

Across the square, an incoming trolley trundled in and disgorged a stream of black-clad figures, country folks in their best clothes for a Sunday afternoon visit to relatives in town. At its arrival, the two clusters across the square began to drift towards the outbound stop, while the driver and conductor left their empty *vehicle* and ambled over to the *Café-Bar* on the square, to re-emerge some minutes later, glasses in hand, to settle down at an outside table. Ten, fifteen minutes went by before the two men dragged themselves up and strolled over to their bus, closing its doors for the short run around the square to the departure line. The crowd surged forward, stampeding towards the coveted seats.

Lena claimed a seat by a window, halfway down the bus, and Adelaide plunked down next to her, the aisle quickly becoming crammed with bodies precariously hanging on to handles swinging down from the ceiling. Banter of dubious wit flew back and forth.

Guido forced his way through the crush and wriggled himself behind the last seat, where he could watch Lena.

On the half hour ride, he watched her closely: she chatted and laughed, excited, like all the girls. Much of the banter was aimed at her, but it seemed to go by right over her head. She seemed to take it all with good humour and reserve, neither shrieking nor guffawing, as the other girls did.

He liked that. *She is modest,* he thought. And suddenly in his mind his own words took on the quality of what he irritably thought of as his mother's '*convent voice*'.

Annoyed, Guido shook off the intrusion. Still, the thought stayed with him and he found himself agreeing with it: she *was* modest. Not artful, not teasing.

Unexpectedly, he was very happy. But then he noticed the obvious draw she had for the men, and his interest shifted gears.

Half an hour later, the *filobus* hissed to a stop in front of Niclin's town hall. The two friends pressed forward with the rest of the crush, making toward the exit.

With a glance over her shoulder, Adelaide elbowed Lena's ribs. "He's looking at you," she whispered.

Lena shoved her forward, moving with the crowd. Across the square, a troop of Black Shirts, bristling with badges and standards, was gathering around a marching band already blaring a fascist song. From somewhere out of sight, came the fulsome sound of an oompah-pah band.

"A polka," Adelaide cried, her feet picking up the rhythm. They hurried off around the town hall, towards the music and came into the church square. Here a multitude of stalls offered plaster images of Saint Giacomo, the town's patron saint, lace *quefas,* prayer books, rosaries, missals, saints' lives, vessels of holy water, presumed relics of *San Giaco.* Everywhere, people strolled among the vendors, fingering goods, bargaining, rejecting, and occasionally buying. Lesser peddlers with trays hung around their necks thrust their wares at the strollers, images of the saint, rosaries, medals, pinwheels, balloons, pestering them to buy. Disputes arose over price, people moved on. Swarms of screaming children darted here and there among the stalls, cannoning into people in their rush, cursed by weary stallholders on the lookout against their pilfering.

"We'd better get our handbags safely in front of us," Lena said, threading the shoulder strap over her head. The two friends strolled on, eager to spot the dance tent.

Suddenly, somewhere out of sight, a trumpet blared, and soon after a noisy parade came into view on the left of the church, led by marching drums and jingling bells, tumblers doing summersaults, and clowns pulling coloured kerchiefs out of their ears. Behind them came two men on longs stilts, several jugglers, and a middle-aged dancer in a Spanish dress rattling castanets. The parade swept through the church square, then exited right, drawing the crowd in its wake toward the fête's main grounds, the vast meadow behind the church, where the clowns, the jugglers and stilt men skilfully herded people towards a small show ring. while a dramatic roll of drums announced the beginning of the next show.

Lena and her friend followed. Across the ring, a matador with the beginning of a paunch swaggered to the centre of the ring, a contemptuous scowl on his face, where he stopped and snapped his fingers above his head, summoning the Spanish dancer who trotted towards him, skirts flouncing, to join him in a strutting fandango. Drum, trumpet, guitars and castanets struggled to keep at bay the noise of an oompah-pah band blaring over on the left.

Adelaide nudged Lena. "It's over there," she said, eager to get to the *bal*. With an eager look towards a white tent that dominated the fairground, Lena nodded, but paused to retrieve a coin for the clown.

The *bal*'s huge canopy shimmered in the July sun. Underneath it, an eight-piece band easily drowned out all other sound, including the carousel's tinny jingle, across the grounds.

The two girls approached eagerly, bought tickets for one dance and waited for the tune then playing to come to an end. Adelaide's hand beat time on the dance platform railing, and her shoulders jiggled to the rhythm.

The band stopped and the dancers began to shift, some heading for the exit, others switching partners and handing in their tickets for the next dance.

"Come on, let's go!" Adelaide grabbed Lena's hand, dashing to the entrance as soon as the access cleared. Lena followed her in. Behind them, a manly voice called out: "*Ch'a speta tòta, ch'a bala costa con mi!*" (Wait, miss, dance this one with me!)

Lena turned and saw a ruddy-faced young farmer eagerly reaching his hand toward her over the railing. Her hand flew to the cameo at the neck of her sprigged muslin dress. "Eh…" she stammered, drawn away by Adelaide. "I'm dancing this one with my friend. Otherwise…" She fumbled for an excuse: "she has no partner."

The young man stretched further over the railing and grabbed the girls' joined hands. "No problem," he cried, then turned to yell over his shoulder: "Pinòt, come here! There's a pretty *turinèisa* for you."

Before the said Pinòt could join them, the band started to play, and Adelaide jerked their hands free and spun away with Lena onto the dance floor. With an apologetic twitter, Lena looked back over her shoulder.

"*Ah, che balòssa!*" the young farmer cried, good-naturedly – you, naughty girl! "Come back for the next dance then," he added over the racket of the band. "*Sì?*"

Lena laughed and nodded. Adelaide, waltzing energetically, glanced back at the young farmer at the barrier, saw the approaching Pinòt, and gave Lena's hand an enthusiastic squeeze. They were off. Going to a *bal* with Lena was always like this: they needed tickets for the first dance, but after that, partners came out of the woodwork.

At the end of the dance the two young men rushed onto the dance floor to claim them. "Here you are at last!" cried Lena's new partner, taking her hand. "And don't you worry about your friend here; my brother Pinòt will take good care of her. I'm Carlin. And you?"

The music struck up a polka and Carlin swept her off at a good clip. "I'm Lena," she called out above the loud music.

Delight and strenuous dancing soon brought a sparkle to Lena's eyes. "It's put lovely roses on your cheeks," Carlin said, twirling her back into his arms after a *promenade*. "Stay with me for the next one," he urged, pulling her up close.

"Oh, my friend…"

"No worry," Carling assured her, "Pinòt will keep her happy."

Lena glanced over to Adelaide and saw her skipping lustily across the dance floor. "All right, then," she agreed. Delighted, Carlin pulled her in closer, still.

She stiffened, pushing back against his chest. "But then," she said, "I'm going back to my friend."

"Why? Don't you like dancing with me?" Carlin asked, launching her into a spin.

"I like it fine," she said when they were close enough again.

"I should say so!" Carlin laughed, showing good white teeth. "My brother and I are the best dancers in town. We always win all the prizes. You stick with me and tonight you'll walk out with that beautiful doll."

Lena followed the nod of his head to the day's *bal* prize, prominently displayed on a stand above the band.

"And my prize," Carlin said, pulling her back towards him and gazing deep into her eyes, "is that I've held the prettiest girl at the *festa* in my arms."

Lena blushed and lowered her eyes. She was embarrassed, though she wasn't sure why. Maybe it was being held so tight. It had been lovely with Ottavio. But this *fieul*… She'd only just met him, and he wasn't *fin*. It didn't feel right. She couldn't put her finger on what displeased her in him, but something did. *I won't dance more than two with him,* she told herself. *Anyhow, not right away,* she qualified. *Later, maybe.* She concluded her thought with: *That'll teach him.* But she didn't spell out what he was to be taught.

She scanned the dancers for Adelaide and found her beaming in Pinòt's arms. *She'll want to continue with him,* Lena thought, *if he asks her.* She'd have to shake free of Carlin on her own.

Vaguely seeking inspiration, she cast her eyes over the ring of onlookers lining the railing. Clumps of schoolgirls sat in pairs, perched atop the railing, legs dangling over the dance floor. Lena knew just what they were up to. She'd never done it but had often watched Adelaide at it with some other girl. They would sit on the railing, hands locked together, watching for the ticket men to turn their back, then jump in and snatch a free dance. Intent on watching the schoolgirls on the railing, her mind did not register the familiar face above their heads – the pushy young man who, last night, had waylaid her outside the *Lingòt* café. *What's he doing here?* flashed through her mind without registering. The frown caused by the annoying presence quickly dissolved, and the thought was forgotten.

The polka came to an end and Adelaide rushed over to Lena, dragging Pinòt by the hand. "Isn't this great?!" she cried over the crowd's noise. "I'll stay with mine for a while, he's a fantastic dancer. You dance with his brother?"

112

Carlin was already getting her into the frame for the tango that had started. "See," he crowed, "what did I tell you? You friend's happy. So you can stay with me!"

Lena shook her head. She would not be told with whom to dance, not even to please Adelaide. After this tango she'd look around *la festa* by herself for a while, then later perhaps, she might come back to this *fieul* – he *was* an awfully good dancer.

At the end of the tango, she left the *bal* and strolled around by herself, looking in at various stalls. She stepped up onto the slatted platform of the gold fish stand, leaning over the railing to get a closer look at the fish swimming in their bowls. She'd always liked the goldfish and had often tried her luck at winning one. Behind her, a crier was making a pitch for a fortune-teller's booth. Lena looked over her shoulder: she had never dared to have her fortune told, but maybe today she would.

She turned to leave, and disaster struck: her heel, stuck between two slats, came off her shoe. Lena cried out. She stumbled off the platform, struggling to recover her balance, and there she stood, on one foot, inspecting her wounded shoe. The heel was gone.

She looked back to the place where she had got stuck, but it was already crowded with onlookers. She cast her eyes around the crowd in a vague search for help, and there he was again, last night's *fieul,* watching her with a mocking grin. She quickly looked away, but he stepped past her to the fish stall, shoved the bystanders aside, and went to work with a pocketknife to free the trapped heel. A few minutes later, he handed it back to Lena without a word. She took it, nonplussed, not knowing what to do, standing lopsided, one shoe on, the other in two pieces in her hands.

"Now at least you have the makings of a whole shoe," he *fieul* teased.

But he'd spoken politely, not like last night. He'd used the formal third person proper between strangers. Lena just stood there, numb.

"Of course," he continued, "if you were a *country* girl, you'd just take the other shoe off."

"What, and walk barefoot at a *festa*!?" Lena cried, horrified at the impropriety.

"Well," he shrugged, "you could put the broken shoe back on and mince your way on tip-toes to a seat."

Lena considered that option. But then what? She'd still have to get to the *filobus,* and then to walk home from the terminal. She put her broken shoe on and tried a few awkward steps.

"Here," the young man took over, a hand under her elbow, "Let me prop you up. You look like you need it." He led her hobbling back to the mountebanks' ring and parked her on a bench. "Wait here," he ordered, disappearing with her broken shoe in the direction of the caravan. Moments later, she watched him mount the steps to the caravan door, knock and talk to someone inside.

A curtain rattled open across a side window, and the Spanish dancer smirked contemptuously at Lena. The matador came out, closed the door behind him and disappeared with Lena's rescuer around the vehicle. Time went by, Lena sat, getting increasingly upset. Then her rescuer was at her side with her shoe in his hand.

"The gypsy had what I needed," he said, delivering his trophy. "It's only glued, so you'll have to wait till the glue sets. Come, I'll prop you up as far as the café. We'll wait there till it dries."

Lena's hand flew to her cameo, but she rose obediently and tiptoed on her wounded shoe toward the trolley terminal, reluctantly leaning on the *fieul*'s arm. She'd only walked on a man's arm once before, on Ottavio's, the night they'd said goodbye, last June. At the thought her eyes welled up, but she kept tiptoeing her way until her rescuer deposited her in a chair outside the café. The Black Shirts were gone. All that was left now where they'd stood was the wall of the building facing the town hall with, daubed onto it in black paint, two, foot-tall fascist slogans – *CHI SI FERMA È PERDUTO* (he who stops is dead) and *CHI MI AMA MI SEGUA* (if you love me you'll follow me).

Next to her her rescuer said, "Come, it's not so bad. Your shoe can be saved. A cobbler will do a better job than I. Don't ruin your day."

A waitress appeared with the soft drinks he had ordered, and Lena reluctantly took a small sip.

"My mother broke her heel once," the young man said looking at her crumpled face. "In church, getting out of her pew to go to communion."

Lena looked up, horrified, and he grinned at her. "She was very embarrassed," he said. "But these things happen. These days we can even tease her about it, *if* she is in a good mood." He grinned again and Lena found herself smiling back.

Perhaps, she thought, still mistrustful, *he isn't so fresh.* But he wasn't *fin,* like Ottavio. But then, no one could be.

"You know," he said as though returning to an earlier topic, "I know your name, but you do not know mine. I'm Guido Delloria."

"You know my name?!" Lena exclaimed, thinking of last night's exchange by the Lingòt café: she'd certainly not told him her name. "How?"

"This morning after mass your friend called you Lena."

"You were in church? I didn't see you."

He sketched a nod and continued. "And, to finish a proper introduction, I am from the Monferrato, I live in Via Nizza, and I work in the prototypes lab at FIAT."

He waited for her to be impressed, but there was no sign that she was. "Last night…" he started again, "waylaying you like that, it was out of line, speaking to you the way I did. My mama taught me better than that. But tell me about you."

"Me? There's nothing to tell."

"Come, come, you are here, aren't you, so there's plenty to tell. I know you live with your mama." He stopped, waiting for her to speak.

"There's not much else to tell," she said with a shrug.

"Are you happy?" he asked with a half shrug that dismissed the notion.

"*Si, si, mi i son contenta,*" Lena answered. (Yes, I'm happy.)

"Why? Doing what?"

She shrugged at the silly question. "Just living together, *mi e mia mama.*"

"And …you work?"

"Yes, I work," Lena said with pride, "at Fornara."

Guido smiled, superior. "And what do you do, at Fornara?"

"I make safety pins."

He burst out laughing. "Safety pins!"

Lena resented the scorn in his voice: "I'm very good at it," she protested. "I'm the best they have."

"I'm sure you are," he said, dismissing her claim. Then he said, suddenly serious: "It's good to be proud of what you do. *I* am proud of the work *I* do. I chose it for myself.*"* He meant to stop there, but somehow he went on: "My father expected me to take over his business…"

He stopped, annoyed at himself for explaining to this chit of a girl, and lying to booth, to impress her. Well, he justified his lie; he couldn't very well display

115

the family's dirty linen in front of her. He went on: "My mother wanted me to be a priest," he smirked at that silly idea, "but I wanted to work with cars, and *that*'s what I'm doing. I started at FIAT when they were still in Corso Dante; it's the best automobile factory in the world." He bragged with a certain nostalgia for the early days in the small workshop when he'd occasionally worked shoulder to shoulder with Agnelli and Scarfiotti. Nowadays they didn't come around to the lab any more.

He turned back to Lena: "And you, what do *you* want?"

Lena shrugged. "I'm happy as I am," she said.

Guido cocked a crooked smile at her. "How old are you, anyway?" he asked. He still addressed her in the polite third person, but his tone was dismissive.

"Eighteen."

He laughed from the vast advantage of his twenty-six years. "Well, you won't always be eighteen. And you won't always live with your mama. What will you want then?"

"I'll live with my mama as long as I can," Lena said.

"Yes, but in the meantime…" Guido searched his mind for a way to steer the conversation away from her naïve satisfaction, "wouldn't it be better, if you found something more…well, something *with a future* to do? There can't be much future in safety pins."

Lena looked at him, with uncomprehending suspicion: what did he mean something with a future? She would always have a job at Fornara.

"Well," Guido started forcefully, but then ran dry: it was easy to see future possibilities for him, but what was this girl fit for? A girl's natural future was to get a husband and have kids, and with her looks… He stopped: he had better not touch upon that subject with her. "Well," he stalled, "it depends…on what you might be taught to do." He frowned: why was he bothering to talk seriously to this girl, with her eager spaniel's eyes? He shrugged and said, "Just for example, say that you could get a place at FIAT…"

Lena guffawed, "At *FIAT!* What would I want with FIAT? What would I do there?"

"Nothing," he snapped, annoyed, "unless you could be taught. There are women working there now, simple enough jobs, but someone has to do them."

"And *what for*?" she went on, ignoring him. "I'm happy where I am."

"But what if," he blustered, "you could… make more money?"

"Oh, I do very well at Fornara."

"But suppose you could make more? What do you make at Fornara anyway?"

Lena stiffened. It was one thing talking about her pay packet with the girls at work. They were pals, in the same boat. But coming from a *fieul* she'd just met, well, it was really too cheeky.

"OK, don't tell me," Guido snapped. "Just say that you could make..." He thought for a moment about women's wages at FIAT. He had no idea what they made - not anywhere near what the men made, to be sure. He named a random figure. "What if you could take *that* home to your mama every week?"

"That'll be the day," she scoffed. She made more than Adelaide's sister, who was a *commessa* in a flower shop; and more than Cichin-a's daughter, who was apprenticed to a shirt maker, and *that* was a trade that took years to learn.

"A woman can earn that much at FIAT," Guido insisted, "if she gets to be any good."

That silenced Lena: almost a third more than she was making now. With a nervous laugh, she dismissed the possibility: what could she and her mama spend so much money on anyway? The surprising answer swept over her quite unexpected: winter coats, instead of the crocheted shawls they now wore; proper snow boots, instead of wooden clogs; chicken every Sunday; a wool-stuffed quilt for their bed; perhaps even the films every Sunday.

Guido watched desire veil her eyes. "I could look into it for you," he swaggered.

Diffident, she shook her head: "No, thanks." She raised her foot to test the mended heel.

"It'll do to get you home by," he said, watching her.

Lena stood up and took a few steps, testing her mended shoe.

Out on the square people were beginning to stream towards the terminal from the two streets flanking the town hall. She glanced at the clock at the start of the trolley line: twenty past five. Inbound runs left on the half hour. She wished Adelaide would come back in time for the five thirty.

"You're worried about your friend," Guido said.

"Just wondering..."

"I'll go look for her. You just sit here."

He threw some coins on the table for their drinks and went off. Lena sat on, alone with the uneasy company of her thoughts.

117

Pier at ël Caval ëd Bronz

In early July, Pier was struck by the fact that the Sunday attendance at the duomo had thinned out. It puzzled him because in San Dalmass' one saw the same faces winter and summer, except during the big snows when outlying farms were cut off. As July drifted into August, he noticed that *Via Roma* was getting increasingly empty. Bored waiters lounged in café doorways. Then last week new notices in shop windows explained the change: *Chiuso per Ferie* or *Chiuso fino a Ferragosto* – closed for vacations until *Ferragosto* – the 15th of August, the magical end of the summer season.

Then last Thursday, Signora Agiati had announced her departure from the city. *"Vado in montagna. Ci vediamo dopo il Ferragosto."* (I'm going to the mountains. We'll see each other after *Ferragosto.)*

Like most middle- and upper-class Italians, she and her family were off to some vacation spot at the seaside or in the mountains, not to return until after the end of August. So, Pier was on his own, at loose ends in the city.

That Sunday afternoon, he strolled down Via Roma towards Piazza San Carlo. The sun was shining, and he was feeling smart and proper in his sand-coloured gabardine trousers, open-necked white shirt and blue linen blazer. He was in a perfect mood for the new adventure he'd been hatching, a cool drink at an outdoor table in the *Caval ëd Bron.* But suddenly he was brought up short: fascist slogans had appeared overnight, slapped on in black paint, defacing the polished granite of the arcade – *VIVA IL DUCE.* A few arches further he saw another one – *CREDERE OBBEDIRE COMPATTERE* – Believe, Obey, Fight.

Long used to these intrusions on lesser walls, both in the city and the countryside, finding one here, on the privileged elegance of the *Torino bene,* shocked Pier; it took his breath away.

He walked on, refusing to acknowledge these obscenities. He would not let them spoil his mood. He would go to the *Caval ëd Bronz,* and sit down at a table in the private outdoor enclosure he had never yet dared to enter. He'd sit down alongside the privileged clientele sipping tea or aperitifs out there, under the white sunshades; he'd study their clothes, their gestures, their mannerisms, eavesdrop on their conversation, hear them speak Italian.

Still somewhat anxious about pushing in where he had never dared before, he reminded himself that since his sartorial transformation he had experimented at the lesser downtown cafes in preparation for this great test. Today he did feel ready risk this most elite of Turin's cafés.

He strolled out of the arcade into the dazzling sun of Piazza San Carlo and made boldly for the entrance to the café's *dehors*. It was sparsely attended, as was to be expected at the height of summer, with just enough parties under the sunshades to make it worthwhile without being too intimidating. He selected a target party: tanned bare shoulders under lavish summer hats; straw bowlers and white linen suits; musical laughter.

Nonchalantly enough, he strolled to a nearby table and settled back in the wicker chair, crossing right leg over left. A waiter hurried to his side. Pier ordered a *gaseus*, casually glancing around him, but listening intently to the chatter at the next table.

"The Riviera's so impossible in August," a woma's voice said, "The mountains are vastly preferable."

"Yes, we came back yesterday. We're leaving for Valtournanche on Wednesday, just the time to repack. The Monteghi are meeting us there…"

Yes, this was good Italian. Pier stole a glance at the speaker: bright red cherries and a cloud of tulle on a black straw hat. A chiffon scarf fluttered to the ground. The gentleman in the next chair reached down to retrieve it – yes, that was it, bending sideways from the waist, spine erect, shoulders squared, just like Signora Agiati had shown him.

The waiter returned with Pier's *gaseus.* Pier took a modest sip, enjoying the fizz on his lips. His eyes spotted a couple at a secluded table: he portly, bald, an impressive gold chain looped across his paunch; she young, blond, willowy, flirting; he bedazzled, lapping it up.

From somewhere down Via Roma came the sound of a marching band. A rumble of thunder coursed the sky; then sudden, heavy raindrops splattered the hot cobblestones. A sudden rush of wind tore at the shades and snatched at the hats. The calm of the private enclosure erupted into a noisy scramble for the shelter of the arcade. Agitated waiters rushed out with open umbrellas to save the elect from the sudden summer storm. The elegant figures that a few minutes ago had lounged, invulnerable, in their privileged grace now huddled, pall mall, under the arcade around the café's doors, white jacketed waiters bustling to escort them to inside tables, mumbling abject apologies for the summer weather.

The Niclin marching band was now in the square, its noise mingling with the thunder and the roar of the downpour, the phalanx of Black Shirts trudging undaunted under the crashing rain, storm-battered banners flapping madly in the wind.

Pier too took shelter under the arcade, but he drifted away to peer at nearby display windows through security grills. A single large painting, gold framed, set up on an easel. Pier gazed at a loaded hay wagon in a harvested field: ominous sky; nervous looking horse; three peasants rushing to stow their last few forkfuls onto the wagon before the skies let loose. On the other side of the gallery's door, a dour-faced woman in a gilded frame stared at him censoriously.

Pier moved on to the next shop: books. He glanced at the gold legend above the display windows: *Libreria Paglieri*. He peered into the dim interior: rows of book stacks lining the walls; a centre aisle, long tables covered with books. In the brightly lit window, titles that meant nothing to him: *Principi di Chimica Organica. La Geologia delle Cozie. Biologia. Fisica Nucleare.*

He moved on to the second window, and here his eyes fell upon a display centring on a folio-sized period scene; next to it, a closed book, *L'Opera nell'Ottocento.* Pier drew closer, studying the illustration: yes, a stage scene. He tried to figure out what opera it came from. Next to it, another title read: *Giuseppe Verdi, l'Uomo e la Musica.* Pier longed to enter the bookstore, but it was closed. Of course: *Chiuso per il Ferragosto.*

No matter. He would come back in a few weeks, when it reopened.

Guido's malaise

The encounter with Lena at the Niclin fête left Guido out of sorts. A vague discomfort plagued him all week, until on Saturday he caught himself thinking that he'd see her tomorrow and was angry with himself: it was not as though he intended to court her. Drawn to her as he was, something about her provoked him and made him want to slap her, to put her in her place.

Ever since he'd first seen her, that evening in front of the Via Passo Buole café, all with the banter and innuendos that had followed, he had been obsessed: he had to find out about her. And finding that she lived on Strada delle Basse should have put her beyond the pale, so he despised himself for ever having thought of her as a potential wife. She *was* beautiful, but she was a nobody, dumb, a bird brain. The image he had entertained before he knew better – Lena sitting by his side at the *Colin-a Longa* dinner table – now made him cringe and flush with anger every time it came into his mind. And yet he couldn't get her out of his mind: she was a thorn in his side, a thorn that pricked again and again when least expected.

Even today, he couldn't get Lena to leave him alone. Worse yet, he had a gnawing suspicion that all along she'd been laughing at him behind her simpleton act, laughing at his patronising her, at his big man talk. The thought stung deep. It put him on his mettle; it made him want to show her, that chit of a girl, that *stupida,* that piece of trash, that no one fooled around with Guido Dellaria.

Another part of him was simply put out that she was taking up so much of his energy. He knew she wasn't right for him, and that should be the end of that. But here he was right now, alone in his beloved lab at FIAT, inspecting the experimental engine that had disappointed the designers' hopes in yesterday's test drive. It was his job to find out which part had failed, to give his feedback to the engineers, and there *she* was, distracting him, while all he wanted was to dismiss her from his thoughts. He wanted to dismiss the whole encounter as trivial, as a momentary game he'd played for his amusement.

But it didn't feel like a game. Time and again he banished her from his thoughts, and time and again her full mouth and smiling eyes came back to taunt him. Time and again he heard her cheerful voice saying, "I'm happy as I am."

Those words made him feel small: *he* wasn't happy. And her laughing outside the Niclin café, her scoffing words, "What do *I* want with FIAT?" The whole scene infuriated him and made him cringe. It made him want to strike her. She had laughed at him. He had to put her in her place.

He flung down the wrench he'd been wrestling with, wiped his hands on a rag, then searched his pocket for his handkerchief and dried the sweat on his forehead. A humiliating thought flashed in his mind: *I want her.*

No, this was no game. Or, if it was, he was the loser. Teeth clenched, staring unseeing at the intake manifold he had just disassembled, he flushed: the tart had taken him over from the inside. Would she ever leave him alone? At that thought, his eyes widened, and he stopped dead, handkerchief in hand. This couldn't happen to him, not to Guido Dellaria! He had to turn the tables on her, take her, *own* her, turn her on, and then thrash her, break her body and soul. It was now a duel between them, and he was a sore loser.

"So, what does it look like?"

The unexpected question swung Guido around, his sweaty handkerchief still in his hand. It took several seconds for him to come back to the here and now of the lab. He picked up the manifold, shrugging, to give himself time to rally. The newcomer, Claudio Dolti, the young engineer overseeing the test, peered inquisitively at the *disjecta membra* of their new model, scattered all over the workbench.

"Carburetor looks all right," Guido said. "Could be the intake manifold." He proffered the suspect manifold for the other's inspection, and soon the two were immersed in the dissection of their engrossing engineering problem, images of Lena momentarily kept at bay.

Later that evening, way past the six o'clock whistle and the homeward exodus of the line workers, the two young men stood side by side at the lab's sink, scrubbing grease off their hands.

"I say," Guido found himself saying, "what are the chances of a FIAT job for a young woman?" He cursed himself, but the question was out.

Somewhat surprised, Claudio glanced up from his soapy hands. Guido had never talked about anything but engines, never about women. "A typist?" he asked.

Guido shook his head. "Someone from the Lingòt crew," he said evasively, implying a reference to his involvement at the neighbourhood *Fascio*. "Works at Fornara now," and added with a smirk. "She makes *safety pins!"*

Claudio went on scrubbing grease off his hands, thinking. "Might check with *Carrozzeria,*" he suggested. "They do use women in bodywork." He looked up at Guido and winked. "Spot of Don Juaning?"

"Nah!" Guido brushed it off. "Doing someone a favour."

A flea in Lena's ear

All that week, Adelaide had been full of last weekend's excitement, of the young farmer who had danced her off her feet and walked her to the *filobus* with the confident assertion that he would see her again soon. At Fornara, she had spoken of nothing else, and as a result Lena had been teased almost past bearing about her broken heel and the lost opportunity of hooking the dancer's brother, who, Adelaide insisted, had danced the whole afternoon craning his neck on the lookout for her.

"If he wanted so much to find me," Lena had finally snapped, "he could have left the *bal* and come looking, I wasn't far away." About Guido she just said that some *fieul* from the bus had helped with her shoe.

Now, on Thursday, on the way home from Fornara, arm in arm with Lena as usual, Adelaide gave her friend's ribs a violent jab. "Look! Look! There he is!"

And there Pinòt was, waiting across the street on the lookout for them.

122

"What did I tell you?" Adelaide whispered excitedly in Lena's ear. "And I bet you Carlin isn't far."

Lena shushed her. Pinòt was crossing the road towards them, a broad smile on his face. On the strength of the Sunday afternoon spent together on the Niclin dance floor, he stooped down and planted a loud kiss on Adelaide's cheek.

"Told you I'd see you soon," he grinned. He stepped between the two girls, and hooked his arms through theirs, drawing them in close.

"So you did," Adelaide laughed. "And here you are! What're you doing in Turin?"

"You need to ask?" Pinòt said and winked at Lena. "She always this coy?"

Lena shook her head, blushing, and lowered her eyes.

"Which way are we walking?" he asked. "Hope it's a long way, because I've got a lot to say."

"Well, then," Adelaide said, flirting, "stop wasting time and talk. You've already wasted three steps."

"Well, then," he started, as they headed towards via Nizza, Lena feeling uncomfortable in the arm-in-arm threesome. "First of all," he said to Adelaide, "in two weeks there's *la festa ëd San Lorèns* and I want you to go with me."

"Where is this *festa*?" Adelaide asked.

"It's in *Non.* And," he added, turning to Lena, "my big brother told me to not come home without your promise that you'll go to *la festa* with him. "

Lena blushed furiously, eyes down, and shook her head. Pinòt tightened his hold on her arm so she wouldn't pull away. "Don't say no," he urged. "He is my *big* brother, you know, so I must do what he tells me. Come, don't get me into trouble."

Lena stole a quick look at his face, saw the wrinkled, mock-worried look and giggled, immediately lowering her eyes again.

"All you are promising is one afternoon on the dance floor," he wheedled. "Don't say no."

Lena kept shaking her head. She didn't know these *fieuj;* they seemed all right; and Adelaide would be there, but...

Pinòt pulled her in closer: "Please," he pleaded. "You wouldn't want me never to be able to go home again, would you?" Lena giggled, still shaking her head.

"Oh, come on," Adelaide chipped in, "you know it'll be fun!"

"But...but," Lena stammered, "Where is this *Non*?"

Adelaide turned to Pinòt. "That's right, where is it, how do we get there?"

"It's not the other end of the world," Pinòt assured them. "Less than an hour on the train from *Pòrta Neuva*, and you needn't worry about that. Carlin and I'll pick you up in Niclin with the *dòma."*

"But," Adelaide said, frowning, "isn't the *dòma* just for two?"

"You leave it to us," he waved her concern aside. "Two up front on the proper seat, and on the luggage rack…" he gave Adelaide's arm a quick squeeze, "a soft cushion for you and me. Much cosier back there. So, what do you say?" he asked, turning to Lena. "Say yes, *yes,* for pity's sake!"

Lena demurred. It sounded like fun and Carlin was a good dancer, but there was a cloud on her memory of the Niclin fête, something that had made her leave the dance floor. She remembered thinking she'd teach him a lesson, but she couldn't remember why. Still arguing with herself, she said, "But how would we get back, how far is it?"

"With the *dòma,* it's half hour from Niclin. You say when you want to go home. We'll bring you back all the way, if you like."

"Oh, come on, Lena!" Adelaide scolded. They had reached the corner of Adelaide's street and she spoke jiggling up and down, impatient for her friend to commit. "Don't be such a stick in the mud!"

"Do say yes!" Pinòt chimed in.

"I don't know…" Lena said, tempted. "I'll have to ask my mama."

Adelaide rolled her eyes then jabbed her elbow into Pinòt's side with a silent message: leave it to me. She'll come.

Pinòt politely shook Lena's hand in farewell. "Hope I'll see you at the *filobus* terminal, then," he said. "One o'clock, Sunday after next."

He and Adelaide walked up her side street and Lena headed homewards, trying to recall why she'd left the *bal* at the Niclin *festa.*

Via Nizza was buzzing with FIAT workers heading out of Turin on their bicycles, mostly men, the few women riding in tight little groups, small, vulnerable islands in a sea of maleness. Lena watched them pedal by.

I wonder, she thought, *if they really make more than I do at Fornara.* Her mind had shifted to Guido's talk outside the Niclin café. *I wonder if I* could *get a job at FIAT.*

Her thought brought on a frown. She wouldn't want to owe it to *him.* Deep in thought, she approached the corner green grocer's shop.

"Finished your work for today, Lena?" the grocer greeted her from among the produce baskets displayed in front of his store.

Lena smiled good evening and walked on, then suddenly stopped and turned back. "I wonder," she said, "would you perhaps know how to go about getting a job at FIAT?"

The man pinched his lips and shook his head. "Not off hand, no," he said, regretfully; but then he brightened. "But I will ask around," he promised.

Lena walked on, the thought of FIAT receding in her mind. More prominent now was her recent walk homeward with Adelaide and Pinòt, and the *festa* coming up: should she go? She'd really missed out on the dancing in Niclin on account of that shoe, and she'd love to *really dance* the whole afternoon; and Carlin *was* a good dancer, and she might actually like him if she got to know him a bit. His brother, Pinòt, *was* a nice *fieul,* well brought up, so probably he was too. She'd ask her mama.

With this last thought, her mama appeared in Lena's mind wearing a red wool coat, brass buttons and all. Lena laughed. Red! Her mama would never wear red! Grey, maybe, or dark blue.

Her hand flew to her mouth as though she'd caught herself doing something naughty. Her mama in a wool coat! She must have been thinking of FIAT after all. But was it true, what that Guido had said, that she could earn a lot more at FIAT? Somehow, she didn't trust that *fieul.* She must look for some other way to find out. She crossed into Strada delle Basse, her mind back on asking her mama about the *Non* ball.

Hammer and Sickle

With Don Marco's embargo on bike riding, Pier started to ride the trams to work. The tramline from Santa Rita to Via Nizza travelled in a tunnel under the railroad and resurfaced just at the start of the extensive FIAT perimeter wall. Riding his bike, Pier had long ceased to pay attention to the bold fascist slogans and emblems – the *Fascio* of the ancient Roman legions – painted at regular intervals on the plastered factory wall. But riding in on the trams, he had started to notice them again. The black, foot tall daubs proclaimed, **CHI MI AMA MI SEGUA** – if you love me you'll follow me, **CREDERE OBBEDIRE COMBATTERE** – believe obey fight, **CHI SI FERMA È PERDUTO** – when you stop you're lost. But today there was something new on the buff plastered walls – a broad, wet-looking line of red paint, ran boldly across the black slogans.

Its violent red seemed to grab all the light of the pale winter dawn. And, above each cancelled black *fascio* or slogan, a gory red hammer and sickle, a defiant challenge to the reigning Fascist regime. The two-foot tall daub – the emblem of the outlawed Italian Communist Party – threatened bloodshed. Pier's eyes widened, and a shiver ran down his spine, hackles stiffening on the back of his neck: he recalled the heated lunchroom disputes, when he'd first come to the newly opened FIAT factory in Via Nizza, three years ago. And still last year, though the debates had got more guarded. He remembered the noisy gatherings outside the FIAT gates and at many street corners. And the soapbox speeches in the squares around Santa Rita and Lingot, the hackling, the sudden fistfights among overwrought listeners in the crowd.

But since the beginning of the year, all that had disappeared. Serious talk had vanished from the lunch- room. Or, if at times there happen to be a semblance of the old intensity, it was in tight little huddles, wary eyes tracking the whereabouts of various station bosses in the room, sudden silence and dispersals occurring as soon as one appeared on the horizon.

The Santa Rita tram trundled its way toward the FIAT gate. Standing by one of the rear windows, Pier stared: even in the drab morning light, he could see the ominous little runnels of red that had dribbled down from each sickle and hammer, and now scored the walls below with a threatening suggestion. On one of the panels, the dribbles, bolder and intentionally shocking, reached the sidewalk, and there they spread out into a broad, thick puddle of red, as though a paint can had been tipped over, its contents trained to run across the whole sidewalk and over the curb, onto the tram tracks, flooding them with a thick, wet-looking red coat – an obvious and deliberate intimation of a blood bath to come.

Workers heading for the entrance gate on foot halted at the gory mess, shocked, they hesitated, then tipped-toed off the sidewalk, circled out past the tram rails and out onto the roadway, risking being run over, to avoid the red mess.

Once past it, they still cast fearful backward glances at it, over their shoulders. Between the spillage and the entrance gates, agitated little knots gathered, excited, wary, speculating, asking wild questions of each other: were the communists planning a clandestine demonstration? Where, when, and what about?

All along the stretch of street along the factory wall, on both sides of the road, the tension of hope and dread ran high. As Pier's tram approached, the strain reached into it through its closed windows and doors, quickly galvanising the passengers' attention.

Pier's tension reached fever pitch. Warily, he got off at the stop opposite the gates, hurried across Via Nizza, making for the gates, craning his neck right and left to catch a glimpse of what was going on. A distant scream of sirens reached him from somewhere further in the city, approaching fast. The crowd began to run, scrambling to get into the factory gates, away from the street and into some semblance of safety.

At the back of the FIAT forecourt, two security officers guarded the door, frantically urging the workers to hurry in, eager to lock up the heavy sliding doors. The sirens were now screaming right at the gates.

"Quick, quick, get in *fast!*"

On the street outside, shots sounded right at the factory gates – loud, rattling explosions, shocking, mixed with shouts, then a high pitched scream evolved into a woman's desperate wail. At the scream Pier stopped, looked back over his shoulder. A guard grabbed his arm, dragged him back into the stampeding herd, shoved him indoors, but not before Pier saw a man crumble to his knees, protective arms raised to screen his head, and *Milizia* men, truncheons raised, hitting and hitting him, then kicking him with steel-tipped boots. Then the steel and glass doors slammed closed behind him and Pier was driven up the ramp by the panicked crowd.

On the second level men and women crowded at the windows, shoving, necks craning for a look into the forecourt, out into the street. More shots were fired. A sudden CRACK sent a window exploding inward, splintering glass shards onto the human press. Cursing and screaming the crowd stampeded away from the windows. A woman remained crumpled on the floor, screeching, and holding on to her stomach. Another woman stopped, turned back, started toward her. "Get back! Get back, you fools," a station boss yelled, gesticulating ineffectually.

"She's hit! She's hit," cried the woman who'd turned to help. "Somebody help her!"

Pier started toward the fallen woman, was grabbed by his overalls, yanked back. "Get back to your station," barked the frantic station boss, "I'll take over here!" But he stood rooted where he was, petrified. Pier tore himself free, made a dash toward the fallen woman. The boss went after him screeching, "I told you to get back, I'll report you, you fool!" He grabbed Pier again, this time by the scruff of the neck, and sent him sprawling with a kick in the pants. Pier sprung up, fist drawn back to strike, but restraining arms held him, dragged him back, shoved him into the screaming mob.

Outside, the row was subsiding. A few minutes later sirens wailed again, down in Via Nizza, their sound rapidly diminishing in the distance. Ambulances, Pier thought, taking the injured to hospital. Or *Milizia* vans, taking the arrested to jail.

Chapter Six

Guido obsesses

For weeks, Guido continued to obsess about Lena. An immediate problem was how to get to her, guarded as she always was by either friend or mother. As a last resource, he started to pose as a member of the *Lingòt* church the two attended, taking his Sunday morning coffee at the corner café where he could see them coming. The second week he risked approaching them, asking politely, "Mind if I walk to church with you?"

Gioana felt Lena's hand tighten on her arm and answered coldly, "Suit yourself."

Undaunted by her coldness, Guido fell into step and made an unsuccessful attempt to start a conversation. At the church door, the three filed in one after the other. The two women marched decisively to their usual pew, leaving Guido standing in the aisle. He turned on his heels and went to join the men clustering just inside the church door.

When the congregation dispersed after mass, he hung back in the shadow of the portico, trying to find out from Lena's chat with her girlfriend what they'd be doing that afternoon. It had puzzled him, the past few weeks, that the two girls didn't discuss plans anymore. Adelaide simply said: "I'll pick you up in half an hour."

He didn't want to hang around too close to the girls because he was well known in the neighbourhood. All he could do was return to his outdoor table at the corner café and watch for Adelaide to go by. But last Sunday he'd watched her walk to Lena's, but they hadn't come back his way. He sat considering a more effective approach. Somehow it went against the grain. It was beneath Guido Delloria. He had no business being strung along by two dumb girls. But he did want to know, so he followed Adelaide to the Le Basse corner, snapped his newspaper open and, leaning against the wall, pretended to be engrossed in his newspaper, all the time peering around the corner: Adelaide disappeared into the third gate.

Some fifteen minutes later, the two girls emerged, heading away from him. *They are going to the filobus*, he guessed. He turned on his heels, and hurried down the street toward Via Nizza: he would get to the terminal before them.

But on the way a second thought swamped him: maybe they were *not* going to the *filobus*. Maybe they were going to the river.

No, he reassured himself. Too dressed-up for a stroll on the Po. Then he cursed, as yet another thought struck him: maybe they were going to meet their beaux at the Junction. He speeded up: he'd just have to watch and see.

At the terminal corner of Via Nizza he stopped by the newsagent, peeked around the corner and saw the two girls just emerging out from the Le Basse lane, making for the little knot of travellers waiting at the *filobus* stop. He hung back until the girls had settled into seats near the front of the bus, then made a dash for the open rear exit and stood at the back of the bus, watching them, fretting and fuming. At a rough stop a passenger accidentally jostled him and he shoved him away with a curse.

"*Ohilà, che manere,*" protested the bystander, "*I l'hai nen falo a pòsta!*" (Really, what manners, I didn't do it on purpose!)

Guido growled, teeth clenched, staring out of the window.

On the Niclin square, he let the bus empty out before he got off with the last cluster of passengers and scuttled into the shadows of the town hall portico. From there he watched the two girls. He saw a grinning young man welcome Adelaide with a hug and a kiss, then a second young man on a smart rig, the horse's reins loosely in his hands. He watched him reach down to help Lena up into the seat next to him, watched her smile at him as she climbed onto the rig.

Cursing under his breath, Guido watched as the four settled on the *dòma* – Lena up front with the driver, Adelaide with her date on the improvised dicky seat on the luggage rack. He watched, glowering, as the driver shook the reins and the handsome bay picked up a lively walk. Cursing, he stormed off the portico and crossed the square to the café where he'd sat with Lena and her broken shoe.

"A cognac!" he snarled at the waitress, throwing himself down into an outdoor chair. "Double!"

Town and Country romance

Feragost and the rush of saints' days during the month of August touched off a frenzy of town fêtes in the Turin countryside. Every weekend there was a *bal* in one town or another – *Non, Vineuv, Candieul, Volvera.* All were within easy reach of Carlin's *dòma,* and he and Pinòt made sure their two *Turinèise* did not miss a single one. On the day of the *Non fête,* Adelaide sprung to her feet before the *filobus* had even turned into the square, and stood by the exit, on the lookout for the waiting *dòma.* Lena kept to her seat until the bus came to a stop in front of town hall, in part out of trepidation about the date.

"There they are!" Adelaide yelled back to her from the ground. "Come on, come on!" Lena joined her, saw Pinòt hurrying to greet them, Carlin sitting in the driver's seat, holding the horse's reins.

"You came!" Pinòt called out to Lena, after planting a kiss on Adelaide's cheek. He turned to wave to his brother, who waved back, pleased that Lena had come.

"Here she is," Pinòt said, handing Lena up to the *dòma*'s front seat. "Told you she'd come."

He trotted around to the back of the *dòma.* Adelaide stood by the improvised dicky seat. He hoisted her up and settled himself next to her, threading his arm affectionately around her shoulders. "Not half bad, is this?" he said.

"Not half!" she giggled and snuggled closer to him.

Up front, things moved more slowly. Carlin shook the reins and the horse stepped out smartly, heading for the main road, where the arc of the Western Alps defined the impressive horizon in front of them. Lena sat stiffly, holding on to the seat's wrought iron rail. Along the road, houses straggled farther and farther apart, until very soon the *dòma* was traveling through open farmland. Carlin clicked his tongue and the horse picked up a steady trot. Alarmed, Lena clutched the edge of her seat's rail more tightly.

"It's quite safe," Carlin assured her, with a sideway glance at her scared face. Stiffly, she smiled at him: he wasn't nearly as forward as she had thought him. She relaxed a bit, began to look right and left at the unfamiliar landscape.

"You haven't been *'n campagna* much, have you?" Carlin said.

She shook her head with a shy smile. He began to name the crops in the fields they passed. "And that," he added, lifting his chin towards the outstanding peak on the horizon, "that is *Monvis.* That's where the Po comes from."

"The Po?" she exclaimed, surprised. "It comes from there?"

He nodded. "Up there, it's just a little creek."

The Po: her hand flew to the cameo at her neck. It was only seven weeks ago she'd last been to the Junction. Almost two months since she had danced with him under the stars. She wondered where *he* was right now, what *he* was doing.

The horse trotted along with a steady rhythm. The countryside slid by, green and well-tended, field after field, irrigations ditches and straight rows of trees revealing their patchwork patterns. Lost in her dream, Lena swayed to the rhythm of the trot until, suddenly, a sweet tang caught her attention. She sniffed the air: the unexpected scent brought back to the here and now.

"Summer Sweet," Carlin told her, reading her body language. He pointed to a double row of linden trees that started at the road's verge and ran into the depth of the fields. The *dòma* came abreast of a trees-lined drive, and Lena saw an open gate, flanked by two stone pillars with resting lions on top.

Spellbound, she inhaled the intoxicating scent and whispered: "It's so beautiful."

"That's the drive to my father's place," Carlin said. "The smell is from those bushes outside the trees. In June and July, you'd smell the linden themselves, but now it's the Summer Sweet."

The horse trotted on, leaving the farm drive behind. Lena sat gazing back over her shoulder, watching the long row of trees rotate behind her, with no house in sight. She did not speak again.

The day at *Non* was wonderful. They danced and danced all afternoon. From time to time, Pinòt or Carlin ran out to get them cool drinks, as none of them wanted to leave the dance floor. At sundown Lena began to get nervous about getting home, so they left at last.

Getting onto the *dòma,* Adelaide whispered in Lena's ear, "Pinòt asked me to be his *morosa,*" and on the ride back Lena was keenly aware of the two in the dicky seat behind her, tightly entwined on their cushions.

They were almost back in Niclin when Carlin's voice broke into her thoughts. "Will you come out with me again next Sunday?" he asked, the reins held loosely in one hand. "There is a *bal* in *Candieul.*"

Lena nodded eagerly, with a shy glance up at him. Carlin shifted a little closer to her on the seat, tentatively slipping his free arm around her shoulders and, when she did not shift away, he drew her closer. Instinctively, she stiffened; but then she loosened up, let her head come to rest against his shoulder, swaying comfortably to the rhythm of the trot.

Stalking Lena

Guido was now hounded by the thought of getting the better of Lena. He dismissed the possibility of personal violence as beneath his dignity. Besides, he had never seen her out on her own. She always walked home from work with Adelaide: and in the last two blocks after they parted, neighbours and shopkeepers constantly greeted her. He, too, was well known in *Lingòt,* as he was still the *Fascio's* drillmaster. He considered the possibility of approaching Lena after supper, if he ever saw her out alone, but that would be impossible as Via Passo Buole was full of peasants come to the city for work, and they continued the country habit of sitting outside their doorways after supper to watch the world go by.

That only left Le Basse. There it was dark and quiet. But that wouldn't do him any good as those who lived there, the city's misfits and poorest workers, enjoyed the cool of the evening in their walled courtyards and would hear any rumpus in the alley. Besides, he saw no pleasure in overpowering her physically. What he wanted was to make her need him, want him. And *then* he would toy with her, punish her, make her grovel.

The thought brought a nasty leer to his face, his lips quivering as he imagined the scene. Could he use the FIAT job to hook her? She had laughed at the idea, but her eyes had widened with greed when he'd mentioned the FIAT wages, real or not. Maybe that was the angle. She was mercenary, after all.

He hadn't as yet come up with a plan, but he started to show up at the Passo Buole café after work, lounging at an outdoor table with the neighbourhood lads, but always maintaining the superior camaraderie of the gang leader. There he waited for her to come along that last block.

Since the night, weeks ago, when he had waylaid her and she had snubbed him, she had taken to walking up the street on the opposite sidewalk, only crossing the street well beyond the outdoor tables. *At least she's afraid,* he thought, the left corner of his mouth twisting with satisfaction.

The banter of the lads at his table distracted him: they no longer presumed to tease him about her. His position at the *Fascio* had quickly established him as out of bounds. He could now sit among them, ignoring them, and keep watch.

Now he cast a glance at his watch: quarter to seven. She was late. He wondered irritably what she could have been doing since the six o'clock end of her workday. Dawdling, no doubt, or jabbering with that other fool, Adelaide.

And then he saw her across the street. He saw the greengrocer step out to meet her on the sidewalk with an eager smile, watched them exchange a few inaudible words, Lena as usual smiling straight up into the man's face, the minx. He watched the man hand her a slip of paper, Lena received it eagerly unfold it, peer at it, then hand it back wistfully, the greengrocer coming around alongside her, focussing on the slip of paper in her hand, his finger moving slowly across it, his head close to hers.

The bitch can't even read, Guido sneered. Somehow, that gave him a bitter pleasure. He watched Lena fold her slip of paper with a kind of reverence, slip it into her pocket and pat it there, as though to bless it and keep it safe.

Watching Guido thought, *Can't be a dunning note.* Across the street, a smiling Lena beamed at the old man, nodded excitedly; the grocer, as pleased as punch, beamed back at her. She walked on at last and the greengrocer took a couple of steps on sidewalk after her, watching her go. Once she turned back and waved to him one more time, excitedly – thank you, thank you so much!

Thank you for what? Guido wondered. He sat there wondering, glowering, following her with his eyes until she disappeared around the Le Basse corner. Then he jumped up, upsetting his chair and leaving it to Toni to set it back on its feet. He stormed into the bar and ordered a double cognac.

Her hand clamped onto the pocket where she'd stowed her precious note, Lena ran all the way home, eager to tell her mama the greengrocer had come through, he'd got the name of the person to whom she could apply for a job at FIAT.

"*Mama, Mama*, look!" she cried, rushing in through the kitchen door. Gioana turned from her supper preparations, surprised at Lena's irruption. "He did it, *Mama*! Look! Monsú Paolin has found out for me!"

She waved her slip of paper at Gioana, who took it, stared at it helplessly and handed it back to her. Lena knew perfectly well that her mama could not read, but in her excitement she had overlooked the fact. Now, she took back her slip of paper and sat down at the table, smoothing out the folds to make the lettering clearer, bent eagerly over it.

"Oh!" she moaned, her face crumpling: she could read printed capitals, but the note was in cursive writing.

"What are we going to do?" she whimpered. There in her hands was what she'd so hoped for, and it was no good to her: she could not read it. She could guess that the first line must be a person's name, and the last line clearly spelled out FIAT, in the same capital letters as the big legend above the Via Nizza factory, some fifteen minutes away. But what of the two lines in between, what did they say?

For a moment, mother and daughter stared at each other nonplussed. Then Gioana saw tears begin to gather in Lena's eyes. "Never mind," said briskly, "put the note safely away, and let's have supper. Afterwards we'll go ask Don Paolo to read it for us. He'll know what to do."

Lena at I Tigli

By San Michel's day, at the end of September, the two *Lingòt girls* had spent half a dozen Sunday afternoons with the two brothers. Besides, Pinòt had twice taken Adelaide to the *Lingòt* cinema, just the two of them alone.

"We sat in the gallery," Adelaide had reported excitedly, adding with a smirk, "way up, at the back." And had concluded her report with: "He is great!"

Lena was mystified by Adelaide's effusions. As usual, her friend had made a mystery of her date, so that Lena had been unable to get any idea of what the new film was about. She wished she could see it for herself, but she and her mama had just been to the cinema the week before, and would not be going again until next month.

Then, on the ride back from the *Volvera bal*, Carlin said: "My father is called Michel, so on San Michel's day we are going to have a big party for him at '*I Tigli*'."

"Under those trees?" Lena asked, recalling the now familiar double row of linden they passed coming and going to the country fêtes.

"Yes, at our farm," Lena looked confused, so Carlin explained. "It's called *I Tigli*. We always have a big *festa* for my pa's name day. We want you to come." He turned to glance over his shoulder at his brother on the back seat: "*Nèh, Pinòt?*"

"You bet. We certainly do," Pinòt confirmed. "Our sisters are just dying to see our girls," he added with an extra squeeze to Adelaide's shoulders and a quick peck to her neck.

So here they were, on San Michel's day, celebrating rubicund Michel Sella, jovial and prosperous, in his own farmyard. The party sat around a long table on the bank of the pond behind the house, in the shade of the linden trees that gave the farm its name. The lavish feast eaten, the family and guests sat on around the table, sipping wine and nibbling on nuts.

135

Lena sat with Carlin on the pond's verge, watching a flock of white geese glide silently here and there. Nearby ducks bickered, and in their wire pen chicken pecked and clucked, while the farm dogs lounged, satiated, under the long trestle table.

Carlin had eyes only for Lena: it felt so right to have her there.

"Come," he said, "let's get to the dancing." He jumped up and began to rearrange the chairs so the musicians could sit and play, and still have their wine glasses within easy reach on the table. In no time, accordion, guitar and mandolin struck up a polka in the broad farmyard, and Carlin and Lena opened the dance.

Pinòt and Adelaide soon joined them, and two daughters of the house, the boys' sisters, were quickly claimed by two young men. Tune after tune, polkas, mazurka and waltzes, they danced and danced, on the packed dirt yard, until the musicians begged for mercy, and reached for more wine. In the pause, the dancers returned to the chairs by the table, or flopped down in couples on the pond's grass verge, sipping wine or lemonade.

Suddenly, a slightly tipsy baritone rang out at a ferocious pace,

> *"A-i é Gregòri ch'a fà ij sòco.*
> *S'a lo fà mach al meis ëd Gené*
> *Col povròm na ciapa pòchi*
> *A l'ha gnanca da mangé."*

There goes Gregory, maker of clogs.
If he only makes them in January
The poor man won't earn enough to feed himself.

Despite the torpor of repletion, voices around the table quickly answered with the refrain,

> *"Disie ch'a vendo na lira le bròcole,*
> *Na lira le bròcole, na lira le bròcole,*
> *E ij caulifior…"*

You tell him broccoli sell for one *lira*,
One *lira* for broccoli, and for cauliflower…

Laughter and loud applause greeted the end of the ballad, and the thump of heavy glasses on the table demanded more singing. Several more ballads followed, mostly love songs and tunes the *Alpini* soldiers hollered on their long tramps up the mountain valleys. In a momentary lull in the singing Lena became aware of birds twittering in the trees, then of the tranquil cackle of hens nearby, sounds so different from her familiar city noise. Then one of Sella girls, Pina, intoned, *Quel mazzolin di fiori...* – that little bunch of flowers. A sparse chorus answered...*che vien dalla montagna* – that comes from the mountains. Her sister Carla joined in and soon the full table was singing the tragic-comic ballad of unrequited love and betrayal to its dismal conclusion.

> *"E sol perché son poverina*
> *Mi fa pianger e sospirar."*

> And just because I'm poor
> He makes me weep and sigh.

The sun sank low behind the trees, and the women began to clear the debris of the feast away. Adelaide vanished with Pinòt, somewhere. Carlin and Lena sat a long time, holding hands, in the relative seclusion of the bench wrapped around the trunk of a massive linden tree, overlooking the pond, until his sisters peeked around its trunk.

"Hey, you two love birds!" Pina called out and her sister told Carlin: "We want to borrow your girl for a minute."

"Yeah, we want to talk girl stuff," Pina echoed her. Lena stood up, and the three girls ran across the yard holding hands and giggling.

In the kitchen they ran past their mother. "Lena's going to show us how to do our hair," Carla called out as they romped up the stairs to their bedroom.

"But I'm not sure I can," Lena protested. "My mama always does my hair for me."

In the bedroom, Pina sat down at her dressing table. "Try anyway," she said, undoing her bun. Carla stood by, watching Lena at her work, admiring the mass of curly hair piled up on Lena's head. "You have such beautiful hair," she said with a touch of envy. "I bet *you* don't have to bother with curlers."

By and by, *Madama* Sella walked into the room and stood watching. Carla was now seated in front of the mirror, with Lena busily working on her hair.

"Any good?" the mother asked with friendly interest, sitting down on the edge of the nearby bed. Pina came over to her to display Lena's handiwork. "Lena showed Carla how to do it for me," she explained. "Now I'm watching so I can do Carla's." The hair dressing session went on with much giggling and banter, until Carlin's voice boomed up the stairs.

"Hey, you two, I want my girl back," he yelled, romping up the stairs. "It's almost time to take her home, worst luck."

"It's been such a wonderful day," Lena cooed getting up, her happy smile taking in the whole group. "You must come again," Madama Sella said, standing up, "and show my girls some more beauty tricks."

Carlin grabbed Lena by the hand and together they ran down the stairs. On the way down Carlin whispered in her ear, "Pinòt's asked Adelaide and she's said yes."

"You mean…" He nodded excitedly. "They are engaged. But they won't tell the folks yet for a while: can't have the younger son married before the first born, now, can we?" He gave Lena a sideways hug and a kiss on the neck that made her blush and look over her shoulder, to make sure no one had seen.

Lena changes jobs

Several weeks had passed since Lena and her mama had consulted their pastor about approaching FIAT for a job. His letter had gone out and Lena knew he had said nice things about her because he had read her the letter before mailing it. But weeks slid by without response.

At first Lena could think of nothing else. Day after day, she stopped by the church on her way home from work, hoping for news. She did so after she had left Adelaide at her corner, so she felt sneaky about doing so. She was dying to tell her friend about her hopes, about the possibility of bettering her and her mama's lot with a job at FIAT; but she dared not, because Adelaide would be sure to blurt it all out all over Fornara, and then what? What if dear *Monsú* Nandin, her boss, was hurt that she wanted to leave, what if he got mad at her and she got fired, and there was no FIAT job? No, better leave well enough alone: she'd better keep her secret to herself until she was sure. She was happy enough at Fornara, she reflected. It was just that…well, what that *fieul* had said in Niclin, that they paid so much more at FIAT. She kept thinking about what she and her mama could do with the extra money. But now Adelaide would be angry with her when she found out, she thought sadly.

The thought of the extra money brought to her mind the Via Nizza draper and the bolts of wool fabric already displayed in its windows, even though winter was still some months away. Winter coats, she thought, that would be so nice. Their very first winter coats.

Meantime, September was drawing to a close, and with it, the season of town fairs in the countryside. The last outing, Carlin's papa's party on San Michel day, had been the best home *festa* she'd ever seen. Actually, she considered, she'd never seen a family party before. There were no parties on Le Basse. People ate and drank behind closed doors, though the women gathered under the medlar tree to darn and knit and gossip. And when one of them was in trouble, they did share what food they had to spare.

Now, she thought, with the fall closing in, there would be no more *bals* until next May, no more rides on the *dòma.*

Carlin had promised to come in on his bicycle instead, she reminded herself. The thought cheered her up: he had already asked her to a film, for next Sunday; the four of them, she with Carlin, and Pinòt with Adelaide.

She'd never before been to a film with a *fieul.* When she'd told Adelaide of the proposed double date, her friend had nudged her ribs and whispered, "Best we don't all sit together, heh? You two sit up front. Pinòt and I'll sit in the back, as usual."

Lena entered her courtyard and was startled to see their kitchen door fly open and her mama standing on the threshold, hurrying her in.

"There, look!" Mama cried, shaking a sheet of paper at Lena as soon as she got within reach. "It's from Don Paolo. They've answered! He wants us there tonight."

Mother and daughter turned right around and rushed to the church. Don Paolo's letter to FIAT had been answered: Lena was to start her new job the following Monday.

Thrilled at the news, Lena heaved a sigh of relief. Now, at last, she could tell Adelaide!

That Sunday afternoon, the foursome met, as arranged, to go to the cinema.

As soon as they were walking together down Via Nizza, Adelaide blurted out angrily: "You won't believe what this one's gone and done."

"What? What has she done?" asked the brothers in unison.

"And *she* such a little nun," Adelaide grumbled, "all quiet and proper, like butter wouldn't melt in her mouth! And never a word to *me,* her *very best* friend!"

Lena's chin dropped to her chest, and her cheeks blazed.

"What *did* you do?" Carling asked trying to catch Lena's lowered eyes.

"What she's done…" Adelaide snapped out, "she's gone and got herself a new job, that's what she's done! At FIAT, no less!"

"You didn't!?" cried Pinòt and Carlin together, then Carlin laughed. "Well, I never!" he cried, squeezing her arm closer to him. "Well done! How did you do it?"

Lena squirmed, blushing deeper. "I… I… Well, I asked Don Paolo, and he wrote a letter for me."

"Just like *that*!" Adelaide snapped her fingers, aggrieved. "You see? Out of nowhere *he* gets it into his head to write a letter for her, and *she* gets taken on at FIAT!"

"But 'Laide," Lena pleaded, "I only asked him…" She stopped. She had almost said, "Asked him to read the greengrocer's note." But she didn't want to do that. She was ashamed on not being able to read.

Adelaide snorted, the jerky shrug of one shoulder dismissing Lena's explanation.

"Please, 'Laide," Lena pleaded, "don't go and be angry with me. Perhaps *you* can ask him too…"

Adelaide scoffed, not mollified. She pulled ahead, hanging on tight to her Pinòt's arm, drawing him ahead with her, and so putting some length between the two couples.

One behind the other, the foursome strolled the short distance to the cinema, and Carlin bought the superior *galleria* tickets.

Inside, they mounted the stairs to the dark *portières* that protected the projection hall from the stairway's lights. An usherette's flashlight swept down the *galleria*'s broad steps.

"Where do you want to sit?" Carlin whispered to Lena. She glanced at Pinòt and Adelaide, already making their way towards the upper rows. She pointed downward.

Carlin escorted her down to the first row and sidled in ahead of her, squeezing past the already seated couples with muted "excuse us", and held a seat down for her. On the screen, the newsreel flicked light and dark. At the foot of the stage, a gramophone blared out the strains of a marching band. They settled in their seats, the whole row resetting after their passage. On the screen, Mussolini strutted about with a knot of impressive uniforms and morning suits.

After a while, Carlin slipped his arm through Lena's, the way he had started doing on their recent *dòma* rides. The armrest between them kept them apart, so he slipped his elbow off it and sought Lena's hand, loose in her lap. Her hand turned upward and closed on his. They watched the film, fingers intertwined.

Pier meets Lena

Next morning, Lena got up earlier than usual for her first day at FIAT. This wasn't necessary, since the walk to FIAT was no longer than the walk to Fornara had been, but she wanted to be sure to be on time. Yesterday after mass, she and her mama had walked up to the huge factory to see where she'd be working, and they had stood side by side outside the iron palisade, gazing up at the vast expanse of concrete, glass and metal.

"It's huge!" her mama said, scanning the five rows of steel-framed windows. "Wonder where you'll be."

"Don't know," Lena said, gaping.

And now here she was. Next to her, a middle-aged woman in a stiff khaki overall scuttled her morosely up a spiral ramp as wide as a street: she'd been ordered to get Lena started, and she resented the fact that it would slow down her own piecework.

Next to her, Lena trotted awestruck, peering right and left. Workstation followed workstation all the way up the ramp, with at each station different crews, different machines. The place boomed with the roar of machines and the shouts of men, the noise echoing up and down the ramp. Lena tried to guess what was being made at the various stations, but she couldn't make anything out that she could connect with the cars she saw on the city streets, though she assumed it was all automobile parts. Then at one station she spotted a low tortoise shell-like thing on squatty wheels, with gaping holes in its sides and a half-moon hole in the back. *That,* she thought, *might become an automobile.*

"Come on," yelled the crackling overall next to her, "keep up! I've got my quota to make, as well as you to break in." Lena ran to catch up. In a sudden lull in the roar, a wolf call rang out behind her, and a coarse voice declared, "That one, now, she's a looker."

A machine screech drowned out the last word, but Lena had spotted the speaker - a stocky body in baggy blue overalls behind a machine, a worn beret pulled down to his eyebrows. Next to him, a tall, slim figure glanced up, uninterested, from his work, went back to it. The woman shoved Lena into the women's station and her bulk blocked out Lena's view.

In the adjoining workstation, Pier ran his fingers delicately along the inside edge of the oval window frame he had just fashioned on his lathe, feeling for burrs on the tricky shape, all curves and grooves.

Later, in the lunchroom, Pinin, the stocky young man who had spotted the newcomer, shuffled forward behind Pier in the line of workers cueing to retrieve their lunch pails, from the steaming vats of hot water. He nudged the small of Pier's back: "There's that looker," he said staring at a clutch of women sitting at a nearby table. "Where did she come from?"

Pier glanced up, absently. Pinin jabbed his ribs again, and his chin lifted towards the women's table.

Pier saw the cluster of stiff khaki overalls, elbows splayed wide on the table. He took in the open lunch pails, the scarf-wrapped heads with two knots on top, like stubby goats' horns. He watched the fat one tear off a chunk of bread, dunk into her pail and stuff it into her mouth while she tore and dunked the next, then stuff the second one into her mouth as well, before she'd swallowed the first, her thumb shoving the whole lot in to make room for a third. He looked away.

The line shuffled forward along the aisle, driving Pier and Pinin, now in possessions of their pails, along with the press , looking right and left for a place at a table as they inched their way along. A high pitched shriek of laughter drew Pier's attention back to the women's table. His eyes landed on the newcomer, seated next to the large woman who'd led her in this morning. She sat upright, eyes flitting from speaker to speaker, attentive to the others' chatter.

Pier stopped transfixed, hot lunch pail in hand: curly brown hair pinned back close behind her ears; no horned scarf; a small pink earlobe, dark smiling eyes, pink lips closed to a rose button, calmly chewing.

Lena felt his gaze and looked up, her eyes met his. Her smile brightened. He smiled back.

A rough shove in the back jostled Pier forward and he had to shuffle to regain his balance. He was pushed on. When he looked back, he no longer had a view of the newcomer, now submerged in the sea of overalls. He craned his neck, managed to catch a brief glimpse of brown curls before the scarf-horned heads shifted, closed in, and hid her altogether.

Pier scanned the tables nearby for a place, but the noisy crowd forced him onward to the far end of the room. Still craning to spot the newcomer, he finally slammed his pail down on a table and shoved himself in at the end of an already crowded bench, the eating men grumbling and shoving each other tighter to make room.

Once seated, Pier glowered in the direction of the women's table, now lost in a sea of blue overalls. He manhandled his lunch pail open. Then he remembered: she worked at the station next to his.

His frown relaxed. He straightened his spine, squared his shoulders, and almost smiled as he dipped his spoon into Nina's excellent stew: he would see the newcomer there; she'd be under his eyes all afternoon.

Chapter Seven

Tornami in mente il dì che la battaglia
D'amor sentii la prima volta, e dissi:
'Oimé, se questo è amor, com'ei travaglia!'
Giacomo Leopardi

Falling in love

If Pier had been struck by the newcomer, Lena on her part, had noticed the bright head above the sea of dark ones. In her work clothes, she was not wearing Ottavio's cameo, but her hand rose to the base of her throat where it would have been. Something in that *fieul* reminded her of her lost beloved.

It wasn't looks, she thought. Ottavio had curly chestnut hair, while this *fieul*'s hair was light and straight. In fact, he did not look like Ottavio at all. Other than that he, too, was tall, slim and straight.

No, it wasn't looks, she thought again, trying to pinpoint the elusive similarity: it was…a certain air about him.

Then she got it: it was the way he carried himself.

He looks *fin*, she thought. He looked refined, like Ottavio.

She glanced around the lunchroom, at men wolfing down a hurried meal, backs humped, elbows splayed out, mouths at the rim of their pails, and chins greasy.

She'd never given any thought to the way people sat or ate; but now it struck her. That *fieul*… Her eyes flew back to where Pier sat, straight-backed, at his table, spooning his food up to his mouth, not diving into his pail. It was the way Ottavio had eaten his ice cream that night, dancing under the stars.

Unconsciously, she straightened her spine and lifted her spoon while her left fingers toyed with the absent cameo. The second Saturday in June, it had been, and now it was October. Over three months. She'd never see Ottavio again.

144

It had all been so lovely, all the times with him, their Sundays on the Po, the walk from Fornara… And then their last night, the ride in the cab, dancing in his arms, her lovely, lovely gift, even the way he'd told her he was leaving. Suddenly, she stiffened. Her mind blocked out the end of their drive, the drunken woman next door, her appalling song.

Her eyes returned to Pier.

Pier, in his seat at the far end of the lunchroom, felt himself stared at and looked up: a gap had developed in the close-ranked, stooping bodies, and now he could see, at the far end of the gap, the newcomer looking at him.

She smiled at him and he smiled back. For a moment their eyes rested in each other's. Then the seated crowd shifted again, and the gap closed.

Lena craned her neck, but could no longer see the bright head. Disappointed, she scanned the seated figures: like bears, they were. Clumsy, clumsy bears. *Even Carlin*, the thought came unbid, *"Nice as he is, and so light on his feet on the dance floor, he's as thick as a bear."*

And suddenly she squirmed at the memory of yesterday afternoon, of holding hands in the dark cinema. Her mind drifted back to earlier yesterday afternoon, and to Adelaide's scolding. Carlin was very nice about it, though, she thought. He'd been glad for her, surprised but *proud* of what she'd done. "Well, I'd never!" he had cried, "good for you!" His words now echoed in her mind and she smiled: there'd been no scolding in his voice. Yes, Carlin was a nice *fieul*. And so was Pinòt. Their whole family was nice, not stuck-up at all; for all that they were so rich.

Next to her on the bench, her chaperone nudged her."It's time to go. Rustle up your stuff." Lena rustled, then sidled out behind the woman. In the aisle, she cast one last look in the direction of the blond head at the far table. He caught her eyes and smiled. She smiled back, holding his gaze. The back-to-work whistle shrilled, and the bears surged and lumbered toward the exit, the blond head outstanding above the blue flood. "Come along, then," the tan overall next to her scolded. Her rough tug on Lena's sleeve broke the enchantment.

It was a full five days before Pier got up the nerve to approach Lena, five days of anxious eye pursuits and shy evasions. Across the space between work-stations, above the noise, above the bustle and clatter, their eyes played hide and seek. By the fourth day, what had been secretive, elusive contacts now boldly declared themselves: their eyes met across the distance as though by appointment: first thing each morning their eyes said 'hallo', last thing at night

145

they smiled 'see you tomorrow'. The two had not yet spoken to each other, but on Friday night Pier's last glance clearly said, 'I'll wait for you outside,' and Lena's answered, 'Yes.'

That evening Pier stopped to wait for Lena right outside the factory gates. Before Lena's arrival at FIAT, he had always run across Via Nizza to catch the first oncoming tram to the duomo. Now he stood a few yards from the gate, the way he'd watched Lena walk home the previous four nights, and there waited for her. A few minutes later he saw her approach, craning to spot him above the blue and khaki flood. He, squared his shoulders, and stepped out toward her. "*Bon-a sèira*," he said with a smile.

Lena's face lit up with delight: they were talking, at last! A few feet apart, they stood speechless, gazing into each other's eyes, and causing a snag in the flood of homing workers. They were jostled and cursed, and Lena laughed and lowered her eyes. Pier took her arm, steered her closer to the wall, out of the rushing stream. There they stood facing each other, at a loss for what to do next until, at last, Lena returned his greeting.

"Good evening," she said, with a quick glance from under her lashes. Neither of them knew what to do next. Then Lena, feeling awkward, stepped out into the pedestrian stream of traffic, heading home.

Pier rushed into speech. "I wonder," he said, falling into step at her side. She looked expectantly into his face. He tripped on the uneven pavement and had to shuffle to regain his balance. He coughed and cleared his throat to cover his embarrassment, but then Matilde Agiati voice surged in his mind, *straighten your spine, square your shoulders*. He obeyed her orders. With a deprecating grin at his clumsiness he finished his sentence, "May I...walk along with you?" he heard the pleading in his voice and cursed himself. In his head, Matilde's voice ordered: *Masterful*.

Lena was beaming at him. He added, *"con chila,"* – with you, in the formal third person pronoun, the proper form of address between people who'd just met. And he was shy, too, she noted, and that was lovely!

Pier leaned down towards her, eager for her answer. *Chin up,* Matilde's voice hissed in his ear, like a prompter from his box. *Masterful!*

He straightened up. He didn't *feel* masterful, but he shouldn't beg, either. His head found a proper, dignified angle. "Since last Monday," he said, "I've wanted to...to... ask you your name," he ended, lamely. Hearing himself, he continued more firmly, "My name is Pier."

"Pier," she said. "Not …Piero?"

"No," he answered with a deprecating grin. People were always asking him about his name. "Just Pier. My ma…" he cleared his throat and started again: "My mama sometimes called Pierin, when I was little."

"But it is…the same name as the saint's, isn't it, San Pietro? I've never heard it said like that before."

"It is. But my…" Pier caught himself just as he was about to say 'my pa'. "My father comes from…" his chin motioned towards the Alps, now invisible in the October dusk, "and that's how he says it. I guess it just stuck. And you?"

"I'm Lena," she said. He actually knew her name: his station mates had got it out from the women in the next workstation.

"Lena," he repeated, lenghtening the vowels, letting their sound linger on his tongue. They walked side by side, now and then exchanging a remark, guarded titbits about their daily lives, until at the corner of Via Passo Buole, Lena stopped.

"I'm just over there," she said, motioning vaguely up the street. She didn't want him to come to Le Basse.

"You live in the new housing?" he asked, for something to say, glancing at the four-storied buildings around them.

"No," Lena shook her head, reluctantly motioning towards the start of the alley.

Pier stepped along the street in the direction she'd indicate, and Lena anxiously walked along with him. But at the corner she stopped. Watched him, take in, in the fading light, the dirty alley, the row of low farmhouse roofs that butted up to the multi-storied buildings of Via Passo Buole. Beyond the low roofs trees tops suggested open land.

"You live on a farm?" Pier asked, surprised.

"It *was* farms, once, I think." Lena answered, uncomfortable. "Now it's just…people's homes." There was a silence, neither knowing what to say. Then Lena said in a very small voice, "Well…then, good night."

"Yes!" Pier almost shouted, and then he added in a normal tone, "Good night!"

Lena sighed and slowly turned to go.

Pier stopped her, "And…" he called out, his hand reaching for her, "see you tomorrow?"

Lena laughed with relief. They couldn't help but see each other tomorrow.

She looked into his face, heart singing. He was now no more than a vague ghost in the dusk, but it thrilled her that he was there. "Yes, see you tomorrow," she answered, breathless, and walked to her gate with a new bounce in her step.

At quarter to seven Pier finally ran across Via Nizza to catch an approaching tram to the *duomo*. He'd be thirty minutes late for his session with Don Marco, but, somehow, he did not care.

Lena's dilemma: Carlin or Pier

The following week brought fast progress to Pier and Lena's romance. Working in adjoining stations, they were constantly in each other's view. By Tuesday, Pier had found reasons to drift in her direction in between his noisy stints at his lathe. Lena, whose job kept her seated at a workbench, was not free to move about as the crew leader brought the parts to be worked on to the bench and collected them when done.

But if Lena was stuck in place, her eyes were not, and her seat faced Pier's station. Hour after hour, her hands generated a cloud of dust sanding and smoothing the rough wooden shapes Pier's station fed to hers. Pier's, she now knew, were the small oval rear window frames. Her fingers soon flew at their tasks of their own accord, as they had at Fornara, so her eyes were free to roam, and they always roamed in Pier's direction. Soon she developed an uncanny sense of the rhythms of his work, the phases that brought him closer to her station. Time and again each day, their eyes met. She instantly lowered hers, but a moment later there they were again, those busy eyes, drifting back to the next station, searching for Pier.

On that Tuesday, when the lunch whistle blew, Pier stood puttering at his lathe until the women's crew began to file down the ramp, and then along he trotted like a sheepdog herding his flock, and deftly cut Lena off from the rest of her crew.

"Mind if I walk down with you," he whispered politely.

Lena glanced around her, uncertain. "I'm not sure it's…done," she whispered back, anxiously looking at the hordes of men around them.

Pier thought of the lunchroom, the few isolated female crews, those tight little knots leaning protectively inward, shoulder to shoulder, shutting out the noisy male throng at the other tables. He read her anxious glances, and remembered the wolf whistles, the hints, the clumsy attempts at flirting, the crude man-to-man banter at the women's expense: he hadn't thought of that and he didn't want to expose Lena to that unpleasantness.

"Well," he whispered, "let's go in close together and I'll just try to sit at a table near yours." With a last surreptitious glance over her shoulder, Lena agreed. Pier fell back and walked down alongside a knot of men, while Lena trotted ahead and caught up with her crew.

That evening, he again waited for her by the gate. Lena came around, saw him, and beamed, her hands reaching eagerly for his. Delighted, he grasped them and held them.

"I'd like to walk you home again tonight," he said, "but I can't!"

"Oh?" she murmured, her face crumpling with disappointment.

Pier's shoulders rose in a sheepish shrug. "Got into trouble last time," he said. Lena's face puckered into a mask of concern. "Not as bad as that," he said, making light of the problem. "It's just that I have another…job, in the evening, you see. Last Friday I was late, and Don Marco, he's my boss, was upset. So…" he chuckled, waggling a mock-scolding finger. "Mustn't be late again, you see?" Lena nodded understanding, but still looked disappointed. "But," Pier hastened to reassure her, "I *can* walk you home on Mondays and Wednesdays. Well," he had to correct, "usually I can, but not this week. I'll explain on Monday."

At the promise, Lena perked up. "Well, then, till Monday," she said, then added, "Good night." She cocked her head at him, smiled over her shoulder and walked away.

Pier stood there, watching her go down the street. She looked back over her shoulder once more, gave him one last bright smile, and merged with the hurrying crowd of homing workers. Pier waited until she had quite disappeared in the crowd, then ran across the street and leapt onto a departing tram, happy.

The following Sunday, promptly at 1:30, as arranged, Carlin knocked on the glass pane of Lena's door to pick her up for the film at the *Cine Lingòt*. "Ready?" he asked when Lena opened the door. He caught sight of Gioana in the kitchen and touched his cap to her. "Good afternoon, Madama Gioana," he greeted her. Lena stepped back from the door.

"Come in, I'll just be a minute." She trotted back to Gioana and bent her knees so her mama could fit the last comb in the back of her hair. "Ready," she cried with a quick peck at her mama's cheek. She tripped over to the door and smiled, grateful that Carlin was so respectful to her mama, and that he did not mind Le Basse. *She* loved her life with her mama, but she saw that other people…*changed* when they saw where she lived. Carlin took her arm and walked with her up the lane, then to the corner café where Pinòt and Adelaide were waiting for them, to have a cup of coffee before the film.

In the café, Carlin pulled out two chairs at their table and settled Lena in hers, then ordered their coffees.

"So, how's your new job?" Pinòt asked Lena.

"It's fine…" Lena lowered her eyes. Adelaide leaned across the table.

"What's it like? What do you do?"

"Oh, I just…sand wood frames," Lena answered.

"Wood frames?"

"Yeah, frames for car windows."

"That's all you do?" Adelaide scoffed.

"Is it hard work?" Carlin asked, interested.

Lena shrugged. "Not hard, no, just…different. It's such a big place."

The inquisition about her job continued. Adelaide wanted to know whether it was worth the change, whether she was making a lot more than at Fornara. "Don't know yet," Lena said. "It depends on how quick I can get."

"You mean…it's *a cottimo,* too?"

"Sure, its piece work, just like Fornara."

Adelaide dismissed FIAT with a disgusted shrug. "So there was no point in changing."

"Oh, I'll do all right. I'm getting faster already," Lena protested, "and besides, I get *le marchette* and *la mutua.*" At Fornara there was no health insurance and no old age pension. Adelaide snorted and sat back, very much on her dignity.

In a lull in the conversation Pinòt, frowned, glaring past his brother's shoulder. Carlin asked, nudged Pinòt's knee under the table. "What's the matter?" he asked.

"There's a *fieul* over there, keeps staring at us."

Lena turned to look, and flushed red. Carlin glanced at her, then at the young man across the room. "You know him?" he asked Lena. He did not like the sneer on the man's face. "Who's he?"

"He is…" Lena stammered then pulled herself together: "It's the *fieul* that helped me with my heel, that day at Niclin."

Carlin turned again to inspect the fellow, saw him smirking. Silently, Carlin summed him up: a *borious,* arrogant, self-important, full of himself. "What's he to you?" he asked Lena.

"Nothing," she mumbled. Carlin studied the man: the jerk didn't belong here. He was no factory worker, not with that suit and that smirk.

Disgruntled, he beckoned to the woman at the bar. "Check, please," he said loudly. Then, as he spread out coins to pay what he owed, he said to the waitress leaning next to him, "Don't look now," he said, "but that *fieul* over there, by the wall, you know who he is?"

The woman scooped up the coins from the table and glanced across the room. "That's…a big cheese over at the *Fascio.*"

Carlin added an extra coin to her tip. "Let's go," he said, scraping his chair back. "*La comica* starts in ten minutes."

Inside the cinema, the four went through last Sunday's procedure: as soon as the portières fell closed on the stairs light, Adelaide and Pinòt disappeared to the top row while Carlin led Lena down to the *galleria's* first row. The newsreel was running – Mussolini strutting in front of a cheering crowd. Carlin held Lena's seat down while she sat down, then settled next to her and slipped his arm through hers. Her hand moved from her lap to settle on the armrest. He found it there and twined his fingers in hers. The farce was on now and the downstairs crowd in the *platea* was hooting with laughter. Lena, stiff at Carlin's side, laughed at *Ridolini's* antics.

The light came on for the first intermission. Carlin gave her hand a squeeze, and sought her eyes. She gave him a quick smile back and looked down. His hand dipped into his pocket, emerging with a slab of chocolate. He ripped back the silver wrapping and offered Lena the tablet to share. Munching, he settled his elbow back on the armrest and found her hand again. The lights dimmed. Down by the screen, the piano erupted into a storm of sound, then Rudolph Valentino strutted across the screen, eyes flashing, Arab robes flowing. A pale-faced woman swooned in his arms, and he engulfed her in a kiss.

Lena withdrew her arm. She covered her action with a quiet sniffle, pressing her hanky to her eyes. Carlin studied her profile in the flickering light. She sniffled again and wiped her eyes. He smiled: she was crying at the romance on the screen. Her hand went down to her lap, her hanky wadded in it. Carlin threaded his arm through hers again, seeking her hand. He felt her stiffen.

"What's wrong?" he whispered in her ears.

"SCHHH!" an angry shush came from behind them.

Lena shook her head: nothing. She raised her hanky to her eyes again.

The rest of the afternoon remained tense. Outside the cinema, they rejoined Pinòt and Adelaide, who were standing arm in arm, closely entwined. "Wasn't that great!" Adelaide gushed, twisting on tiptoes to plant a kiss on the corner of Pinòt's mouth. His lips puckered but missed her cheek and kissed the air.

The two couples said good night in front of the cinema. Pinòt led Adelaide toward *Via Alba,* the side street on the right where she lived in one of the multi-storied tenements; the other two walked left, towards Lena's lane.

"What's wrong, Lena?" Carlin asked gently as they approached the corner. "You're not yourself, today."

Lena tried to laugh it off. "Not myself? Why, that's silly, who else would I be?"

"No, it isn't silly. It is the guy at the café?"

Lena shook her head, denying it, and then abruptly nodded. "He was fresh to me once… It upset me."

"When? What did he do?"

Lena shrugged, pouting.

"Was it that day at Niclin?" Carlin pursued. When she didn't answer, he tried to joke, "I told you," he said, "you should have stayed with me." He leaned towards her for a peck on her cheek.

She jerked her head out of reach. Hurt, Carlin stiffened. They walked on in silence.

But the tension got to Lena and she bleated out, "Oh, I'm sorry… It's not *you.*"

"Well then, what is it?"

"It's… I'm just upset, that's all," she moaned.

They walked in silence the rest of the way. At her gate, she stopped and blocked his way. He stood, confused: he always walked her in and said good night to her mama. "Next Sunday, then," he asked. "Same time?"

Lena squirmed. "Maybe," she wailed, chin to her chest. "I don't know."

Carlin sensed her tears. "Why are you crying? Did something happen? Did I do something wrong?"

Instead of answering, Lena shoved past him and ran, sobbing, across the yard and slammed her door behind her. Carlin, who had started to follow, stopped short, swearing under his breath. Through the thin cotton curtain, he could see the outlines of Lena and her mama clutched together in the faint yellow light of the kitchen. He watched them: they did not move. He searched his mind for anything he might have done to cause all this and came up empty. Whatever had happened, he was at loss for what to do. Better let her calm down in her own time, he decided. Her mama would take care of her. Next Sunday he'd be here, and he'd try to sort things out then. He turned on his heels, and strode off, unhappy, to meet his brother for the six thirty *filobus.*

Pier asks Lena to the Duomo

The following Monday evening, Pier and Lena met at the gate after a day of eye catching across workstations. Side by side, surrounded by the humming swarm of homing workers, they headed towards *Lingòt.* They walked in silence, content with the other's presence.

Some ten minutes into the homeward journey, the throng began to thin out. With groups of people clustering at tram stops and others speeding home on their bicycles, a little pool of relative quiet formed around Pier and Lena, and in one of these moments of calm Lena, broke the silence.

"You said Don Marco," she said as though continuing an ongoing exchange. "Your boss is a priest?"

"Hm," Pier mumbled, suddenly embarrassed.

"You work in a church?" Lena queried. "Doing what?"

"I sing," he answered.

"Sing?" she echoed, then paused. "Like…in the mass," she asked after a moment's thought.

"Yes, mass, and other things…"

"You mean…you stand by the altar. Are you an altar boy?"

"Not anymore," he said, stung.

"But you are one of the men who sing inside the communion rail…"

"I sing with the choir, yes," he said.

"The choir," Lena repeated the new word.

"Yes," Pier explained, "I've been singing with the choir since I was a kid. Now I'm a soloist, a tenor."

"But you still sing mass?"

"Yes, I do. I sing at the duomo," he said, then stopped. Not knowing what Lena's church was like, he didn't want to give an image she couldn't relate to. At San Dalmass' the choir did stand on one side of the altar, like she had said; at

153

Santa Rita's it had its own section next to the harmonium, while at the duomo the choir sang in the organ gallery. He wondered if Lena knew what an organ was. He had not, until he had got to the duomo. He glanced at her and seeing no recognition he explained: "At important *Messe Cantate,* there's the choir and then there are the soloists. I'm one of the soloists."

Too shy to ask what a soloist was, Lena she just said: "Why?"

Not knowing how to answer, Pier said lamely: "It's just the way the music is written."

"But why?" she asked again.

Pier squirmed. "It just *is.*" He hated not being able to explain, so her questions annoyed him.

"Don't the…soloists sing with the others?" she insisted, and Pier's impulse was to cut her short; but just then the light from the draper's display window caught Lena's face, eagerly turned up to Pier, the shop's light creating a halo around her. Enthralled, Pier stopped, his irritation quite defused. He faced her, enchanted.

"Well," he explained, "it's like…you know, when the priest at the altar says '*Agnus dei qui tollis peccata mundi',* and the congregation answers '*ora pro nobis'?"*

Lena nodded, familiar with the ritual, if not with the meaning of the words.

"Well," Pier went on, "the choir and the soloists are a bit like that, sort of." He paused, then added, "Only not quite."

She was still looking up at him, waiting for him to say more. He squirmed, dissatisfied with his explanation, so he dodged. "It's easier to explain with opera," he said. "There, it's just like people talking to each other, see, only they are singing. At times it's just one person singing out loud what's on his mind."

He saw Lena gaze vaguely in the gathering dusk, and he thought he had lost her. But then she spoke, so softly into the night that he barely heard her: "And you're one of those?"

"Yes, I'm a soloist, at the duomo."

Lena walked on and for a second Pier was left standing in the draper's light. He took a quick couple of steps and caught up with her. "I could show you sometime," he blurted out, falling into step with her again, "if you want to come to the duomo."

She strolled on. "And the opera," she asked, "what's that?"

"Oh, opera…" How did one explain opera to someone who'd never seen it? He started: "It's like…" He searched for a parallel she might relate to. "Well, it's like the films, you see. It's a story, but… it's… sung rather than spoken." He stopped, dissatisfied again. "But in opera stories are…well, they are different."

"And you sing that too?" her voice was almost a whisper.

"Not yet…" Pier demurred. "I am just studying for it.*"*

Lena's eyes dropped to the pavement. Ottavio had been studying, and now he was gone.

Lena stopped at the corner of Le Basse. Pier said: "See you tomorrow."

She answered, "Yes, see you tomorrow," but she did not walk on.

"And," Pier asked, straining to see her in the deepening dusk, "can I walk you home again on Thursday?"

Her 'yes' was so soft, he barely heard it, and still she lingered.

At last, she said: "Till Thursday, then," and, with a lingering look over her shoulder, started down the lane.

Pier stood watching until her form dissolved in the gloaming, then ambled his way back to the trams, inexplicably weighed down with sadness.

Next morning, on the tram to work, he forced himself to a decision. All night he had tossed and turned, distressed by dreams and abrupt wakings. The duomo, FIAT, Lorèns, the *Regio,* Lena and his ma had jostled each other in his brain. At breakfast, he had sat, morose, at his *cafelàit,* tormented by the feeling that there was something he should have done and had failed to do. Now at last he thought he knew what that was. He would do it at lunchtime. When the midday whistle shrilled, he lingered at his lathe, watching for the women to pour out of their station, then sidled up to the group and herded Lena to one side.

"Listen," he whispered, bending down to her ear, "what if I pick you up this Sunday and you come to mass at the duomo?"

Lena's head swivelled, her eyes locked on his. He saw anxiety and hope in them, and his heart sang.

"Let's talk about it tonight," he whispered, "I'll wait for you at the gate."

"But you're not walking me home tonight," she pointed out.

"No, but we can talk for a few minutes."

Lena beamed yes, then caught up with her crew with a new bounce in her step.

The six o'clock whistle went, at last. Pier caught Lena's eye across their stations, and she signalled yes. Ten minutes later, he shepherded her away from the crush in front of the gate and across Via Nizza. There they worked their way through the crowd waiting for the next tram and went to stand with their backs to a spice store's window, insulated in their own private world.

"I'd like you to come to the duomo this Sunday," Pier began, speaking softly, close to her. She was looking eagerly into his face. "But," he went on, "I'll be up in the gallery, singing. I hope you don't mind."

"Oh, but I'd love to hear you sing!" she cried.

"You would, really!?" He leaned closer. "But, you see," he stressed, "I'll be *upstairs,* with the choir, so I won't be able to sit with you. You'll be alone all through mass."

A screech of steel on steel drowned his words – a tram grinding to a halt on the tracks, sparks shooting out from the rails. The eager crowd surged.

Somewhere behind them the shop's doorbell rattled, and a woman burst out of the door in a mad dash for the tram. She cannoned into Pier, roughly shoving him out of her way, and boarded the tram, which trundled away with a clatter of wheels, bell clanking, leaving the sidewalk momentarily empty. On the relatively quiet sidewalk, Pier rejoined Lena and led her a few feet down the street, away from the store's entrance.

"But that'd only be during mass, right?" Lena asked as though there'd been no interruption.

"Yes, I'll come down right after it and we can be together. But listen…" Pier rushed on, "You said you live with your mama. Do you think your mama would like to come too? That way you wouldn't be alone during mass."

Lena demurred. "Perhaps," she said, "I can ask her. But she'd probably rather go to our church where she knows everybody."

Pier caught up both her hands and pulled her closer. "Either way, you'll come?"

A restive crowd was again milling at the tram stop, shoving and pushing. Someone bumped Lena into his chest. She laughed, embarrassed at the unplanned embrace, and nodded Yes, YES, she'd come, inches from his face.

Another tram was approaching, one of the older models with open platforms and no doors. Even before it stopped, the waiting crowd surged forward, blocking the exit of the disembarking passengers. Other people were running across Via Nizza to catch it. Its narrow doorways forced the throng on the sidewalk into two single files, but still it shoved and elbowed itself into the already packed tram. Against the wall, Pier and Lena, her hands still resting on his chest, watched the onslaught. The tram clanked its bell and began to chug forward.

"I guess I'd better catch this one..." Pier said reluctantly, suddenly remembering Don Marco.

With a wistful little smile Lena nodded. Pier dashed his first kiss onto her cheek, and sprinted for the already moving tram, caught hold of the pole that served as a handle for its rear platform, and leapt on, instantly turned and waved to her, saw her hand still on her cheek, treasuring his first kiss. A joyous smile transformed his face, his spine stretched tall and his shoulders squared themselves. Chin high, he weaved himself more securely into the crush in the tram's aisle.

Suddenly, there was a scream of tortured steel, and a violent jerk thrust the tram's human cargo forward. Cursing and screaming, the passengers fell pell-mell on each other, The conductor cursed, *"Dio fauss! Lòn ch'a fa stó cretin!"* (Goddamit, what's that idiot doing!) On the tracks a cyclist was hustling his machine out of the tram's way, screaming obscenities back. On the tram the passengers struggled to disentangle themselves along the length of the tram. *"Ahi, me pé,"* a middle-aged man cried out nursing his instep.

In the sudden stop, Pier had stepped on it. *"Am dispias tant,"* he apologised. The irate man had dropped his battered leather briefcase to the floor. His overcoat, too, had seen better days. *A clerk*, Pier thought, going home to his dinner. *"Ch'a scusa, Monsù,"* he apologised again, retrieving the briefcase and handing it to the man. *"Cretin!"* the man snarled at Pier's with a shove chest, *"Fa atension a cò 't fase."* Pier staggered back, stepping on a second foot, this time a young woman's. He turned to his new victim.

"Pardòn, Madamín," he said courteously. (Pardon me, madam). The woman gave him a rueful little smile: it wasn't his fault.

Pier turned back to the man, who was still cursing, standing on one foot and nursing the other.

"Ch'a scusa tant." (All my regrets.) Pier said again, *"Ma i l'hai pròpe nen falo a pòsta."* (I really couldn't help it.) The other continued to rub his foot, scowling and cursing under his breath. Pier sketched him a small bow. A smile was back on his face. He turned away, threaded his way through the crowd to a rear window, unsinkable.

Lena's dilemma: Carlin

Pier's including Gioana in his invitation to the duomo forced Lena's hand. She sat at her workbench deep in thought, oblivious to the noise and dust, her fingers whizzing at their task. She had now been at FIAT two whole weeks and she had never yet mentioned Pier to her mama. She'd wanted to. In fact, with her head so full of him all the time, it had been hard *not* to mention him. But there was Carlin, and she knew her mama was partial to him. Of course, Lena, liked him well enough, but Pier…Lena's eyes lit up at the mere thought of him.

The problem was that, since *San Michel's* day at *I Tigli,* her mama had set her heart on Carlin. Nothing had been said, but Lena had been so well received by his family that her mama nursed the hope that she and Carling might get married. *I Tigli* was a prosperous farm, and one could tell Carlin wasn't stingy – the *galleria* seats, coffee before, the chocolate at intermissions… Lena herself had felt quite spoiled by the way he was treating her; and her mama wanted to see her Lena well married, well cared for. Lena herself had begun to think that it might happen. And why shouldn't she hope, she thought rebelliously, suppressing the memory of Ottavio. Adelaide was engaged to Carlin's younger brother, wasn't she? So why not?

True, Adelaide did not live on Le Basse*; h*er father was a skilled craftsman who worked for a joiner, and in church, the family sat well forward, with the respectable artisans. But Carlin did not seem to mind where Lena lived. He picked her up at Le Basse and walked her back, and he was always nice to her *mama*, brought her small gifts from their farm – a basket of grapes, some pears. Last week he'd brought her quince. And each time he'd handed her his gift saying, "*Mia mare* thought you might like some of these. Just ripe this week."

So how was Lena going to tell her mama that she'd seen somebody else? How was she going to explain what was happening to her when she didn't understand it herself? Last Sunday, when she'd run in crying after the cinema with Carlin, she had been so scared and confused all she could do was cry harder each time her mama asked her what was wrong.

"Had a fight with Carlin?" her mama had asked at last. Lena wanted to tell her no, it was not Carlin, it wasn't his fault. But then again it *was!* He had…well, he'd become a problem, simply by being there!

So, poor Lena didn't know what to do. She needed time. As yet, she knew so little of Pier, and yet she was so sure! She was so happy when she saw him, or even when she just thought of him.

And now Pier had asked her mama to the duomo, and Lena didn't know what to do. Last June, when Ottavio had asked her to the dance, she hadn't wanted her mama to go with. She felt like that now, and yet it was different. All along, Lena had known she could not let Ottavio see where she lived; but Pier did not mind. She'd worried about this, that first time he walked her home, but he hadn't minded at all.

Right now, in her mind's eye, she saw that scene, standing on her corner, that first night: Pier squinting down Le Basse in the dusk and saying, "You live on a farm?" He sounded surprised but not a bit upset. No, he'd almost sounded pleased.

That first night she hadn't let him come past the corner. But deep down she'd felt even then that it would be all right, only, not quite yet, not until she had… well…sorted herself out about Carlin. But now Pier had invited her mama and she had to decide.

She cringed: her mama would be hurt that she hadn't told her about Pier. And *he*… What would *Pier* think if she told him that her mama *didn't want to* go to the duomo to hear him sing? Would he be hurt, offended? Would he think that *she* didn't want her mama to see him? Of course, she wanted her mama to see him, he was…wonderful! So why had she told him that her mama preferred to go to their *Lingòt* church? She had no idea what her mother preferred. The question had never come up before; they had just always gone to mass in *Lingòt*.

Suddenly, a horrible though struck her: what if Pier should think she was ashamed of her mama, like she'd been ashamed of Le Basse with Ottavio?

Oh, but she wasn't! Her mama was a darling and she loved her with all her heart, loved living with her, doing little things together! She was so happy with her mama, at times she got scared at the thought that things might change.

More calmly, she reminded herself that things had become comfortable since they had their two wages, and it would get even better after next Saturday, when she got her first pay packet from FIAT. She had great hopes of FIAT, and the thought of winter coats and proper boots stirred her heart. But she had promised Pier she'd tell him tonight, about mass at the duomo, and she hadn't asked her mama yet. *I'll tell her tonight,* she told herself firmly. She'd tell her about Pier as well, and about the big church where he sang.

A sudden draft ran through her workstation and made her shiver. That sent her thoughts off in a different direction: what did one wear to mass at the duomo? At the *Lingòt* church everybody wore shawls – well, in the back pews, anyway.

Would there be anyone in shawls at the big church, or would they all come in wool coats and hats? A stray thought added: *"Hats with feathers, like in the films."* This was something she could ask Pier. He would know. He sang there.

But how could she tell him she hadn't asked her mama yet? Would he think she was putting him off because *she* didn't want to go? *I'll tell him my mama hasn't decided yet*, she thought. *Then I'll ask her tonight.* She felt easier, and concluded: *Tonight I'll just ask him what one wears.*

That night, she tackled her problem as soon as she got home, in case she lost her courage.

"There's this *fieul*," she said casually, while eating supper, "he works in the station next to mine. He sings at a big church downtown, the duomo, he called it." She lifted a spoon of *ris e faseuj* to her mouth. "He's asked me to go hear him this Sunday." She threaded her spoonful into her mouth.

"Would you like to go?" her mama asked her.

"Think so," she edged. "What about you? Would you mind?"

"Not at all. I can go to mass with Cichin-a."

"No, I mean…" Lena said, shaking her curls, "would *you* like to go hear him in this big church?"

"Me? Why?"

Lena shrugged, "Well, to hear him sing."

Gioana cocked her head sideways, looked her daughter in the eye, "So," she said, "*that's* what's been happening!"

"Nothing's been happening!" Lena protested hotly.

"And the tears, last Sunday, hey? And Carlin not coming in to say good night?"

"Oh, Mama!" Lena's hands joined fervently in front her mouth. "He's *so nice!"* Gioana kept her sideways squint on Lena's ecstatic face, encouraging her to go on. "He's tall, and blond, and…and…ever so *fin!"*

"So what's he doing at FIAT?"

If there was a challenge in Gioana's voice, Lena did not hear it. "He works at a lathe. He mills the rear window frames I sand…"

Her eyes came down from their ecstatic contemplation of the new *fieul*'s perfections and caught the teasing glint in her mama's eyes. "No, really, Mama," she cried, "he is!"

"I believe you, child," Gioana laughed; then she added, seriously: "But what about Carlin?"

Lena's face fell. "Oh," she moaned her rice and beans forgotten. "What am I going to do!?"

"Tell him you don't want to rush things."

"Pier!?" Lena cried, horror-struck.

"Well…who is it you don't want to rush things with, Carlin or this new *fieul?"* Lena didn't answer, but there was no doubt in her mind.

Her thoughts turned to Carlin: Adelaide and Pinòt were rushing things with that secret engagement just two months after they'd met; and Pinòt hadn't even done his military service yet, so he'd be gone for a whole year. They *were* rushing things, so maybe Carlin would accept that *she* didn't want to rush things. Her face brightened and she finished her now cold *ris e faseuj.* A moment later she frowned again: why would Carlin want to wait when his younger brother wasn't? Carlin had finished his military service three years ago. "Oh, but Mama…" she pleaded for help.

Gioana was serious now. "What's worrying you, girl?"

"Will he accept *that,* now that Pinòt and Adelaide are engaged?" Gioana's eyebrows rose. "They are engaged?! I thought you said he'd just asked her to be his *morosa* a month ago!"

"Well, yes, but that was *before!"* Lena said, brushing the question aside, then she clapped her hand over her mouth. "Oh, sorry!" she cried, shocked. "That was a secret. I wasn't supposed to tell. But it just slipped out. Promise *you* won't tell anyone."

Gioana's mouth tightened, but after a moment she said, "It's none of my business."

"Yes, but promise!" Lena insisted. "Adelaide will never forgive me."

"All right, I won't say anything. But what are *you* going to do?"

"I'm going to the duomo to hear Pier sing."

"So, his name is Pier. But what about Carlin, what are you going to do about him?"

Lena's face crumpled again, and her eyes filled with tears. "What *am* I going to do?" she sobbed.

Gioana waited in silence. After a while she poured out a glass of water and slid it across the table, nudging Lena's hand with it. Still crying, Lena drank it. "Blow your nose," Gioana said, handing her handkerchief to Lena over the table. Lena blew her nose.

"What *do* I do, Mama?"

Gioana thought a while, then said, "Tell him you need time. You've met someone at work you want to get to know better before going any further."

"Oh, but that will hurt him!"

"Whatever you tell him, child, hearing *no* always hurts. Better hurt him with the truth than with a lie."

"But I can't, oh! I can't!" Lena wailed, crying harder.

By and by, she calmed down and got up, sniffling, to dry the dishes Gioana was washing.

Later that night, lying close in bed, Gioana raised the question again. "What have you decided to do about Carlin?"

"I guess I'll have to tell him," Lena moaned.

"But *what* will you tell him?" Lena sighed, then murmured, "That there's someone else…"

After a moment's silence Gioana asked, "When are you going to tell him?"

"I don't know, I don't know," Lena whimpered, pulling the covers over her head.

"Don't leave it too long," Gioana said firmly. "He's got a right to know where he stands."

Lena turned away from her and covered her head with her pillow. She didn't want to think about all this anymore. She just wanted it all to go away.

Gioana sighed and lay staring into the dark. "He is a good man," she murmured regretfully to the night.

Lena at the Duomo

On Sunday morning, Pier picked Lena up in good time. His *Messa Cantata* was not until eleven o'clock, but he had to check in by ten thirty. The morning was soft with a mild October sun and a faint, high haze. Lena met him at their corner, wrapped up in her best shawl, her missal and her rosary in her matching crocheted bag. Pier stepped forward to meet her, dazzled by the copper lights the morning sun scattered in her dark chestnut hair.

Half an hour later, they walked up the duomo's broad flight of steps side by side. Halfway up Lena stopped, her hand screening her eyes from the morning sun, awed by the ancient façade. Pier stopped with her, glorying in her nearness. She turned around to gaze at the irregular square below, and her hip brushed against his thigh. Pier caught his breath, shaken by the strange quivering inside him. Lena stood, oblivious, watching the Sunday scene below, the cobbled

162

square, pedestrians strolling in their Sunday clothes, a tram clanking on its tracks, disappearing through the ancient Roman arch. She had never been to this part of Turin, though it was only minutes away from the Via Po arcades where she often window-shopped with Adelaide, or with her mama. She caught Pier gazing down at her and smiled, then quickly lowered her eyes.

Side by side, they resumed their climb towards the vast carved portals. Here Pier said: "In a moment I'll have to leave you. But I'll come down right after mass. It will be over by twelve thirty."

"An hour and a half!" Lena cried, surprised. Mass at *Lingòt* never lasted more than an hour. She wouldn't be home in time for midday dinner, and her mama would be waiting for her, worrying. But she hadn't known... Pier was explaining, "It's a high mass, you see. There's lots of singing. I hope you won't be bored..."

"Oh, no, not bored," she beamed at him. But he caught the shadow of discomfort. Maybe it had been a mistake, he thought, asking her here on their first time out together. And now he had to leave her alone.

"Afterwards," he said, trying to make things better, "we could walk across Piazza Castello. It's just over there, not far. I could show you the Teatro Regio, where I study opera." Lena smiled, but looked away without answering. She should have told her mama not to expect her for lunch, she thought. Now she'd worry. But she *hadn't known*, she'd thought it would just be a regular mass and she'd be home in plenty of time.

Confused by her silence, Pier apologised: "I'm so sorry to leave you, but I have to go in now. Do you want to walk about out here awhile, until the ten o'clock mass ends? It shouldn't be long. Or I could walk you in now, settle you in a pew..."

Lena glanced around the square: no shops, no lights, just somber, three-storied stone buildings. "I'll go in now," she said, lifting the top layer of her lacy wool shawl to cover her head, aware that it lay becomingly on her dark curls, and framed her face to advantage. Pier held the side door open and she walked in, the door closing silently behind her, excluding the daylight. The holy breath of the church enveloped her with its deep scent of wax and incense, awesome, yet familiar.

Inside, in the shadow of the choir gallery, she stopped, awe-struck by the eerie light and the immense length of the nave, the vast carved portals behind her precluding retreat. From on high, mysterious shafts of light crisscrossed the holy dusk of the nave. A phrase from last Sunday's sermon seared her mind: "The sight of God."

Feeling very small, she turned to Pier, but he was no longer there.

Instantly, she was swamped with panic, until, a few feet away, she saw him, dipping his fingers in the holy water font, to bring back to her a touch of holy water. She reached out her hand to receive it, and their fingers touched, shooting a galvanising thrill though her.

Slowly, very slowly, their hands withdrew. He took her arm and, solicitously, led her to a nearby pew.

"I'll be down at twelve thirty," he whispered as she sat down. She nodded assent and watched him scurry off to the back of the church, where he disappeared through a small side door. Lena's last glimpse of him saw him running up a narrow spiral staircase while the door he'd opened swung slowly and silently to.

Alone, Lena checked that her shawl covered her head properly, she smoothed her dark skirt modestly over her knees, then she peered around her, gradually taking in the details of the vast holy place. She now spotted the source of those uncanny shafts of light: there were windows high above those deep recesses that lined the nave.

Her curious eyes explored those recesses: inside their balustrades, ranks of pews before candle-lit altars, paintings, statues. Next to the balustrade, on the right side, the statue of a saint or a holy virgin; and beneath the effigy brass trays with candles set in golden sand, an offering box next to them.

In one of the chapels she watched a woman get up from her knees, stop before the illumined statue by the balustrade, kiss her fingers, and reverently lay her kiss on the virgin's naked feet. Lena watched her light a candle and drop a coin into a slotted box.

Lena looked closer at the statue. "*Mater Dolorosa*," she whispered to herself, recognising the image from her prayer book, the words surfacing from the litanies of her novenas.

Around her, people were now rising from their pews and filing out: the ten o'clock mass was over. Soon she would hear Pier.

After some minutes of stillness, new people began to file in. Lena watched their progress down the aisle, noting their apparel: men in mid-season tailored overcoats, felt hats in hand; ladies in heavy wool suits and hats, tiptoeing towards the forward pews – the clip-clopping of high heels out of place in the house of

God. Others, more modest, slipped quietly into the midsection pews. Here, the women wore crocheted hats with wool suits or coats. A few had on lace a *quefa*. Only in rear pews could she spot any shawls or black scarves. Lena crossed her shawl more tightly across her chest.

In the silence that followed the new arrivals, she had begun to roll and unroll the edge of her shawl between her fingers, when an explosion of unearthly sound erupted throughout the church, making her jump in her seat. With no apparent source, it shook the vaulted ceiling, the nave, her very being. Lena cowed with dread.

Then she remembered: the organ. Pier had spoken of it, but she had no idea. It must be up there somewhere in the choir gallery. Where *he* must be now.

A private smile dawned on her face. She would hear him soon.

From the altar came the tinkle of a bell, and worshippers rose to their feet: the mass was about to start.

Her attention turned to the altar, her breath catching up short: not *one* priest filed in, but five; and several altar boys, swinging censors.

Around her the faithful opened their missals, some kneeling, others remaining in their seats. Lena kneeled, her little book open in her hands – the parish's gift to each first communion child. She could not read her little book, but she knew it by heart. She knew, without understanding them, the Latin responses. She knew them from years of weekly repetitions, and she was stirred by the hypnotic rhythms of the sonorous Latin sounds. To remind her of what each section of the mass was about, she had inserted holy images between the pages, The Last Supper, the glory of God, the Offertory, the communion of the faithful…

At the altar, the officiating priest intoned: "*Kyrie eleison; Kriste eleison; Kyrie eleison.*" Invisible male voices answered with elaborate volutes of sound.

When the chanting stopped, the congregation sang "A–me–n", and Lena joined in, restive: she had not been able to pick out Pier's voice in the resonant chorus.

The organ sounded again, swelling into ripples and waves, a veritable cascade of sound. When it subsided, the officiating priest intoned: "*Gloria in excelsis Deo,*" then he went to rest on a padded seat at the left of the altar, and in the eerie silence that followed a full, clear voice rang out on high: "*Glo-o-o-o-o-o-O-o-o-o-o- O-o-o ri-a-a-a.*"

Pier! Lena had never yet heard him sing, but she knew it was him! She sat transfixed, spine tingling, eyes fixed on the altar she barely saw, unseeing. Whenever the choir joined in, or the organ took over, she waited, holding her breath until she heard *him* again, in awe both of what she heard and of what was happening inside her.

Over the next hour, organ and chorus again and again intruded, using up time she could have been hearing Pier, but it did not matter, he'd soon be with her. All worries about her mama vanished, she waited for Pier.

The officiating priest raised the host. All heads bowed, some over folded hands on crimson padded leather. Her head bowed, Lena still gazed vaguely forward. Somewhere in a front row, a long, thin feather rose straight up from a wintergreen hat, above a brown fur collar. Head still bowed, Lena now, again, studied the congregation, taking in the few lace *quefas*, and, in a side chapel, a *mater dolorosa,* all in black, head collapsed over hands clutched in prayer. It brough to her mind her poor neighbour, whose daughter had been run over on Via Nizza by a speeding car, the way the desolate woman had looked on the day of the funeral.

"A-a–gnu-u–us De-e-e-i-i..." Goose pimples stiffening on her skin, Lena's head jerked up, sharply alert: Pier was back! *"...Qui to-o-o-ol—li-is pec–ca-a–a—ta-a mu–u–un-di-i-i..."*

"It's Pier! It's Pier," Lena's soul sang. A pleasurable *frisson* enveloped her, the sacred ritual dissolved in the miracle of his unseen presence. Whenever the organ again took over, she waited impatiently for the sound she longed for. Each time the glorious voice returned, she hung upon its magical music. Whenever it stopped, she longed for its return, anticipated it, pined for it.

The mass over, Lena twisted around in her seat, searching the spiral stairs where Pier had disappeared. But its door, in shadow, remained closed. People began to file out of the pews and into the aisles. On her right, a voice whispered, *"Scusi,per favore,"* excuse me, please. A woman stood next to her, wanting to file out toward the centre aisle. Lena half rose, pressed herself back against the pew 171

Soon the church was empty. Lena sat on, indecisive: Pier had said he'd come to get her. But had he meant here, in the pew, or outside the church? Repeatedly, she twisted in her seat to check the closed door under the organ gallery, waiting for Pier, longing to see him scurrying along the nave to meet her. The empty nave now became oppressive. And she was cold. She longed to be outside in the sunlight, but…would *he* want her to do that, to wait for him outside? He hadn't said. So she sat in her pew until an awful thought struck her: *Has he forgotten me?* In near panic, she peered towards the choir stairs, then scolded herself, *Of course he wouldn't forget me.* With that, she sidled out to the centre aisle, skimmed the stone floor with her right knee and walked out, trying to look composed.

Outside, the sunlight dazzled her. The light morning haze had dissolved, and the sky now stretched out, a deep, brilliant blue. She heaved a sigh of release. And, suddenly, there he was, Pier, at her side! "Oh!" she cried. "But…you didn't come down the same door!"

"No," he explained, "I had to put my vestments away in the vestry. I came out a side door. So, what did you think?" he asked eagerly, searching her eyes. Lena's face, hands, her whole body expressed wordless ecstasy. Then, needing more, she grabbed his hand in both of hers, and cradled it against her cheek. With a half-choked laugh Pier said, "Anyway, now you know what I do on Sundays." He took her arm and guided her down the steps to the square below. "Let's walk," he said. "I want to show you the *Regio*." She snuggled up close, hanging on, ecstatic, to his arm.

Behind them, in its square tower, the duomo's bell struck one o'clock. Lena cringed with a pang of guilt. *Mama will be waiting for me,* she thought. But, trotting at Pier's side, her guilty feeling was short lived. She had no desire to go home. Then another unwelcome thought flashed through her mind: *In half an hour, Carlin will be there.*

She shooed the disturbing thought away. Her stomach growled, so she rushed into speech to cover it up. "Where is this theatre?" she asked.

"Not far," Pier assured her, gazing as her smiling, up-turned face, "just over there, across Piazza Castello." His hand covered hers on his arm. "And afterwards, if you like, we can grab a bite at the café where all the artists eat."

Lena's dilemma: Carlin again

It was getting dark when Pier and Lena said goodbye on the tram island in front of Porta Nuova. He wanted to see her home, but she wouldn't let him.

"It's so late," she protested. "You'll just have to come back here to catch your tram to Santa Rita. I can catch mine right there. It's no problem."

In the end, Pier gave in and saw her onto her tram before running across Corso Vittorio to catch his own. Still dazed from their first day together, he waited for his ride home, going over their first date: it had been a good day, despite the uncomfortable beginnings. He could see how she could have felt *dëspaisà* in the duomo, disoriented among the city's well to do. She needn't have, he smiled to himself, remembering the sunlight in her hair on the duomo steps: she was easily the loveliest girl there, shawl or no shawl.

On her tram, Lena sat demurely in her seat, gazing out of the window. The sun had disappeared behind Monviso some time ago, and the light was growing sombre. Her thoughts turned to what was waiting for her at home: she'd never stayed out all day before, and her mama would be upset that she hadn't told her, so she had a scolding coming. She did not want her mama to be cross with her; she should have gone home right after mass, but the day had been so…dizzying, she sighed, with one thing following another, and she hadn't wanted to give up a single moment with Pier. And he had taken her places, not just looking in at things from the outside.

For a moment, she was back in front of the Regio: it was amazing that he sang at that big church, but this *theatre* – it was just like the movies. And to think that one day he might sing there! He'd said he wanted to, and she believed one day he would. In her mind, she saw Pier's face on the billboard, with his name, Pier Venturi, in big, bold letters underneath. She smiled happily and sighed. One day, maybe…

Her thoughts returned to their walk arm in arm, their stop by the stage door, Pier's tale of his first time there; then their lunch at the *Tampa Lirica*. She relived walking in on his arm, being led to a corner table, a chair being pulled back for her, people at other tables calling out to Pier like they were old friends.

"Stage crew," he'd explained. And he had told her what went on in the theatre, a whole new world, so many things she knew nothing about. She sighed, overwhelmed with blissful excitement.

But then a distressed sigh broke out from her: Carlin might still be waiting for her at home. She hadn't actually promised to meet him today. Her fingers tortured the strap of her crocheted purse, fervently praying he wouldn't be there. There was nothing she could tell him that would not make him angry, and she didn't want her lovely day spoiled. Why couldn't he just go away and leave her be?

Her tram ground to a stop by Cinema Lingotto and she got reluctantly off, stopping to stare absently at the cinema's future attractions as the tram trundled noisily on. Home was just minutes away, and now a threat. At last, she began to crawl homeward, fearing at every step that she'd run into Carlin, coming the other way. She stopped at the gate, still wide open, anxiously studying the small rectangle of light that was her mama's kitchen door, dreading she'd see *two* silhouettes inside. Still putting off the inevitable, she stopped to close the gate, threading the night chain through the iron bars.

"Lena? Is that you?" she heard above rattle of the chain: her mama stood in her open doorway, peering out into the dusk.

"It's me," Lena called back in a small voice.

"*Tut bin?*" came the anxious inquiry from the door. "You're all right?"

"*Sì, tut bin,*" Lena answered, approaching.

"You had us worried," Gioana said from the doorstep. "Carlin's been here all afternoon." Carlin's bulky shape now loomed big behind Gioana.

"Oh, no," Lena moaned, shuffling towards the threshold. The two figures drew back to let her in.

"Where have you been?" Gioana asked urgently, exchanging their customary welcome kiss on the cheek.

"Your mama was sure you'd been run over," Carlin said.

Lena sidled past them, heading for the bedroom door.

"You had me worried to death, child," Gioana said, following her. "Carlin went down to the café and called the hospital to ask about accidents."

"What did he want to do that for?" Lena muttered, closing the bedroom door on them.

"We were worried, child," her mama scolded through the door. "I expected you home for lunch, and it's after six…"

Lena clapped her hands onto her ears, kept them there until the voices subsided. Then she went about folding her Sunday shawl and putting it away in its drawer. Still delaying the confrontation, she kicked off her shoes and was stepping into her slippers when her mama knocked, then walked in.

"Do you have any idea what you've put me through?" Gioana challenged. "I swear I saw you lying on the ground all broken up and bloody, like Teresina's daughter. I was quite beside myself when Carlin came to pick you up for the film. And it was *good of him* to go and telephone."

"Well, I'm not dead," Lena whined, petulant, pushing past her and into the kitchen. "I'm quite all right."

But Gioana wasn't done. "And poor Carlin, here," she said laying a motherly hand on the young man's arm. "He's been waiting for you all afternoon, and as worried as I was."

"Well, he shouldn't have. I never promised I'd go out with him today."

"You never said you wouldn't," Carlin put in. "We've been seeing each other every Sunday since August…"

"I said I didn't know…"

"You could at least have left word with me this morning…" Gioana put in.

"But I *didn't know!"* Lena wailed. "I thought it was just for mass, one hour, but it was so much longer…"

"I thought maybe you'd had your purse snatched," Carlin said, "and couldn't take the tram. A girl alone…It isn't safe."

"But I was never alone!"

"Well, even two girls…" he said his tone implying. "Easy targets."

"I told Carlin you'd gone to mass at the duomo," Gioana explained, "with your new friend from FIAT."

Lena's eyes flew to her mama's face. "Oh," Lena moaned: so now she had to tell Carlin that her new friend was a *fieul*; and *that* she couldn't bring herself to do. Her chin quivered and tears flooded her cheeks.

"What's happened, Lena?" Carlin asked, bending towards her. "You all right?"

"Nothing happened!" she screamed. Why did they keep asking? Why couldn't he leave her alone!

"But *five hours*," Carlin persisted. "What were you doing all that time?"

"Walking, we were just walking."

"For five hours!?"

"And then we saw this place and we were hungry, so we went in for a bite to eat."

"Just you and your girlfriend?"

"Oh, why do you keep asking me all these silly questions? Why can't you just go away and let me be!" Lena threw herself down on one of the chairs by the kitchen table, hid her face in her arms.

"Just like that!" Carlin cried bitterly. "You just want me to go away! And I'm not to ask for the reason?"

Lena howled.

Hurt, confused and angry, Carlin turned to Gioana: what had he done to deserve this brush-off? Search his mind as he may, he could see nothing that justified Lena's change towards him from one week to the next. Gioana hunched up her shoulders, as helpless as he. Both fell silent, stunned by Lena's violent sobbing.

"Is there someone else?" Carlin asked after a while, almost ashamed of asking. Lena was so modest...

"Oh, leave me alone!" Lena howled through desperate sobs. "Go away! Just leave me alone!" Her face turned in her arms to hide from him.

Gioana stepped to her side, gently stroked Lena's shoulders, like one soothes a colicky infant. She glanced at Carlin who stood by, nonplussed, scared at Lena's paroxysm: something dreadful must have happened to his sweet Lena, to make her act like this. He sought Gioana's eyes and she shook her head, silently mouthing, "Let her calm down."

Helpless, shoulders rose, palms up-turned in silent questions, he mouthed back to her, "What happened? What did I do?"

Gioana shook her head in infinite regret: he had done nothing. Carlin withdrew, stopping at the door to retrieve the cap he'd hung on the usual peg. With a last distressed look at Lena, still collapsed on the table, he raised a finger to his cap in farewell to Gioana and left, quietly latching the door behind him.

It took another good ten minutes for Lena's sobs to subside and for her to sit up in her chair with a frightened look around the room. Relieved that Carlin was gone, she searched her pocket for her handkerchief, blew her nose and wiped her cheeks. At last, she dared to look at her mama, who sat across the table, waiting for her to speak. The mask of sorrow she saw stirred up her guilt.

"Oh, don't, please," she cried, "don't look at me like that!"

Deeply distressed, Gioana only shook her head.

"I didn't do anything wrong, Mama, I promise!" Lena cried.

"I know, child. I know. But that poor Carlin...he cares for you, Lena. He was really scared this afternoon."

"Don't, Mama, please!"

"You'll *have to* talk to him. Whatever it is, you'll *have to* tell him. This way you are treating him very badly. "

"Don't, Mama!" Lena wailed, bolting from the kitchen. The crash of her chair onto the stone floor merged with the slamming of the bedroom door.

Chapter Eight

...Chaos of thought and passion all confused...
Alexander Pope

Matilde and Rexel: Pier's audition

With the approach of autumn, Matilde's thoughts turned to the new opera season, and to the next step in Pier's training. All through the summer, he had worked hard and made considerable progress, even during her vacation. His Italian diction still had a long way to go, but when he sang rehearsed lines, it was now quite acceptable. And his voice was truly remarkable: she had been sure of that since she'd first gone to hear him at the duomo. She was equally confident of his acting talent. Raw as it still was, it had depth.

Last July she had started to work with him on dramatic duets – Rodolfo and Mimi, Alfredo and Violetta, the Duke and Gilda. Then one day Pier had asked to try the Azucena-Maurico prison scene. It had surprised her because that scene is really the mezzo-soprano, not the tenor's. But when she heard and saw his "*Se m'ami ancor, se voce di figlio...*", she sensed a dramatic depth in him that she hadn't suspected. That and his anguish in *Di quella pira* decided her to bring her protégé to the attention of Professor Horst Rexel, the resident music master of the Regio. If Rexel liked what he heard, Pier would get the training his voice needed for dramatic roles. Later he might be brought to the attention of Maestro Gui, and if Vittorio Gui took him under his wing, well, Pier would at the very least get the guidance needed to navigate the operatic labyrinth in which *she* had run aground in the chorus.

Leery of raising unwarranted hopes, Matilde had not mentioned her thoughts to Pier; but, before she left on her vacation, she had assigned him the task of working on the dramatic aspects of the scenes they had been practicing together, among them three arias she thought would show off to advantage both his voice

172

and his dramatic scope, *Che gelida manina,* from *La Bohème, Lungi da lei,* from *La Traviata,* and *Vesti la giubba,* from *I Pagliacci.*

This summer work had paid off and, after their last session, Matilde knew that Pier was ready. She expected to run into Professor and Frau Rexel on the following Saturday, at a pre-season gathering. She would buttonhole him and try to get Pier an audition. Once she had a date, *then* she would tell Pier. Professor Rexel had set the date for Pier's audition for nine o'clock on the third Wednesday evening of October. By then, the new season's opening night would be behind them.

On the appointed evening, Matilde met Pier at the Regio's stage door a good hour before the audition, and led him through his warm-up, devoting the last ten minutes to deep breathing, eyes closed, mind, hopefully, blank. At nine, precisely, the rehearsal room door swung open and Professor Rexel bustled in: a round, little man, with a shock of reddish hair tumbling over bushy eyebrows at each brisk step.

"*So, mine Frau,*" he shouted in a strong Germanic voice, "this is your *Wunderkind.*"

"He is, Professor. Pier Venturi," Matilde introduced him.

"Professor," Pier said with the small bow she had taught him.

"*Gut, gut. So,* what am I going to hear?" Matilde handed him a card on which she had written out Pier's name and the arias he was going to sing. "Hum... I see..." Rexel muttered peering at the card, his shock of reddish hair quivering as he read.

He turned his back on them and bustled across the room to one of two armchairs set against the far wall. "Whenever you're ready..." he called out throwing himself down into one of them, his plump, freckled hand fluttering an impatient 'get on with it'.

Matilde sat down at the piano and glanced at Pier, standing tense next to the instrument. Discretely, she mimed 'deep breaths from the diaphragm.' Pier followed her cue and his body relaxed. Matilde smiled encouragement, closing her eyes and miming 'into the scene'. Pier closed his eyes, withdrawing from the here and now. Soon, his mind evoked a moonlit garret in Paris, a cold stone floor, hands groping about in the dark after a lost key. Next to him, on all fours, Mimí turned her face towards him and, inexplicably, it was Lena's face on the steps of the duomo.

He opened his eyes, caught Matilde's poised at the piano, waiting for his signal, and nodded. She played the introduction to his first aria, then Pier sang, "*Che gelida manina…*"

Matilde heard the difference instantly: there was in his voice a new lightness, a joyousness she had not heard before. She looked at him as Rodolfo proceeded with his introductions: despite the sober blue suit she'd had him wear to the audition, for the first time, she saw the young poet of *La Bohème* – carefree, tongue-in cheek, imagination soaring, making light of his poverty as he flirts in the moonlight with the pretty new neighbour. Pier sang, "*Per sogni e per chimere e per castelli in aria L'anima ho millionaria.*" (As to dreams and wild fancies and castles in the air I have a millionaire's soul.) His voice sailed with ease through the poet's airy conceits, then, gently, eagerly, he coaxed, "*Or che mi conoscete, Parlate voi, deh! Chi siete?*" (Now that you know me, speak, do! Who are you?) Matilde ran off the closing notes. She turned to check Professor Rexel's reaction.

"*Nicht schlecht*," rumbled the deep voice from the far wall. "Not bad at all." Half-rising, he sketched an acknowledging bow in Matilde's direction and sat down again. "Vhat next?" he demanded.

Again, Pier closed his eyes for a moment, withdrawing from the rehearsal room into himself. Then he caught Matilde's eye and they went through his second selection, *Lungi da lei*.

Again, Professor Rexel listened, attentive, and at the end, he again nodded approval. Matilde smiled her thanks to the Regio's music master. She sought out Pier's eyes and smiled, sending the wordless message: "He likes it. You're doing well."

From the far wall, the deep rumble again demanded: "Vhat next?" Pier gathered himself together for his final effort, a radical shift in mood, then looked to Matilde and nodded. Matilde played the wrenching opening phrases, then Pier sang, "*Recitar! Mentre preso dal delirio… –* to act! While seized with delirium…" Gone was the bonhomie, the playfulness of Rodolfo. Alfredo's slender frame, that in *Lungi da lei* had lounged, languid with love, was now gnarled and cramped with Canio's frenzy of despair, betrayal and self-contempt. Pain thickened the clear young voice, until it was a broken old man's, his notes ringing true and clean despite the agony.

Professor Rexel sat up on the edge of his armchair, his eyes on the clown's face. Pier sang, "*...tramuta in lazzi lo spasmo e il pianto.*"(Transform into jokes your pain and tears), and a *frisson* ran up the professor's spine.

Voice and piano fell silent, and Matilde and Pier turned to face their judge. He sat silent; a gnome huddled in the vast chair by the far wall, bushy red hair obscuring his features. Pier's eagerness flared into panic and he sought Matilde's eyes, seeking reassurance. She raised her shoulders, eyes wide, brows up, nonplussed. Then from the far wall came a thump, a hand slapping leather upholstery, over and over again. Their eyes flew to the huddled figure by the far wall: Professor Rexel, slumped in his chair, kept slapping and slapping the padded armrest.

Matilde looked at Pier and again gave her helpless shrug: she couldn't read the verdict.

At last, the professor rose from his chair and slowly crossed the room.

"*Ach, so,*" he sighed, still a few feet away. "Your protégé, Matilde," he reached out his hands to her, "he *can sing!*" He gave her hand a vigorous congratulatory shake.

Matilde burst into a laugh of relief, and Pier let out his pent-up breath with a hiss, then laughed and started to breathe again.

Then the oracle turned to him. "I'm told, young man, that you sing for Don Marco."

"Yes, sir," Pier said.

"I must come hear you there sometime. But, your teacher, here," his glance included Matilde, "tells me opera is what you want…"

"Yes, sir," Pier answered, tongue-tied, suddenly alarmed at the possibility of the professor meeting Don Marco, thus revealing his carefully guarded secret – his clandestine visits to the theatre. The oracle nodded wisely.

Unexpectedly, he raised one bushy red eyebrow at Matilde and added, "And, by Giove, he *can act,*!" A click of the tongue accompanied the toss of his head. But then he frowned and turned away, started to pace back and forth across the room. A few moments went by, then his tongue clicked again.

"Hmmm," he muttered, "but no money." Head shaking, without a word, he turned and made for the room's door.

Scared, Pier looked to Matilde. Her expression said, "Hold on." At the closed door, Professor Rexel turned around, ponderous as an old man, aimed his finger at Pier's chest. "When sing you at the duomo?" he demanded. Pier told him. "I come to hear you there," the oracle said, then turned, swung the door open and walked out.

Matilde shook Pier excitedly by the shoulders. "You've done it!" she cried. "You've done it. He's interested!"

"But…" Pier stammered, confused.

"But nothing!" she laughed, clapping her hands in excitement. "Don't let his ogre ways scare you. He enjoys them. But he's impressed. You've got him!"

"But," Pier all but wailed, "but I've no money!" Matilde shushed him, her hands brushing non-existent specks from his sleeves.

"He *knows* that. It was the first thing I told him, before I asked him to hear you. So give him time."

"Time to what?"

Matilde shrugged the question aside.

Pier groaned, looked around the room, deflated. "So now what?" he all but whimpered.

"So now *we wait*," she said emphatically. "You go on with what you're doing and show up here as often as you can," her hand brushed a last invisible speck from his sleeve, half motherly half proprietary, "and keep your chin up," she added, seeing his downcast air, and running an affectionate finger under his jaw. "The first rule of the theatre, my dear, is 'be on time and wait'."

She glanced at her watch, pulled a face, hurriedly grabbed her mid-season coat and pulled it on. "I must run," she said, tipping her hat over her left eyebrow. She reached up on tiptoes, placed a proud peck on Pier's cheek, and left.

Pier stared at the inexorably shut door. Signora Agiati, his guide, his mentor, *his courage,* was gone. Out of his sight, for him, Matilde Agiati ceased to exist. She *had left him,* suddenly and alone in the now threatening room. The professor's ambiguous response to his audition had left Pier so shocked, so disoriented that he experienced his guardian angel's departure as a cataclysmic loss. The door that had closed behind her had shut on the new world she'd given him a glimpse of – a world of discovery, of possibility, of hope.

Trembling as with a sudden chill, he felt himself sucked into a dark, desolate vortex and his mind flipped back to a childhood disaster – to the day his mother's heart had turned cold to him, the day he had failed to share with the family a tip received for running a neighbour's errand, the day *his ma had made him watch*, excluded, while his siblings devoured a rare after-supper treat – the delicious apple fritters his ma had made especially *to punish him*.

Today, the shock of his guide's departure had flipped his newly discovered world of possibility on its axis; it had hurled it into the orbit of his old, familiar world of negation, brutality and mistrust. He had staked his all on this bid for admittance to that privileged world and *experienced* rejection had destroyed his inner balance. He felt hurled, alone and tether-less, into a dark, eternal void, his very senses unhinged. The rehearsal room he'd entered less than an hour ago with such eager anticipation now taunted him with a *physical reversal:* it had *flipped on its axis*, its right flipped to its left, the piano now appeared to be where the professor's armchair had been, and vice versa; door and windows had switched places on their respective walls. Pier stared at the armchair where the professor had sat, watched the hand slap the armrest after Pier's last aria. It slapped and slapped and slapped *now*, mocking his deluded attempt.

Frightened, feeling his reason foundering, Pier crossed the room, trying to realign his perception with his memory, changing *his* position to make the room come right again.

It didn't work. The room remained stubbornly turned around. But Pier refused to be swindled. He forced himself to trust to his reason, since his senses were betraying him. He crossed back to where he thought he had started from. The room still looked wrong. Obstinately, he argued with himself: *that was* where the door had been. He stood across the room, reached for where the door handle had been. Then his eyes fell on his briefcase, propped open against the back of the chair next to the piano. He walked over to it and, clutched it, eyes closed, clinging to that one piece of reality, afraid to open his eyes, lest the room played some other nasty trick on him.

Suddenly, he became aware of his choppy, gasping breath. An inchoate thought came through his mental fog – *Signora* Agiati's injunction, "*Breathe! Deep...slow...breaths.*" Eyes closed, he obeyed her. He laid his hand on his diaphragm, went inward, attending to the rise and fall of his belly with each breath.

When he, at last, reopened his eyes, the room had righted itself. Still mistrusting it, Pier looked all around him: yes, windows, door, piano, they all were where they had been when he and his guide had walked in for the audition, an hour ago. For a moment, Pier stood stock-still. His scores were still propped open on the piano. He gathered them up, shoved them pell-mell into his briefcase and dashed out.

Outside, by the stage door his old friend, Paulin, stood as usual, one shoulder propped against the doorjamb, dragging away at his fag. Catching sight of Pier, he straightened up for a chat and called, out, *"Òhi, Pier, how is it going?"*

Pier dodged past him, barely lifting his chin in salute. He struck down the street at a run, heading for the river.

"Òhi là, what's the matter?" the old man out called after him, stepping down the few steps on stiff knees.

Pier just kept running in the late October night, fog drifting here and there in thickening patches, catching at his breath as he ran. In his distraught state, Matilde's caution not to get too worked up about the audition, now pounded at him. What she'd told him about the audition was that the Regio's singing master *might* be willing to give him some pointers. But the intensive work she'd put him through on his three arias had given far more weight to the event than her cautious words had implied. So tonight's disappointment was entirely his own fault. He was the fool who'd let wishful thinking run away with him. *He* was the fool, the *pagliaccio,* the stupid, ridiculous clown who'd given way to foolish hopes.

At a run, he reached the *murazzi,* scrambled down the stone flights of stairs two, three steps at a time, came to a stop, breathless and sweating, at the edge of the Po, its waters lapping at the promenade's stone walls. Fog rose, cold and dense, from the sluggish waters, enveloping riverbanks and city blocks in misty, shifting layers. It caught at his throat, it made him cough. His throat felt raw.

His wrist rose to cover his mouth. He must not catch cold. Tomorrow night he had his session with Don Marco. But he could not bear to go home. He ambled, unseeing, upstream along the water's edge for a long time, until in a momentary thinning of the fog he saw one of the promenade's flights of steps that rose to street level. Listlessly, he dragged himself up those stairs, then along the corso towards the tramline for home, his disillusion turning to anger as he walked.

Once again, kept pounding in his head, *once again, almost, but not quite.* Foolishly, he'd hoped… yes, he'd really hoped that *this* time…but no. *Others* got what they wanted, they got breaks they needed, the help, the education… But *not he.*

Once again, he had wished, and tried, and given it his all. And all for nothing! And yet he *had succeeded,* the professor had liked his singing, had *been impressed.*

A snarl, half laugh half curse, broke from him. "Yeah," he cried out loud, "but not enough!" The retreating Germanic voice echoed inside him *now*, taunting, *But you haf no money...no money...no money...no money...* The ultimate indictment. In its mind's eye he saw again the shock of red hair, the plump little man that had become his hope, his chance of a glorious future, turn his back on him, and waddle, indifferently, out of the room. He heard the door click latched behind him.

In that image he saw a brutal fact: whatever he did, whatever his talents, whatever he accomplished, he'd *never* be good enough. He'd never be *one of them.*

Pier's bad mood and Adelaide's anger

The next morning, Pier barely made it to FIAT on time. Nina had to prod him out of bed to get him going. She wondered if he was having one of his migraines, but soon realised that wasn't it: the signs were wrong. Pier was upset. Something must have happened and now he was upset. But he still had to get to work on time, or there'd be more trouble.

When he was finally dressed and sitting at the kitchen table, morose, shoulders hunched, Nina nudged his hands with his ignored bowl of *cafelàit*, but got no response.

He punched in at FIAT ten minutes late. It would be a mark against him, and they would dock his pay, but he didn't care. By the time he dragged himself to his lathe, the rest of the station was already loud with the buzz of machines.

"What was it, Romeo?" the foreman taunted him, casting a lewd glance in Lena's direction. "Out late on the tiles?"

At her workbench in the next station, Lena blushed. She was alarmed because Pier had never been late before, and today he had gone to his lathe without catching her eye. She waited for the foreman to turn his back then tried to catch Pier's eye. To her distress, he refused eye contact, stooped to pick up his first board and walked back to his lathe without looking up. She was stunned. She hardly recognised her Pier in the hostile, closed in, almost ugly face.

All morning she tried to catch his eye and failed: he simply wouldn't look at her; he just stooped over his lathe, grim, his every move resentful, angry. Lena got scared. What had she done to offend him? She searched her mind, but the last time they had walked home together, last Monday, everything was lovely.

Last night they hadn't walked home together because he had an extra session with his teacher. So it couldn't be her fault. Or could it?

All day she wracked her brains to divine what could be wrong. Sunday afternoon they had strolled *al Valentin* and it had been lovely; they'd stopped for coffee before catching the tram home, and everything had been fine. A lump in her throat, she waited anxiously for the midday whistle: maybe he would speak to her then.

At last, the midday whistle shrilled, ear-splitting. The last whine of the machines merged with the hubbub of voices and boots and clogs, trampling down the ramp. Lena stood up, but lingered by her bench, waiting for Pier to leave his station, half-hoping he would wait for her, as usual.

He didn't: shoulders hunched, chin tucked into his chest, he merged with the crowd and trundled down, his head a vague bright spot bobbing among the dark ones.

Lena ran the few yards to catch up with him. "Pier," she called out. "Are you all right?"

"I'm fine," he muttered with a brief sideways glance, and kept plodding.

Lena trotted at his side. "You don't…look yourself today," she whispered. "Has something happen?"

Pier kept walking without responding.

Lena tried again. "You were late this morning…I thought, perhaps…your bike, a flat tire? It was mean of the foreman…"

"Leave it!" Pier snapped, speeding up. "I've got a headache, that's all."

He left her standing there, stunned by his tone. "Oh…I'm sorry," she murmured, voice fading, "I didn't mean to…"

Toni, Pier's station mate, walked past her. "*Tò pistin al cafelàit* – your finicky dandy is in a bad mood today," he taunted. "Better get used to it."

Lena's bench mate stopped to wait for her. "Never mind him," she said, taking Lena's arm and walking down with her. "He's just jealous."

But Lena was not comforted. From her seat at the women's table, she searched the lunchroom for Pier, but could not see him.

After the midday break, it got even worse. Pier worked at his lathe, his face stormier than ever. He simply wouldn't look her way. He thrust his work at the machine as though to destroy it. During the afternoon, one of the men accidentally bumped him with a long plank he was fetching to his lathe, and Pier swung around, fist back, just short of striking. At the other's apology, he re-coiled himself in, and returned to his lathe, darker than ever.

Lena watched, scared. That night, she walked home heavy with a sense of doom. It couldn't be over, and she had no idea why. Pier had always been so gentle, so *fin*...

For a moment the image of Ottavio rose in her mind next to Pier's. *Like brothers,* she thought. But then today... Today she'd seen, pent-up in Pier, the violence that had wrecked her childhood. But Pier *wasn't* like that! Today he was like a different *fieul.* She shook her head, defiant, and swallowed her dread.

"No," she cried. "Something must have happened. But what?" She searched her mind for what could possibly happen *to her* that might upset her that much.

A shiver ran down her spine. Something could happen to my mama. She stopped dead on the pavement, her mind suddenly blank. She fought down her panic: nothing was going happen to her mama. She crossed herself, and under her shawl, four fingers crossed tightly over each other.

She walked on, her mind back on Pier. No, she thought, it couldn't have to do with *his* mama. If something that bad had happened to *her*, she'd have turned *to* Pier, and *he* had turned *against* her. Disconsolate, she hurried home, eager to be with her mama.

But it was not to be: at home, she found Adelaide at the kitchen table, stiff as a board, glowering, waiting for her, taught and thin-lipped.

Lena glanced at the supper table set for two. The sweet smell of her mama's *ris e castagne* filled the room, but on the stove the cast iron pot was pushed to one side to keep warm. Adelaide hadn't come for supper. In fact, she threw Lena an angry, disgusted look. "Oh no," Lena moaned, not now. She needed comfort, not more anger.

"Ciao," she said tentatively. *"Com a va?"* (How are you?)

"You need to ask?" Adelaide snarled.

"Adelaide's worried about Carlin," Gioana chimed in gently, cueing Lena in.

"Oh...?" Lena moaned again, making it a question.

"Don't play the innocent!" Adelaide shot back.

Lena approached the table, mindlessly shifting a spoon about. "Is he sick?" she added lamely.

"You know perfectly well what he's sick of! He's sick of being played for a fool!"

"What do you mean...?"

"You know perfectly well what I mean: one day you're all over him, lovey-dovey, and the next time he comes for you – to take to the films, mind you, and to the café before, and chocolate during, treating you like a queen – and you're not even *there!* And not a word to explain! No, *not you!* You don't even tell him 'thank you, but, no, I'm not interested'. How do you think that makes him feel? What're you playing at?"

"I'm…I'm *not* playing at anything," Lena whimpered. "I…I…" She turned to Gioana, for help. "Mama?"

Gioana tipped her head sadly: "You did treat him rather shabbily, child."

Wide-eyed with disbelief, Lena stared at her: her mama was turning against her! "Mama!" she pleaded.

Adelaide jumped up from her chair and rushed at Lena. "And why," she demanded, "why? What did he do to deserve your casting him aside," she snapped her fingers, "just like that, and no explanation at all?"

"You're mad at me!" Lena howled. "Both of you, you're mad at me! Everyone's mad with me!"

"What do you expect, you fool?" Adelaide railed. "How would you like it if some *fieul* had done this to you?"

Lena wailed.

"You surprised Carlin's upset?" Adelaide went on, relentless. "You should hear his sisters! And his parents! They thought the world of you, and you've let them *all* down. Carlin's been a bear, can't go near him without having your head snapped off. He can't tend to his work; he's talking back to his pa. He's even got into a scrap with Pinòt because of you. And now Pinòt is leaving *a fé 'l soldà*, (military service), and he can't tell them of our engagement. And all because of *you!* He can't tell them *now*, not with all of them upset like that. And he'll be gone for a whole year!"

"I'm sorry, so sorry…" Lena whimpered between sobs.

"He wanted so much to tell them before going away, so they'd look after me while he's gone, and now *this* is what he's leaving behind!" Tears flooded her, so she turned angrily aside.

"Oh, 'Laide," Lena pleaded, "Please don't be anger. I'm sorry. I'm so sorry…"

Adelaide turned back, dabbing at her wet cheeks with the back of her hand. "Sorry won't do it, you ninny! You've got to set it right."

"But what can I do?" Lena whimpered, baffled.

182

"Make up with him, you stupid!"

"Oh, but I can't," Lena wailed, "I can't…"

"Why on earth not? He *cares for you*, don't you get it? And you'd be in clover at *I Tigli!"*

"I can't! I can't!" Lena keened, collapsing on a chair by the table. Gioana stepped up to her daughter, now sprawled over the table settings, shaking with sobs. She stroked her shoulders, trying to soothe her. Adelaide glared from one to the other, then turned to Gioana.

"She *likes* Carlin," she affirmed. "I know she does. All summer, double dating, you could see it a mile away…"

Suddenly, an unwelcome thought furrowed Adelaide's already stormy brows. Had Lena been playing Carlin for all she could get? She brushed the thought aside. No, that just wasn't Lena. She was not smart enough. No, Adelaide was sure, Lena had liked Carlin, even just three weeks ago, after the film, the way she'd looked up into his face…

"So…what's happened?" she demanded, dumbfounded. She looked from Lena's shaking back to Gioana who was still stroking it, trying to comfort. "What happened, Gioana? Can you make any sense of this?"

Gioana's shoulders shrank in a helpless gesture. "She…has met someone else," she said in a regretful voice.

Adelaide stood speechless, glaring in disbelief. "That's it?! Just like that?" she said at last. "Still waters run deep," she mumbled. Then her anger flared up again. "Who?" she demanded. "Who is he, where did she meet him?"

Lena howled.

"At FIAT," Gioana said. She didn't want to tell on Lena, but poor Carlin was a good man and he was being hurt. He had the right to at least know where he stood. So, if Lena couldn't tell him, she'd have to.

"N'operai?!" Adelaide cried, glancing down at Lena in disgust. "Does she know what she's doing?" Lena was giving up Carlin and *I Tigli for* a labourer!? She glared at Gioana, like it was her fault. "You've met him?"

Gioana shook her head. She had gone as far as she would go: she'd said enough so Carlin would know. She hoped he wouldn't take it too hard, that knowing would help him to recover. The rest was up to Lena.

At Gioana's stony silence, Adelaide reared herself up to her full height and, chin in the air, stomped to the door, where she stopped and swung around.

"You, fool!" she spat at Lena, still blubbering, head in her arms on the table. "You, stupid, stupid, *stupid* little fool!"

She flung the long bight of her shawl over her left shoulder and stormed out, slamming the door behind her.

Lena's nightmare

That night, Lena cried herself to sleep, but sleep brought no relief. After the first collapse into oblivion, snatches of dreams haunted her. Eventually, she was chased down Le Basse by an unseen presence. She ran desperately towards her home gate and the safety of her mama's rooms; but her familiar street, which in reality housed only five courtyards, in her dream stretched on and on without end. She ran until, heart in her throat, lungs on fire, she could go no further. At bay, she collapsed by a locked gate, huddled against the cold metal, and peered back at the infinite length of the now-strange lane. She heard the harsh breath of her pursuer closing in on her, but could not see him. In an unsteady light, the empty lane stretched out to infinity, utterly desolate. Terrified, she battered at the iron gate with her fists, begging without hope for someone to help her. No one came.

Whimpering with exhaustion, she peered down the lane again. Then, startling, she heard the chain rattle above her head, where the gate's solid lower half gave way to iron bars. Holding her breath, Lena raised herself to her knees, watched, hope contending with fear, as the chain slowly slid through the bars: someone was there; someone had come. This *was* her home gate after all. Hope shifted to relief.

"Mama," she whimpered, gathering herself together with almost unbearable joy.

The gate groaned with the familiar grinding of hinges and Lena rose to her feet, her hands pushing to open the gate. It resisted, barely ajar, it stopped, held firm by some unseen obstacle within.

Somehow, Lena could not see through its iron bars and could only peer in through the narrow opening between the gate's two panels: Adelaide was there, *not* her mama. Yesterday's Adelaide, cold and vengeful.

"Adelaide, please, let me in," Lena pleaded. But as she watched, Adelaide lost all colour, became translucent, a human block of ice.

Now Lena could see through the gate's bars: behind Adelaide, the courtyard was shifting: the medlar tree, in whose shade, on summer days, the yard women gathered for companionship, was twisting and groaning, its trunk growing gnarled, daggers-like thorns sprouting from its bark. They dripped blood; they moaned. And in that moan, Lena recognised the laboured breath of her pursuer. Adelaide was no longer there. The gate, still ajar, screamed on its hinges, the noise merging with the tree's groans and the pursuer's breath, then, violently, swung open. Lena screamed and ran.

She woke up bolt upright in her bed, in the predawn dark, drenched in cold sweat, her heart in her throat, struggled to catch her breath. The chill of the room echoed the arctic cold of her dream. A soft rasping breath next to her triggered her nightmare panic: her pursuer was still with her, right here in her bed!

Then the rasping breath became a soft snore. Lena's left thigh sensed warmth under the bedclothes. Her foot crept timidly toward that warmth, checking it out. The warm emanation giving it courage, it dared a bit further and found her mama's warm leg.

With a moan of relief, Lena slid down under the covers and snuggled close to her mama's sleeping back. In her sleep, Gioana turned onto her side, and her arm curved to draw her child into her own comforting warmth.

Don Marco's offer

That night at the duomo, Don Marco heard the strain in Pier's voice as soon as he approached the practice room where Pier was going through his warm-up routine. It had long worried him that the lad spent his days in the drafty, unsanitary conditions of the *carrozzeria* department at FIAT. He'd long wanted to get him out of there, to get him away from all that dust and fumes. He entered the room and took a hard look at Pier: tonight, he looked positively haggard. There were dark circles under his eyes and his shoulders hunched over, constricting his chest. He'd looked fine when he'd last seen him, two days ago.

Pier finished his warm-up and faced Don Marco for instructions.

"You look tired tonight, Pier," Don Marco said. "You feel all right?"

Pier worked his chin left and right, clearing the kink in his neck. His hand cradled his throat.

"I'm all right," he said.

Don Marco squinted at him, unconvinced. "Perhaps we'd best give your voice a rest tonight," he said, strolling away from the piano and pulling out two chairs from the table at the other end of the room. "I've wanted a chat with you, anyway. Come sit down."

Warily, Pier followed him and sat down.

"You've been singing in church a long time, now, man and boy. How long has it been?"

"I was with Don Carlo eighteen months last Christmas," Pier said.

Don Marco nodded, settling back in his chair. "And before that? How long did you sing at San Dalmass?"

Pier shrugged. "Don't know," he said. But Don Marco kept looking at him, like he was waiting for more. When Pier went no further, he prompted: "How old were you when you started?"

Again, Pier shrugged. "Don't know."

"Ten? Eleven?"

"Well before that," Pier said and, after a brief pause, continued: "I was still in school."

He bit his tongue: he'd not meant to disclose how little schooling he'd had. To cover up, he rushed on. "Must have been when I was going to catechism for my first communion…" That was the only period he'd been at church every afternoon, until Don Michel had talked his pa into letting him off late chores, a couple of days a week.

Don Marco's chin went up as he put two and two together. "So…you must have been, what? Six, seven…"

"Guess so. First Communion service was the first time I sang all by myself."

Don Marco smiled at Pier's way of putting together the events of his childhood by farm or church landmarks. Like last June, he thought, when Pier had said '…when the winter wheat's in.'

Still smiling, he said: "And now you are…what, twenty one? So, you've been with us for fourteen years." After a brief pause, he added: "Have you ever thought that you might want to…"

He stopped abruptly, eyebrows creasing together. "And your military service?" he asked.

Pier twitched an indifferent shoulder. "They didn't want me."

"Oh? Why's that?"

The shoulder twitched again. "Don't know."

"You mean…They didn't tell you?"

Pier shrugged: "My feet, maybe."

"Something wrong with your feet?" Don Marco inquired, looking down. Pier raised his right foot, pointing to the small spur of bone that distorted the upper edge of his shoe.

"Yes, I see," Don Marco grinned. Flat feet. That wouldn't stand in Pier's way in the church.

"Well, all the better for us," he said, returning to his earlier train of thought. "As I was saying, have you ever thought of joining us?"

Pier was startled. "You mean…becoming a priest?"

"Well, maybe, but not necessarily. Not everyone's cut out for it. One doesn't become a priest just because one decides to. One starts with years of study in a seminary, then, if the vocation declares itself…" he spread out his hands and raised his eyes to the sky, as though submitting or giving thanks.

His eyes went back to Pier's face: they found the lad's grey stare fixed on him, tense but no longer haggard. "Now, in your case," Don Marco went on, "with your voice, you most likely would be steered to a *Schola Cantorum*."

"What's that?" Pier asked, leery.

"A music school," Don Marco said, watching Pier closely. "A lot less dusty then FIAT," he joked.

"Is that a *real* music school?" Pier asked a deep flush rising to his ears, turning them a dark red. Don Marco saw his work-coarsened hands clutch the edge of the table, knuckles white.

"It is," Don Marco said, touched by the boy's intensity, adding, "to train fine voices like yours for sacred music."

"And…and what else would I…have to do?" Pier asked.

"You'd have to study a lot of different things, like all seminarians. Other subjects as well."

"And would I have to…to…" Pier fumbled.

"…To take orders?" Don Marco supplied *one* applicable question. "That might come later, if you find you have the vocation. But there are many ways to serve God without taking orders. You could sing for the glory of God."

Pier relaxed slightly and asked: "And…what would I have to do *now*…to…to…"

"To be a candidate?" Don Marco finished for him. "For right now, all you have to do is consider whether going to a *Schola Cantorum* might satisfy your heart. If you find it would, we could have you admitted next January."

"Next January!" Pier sputtered. "But that's just weeks away!"

"That's right," Don Marco said with a smile. "No more FIAT dust."

He stood up, and Pier rose too. He placed an arm around the boy's shoulders and steered him affectionately towards the door. "You give it some thought," he added, ushering him out. "And now take the night off. Go home and have a good sleep."

Sleep did not come easy to Pier that night. Alone in Nina's dark *retro,* he wrestled with warring thoughts and desires. He still smarted from last night's cruel let down: he'd worked so hard for that audition, he had had such hopes of it; and then to have it all fizzle to nothing… The Germanic voice, like a voice from hell, again taunted him: *You've got no money…no money…no money…*

And then, again, out there by the stage door, – Pier tossed and turned in shame in his cot – he'd run out on old Paulin without a word, the old doorkeeper without whom he would never have penetrated the magical world he craved.

And now, instead of his dream, instead of opera, Don Marco was offering him the opportunity to study music at a seminary. It was not what he wanted, but it might be as close as he ever could come to his dream of a life of music. He recalled Matilde Agiati's words, *You're getting excellent training with Don Marco.* He'd learned a lot from her, and he trusted her. Well, he *had.* But after last night…She'd encouraged him to hope, and it had all come to nothing.

He tossed in his bed, fragments of conversations heard in the dressing rooms both at Santa Rita's and at the duomo came back to him, references to *years of study* in this or that *conservatorio.* He wondered if Don Marco's *Schola Cantorum* was anything like a *conservatorio.* He wondered whether studying music at a seminary school would ever make him *one of them.*

He tossed again with a sneer that, to his horror, sounded just like his pa's: nothing, *nothing* would ever make him *one of them.* He was doomed to be the outsider. Forever.

Then another thought intruded: a seminary? It had never crossed his mind to become a priest, but if it meant that he could sing for a living… Sure, it was *opera* he wanted to sing, in a theatre, and then to go out and celebrate – with friends, admirers, toasting *life,* sparkling, long-stemmed glasses, *viva il vino spumeggiante nei bicchieri scintillanti…*

He drifted off: he was in the brilliant Piazza San Carlo café. Around the table, elegant people lifted their glasses *to him.* On his left was Matilde, and on his right, Lena, beaming admiration up to him.

Lena! He woke up with a start and sat bolt upright in the dark. What had he done! Her lovely, frightened face tugged at his heart. He'd been miserable to her. Time and again she'd tried to approach him, and he'd pushed her away, just shut her out. He'd seen the hurt in her face, and it hadn't stopped him. He'd *wanted* to hurt her because he was hurt, in despair, all his hopes, his dreams, in ruins…

And now, what would happen now? Would she let him make things right between them? Oh, she must, she must! And he must try! Tomorrow he would. He would try to explain what had upset him so; make her see what it had all meant to him.

Another concern stormed into his mind. If he went to a *Schola Cantorum* what would happen with Lena? Would they allow him to see her?

And was there one in Turin? He'd heard there was no *conservatorio* in Turin, but perhaps there was *Schola Cantorum,* in some seminary. But even if there was one, would it be allowed – seeing a girl? Seminarians were studying to be priests, weren't they? So it probably wouldn't be.

At that thought, his nascent excitement about studying at a music school, and the promise of a life of singing collapsed, and he was again deflated, the second time in two consecutive nights.

With a strangled curse, he buried his face in his pillow, bit into it to keep himself from howling. He couldn't bear the thought of a life without music or without Lena.

Pier and Lena's first reconciliation

That Friday morning, Pier approached FIAT, torn between eagerness and fear. On the streetcar, his back against a rear window in his usual stance, he stared without seeing at the recurring Fascist slogan defacing the buildings' walls. He looked forward to seeing Lena and at the same time dreaded the scene he imagined. He was afraid of her hurt, of the frightened look he'd seen on her face yesterday afternoon. He imagined waiting for her at the gate and talking to her on the way to their stations. But he couldn't do that: everybody would see them, and sneer.

As it was, his singing was a joke to them, something to taunt him with. Yesterday his world had lain, shattered, at his feet, the rubble of his dreams, and he'd been numb, frozen with loss and shame. He hadn't told Lena about the audition because too much was riding on it, and he feared he'd be laughed at if his attempt went nowhere. So, to explain not walking her home last Wednesday, he'd told her that he had an extra session with his teacher. So how could he, today, confess to yesterday's despair? He was too ashamed of having entertained foolish hopes, and of having shown his hurt.

A snarl of self-contempt broke out from him. He covered it up with a cough. Then a painful grin twisted his mouth: the irony of it! Don Marco's consolation prize! A year ago, he would have jumped at the offer of a *Schola Cantorum,* or of any school, for that matter, where he could get an education that put him on a par with his fellow choristers, no longer ashamed of his ignorance, no longer rough at the edges. A year ago, he had cherished his place at Santa Rita's, even though he bristled at the way others treated him. Last winter, the thought of trying out for a place with the duomo choir had been overwhelming, and now Don Marco's offer had become no more than a consolation prize.

His mind switched back to Lena, to the first time he'd walked her home, then to the night he had told her, half joking, *I got into trouble the other night,* and her face had crumpled with concern.

No, he couldn't speak to her of the collapse of his dream: the pain in her face would mirror too plainly his own, and leave it exposed. She would be crushed with disappointment *because he was.* It had been a mistake to reveal his passion for the theatre to her. Don Marco's offer might give him a chance to save face, allow him to pretend that *he was choosing* the *Schola Cantorum.*

Last night's conversation at the duomo flashed through his mind. Don Marco *didn't* expect him to become a priest, but what about Lena? He blinked hard, forcing his mind back to today's problem, to making up with Lena. He would start today; he'd be extra nice, not saying too much about yesterday, just telling her that he was subject to bad migraines, and that yesterday's had been an especially bad one. Today he'd be extra nice and convince her that he'd just been ill and that nothing was wrong.

Lena got to her workbench that morning still weighed down with last night's strife, and her subsequent nightmare. The dream itself she did not remember. What persisted was the sense of endangerment. Several times, as she walked up the ramp with her work mates, she cast furtive glances over her shoulder, checking behind her. When the little group of women reached Pier's station, Lena's eyes flew to his lathe and her heart flipped over: Pier was puttering about his machine, obviously on the lookout for her. Anxiously, she searched his face and caught his eye. He held hers with a sheepish, adoring, pleading smile.

Lena's heart soared: it was OK! Pier, *her Pier* was back! Whatever had happened yesterday was erased, Pier was back. She soared on her relief as on a spring breeze, her eyes brightening with a broad smile.

Pier unfroze and drifted towards the little cluster of women passing his station. "*Bondì* " he called out as Lena stepped into her own station.

"*Bondì,*" Lena answered, lingering in that first contact. The other women went on to their respective workplaces, nudging each other.

"I thought," Pier ventured, "we might walk down to lunch together?"

Lena searched his face: his whole frame, shy, eager, yearned towards her. She nodded yes without a word, breathless, as eager as he.

Throughout the morning their eyes played catch with each other, nurturing their re-connection, both still wrestling with apprehension about what would have to be said, what couldn't be.

For hours, Pier waited for the hated midday whistle, and dreaded it. He knew now that things would be all right with Lena, but worried about the questions she might ask, torn between the longing to tell her about the ordeal he'd been through and the deep shame he felt about its failure. All morning he hovered between wanting to tell and wanting to hide.

On her part, Lena wrestled with the pressing need to know what had happened yesterday, and the need to be reassured, ultimately, the need to close her eyes to the fright, not to know it had been, to erase it from her mind, to make it *never have happened.*

When the midday whistle shrilled, Pier shut off his lathe and made for the ramp to wait for Lena. She was there as fast as the line of women, shuffling out of their narrow work benches, would allow her.

"Back in his lordship's graces," Toni sneered in her ear, as he passed behind Lena on his way down.

Lena blushed and shyly smiled up to Pier. He glowered after Toni's retreating back: the taunt made it impossible to talk to Lena on their walk down.

After a few moments of tense silence, they caught each other's eyes in a furtive sideways glance, and Pier grinned at her. He drew a little closer and they walked down, side by side, in silence.

That evening, Pier waited for her at the gates, falling into step with her as soon as she appeared, walking her away from the crowd and towards her home. "Can't talk now," he said softly, not to be overheard, "I have to catch the next tram to the duomo, but I'd like to pick you up Sunday afternoon, if that's all right."

Lena nodded: it was, it was. She knew that Friday was one of his nights with Don Marco. "In front of the *Cine Lingòt?*" she asked.

"Fine," Pier said. "At two?"

Again, she nodded, and he leaned down to place a timid kiss on her left cheek. "Good night then," he said. "See you at work."

"Good night," Lena answered.

He ran across the street. "Good night!" she called out again after him, watching him sprint to catch the oncoming tram. The threat was gone.

She headed homeward light-hearted, a smile on her lips, in her mind images of the life her date with Pier had given her a brief glimpse of – the duomo, the theatre, the restaurant, the elegant people, a world which, until then, she had only gawked at from the outside on her window shopping rambles downtown, so different from the drab *periferia* routine of *Lingòt.*

On her way, she lingered dreamily in front of the Via Nizza draper, looking in at the window display she had been studying since she had started work at FIAT. The winter wools were in, bolts of cloth upright in the background, flowing in broad swathes of colour from the depth of the window to its front, like streams flowing across the display's floor, then gathered into soft pleats against its glass.

Lena ran her fingers on the glass along the coloured pleats, envisioning overcoats made out of one or the other colours. Her eyes lingered on the scarlet wool that seemed to catch all the window's light, and she saw herself in the duomo pew, wearing a bright red winter coat.

With a sigh, she tore her eyes from the lure: that dark green would be nice on her mama.

Discreet price tags nestled among the coloured wools and the amounts alarmed her. It would take a lot of extra earnings to buy winter coats. She walked on.

But the image of the tailored ladies in the duomo, and along Turin' smart streets, persisted. Pier had worn a blue suit to the duomo, not the work clothes she was used to seeing him in. She wouldn't want to shame him, going places in the smart town centre without proper attire.

Her light-heartedness slightly dampened, she walked home to her supper. Over their *polenta e bodin,* Lena said casually: "Mama, those tags in the draper's window, are those the price of the cloths?"

"Yes, they are."

"For…how big a piece?" On the street markets, prices were for lengths of cloth, usually enough to make whatever garments the fabric was meant for.

"Prices are by the yard," Gioana said.

"How many yards does it take to make a winter coat?"

"Winter coats?" Gioana said, spoon in mid-air. "I don't know. Why do you ask?"

"Who would know?" Lena countered.

Gioana mashed her *polenta* into the blood pudding and onion sauce in her plate. "Cichin-a's daughter might know." The young woman was apprenticed to a shirt-maker.

"Could we ask her?"

"We can," Gioana nodded, eating. "But why do you ask? Do you want a *paltó?*"

"I'd like us both to have proper winter coats," Lena said, stirring her fork around in the thick mush on her plate, suddenly uncomfortable. That had been true enough when she'd first contemplated the possibility of a job at FIAT, but now, *she* wanted a winter coat. She wanted to be dressed like a proper city girl when she went out with Pier, not like someone from Le Basse.

Chapter Nine

Matilde's misgivings

In the week following Pier's audition, Matilde was surprised at not seeing him backstage. She was aware that he'd felt let down at the immediate outcome of the audition: he had looked positively scared when Professor Rexel had walked out of the room. She'd made it clear that the audition had gone very well, that the professor *was* impressed, that now they just had to wait. Obviously, that had not been enough for Pier, since he'd not been around for a whole week.

Beside her worry about Pier's absence, Matilde was becoming aware of an unwelcome discomfort, of a sense of something lacking. *I miss him,* she thought, surprised. She had gotten so used to spending two evenings a week with him during the summer, and seeing him backstage several times a week since the beginning of the new season.

Discovering that she missed him made her realize how important he had become to her. His *success* had become important to her, she told herself. She *wanted* Rexel to take Pier on, to steer him through the hurdles of an operatic career.

She was almost sure the professor was going to, but it appeared that her reassurances last week had not been sufficient, that Pier had lost faith. "I should have stayed closer," she scolded herself, "maybe scheduled one of our sessions while we wait for the answer." She had been wrong to assume that she'd see him at the theatre. She knew his tendency to come down hard on himself, and it wouldn't be surprising if he had kept away, believing that… he had 'made a fool of himself', she finished, quoting him.

She would hate to see their hard work go down the drain. His diction was especially vulnerable, surrounded as he was all day long by *Piemontèis* speakers. He needed to keep up his work; otherwise he ran the risk of being reabsorbed into the coarse milieu in which he, unfortunately, still spent most of his days. His talent for opera had been both an antidote and a catalyst for change, and his range, actual and potential, was one of his key assets. He couldn't afford to jeopardise its development now, because of a temporary disappointment.

Her first glimpse of him in the wings, last season, came into her mind – a lanky, clumsy innocent flattening himself against a painted flat to let her voluminous costume pass him in the narrow backstage passage. She smiled at the memory. A great deal had been accomplished over the summer: his posture had straightened, and with that, his entire presence had changed. Brief moments from their work together came to mind – Pier as Alfredo, in their last rehearsal of *Lungi da lei,* the young lover returning from a stroll in the countryside to throw himself into an armchair and revel in his love for Violetta. That young man had been a gentleman, *not* last winter's country bumpkin. Matilde smiled, proud of Pier's new presence: *that,* she thought, *was* her doing.

"I must get hold of him," she concluded. "I must make sure he doesn't get himself into a funk and mess things up." He needed to be under Rexel's eye at the Regio every day, a living reminder. On Sunday she'd go look for him at the duomo.

Don Marco follows up

A week had gone by since Don Marco had broached the subject of the *Schola Cantorum.* Pier seemed to have recovered from last Thursday's exhaustion, the purity of his voice restored. Tonight's practice had been so satisfying that Don Marco was moved to return to last week's topic.

"Are you giving some thought to what we talked about last Thursday?" he asked, gathering his scores.

Pier nodded, but did not speak.

"Good, good. And…?" Don Marco encouraged him.

Pier flushed red and shuffled his feet. "I… I'd like to," he said. "Very much…"

Don Marco heard reservation in Pier's manner and enquired: "But…?"

"Well… It's just that…well, would I have to leave Turin?"

"Would that be an impediment?" Don Marco inquired with a slight frown.

Pier's shoulders shrugged the impediment aside. He shuffled his feet again. "Well, I…" he racked his brain for reasons not to leave Turin without mentioning Lena. "There's my job…"

Don Marco smiled. "You wouldn't have a job, remember? No more FIAT dust?"

Pier slapped his forehead. "No, of course, not." He laughed.

But it did not sound like his concerns had been addressed. Don Marco cocked his head in inquiry and waited.

"It's just…" Pier fumbled. "It's just… I've never…you know, not had to work…" he drifted into silence. Don Marco waited, eyes on Pier's face. "And… And there's Nina, my sister. I live with her, you see, and her little daughter, Anna. And she's pregnant again. She needs me."

"Doesn't she have a husband?"

"She does…" Pier's shrug dismissed the husband.

"I see…" Don Marco read the rest of the story in that shrug. It was common enough.

"Well," he continued, thinking of nearby seminaries. "You'd be living at the seminary, of course. But you wouldn't have to be too far away. A short train ride. You could stay in touch, visit often."

"Every week?" Pier asked eagerly.

"Possibly."

Pier heard irritation rise in Don Marco's controlled Florentine Italian. He mustn't push too far. He dropped the subject, but stood still, slowly winding his scarf around his throat.

"You give it some more thought," Don Marco urged. "But keep in mind that, if we are to get you started in January, you need to make up your mind before the end of this month."

Pier left the duomo in turmoil. He still hadn't found out where he would be sent. Don Marco had said a short train ride, but that could mean anything. Don Marco often travelled to Rome and Milan, and sometimes went abroad. There was no telling what 'a short train ride' meant to him. And there would be the cost… And that *'possibly'* every week worried him. He couldn't imagine not seeing Lena for a whole week, let alone less often. He would miss her, but if at least he could think of seeing her each Sunday… He clicked his tongue at the uncertainty. He was so used to having her always under his eyes; he almost minded leaving FIAT because they would no longer be in the same space.

With a sigh, he refocused his thoughts. There was the other side, of course. He would be rid of the factory and of his hateful foreman, of Toni, and of the smell, the noise, the crush of people everywhere. He never really *breathed* except when he was out of there. He didn't mind the crush on the trams when he was going where he wanted to be, to people who seemed to want him.

Other images crowded in: Lorèns in Nina's kitchen; his pa and Clot at *La Speransa*. Vigin-a, too, was a nuisance, but she didn't count; and his ma with her untouchable mistrust of the city and of everything in it. She still hadn't given him a chance to tell her about Lena, and as for the theatre... Well, to her the theatre was simply a den of iniquity, *sin,* pure and simple.

Lena. Pier tensed up. What would Lena think about this going to a seminary? He'd have to make her understand that he was not going there to be a priest, but only to study music. But would she be willing to be his girl if he could only be with her every few weeks?

At the thought, he bristled. A man had to do what a man had to do. She'd accepted it if I were going *a fé ël soldà*, he told himself. She'd accept not seeing me for a whole year. She'd have to. Women had to accommodate themselves to their men's lives.

With that, he tried to set his apprehensions aside. But he continued to obsess: singing in church, even at the duomo, was no longer enough; and Rexel had turned his back on him, walked out of the room and out of his life. To Pier that said clearly, *'you'll never be one of us.'* So, how could he go back to the theatre?

Until this moment, he hadn't known why he'd stayed away. He'd known the hurt and the impossibility of being where he longed to be. Now the humiliation of that *'you've no money...'* flooded him with its persistent meaning: *'you can't be one of us.'* He barked out a defiant, strangled laugh.

"Don Marco, at any rate, wants me," he countered. "For him, I *am* good enough." But it stung deep that Rexel, impressed as he had been with Pier's performance, had just turned his back on him, and walked away. It stung deep that he was rejected for the wrong reason, for a reason over which he had no control. His anger flared up against the professor, against all the smug, negating people who refused to let him in, against all *that kind of people.*

For a moment his mind went blank. Then his anger switched to Matilde: she'd led him on; she'd caused his humiliation, his disappointment, by urging him on, by encouraging him to hope. Now he rebelled against all that he had learned with her, against the citification she had encouraged and he had eagerly embraced. He shut his mind to his unbearable disillusion.

Don Marco wanted him: at the thought, a bitter triumph stirred in him: he would be a *singer,* despite *all those people*! He would go to a proper school, to a *music* school, even if it was only a seminary. He would have an education. He would learn how to behave in the world – in a world he could *feel good to be part of.* He would not be a labourer anymore, he would not have to live in a world of Lorèns, and Pas, and Clots.

Matilde seeks out Pier

The following Sunday, Matilde went to the eleven o'clock mass at the duomo, intending to catch Pier when he came down from the singers' gallery. It was almost one o'clock when she finally saw him emerge from a side door onto the church's sunlit rampart. "Pier!" she called out, stepping towards him.

Pier stopped, squinting, the sun in his eyes, one hand raised to screen them. "*Signora* Agiati," he said, courteous but cold, just that hint of the bow she'd taught him. "*Buon giorno.*"

Matilde smiled, her head cocked to one side: "Hm…so formal with your old friend?" She stepped alongside and took his arm the way she'd done that night, last May, the first time she'd led him to the café in *Via Po.* "Why haven't I seen you at the Regio all week?" she asked.

Pier shrugged. "What's the good?"

"Don't you care anymore?"

Pier did not respond.

"After all the work we've done?"

Pier shrugged again, morose. "What's the good wanting what you can't have?"

"Who says you can't have it?"

There was that bitter shrug again, and the scowl.

"I told you, you'd have to wait," Matilde reminded him. "You're not *out*; you're just *not in* yet. The professor needs time. Give him a chance. I think he'll come through."

"Has he said so?" Pier's said, eyes scouring her face, hope rising against his will.

"Not yet, no. But—"

"Not yet, no." Pier mimicked bitterly. He walked on and she trotted alongside to keep up.

"Have a little faith, *bonòm*," she urged, inserting the dialect epithet for simpleton into her carefully modulated Florentine Italian. "There are…practicalities you don't understand. He's probably working on them now.

Come now, stop scowling." She took his arm again and steered him towards a Piazza Castello café. "Let's have an aperitif and talk," she said, "There's work for you to do as well, while we wait."

Pier let himself be led, but kept his eyes averted from the theatre across the square. She marched him into the café and, spotting a table just being vacated at the back of the room, she steered him to it and sat down. "Two vermouths," she threw at the approaching waiter to get rid of him. Still morose, Pier settled down next to her.

"You need to keep working," she said, settling her coat across her knees. "You can't let what you've learned slip. Your diction needs steady attention," she told him, very much the teacher. "I'm rather busy right now; but, until we hear from Rexel, I want to see you at least once a week."

Pier scoffed, flinging out a hand in a dismissive gesture. She grabbed hold of it, "He *will* get back to us," she insisted, "and I don't want you to lose ground. It's easy to backslide when all you hear all day long is nothing but *Piemontèis* right, left and centre. Can you still make Wednesday nights?" Pier nodded. "Nine o'clock, as usual?" Again, Pier nodded. "Good," she said, relaxing briefly before going on.

"And there's something else: you need to hear proper Italian regularly. There's a group of people connected with the theatre I want you to join. They speak very fine Italian. They get together every few weeks to discuss plays, and other literature. It's a good way for you to cultivate your ear."

"Me?" Pier scoffed, alarmed. "What do I know about plays and…and literature?"

Matilde brushed his objection away. "You're there to *listen,* to hear *proper Italian.* I will introduce you." Pier sat back, morose, chin to his chest. Matilde gave him a few moments to regroup, then asked pointedly: "Will you go?"

"What for," he shot back, "to make a fool of myself?"

"Why should you make a fool of yourself?"

"What if I don't understand?"

Matilde dove into her capacious handbag. "Listen to this," she said and read out loud, "*San Martino.* You understand *that*?" Pier shrugged, resistant. "What does *San Martino* call to your mind*?*" She repeated the poem's title in Piemontèis, "*San Martín?*" Pier only shrugged. "*San Martin…*" she prompted, "what does '*Fé San Martin*' mean to you?"

"To move house," Pier muttered, "from one farm to another."

"Why? Why move on *San Martin*?"

Again, Pier shrugged again. "It's just when people move," he mumbled.

"But why do they move *then*?"

"Because farm rents run from *San Martin* to *San Martin.*"

"And when is *San Martin?*"

"End of October."

"All right! So, tell me, what is that time of the year like?" She waited, giving him a chance to visualise a fall scene, the way she'd taught him to visualise an opera scene he was going to sing. Then she said, "Now listen to this," and read on in her clear, articulate voice:

> *"La nebbia agli irti colli*
> *Piovviginando sale,*
> *E sotto il maestrale*
> *Urla e biancheggia il mar…"*

> Fog crawls, drizzling,
> Up the steep hills
> And under the mistral wind
> The sea screams and leaps white…

Matilde stopped, her eyes pinned to Pier's. "Do you understand that?"

For the third time Pier just shrugged, resistant. "Come on," she urged, "*see it in your imagination*, like it's the setting of an aria you are going to sing. Describe that scene to me."

Pier sighed, refractory, then he did as she asked. "It's a hilly place," he said, "in the fall. Fog's creeping up the hills, drizzling…"

"Go on," Matilde insisted, twirling her finger demanding that he continue. Pier described the rest of the November scene.

"Anything you didn't understand in all that?" Matilde asked. He shook his head. "All right, then. Listen to the rest."

She read on, or rather recited, the well-known poem, from time to time glancing up at Pier to gauge his reaction, to keep him engaged. By the end of the second stanza it was clear that the image of the mist-shrouded village was so vivid in Pier's mind he could almost feel the damp of the fog on his skin, smell the tang of fermenting grapes pervading its streets. When she was done reading

Matilde nudged him, "There, you've heard your first poem." She handed him the book. "Now you read it yourself."

"What, here?" Pier whispered alarmed, casting quick glances at the crowded café-bar around them. "Why not? Read," Matilde insisted.

So Pier read, *sottovoce,* practically in a whisper. When he was done, he set the book down on the table, his hand lingering on it.

Matilde smiled. "You see? Language can *sing* as well as music." One again she dove into her handbag. "Here," she said, handing him a slim volume, "take this home with you. Read it. You'll find each title is a different story."

Pier scanned the list of entries in the table of contents. Halfway down the list, his eyes whipped up to her face: he had spotted *Cavalleria Rusticana.*

"That's right," she grinned at him, "Giovanni Verga wrote the story that Mascagni later turned into the opera."

Pier now looked at the little book with awe.

"Take it home," Matilde told him, "read it. Then come to my house on Wednesday and we can talk about it. Read a little piece of it out loud every night – a couple of pages. That's all this group I want you to join does. You'll soon catch on." She glanced at her watch. *"Santo cielo!"* she exclaimed, "I must run. My husband will be screaming for his Sunday dinner." She threw a few coins on the table, patted Pier's shoulder and hurried away.

Pier sat on, studying his book.

"Qualcos'altro, signore?" Something else, sir, said a voice at his elbow.

Pier looked up at the supercilious waiter looming over him. Behind him, a small crowd stood by the café's entrance, waiting for a seat. Pier jumped up, his book clutched in his hand, one finger inserted at the page he'd stopped at.

Once outside, he headed for the tram stop, a couple of blocks away. The sun was now hidden behind roiling clouds, and the day had dimmed into a typical November light. *San Martino,* Pier thought as the last image of the poem coalesced in his mind: a farm kitchen, a fire blazing in the hearth, meat turning on a spit; and there, a shoulder resting against the doorjamb, his pa, in his corduroy hunter's jacket, gazing at a cloudy sunset, stridently whistling between his teeth. The last few lines of the poem rose irrepressible in his mind, and he recited to himself out loud in the empty dinnertime street,

> *"Sta il cacciator fischiando*
> *Su l'uscio a rimirar…*

...Stormi d'uccelli neri
Com'esuli pensieri,
Nel vespero migrar."

The hunter stands, whistling,
On his doorstep, watching...
Throngs of black birds,
Like exiled thoughts,
Migrate in the dusk.

Pier and Lena: first exposure to literature

On the tram, on his way to meet Lena for their afternoon date, Pier opened the book Signora Agiati had given him. He soon became so absorbed that, some twenty minutes later, he missed his stop by the Cinema Lingotto, where Lena stood, waiting for him. The tram's jerk as it pulled away from the stop, broke his concentration. He glanced out of the window: his Lena was standing open-mouthed, looking in dismay at the tram that carried him away from her. He jumped up and dashed to the exit. "Stop! Stop!" he cried, hammering on the stop bell, "Oh, please stop!" The tram driver sneered and accelerated faster.

Now frantic, Pier turned to the rear window, pounded on the dirty glass with his hands, calling out to her, "Wait, wait for me! Don't go away, I'm coming, wait for me!" But behind the closed windows, he was inaudible in the clatter of steel wheels on steel rails. He watched Lena take a few uncertain steps after the tram, then sag to a standstill, a living statue of dismay.

At the next stop, two blocks later, he leapt off the tram before its door was fully open and, book in hand, sprinted back towards Lena. She saw him coming and ran to meet him, colliding, in mid-sidewalk, into a frantic hug. "I missed my stop," Pier pleaded breathlessly. "I was so afraid you'd leave. Thank goodness you didn't."

"What happened?" she whimpered, straining her neck back to peer up into his face. Clutched in mid-sidewalk, they created a snag, forcing the stream of Sunday strollers to split around them. "I thought perhaps you didn't want to see me," she cried.

"Not want to see you! Of course, I want to see you!"

Lena laughed, making light of her fears, but she was shaken. "It's just that..." she said, "you've never been late before. What happened? Did mass run late?"

"No, it was Signora Agiati. She was waiting for me after mass, and …wanted to talk."

In each other's arms in the middle of the sidewalk, they stood gazing into each other's eyes, and he saw Lena's anxiety in her face. "There's something else she wants me to study," he explained, waving the book still in his hand. "I was looking through this book, and that's how I missed my stop."

"But…more things to study… Will you have time for it all?"

"It's not more work. It's…well, it's for our Wednesday sessions."

"You mean…you're not going to sing anymore?"

"Of course I'm going to sing!" Pier laughed. "This is to help me do it better. Look," he sidled up to her, opening the book at *Cavalleria Rusticana*. "See this? It's the story that the opera was made from, you know the one." He sang *sottovoce*:

> *"O che bel mestiere,*
> *Fare il carrettiere,*
> *Andar di quà e di là!"*

> What a lovely calling,
> Being a carter,
> Going here and there!

Lena nodded vaguely, pretending she knew what he was talking about.

"Well," Pier continued, "*Signora* Agiati says that, knowing the story, I'll be able to perform my part better." He looked eagerly at Lena, who looked blank. "Here," he said, flipping through the book. "Let me show you."

"*Ch'a scuso,*" snapped an irritable voice behind them: they were obstructing the sidewalk.

With an apologetic giggle, Pier skipped out of the way, drawing Lena with him to huddle up against the wall. He began to read.

"But…" she said, shyly, "we'll be late for the film."

"Ah, già!" (Ah, yes,) Pier said with a short laugh: they were supposed to go to the movies. "Let's go," he said, shutting the book and slipping it into his pocket. "I'll show you afterwards."

Arm in arm, they walked back to the cinema and sat through the film, holding hands. From behind them came the usual heavy breathing and rustles. Lena rested her head on his shoulder, holding hands, eyes firmly on the screen romance. Next to her, Pier fidgeted, his attention divided, uncomfortably aware of the rustlings behind them, impatient for the show to be over; his mind on the book in his pocket. He had read just enough of Verga's *Cavalleria Rusticana* on the tram to give him a sense of what lay behind the frantic passions in the recording he'd been listening to with Signora Agiati. The village square in the short story – church on one side and tavern on the other – reminded him of San Dalmass', devoutness cheek to jowl with carnal, everyday sin. But the central love intrigue seemed far-fetched. Alfio's wanting revenge on Turiddu struck a true enough chord, but…over a woman?

He called to mind times in his life when he'd hated someone enough to murder him, and it had never been about a woman, or about women. Not even Vigin-a, who could get under his skin easily enough. He'd often enough been tempted to slap her into silence her. But, to kill her? No, never. What had driven him blind with hate was the taunting, the being set up to ridicule and humiliation. Only men could do that to him. When Vigin-a tried it, he could shrug her off simply because *she didn't count.*

Oddly enough, he found that the portion of the Verga story he'd read so far had made him feel closer to Santuzza's state, to that state of – what was it, humiliation, helplessness, despair? It was a state in which she *had* to strike back or die of shame. He thought of the opera's plot: Santuzza driven to bring about the destruction of what she hankered for and couldn't have – the faithless Turiddu.

Pier greeted the end of the film with relief: soon he'd be able to get back to his story. He'd take Lena to the corner café and read it to her.

But at the corner Lena refused to walk into the café. "Let's just go for a walk," she urged, snuggling closer onto his arm. Frustrated, Pier slipped his book back into his coat pocket and, lips pinched, walked on with her, down Via Nizza, towards the terminal square: there was another café there; he'd try again there.

At his side, Lena babbled away – the film, their past week at FIAT, tit-bits of *Lingòt* gossip. Pier hovered on the brink of snapping at her, but bit his tongue, remembering his guilt and shame at having shut her out, the Thursday after his audition; remembering also the promise he'd made to himself to be nice to her, not to risk losing her again.

But he fretted: the book in his pocket burned hot against his hip. At the end of Via Nizza, he struggled to restrain himself from dragging her directly to the café. Instead, he let her stroll in her leisurely fashion all around the square, chattering, lingering in front of each shop window, the corner of his eye firmly on the café across the street. When they finally got there, he said casually, "Let's step in for a hot drink. It's got quite chilly." He pushed the door open without waiting for her to respond, and steered her in. Smiling expectantly, she sat down at the small table he'd chosen, near a window. He ordered two coffees, and then took out his book. "Let me read you what made me miss my stop," he said with a sheepish grin. Lena pulled closer to the table, preparing to listen. The coffees came while he leafed through the pages to find the beginning of *Cavalleria.* Lena picked up her cup and sipped the hot, strong liquid through its fragrant, golden froth. Pier started to read, his coffee forgotten. He read slowly, enunciating clearly, as Signora Agiati demanded, though reading aloud was still a challenge for him and, on a first read-through, he often still struggled over unfamiliar words. But righ now it was urgent for him to share with Lena the excitement of today's discovery. So he read carefully, looking up at her every few words, to maintain his connection with her, to see her face reflect his excitement.

But he quickly became engrossed in the story. He looked up at her less and less often, until, feeling ignored, Lena got bored. Twice she cleared her throat. Twice she re-crossed her ankles under the table, the second time jostling the table enough to rattle the coffee cups. Instinctively, Pier's hand flew to his cup to steady it, lest any coffee stain Signora Agiati's precious book. Page after page, he went on reading, his voice getting raw with fatigue, until he at last reached the end of the story.

"Well, what do you think of it?" he asked, closing the book and laying it aside on the table.

"Turiddu," Lena said, tentatively, an image of Guido at the Niclin fête fleeting through her mind, "doesn't seem very nice."

"No, he doesn't. But there are other stories as well," Pier said, eagerly, his hand toying with the book's cover. "Shall we read another one?" Lena brushed a few grains of spilled sugar off the tablecloth. "Yes, perhaps, sometime…"

Sometime, but *not now.* Pier's mood plummeted, disappointed, struggling with guilt: here he was, meaning to be nice to Lena, and instead he was getting angry with her. She obviously had no interest in his stories. He'd thought she *would* be, considering she usually went on and on about the stories in the films they saw. He paid for their coffees and they left the café.

Outside, she took his arm again, snuggled up close, her face smiling up to him, happy again. Somehow it annoyed him. They strolled homewards in silence. Then, out of the blue, she asked: "Is that the story in one of your operas?"

"Pretty much."

"And your teacher wants you to learn it?"

"Well, not *learn it,* like a lesson. She just wants me to read it and think about it."

"And one wouldn't know what the opera's about without reading the story?"

"Well, one would…" Pier said, his irritation deepening: he hated it when he was asked to explain things and he couldn't. They walked on in silence.

Lena felt him pull back into himself, and tried draw him out again. "Back there," she begun, "you said we could read some more stories together…"

"Only if you're interested," he snapped.

"It's not that…" she said, hurt, head down, no longer buoyant. "It's just that… Well, I…can't. I can make out the big letters on the store signs, but the small letters…"

Pier stopped short and swung around to face her. "Oh Lena!" he cried, hugging her close, choked with pity and guilt: he had misjudged her, he had thought her indifferent, and it was just that she couldn't read.

"You…do not mind?" she asked in a small voice.

"Of course not! It's not your fault! I thought you didn't care!" He kissed the top of her head, then squeezed her in a tight embrace. "I can *teach you* to read. My mama taught me."

"Really? You can? Would you?"

"I can bring the books I am reading and we can read bits of them together. Bit by bit you'll learn. We can start with this one," he added, fetching the book out of his pocket.

"What, right now?" she cried, alarmed. "It's getting late. Don't you have to be back at the duomo tonight?"

"Not tonight. Let's stop at the corner café and read some more."

"NO," she said, stiffening. "*Not* the corner café,"

Pier looked at her, puzzled.

She struggled to explain. "It's just that…there are…some people there…I am…not comfortable with."

"Well then, we'll go somewhere else."

"But it's late, and my mama's waiting for me for supper." She felt Pier draw back into himself, and quickly added, shyly, "But you could come have a bite with us. If you don't mind. Then, afterwards, we could sit and read a bit more."

"I'd love to," Pier cried, threading his arm affectionately through hers. "And anyway, I'd like to meet your mama." Arm in arm, they walked briskly toward Le Basse.

Two old foxes: Rexel and Don Marco

As he had announced at the end of Pier's audition, Professor Rexel duly went to hear Pier at the duomo. He went for the All Saints' Mass. What he heard there confirmed his determination to find a way to promote the young singer's development. As he listened to the Pergolesi Mass, he acknowledged to himself the evidence of Don Marco's training: Pier's voice had a solid foundation. Evolving it into an operatic instrument would not be a difficult task.

Nevertheless, he felt a twinge of discomfort. *I'm a fox in my neighbour's chicken coop,* he thought. Here he was, in Don Marco's duomo, recruiting his colleague's star singer.

Granted, Pier had sought him out – or rather, Matilde Agiati had – and opera *was* Pier's choice.

It now occurred to him that he hadn't seen Pier backstage, whereas last spring he had noticed the fair, lean, almost Germanic lad making himself useful among the dark, thickset stagehands.

Then his thoughts returned to his present concerns: Pier's choice or not, he couldn't just take the youngster away from his current mentor. Turin's music scene wasn't so large that he could afford to antagonise one of its chief figures. Besides, he'd known Don Marco a long time, first in Rome as a colleague at Santa Cecilia, and later in Venice and Verona, as an almost friend, a fellow opera devoté. And nowadays, the spare clerical figure of the duomo's music master was a regular feature at the Regio productions. So, Rexel told himself, he owed the old fox the courtesy of at least *appearing* to consult him. And it would be useful to hear what Don Marco had to say about working with Pier.

He made his phone call right after mass, from a nearby tobacconist's. And now here they were, ensconced behind steaming *cappuccinos* in the comfort of Café-Confetteria Baratti, under the elegant Piazza Castello arcade.

"When was that exactly?" Don Marco asked when the Regio's music master finished telling him about Pier's recent audition.

"Ten days ago," Rexel said, struck by the pointed tone of the inquiry, "on Wednesday night."

Don Marco leaned back, spine erect, in his rose velvet chair, visibly putting two and two together and getting five. "And…the audition went well?" he asked again.

Rexel's plump hands flew up enthusiastically, "I was speechless! Matilde Agiati – you know her don't you, she's our diction and acting coach, and sings contralto in the chorus…"

Don Marco waved Matilde Agiati aside. "Not personally, but I think we've met."

"She spotted Pier backstage last spring. You should ask her about it. It makes quite a story. She has been coaching him through the summer and she brought him to me. His voice you *know* – I heard your training in it, this morning," he grinned. "The *Agnus Dei*…splendid, splendid. And he's got range and dramatic depth as well." He shook his head, almost speechless again.

Then he took in the priest's closed expression. He couldn't tell what emotion was creasing the other's usually serene brow and making the right corner of his mouth twitch and twist. It could be anger, but it could also be something quite different.

Don Marco, in turn, saw Rexel's restrained puzzlement and smoothed out his countenance as he asked, "And Pier was…happy with his audition, you say?"

"Must have been, I haven't talked to him since. The problem, of course, iss funding his training…"

Don Marco's chin shot up and his mouth opened in an enlightened AH! This explained Pier's haggard look that Thursday. He'd done well and was left wondering. Pier being Pier, he had of course assumed he'd failed. "That makes sense," he said without explaining. "And you're making headway?" he enquired, shifting the focus back to the other's fundraising tale.

Rexel head nodded and shook at the same time, agitating his red mop of hair: "*Ja, ja,* I zink so. A couple of Regio patrons are interested. Might be able to put somezing together for him. He's got to get out of zat FIAT job, though."

He caught the half grin on Don Marco's face, and pinned an inquisitive eye on him.

"I've been concerned about that, too," the priest acknowledged.

The two music masters studied each other over their *cappuccinos.* Without removing his attention from Don Marco, Rexel caught sight of a waiter in the background, and beckoned him over with a snap of his fingers.

"*Pasticcini,*" he ordered, waving in the direction of the enticing display of pastries on the bar's counter. "With *marrons glacés,*" he added. The waiter bowed and left, and Rexel resumed his conversation with Don Marco. "Would you haf any concern if Pier…came over zo us?"

Don Marco shrugged one shoulder even before Rexel had finished his inquiry. "It's up to Pier," he said.

"So it iss. But you've put a lot of time into him."

Don Marco spread his hands out, then brought them together in an ecclesiastical gesture of acceptance. "He must do what he thinks best," he said.

The waiter returned with the ordered pastries, and Rexel pushed his cup to one side to make room for the tray close to him. "*Gut, gut, danke,*" he muttered, shoving a whole *marron glacé* into his mouth and munching with intense concentration. He transferred two more *marrons,* a *napoleon* and two *bignés* to his plate, before nudging the tray towards his guest. Don Marco declined with a small lift of his fingers. Opposite him, the German munched on with intense concentration, eyes down, brows knitted together.

"So…" Rexel resumed after swallowing and taking a sip of coffee to clear his throat, "how do you see it vork?"

Don Marco cocked his head to an inquisitive angle but did not speak.

"How do ve make this vork?" Rexel pursued, "Do ve share him? I'd have no problem vith zat."

Once again, Don Marco leaned back in his seat, straightening his spine. He heard clearly the real question behind the Bavarian's words: was *he* willing to contribute to Pier's funding?

"Well, that might be a possibility," he said.

"*Na ja,* a possibility. Let's look into it, shall ve? Give it some thought. Yes?"

On that, they parted, each to work out his own view of what that possibility might entail. They agreed to meet again in a fortnight's time to discuss possible terms and conditions.

Don Marco fumes

Don Marco left *Caffè Baratti* in a steaming temper. The encounter with Horst Rexel disturbed him considerably; in fact, it infuriated him. It wasn't the first time the German blighter had made himself a thorn in his flesh.

Lips pinched, Don Marco stepped absent-mindedly off the curb, causing a squeal of brakes he didn't so much as hear. He was reliving their rivalry from the old *Santa Cecilia days,* then through the Verona trouble, and then again the *Fenice* incident. Over and over again, Rexel had managed to throw his spanner into Don Marco's works. And now here he was, interfering again.

What galled him most was the fat Teuton's deviousness, his underhandedness: one never saw him coming, and then there he was, butting in, sticking his oar in, pulling the water to his mill. All the past year he hadn't seen the carrot-head at the duomo a single time and now here he was, praising Pier's 'good foundation', presuming to make a bid for Pier, and making it sound like he was doing Don Marco a favour. And, to top it all off, Don Marco sputtered, the blasted German massacred the Italian language.

"How are ve going to make this vork," he mimicked out loud. The unmitigated gall of the man – he'd actually said *ve!* There was no *ve* here! Pier was his, Don Marco's, find. *He* had spotted the lad last year at a Santa Rita's Christmas rehearsal; *he* had brought him to the duomo; *he* had bought him off his brute of a father; and *he* had lined up a place for him at the Carignano seminary. Rexel had had nothing to do with any of this! And *he*, Don Marco, would get Pier out of the poisonous atmosphere of factory work. *And from his impossible family,* he added as a powerful afterthought. He'd heard from Don Carlo at Santa Rita's that Pier's sister had delivered her baby last July, and her mother had sent in a sister to help, but she sent the one with whom the new mother didn't get along. "What was the old woman thinking of?" Don Marco harrumphed in disgust; why couldn't she send the younger sister, as the pregnant mother had requested? Of course, it had backfired and the two sisters were now at each other's throats, fighting over turf in the woman's miserable little establishment.

He shook his head: four grown-ups and two babies in two measly rooms. Pier had had to give up his makeshift bed in the kitchen-*retro* to the intruder, so that, since July, he'd been sleeping under the counter of Nina's *lavanderia.* Small wonder, he thought angrily, he'd been looking so ragged.

And here was Rexel once again, with his spurious concern, his transparent pretence of friendliness and his ludicrous 've'. "How do ve make zis vork? The *good foundation*," he snarled, recalling the German's praising words, of Pier's voice had nothing whatever to do with the blasted *Herr Professor*. It was *his* own doing, Don Marco's. The presumption, the offensive, patronising air of the man galled him, and his shifting the blame: "Pier sought me out," he'd said, "or, rather, Matilde Agiati did." – Whoever the blasted woman was – as though that excused everything. It excused nothing!

His irritable mind went back to a snatch of the conversation in the *Caffé-Confetteria* Baratti. *She's been coaching him all summer…our diction and acting coach…* Somehow, that brought into focus changes Don Marco had noticed, without giving them much thought: Pier's speech had improved, and so had his presence and manners. He now recalled specific moments of his interaction with the lad: last June, when he'd told Pier he would no longer have to work in the fields for his father, the lad's response had been barely short of boorish: he'd glowered, shuffled and cringed, like he suspected a trap. Don Marco still remembered being annoyed at the uncouth absence of thanks. In contrast, in the last couple of months, there'd been nothing boorish in Pier's manner. The wariness, the reticence – Don Marco scoffed at himself: call it what it is, his distrustful *secrecy* – were still there, but they had become almost civilised, just as his clothes had become citified.

Don Marco sneered at himself: he had been so pleased with Pier's progress, assuming it to be the result of his own influence! He'd gone out of his way to promote Pier as the singer to hire for society weddings and other functions, he had steered many extra earnings in Pier's way, wanting to support the boy's efforts to better himself. Good clothes cost money…

A bark of self-contempt escaped him: and all that time Pier was sneaking from the duomo to the Regio! He wondered how long it had been going on. When Pier's first interview at the duomo had to be postponed, Don Carlo had mentioned that during his two years at Santa Rita's Pier had never found his way downtown. "Well," Don Marco snarled, "it hasn't taken him long to find his way to the theatre."

Don Marco's anger now shifted towards Pier, the deceitful twerp. He'd spent months worrying about Pier wearing himself out, and now it was clear where that exhaustion had come from. *From hanging about at the Regio,* he thought; *from attaching himself to the Agiati woman?* But where had he found the time, since he was at the duomo three nights a week, beside Sunday mornings? And just weeks ago he'd heard from Don Carlo that Pier still put in practice time at Santa Rita's a couple of times a week.

Suddenly, he recalled the lad's home situation: six people in two rooms, with two crying infants, the two sisters at loggerhead, Pier's makeshift bed under the *lavanderia* counter. His anger abated: anywhere would be better than that. He also recalled Pier's reluctance to leave Turin, in their recent conversation. He'd said, "There's my sister. She needs me." No mention of the second sister who had taken his bed; no complaints, just that raised shoulder, dismissing the sister's husband. That conversation troubled him now, in the light of today's discoveries. He'd have to look into it.

His mind turned back to Matilde Agiati and her work with Pier, and he brooded about the nature of their relations. He'd have to find out. His anger now hovered between the woman and Pier: he'd been deceived, and that made him suspicious. He'd have to get hold of this woman, he told himself more coherently.

His mind shifted back to Rexel – blast him! And there was the recent audition: it had taken place the day before Pier came to his session hoarse and haggard-looking. This time, Don Marco positively snarled at his own gullibility. The loud snarl shocked a well-dressed, middle-aged couple, walking arm in arm in front of him, and they turned to stare. Then, recognising him, the man lifted his hat and the woman sketched a courtsey: members of the cathedral's congregation.

With an effort, Don Marco smoothed the snarl off his face and composed it to a benign expression to return their greeting.

He realised then that he was already in *Via Venti Settembre,* just a couple of blocks from the duomo. He wasn't prepared to go back there in the foul mood he was in. He ducked into an alley and re-crossed *Piazza Castello,* this time along the palisade of the royal palace, making for the royal gardens beyond it and the ruins of the Roman wall. Only there, in the patchy sunshade of the November afternoon, he began to calm down. On the well-groomed paths crisscrossing wide lawns, dignified middle-class couples and family groups enjoyed a Sunday stroll. At regular intervals, well-tended flowerbeds proclaimed the All Saints' season with masses of chrysanthemums in bloom. Don Marco inhaled their funereal scent and relaxed. From a stone bench, where they were taking a break from their stroll, two elderly ladies bowed to him as he passed them, one crossed herself.

Don Marco dipped his head to them, his hand sketching an ecclesiastical blessing.

His mind was still on Pier and Matilde Agiati, on their encounters at the Regio and on Rexel's chuckle: *You should ask her…it makes quite a story.* He *would* ask her. He needed to get his mind around what had been going on in the past eight months. He hated the thought that he'd been played; for he was now convinced that, somehow, Pier had been the prime mover behind this mess.

Over the park's almost bare trees, the voice of the *San Giovanni Battista's* bell struck four, calling him back to his All Saints' duties: he had to be back for Vespers. He struck out on a cross-path, heading back to the cathedral. *Back to Pier and Monteverdi,* he found himself thinking.

Unexpectedly, he grinned. The foxy cub! When on earth had he found the time? And how on earth had he managed to get the Regio's diction coach to work with him? He *was* a handsome cub, of course, when he was in a good mood, but even so… And why had he never said anything *to him* about loving opera? He would have enjoyed talking opera with him.

The image of Pier's wary, sideways gaze, last June, when he'd told him he wouldn't have to work on the farm any more came back to him: he had peered at him like he suspected a trap. And a few weeks ago, Pier's caginess about leaving Turin to study at a *Schola Cantorum. It's the Regio, of course,* Don Marco thought, enlightened. The cub couldn't bear to be away from it.

Suddenly, he saw himself a raw youth in Rome, torn between his vocation for the church and the seductive pull of the stage, and he smiled with a certain tenderness for the agonies of youth. *He* had been lucky: for him, it had never been a question of all or nothing. His father, a *liceo* professor, had supported his tastes and his talents, and helped him make the most of both his passions.

In a way, he thought, *the church is a stage.* He saw himself, earlier that day, taking his bow first to the couple on Via XX Settembre, and then to the two ladies on the park's bench.

Another thought crowded in. "I wouldn't be surprised to discover there's a girl mixed in with all this." Pier was twenty-one, so nothing would be more natural.

Then the image of Matilde Agiati resurfaced: the middle-aged woman and the handsome lad! Don Marco chuckled, the notion of her disappointed longings a balm to his own wounded pride.

But Pier's deceitfulness rankled. "I'll have to talk to the woman," he told himself as he trotted up the cathedral steps.

Without quite knowing why, he suddenly felt light-hearted, as frisky as a kid. He steadied himself and entered the church at a dignified walk, heading for the sacristy to prepare for Vespers.

On the way, he stopped in his study and placed a call to Matilde Agiati.

Chapter Ten

...Created half to rise, and half to fall...
Alexander Pope

Pier, Don Marco, and Rexel

The let-down after his Regio audition, with the other upsets it had triggered, left Pier reeling with confusion and self-loathing. Signora Agiati's seeking him out helped to abate his black mood enough so that he was able to return to the theatre and settle into a relatively calm waiting mode. But hanging on to this calm remained a struggle, precariously anchored as it was in a casual comment Matilde Agiati had made when she'd sought him out. *All is not lost,* Pier repeated those four words to himself like an incantation. She was right, he scolded himself when he felt himself wavering. He *was* a *bonòm,* a simpleton: she had assured him that the audition had gone well, so why had he *assumed* that he had failed? "You're not *out,* you're just *not in yet,*" she'd said. Those words, too, he repeated to himself like a talisman, always reproducing her exact tone.

One thing that troubled him now was trying to make sense of his recent despair: his extreme reaction to the professor's perceived rejection made him fear a fatal flaw within himself. He could put no words to the way he'd felt, except an echo of his mother's familiar comment: "All the world is ashes."

A second thing scared him. Because of his black mood, he'd hurt Lena. He'd punished *her,* and that made no sense; she'd had nothing to do with it. For twenty-four hours he'd put her and himself through hell, and the very next night Don Marco had offered to send him to a *Schola Cantorum.* That wasn't the Regio, but it was a chance he would have crowed about a year ago, so why the despair now?

The haunting image of Lena's anguished face, when he'd refused her approaches on his Black Thursday, stirred up in him an inchoate fear that some evil lurked within him that made him cruel and hurtful to the one person he loved

215

in this world. Now he felt an urgent need to make amends, so as to deny that evil within him. He needed to believe that he could trust himself not to destroy what he loved.

He started to make amends the very next day. He gave no explanation (how could he explain?) and Lena required none. All she needed was his renewed tenderness. Pier felt not only forgiven but more deeply loved. And feeling loved, he was loving, eager to share his doings and his dreams with her. He started to spend his Monday evenings – black night at the Regio – with her, coaching her with her reading, talking to her about the readings Signora Agiati recommended, often reading aloud to her at her mama's kitchen table.

After the first couple of weeks, he started to look forward to their cosy evenings together in the warm kitchen. He was touched by Lena's enthralled attention when he read out loud to her, with Gioana sitting by the stove with her mending, a half smile on her soft, old face, her quiet enjoyment a stark contrast to his ma's pinched face and rigid frame. That contrast brought home to Pier that he still had not told his mother about the theatre. In a way, he had *not been allowed* to tell her by the response he anticipated, her dreaded familiar refrain: "Work of the devil."

On those quiet evenings in the warmth of the Le Basse kitchen, Pier knew for the first time a novel sense of wellbeing, and his soul expanded in that quiet comfort. His self-mistrust told him he didn't deserve it, that he would somehow destroy it, as he had almost destroyed Lena's love. It frightened him that all this could so easily be destroyed in a moment of despair, and he worked hard at keeping his anxiety at bay, telling himself that nothing was lost, that Signora Agiati was still helping him, she now planned to introduce him to the *Convivio Letterario,* where he would hear proper Italian. He reminded himself that Don Marco still wanted him and had left it up to him to decide about the *Schola Cantorum*. As to Professor Rexel…well, Signora Agiati assured him the professor was working for him behind the scenes. And, Pier told himself, even if *that* didn't work out, it was easier now to see new possibilities, to be patient, to simply wait and see.

Pier's relatively calm frame of mind stretched well into November. He still put in his workdays at FIAT, still attended his sessions with Don Marco and sang at the duomo. But from time to time, he worried that word of his opera audition might reach Don Marco and upset the apple cart. Mostly, he tried not to think about it. After all, he told himself, the church and the theatre were worlds apart, even though they were, physically, a stone's throw from each other, just like the church and the tavern were in San Dalmass'. God and the devil, as his ma said.

On the fifth Thursday since his audition, Pier trotted up the cathedral steps in a dense November fog for his session with Don Marco. As he crossed the vestibule, hurrying toward the practice room, a familiar voice behind him called out, "Oi!"

Pier looked over his shoulder without stopping and called out *"Buona Sera"* to the sacristan he had met on his first visit to the cathedral. "Don Marco said to meet him in his study," the old man yelled after him.

"Grazie," Pier answered, hurrying down the corridor, as he unwound the long woollen scarf off his neck.

Don Marco, he thought, must want his answer about the *Schola Cantorum. But I still have another week,* Pier argued, remembering the end of November deadline. And, in that week, he might hear from Professor Rexel. He didn't want to commit to the seminary school without knowing what his chances were at the theatre. Yet, at the same time, he was afraid that, if he didn't commit soon, Don Marco might take offense and withdraw the offer. Pier absolutely didn't want to risk that. After all, studying at a seminary was better than nothing.

Then a new and alarming thought came into his mind: why was Don Marco calling him to his study? Why not talk to Pier in the practice room as he usually did? Thoroughly rattled, Pier stood in front of the study door, afraid to knock. He found himself shaking and felt the hated flush spread up his face. He cursed himself, forced himself to straighten his spine as he repeated the mantra Signora Agiati had prescribed for him: *Confident. Masterful.*

He felt neither. He cursed again and closed his eyes, concentrating on his breath, trying to calm down. In front of him, the door handle squeak and the door flew open.

"Pier!" Don Marco greeted him, "I thought I'd heard you. Do come in." He turned on his heels and led the way into his study. Pier was carefully closing the door behind him when Don Marco's voice called out, "I believe you've met Professor Rexel."

Pier froze, aghast: on the stiff leather settee between the study's two windows, the professor's bushy red head bobbed up and down, a wicked grin on his face. Don Marco draped an arm around Pier's shoulders and steered him, passively resistant, to one of the chairs by the settee and sat down across from him. At bay, Pier stared from one man to the other, desperately trying to control the shameful flush he felt burning the top of his ears. In his confusion, he wriggled himself deep into his chair as if to hide in it. Then, to his horror, his right knee jerked up to his chest and his fingers latched themselves tightly around it. Hurriedly, he put his foot back down on the floor and straightened his spine. "You wanted to see me," he mumbled lamely.

Don Marco broke into a laugh: "You could say that, you, sneaky cub! But why couldn't you tell me?"

In his chair, Pier shrank to dwarf size. What could he say? He was caught.

"Well, never mind that now," Don Marco continued, benign. "Professor Rexel has put me in the picture. And we both concur: in church or on the stage, your voice is a God-given gift well worth nurturing. The question is how are we going to go about it?"

He stopped, enjoying Pier's open-mouthed astonishment. *Like a kid on Christmas morning,* Don Marco thought, *staring at two Father Christmases.* He exchanged an amused glance with Horst Rexel, who still sat grinning.

"The problem iss," the deep Germanic voice rumbled, "you've got no money." Pier's heart dropped. "But…" Rexel let the pause stretch out into a black hole before he continued: "Ve've been putting our heads together, Don Marco and I," he chuckled, "and ve think ve've found a vay for you to study and…" his hands flew out in an exuberant gesture "…SING!"

Pier blinked fast several times, staring from one man to the other, left, front, and left again.

"That's right," Don Marco confirmed, grinning. Pier's eyes flew back to him. "I offered to send you to a seminary school to cultivate your voice and get an education. But, if you want to sing opera, that won't do. Professor Rexel tells me *that*'s what you want: opera. Is that right?"

Pier opened his mouth, but nothing came out. He closed it, coughed, and squeaked out: "Well…" But his throat was dry, and he coughed again, trying to focus his voice well forward so he could control it. "A year ago…" he began down in his baritone register, "I didn't even know opera existed. But then…I ran into the Regio and…" He stopped, shaking his head, his shoulders, his entire body, like a dog emerging from water, like he was trying to shake himself awake from a dream: "I was…blown away!"

"And your fourteen years' of work on sacred music?" Don Marco asked.

"It's been my life!" Pier cried. "Especially since I've been here – Palestrina, Gabrieli, Pergolesi, Mozart, Monteverdi…" He heaved a deep, ecstatic sigh.

"But…?" Don Marco persisted, demanding an explanation.

Pier's shoulders rose even more: how could he explain? But Don Marco wasn't about to let him off. So, eventually, when he could breathe again, he tried once more.

"Well, opera is like…everyday life," he stammered. "In church it's…well, it's *Sunday* music! But opera…that's…people…real life!"

. "I see…" Don Marco he said, studying Pier thoughtfully across the few feet of space between them. The silence lengthened, and Pier felt again the urge to run away. But there he sat, glued to his chair, unable to move. He felt tears begin to prickle at his eyes, so he dug his nails into his palms and stared hard at the floor to regain control: he'd said the wrong thing, he'd offended Don Marco.

"And," Don Marco said, a note of ironic amusement in his voice , "everyday life moves you more."

"No!" Pier struggled to explain, "But…well, every day is…well, every day is six days a week!"

For long seconds, Don Marco peered at Pier: opera equated with real life! The cub still had a lot of growing up to do. "So…" he said at last, "you want…what? Both!?"

"Yes! Yes, that's it! I want both!" Pier cried eagerly. "But…"

Rexel's sympathetic bass rumbled on his left, "But you don't know how zat can be made to vork."

Startled, Pier turned to look at him.

"That's vhat ve've been vorking out," the professor said. "And there may be a vay—"

"But we need to hear from you;" Don Marco interjected, "what you really want, how hard you're prepared to work to get it."

"Anything!" Pier cried frantically, eyes flying from one man to the other. "I'll do anything!"

"Careful with promises you may not be able to keep," Don Marco said, teasing.

"*So*! Ve've vorked out one plan," Rexel put in. "Don Marco vill tell you. Then you tell us vhat you zink."

Pier was now on the edge of his seat, right hand clenched over left fist, his whole being hanging on the sentence about to be pronounced.

Don Marco sat back deep in his armchair, pontifical. "Professor Rexel," he said, "has been able to call on some generous Regio patrons who are willing to put together a scholarship for you." He bowed briefly to the professor, who nodded back. "That will allow you to work on your voice and stage craft without having to…do outside work." Pier's jaw dropped. "…But that still leaves your living expenses, and, what's more important, your… *general education.*"

"I don't need much," Pier broke in. "I can live with my sister—"

"Ah… but I'm afraid that won't do." Don Marco interrupted firmly. "And that's where I come in, *if* my plan suits you."

Pier's eyes were now glued to Don Marco's face, a butterfly newly pinned on a display tray.

"Education requires…" Don Marco checked himself a moment, searching for a tactful way to proceed, "steady exposure to an educated way of life. That's hard to achieve among people who are struggling to make a living. You've been at FIAT for two years, you must know…"

Pier's eyes dropped to his knees, an image of mealtimes in Nina's retro vivid in his mind.

Don Marco went on, "What I propose is this; you will be offered a position at a boys' *collegio,* here in Turin. You don't get paid, but you get your room and board. Officially, you will be there as an assistant to the music master, but at the same time you'll receive the tutoring you need to work on your education. You will do your homework, like any other student; but you will turn in your homework and tests *privately* to your teachers. It will be hard work, but you will get the education you need to go out into the world as a singer."

For a long time, Pier sat speechless, overwhelmed and, at the same time, angry that decent, hardworking Nina was implicitly declared not good enough. But he was being offered a chance at the life he wanted, so he couldn't afford to take offence. The two music masters sat in silence, watching the struggle behind his closed face.

At last Pier stammered out, "But…but… What do I have to do for all that?" The two men exchanged glances, then Don Marco said: "You have to do your best…" and, at the same time, Rexel interjected, "Make *us* proud, *ve* who've discovered you."

"…and," Don Marco finished, "continue to sing here, as much as you can."

"I will! Oh, I will, I will!" Pier cried, voice cracking.

Then a frown clouded his face.

"You see a problem?" Don Marco asked.

"It's just…is this… I don't know how to thank you, both of you. But…but…"

"Well, spit it out!" Don Marco urged.

"Will I have any money?"

"So!" Rexel chuckled, a deep, amused rumble. *Der Bube* has his feet planted on the ground, after all!"

Don Marco smiled, then reminded him, "You did quite well this past year, singing at private functions. I'll steer as many your way as I can. But you will have to learn to budget your earnings to make them last through the lean winter months."

This time Pier's silence positively sparked with excitement. He kept gazing from one master to the other, utterly at a loss for words.

"Well," Don Marco said, "if that sits well with you, we can have you started right after the Christmas holidays."

"Right after Christmas! Oh, yes, please!"

"Well, then," Don Marco got to his feet, "The problem is solved. Let's drink to your future." He strolled over to a side table and poured out three glasses of *marsala* from a crystal decanter. "To Pier's singing," he said, raising his glass. "To Pier," echoed the professor, standing up. The three drank.

"And," Pier hazarded breathlessly, clutching the stem of his glass, "is it ok if I have a girlfriend?"

Over his glass, Don Marco's eyes mock-consulted with Rexel. "And vhy vould it not be?" the professor queried.

"Why not indeed!" echoed Don Marco, draining his glass and placing it back on the table. *I knew there was a girl somewhere in all this,* he thought, recalling Pier's reluctance to leave Turin. Suppressing a grin, he turned back to Pier, "And now," he said, "you'd better leave us to work out the details."

Pier hastened to set his glass down on the side table, bowed his thanks first to one man then to the other, and made for the door.

He was on the threshold when Don Marco's voice stopped him. "Oh," he said, "tomorrow you might as well turn in FIAT your notice. I need an assistant here at the duomo for the Advent and Christmas season."

Pier tells his News

Pier emerged from the cathedral in an ecstasy of excitement. Skipping down the cathedral's steps, he leapt up into the air and clicked his heels together. But he came down on the edge of a step and slithered down several more, his feet scrambling in some fast, gigue-like footwork to regain his balance. He landed hard on the sidewalk, but bounced up and straightened his spine to resume some semblance of dignity. "Yeah, masterful," he mocked himself out loud, thinking of Matilde Agiati.

That's what he had to do next: find a telephone and share his news with her right away, she, the one person who knew what he'd been through since the audition, how much this all meant to him. Head high, he strode down Via Garibaldi toward Piazza Castello. And as soon as he was done with the phone call, he'd go to Lena. Lena was the next person he wanted to tell.

At the street corner, he spotted the black and yellow disk that signalled a public phone and walked into a smoke-filled café-bar. "Signora Agiati," he burst out, as soon as her voice came on the line, "It's happened, I am *in!*"

"You are!? Fantastic!" she sang out, "But then, I knew you would be! You heard tonight? How, when, from whom? Tell me." He told her, his voice pitched high with excitement, and with the need to make himself heard over the din of the bar. Laughing at himself and his fears, he told her about the unexpected meeting, about his fright at seeing the professor and Don Marco together. Matilde laughed, delighted, amused, catching Pier's infectious enthusiasm.

"That's so funny," she cried, "Don Marco is as crazy about opera as you are! He's there for every new production! But that's marvellous, Pier! I'm so glad. Now you're on your way! Come right over, we must celebrate your triumph!"

The line went silent. Pier hadn't thought of that.

"Pier?" she queried. He cleared his throat, embarrassed.

"I'd love to…" he mumbled, apologetic, "I had to tell you right away, but…Tonight… I already have another engagement. And I'd like to get home before my sister goes to bed, and tell her as well…"

"But of course," she said. "We'll celebrate your success on Wednesday. Come prepared for bubbles."

Pier hung up, buoyant. Bubbles: *Viva il vino spumeggiante*... The image flashed through his mind: *spumante* being poured behind a café window under an arcade, the elegant party raising their glasses in a toast. He was getting there, this time he really was! He hailed the barman, pointed to a bottle on the rack behind the counter, "A bottle of Martini e Rossi *spumante*," he ordered, confident, masterful. He left the bar, the wrapped bottle cradled in the crook of his arm, an irrepressible grin on his face.

On the way to a Lingotto tram stop he stepped at a *pasticceria* and ordered a kilo of pastries to go with the bubbles. He got to his tram stop just in time to leap onto the already moving tram through its sluggishly closing doors. Shoulders square and chin up, he made for his customary spot against the rear window. The tram clock read eight twenty: Lena would be done with supper, he thought, anticipating her excitement, her delight at his news, at the bubbles and pastry, at the prospect of their future life together. Then a tiny white cloud crossed his sunny heaven: at Le Basse there wouldn't be any stemmed glasses. But nothing could sink his spirits tonight. One day, he told himself, one day they *would have* stemmed glasses of their own. Right now, he just wanted to tell his Lena.

Then, he thought, *I'll run home to tell Nina, if she is still up.* The image of Lorèns floated up in his mind. *Up and alone,* he amended.

The following morning, he waited for Lena outside the FIAT gate. She ran up to him, ecstatic, and threaded her arm through his, snuggling up close.

"I still can't believe it, Pier!" she cried. "You at the Regio! It is too too wonderful!" She cast a defiant glance at the workers crowding in through the gates for the start of another workday. Pier covered the hand on his arm with his own and steered her proudly through the gate. For the first time, they walked into the factory with the morning rush *openly* together, daring the stares, the taunts, and the gossip. He left her part-way up the ramp with a peck on her cheek, while he headed for the labour office to hand in his notice. The head of his section wouldn't be in yet, but he'd written out his notice to leave with the secretary: let the boss come to him if he had to.

The next thing Pier wanted to do was to go home and tell his Ma. He also dreaded doing it, knowing what to expect. *But I'm done sneaking about,* he thought, suddenly defiant. He was proud of his progress in the city, even though he knew that all his mother would see in it was evil. *So be it,* he thought, refusing to let her disapproval spoil it for him. If Don Marco saw no sin in the theatre, surely, *he* must know best. There was no shame in loving the theatre, or in making his living from opera. Well, in time, some day. Maybe. Hopefully.

And then Pier made the big leap: this time, he'd tell his ma about Lena. Last night he'd told Nina. "I'd like to meet her," Nina had answered eagerly, then suddenly stopped short. Pier guessed what had happened: she'd been on the verge of telling him to bring his girl to dinner on Sunday, but dinner meant Lorèns. Pier understood, so he had quickly added, "I thought I'd bring her to

Santa Rita's for *Benedission.* Perhaps you will join us. Then we can stop for coffee at the *pasticceria-bar* on the square." Relieved, Nina had eagerly agreed.

Now Pier began to consider when it would be possible for him to get to *La Speransa.* He'd be done with FIAT on Friday, a week from today, and Don Marco wanted him at the cathedral for Advent, which started the following Sunday, so on that Saturday he would be free. He'd check with Don Marco that he wasn't needed, and then he'd bike out and tell his Ma.

He approached Don Marco after the next choir practice.

"How are you going to get there?" the music master asked him.

"I'll bike over."

"Are you still running around on that bike!?"

"Not in town. But there's no other way to get to the farm."

"Well, you can't ride your bike in December. You can't afford to catch a cold, not with Christmas coming."

"I've been taking the trams, honest I have," Pier protested.

Scowling, Don Marco headed for his office at a brisk pace with Pier trotting alongside, explaining: "I haven't seen my mother since summer, and Christmas is coming…and…and… I want to tell her the news."

"Of course, you do," Don Marco cut in, pushing his office door open. "She'll be pleased to hear."

"No, she won't," Pier thought bitterly. But he found it reassuring that Don Marco thought she should be. He followed his mentor into the music master's office.

"Well, the bike is out," Don Marco decreed, flinging his scores down onto his desk. "No riding in winter," he added, his eyes pinned on Pier's, willing him to accept the fact. "Promise me that."

Pier lowered his eyes, acquiescing. He would have to write the news to his mother. Maybe it was just as well. But he didn't want her to hear about it through the grapevine, like he was sneaking behind her back.

"The cathedral automobile will call for you on Saturday afternoon," Don Marco said. "Will …a couple of hours with your family be enough?"

Pier at the *Convivio*

The following evening, Matilde Agiati took him with her to the reading group she wanted him to join, the *Convivio Letterario.* His first night at the meeting left Pier intimidated and confused. Of the twelve members present that night, two were university professors, one wrote reviews for *La Stampa,* another wrote poetry, and a fifth wrote fiction. Of the remaining eight, three taught at city *licei,* and one was a priest who taught philosophy at a Jesuit seminary. Two more, a man, and the only woman other than Signora Agiati, were *avant-garde* actors from the recently opened *Teatro Nuovo di Torino.*

The initial welcome, when Matilde Agiati introduced Pier to the group, was cordial enough; but Pier, trying to follow their conversation, soon found himself at a loss. His discomfort grew worse during supper, when the group members got passionate about city events Pier had hardly been aware of. At one point, trying to follow their debate, Pier gathered the nerve to ask a question: who was Piero Gobetti? The group had been discussing him with intense passion. He was told curtly, "*Legga i giornali,*" read the newspapers.

The after-dinner discussion of a book he had not read left Pier utterly disoriented: he heard repeated references to the Blessed Cross. His mind replaced the phrase with the more familiar one, the Holy Cross, but the context of the debate remained impenetrable to him. It was only well into the discussion that he caught on to the fact that they were saying Benedet*to* Croce, not *Benedetta Croce:* they were talking about *someone* whose name was Croce, not about the Holy Cross. Later that night, on the way to the tram stop, Signora Agiati explained that Gobetti was a young journalist and political philosopher who had antagonised the Fascist leadership with his articles on liberalism.

Overall, he left that first gathering feeling that he was painfully out of their league. Signora Agiati urged him to keep attending the group because, to correct his *Piemontèis* accent, he needed to get used to the sounds and rhythms of proper spoken Italian. She also insisted that exposure to discussions of current concerns would be good for him. Pier trusted her advice, so he promised to continue to attend – as long as *she* was there as well.

Privately, he was disappointed. He'd expected the group to read things more like the ones on Signora Agiati's reading list. Since his first encounter with Verga and his *Cavalleria Rusticana,* he'd become passionate about the author's work and could not get enough of it. He had told Signora Agiati of this preference. She had sympathised, but had added: *"Per farsi una cultura è necessario leggere anche cose difficili che non ci piacciono tanto. Abbia pazienza."* To cultivate one's education, it was necessary to read difficult books as well, even ones one doesn't much enjoy. He had to be patient.

At the end of that conversation, in response to Pier's trying to tell her what moved him in Verga, she had added two more authors to his list, Manzoni and Zola. Pier went to the city library the very next day and checked out two novels by Zola, *L'ammazzatoio* and *La Fortuna dei Rougons*. He quickly became engrossed in their stories: time and place were different, but he found the characters and their struggles painfully familiar. They reminded him of people he'd grown up with. The young men and women in the novels, with their yearnings and their fears, could have been he, while the rigidities of the old, their obsessions, their violence and despairs evoked his experience of his mother and father. The setting of *L'ammazzatoio,* literally, the slaughterhouse, but, in the context of the novel, the tavern in which the characters dissolved their pain and their minds in *absinthe*, soon came to stand, in Pier's mind, for the San Dalmass' tavern where his pa regularly got drunk.

As to the Manzoni novel, so far he had only glanced at it, but the title, *The Betrothed*, had made him think that it might be a book he could read with Lena. And the rhythm of the novel's opening sentence, *Su quel ramo del lago di Como che volge a mezzogiorno,* had etched itself on his mind. Since then, it kept resurfacing at unexpected moments – on that branch of the lake of Como that stretches towards the South. S*u quel ramo del lago di Como...* The sheer music of it haunted him. The sentence became a refrain in his mind. Yes, he would read this book with Lena.

He smiled at the scene his mind had conjured up: the Le Basse kitchen, after supper; he and Lena at the table, close together, the book between them, the electric bulb under its enamel reflector lowered for reading, its cone of light bright on the book; the crocheted lamp shade casting light and shadow patterns on Lena's curls, and on the room's walls, like moonlight through summer leaves. And at the edge of the scene, Gioana, sitting by the cast iron stove, busy at her mending, but listening attentively to his reading, a soft smile on her kind old face.

He borrowed the book, and that very night started to read it to Lena and her mother. On his own, later at night, he continued to read Zola's *Rougons* saga, and found in this reading the solace of painful recognition.

That solace, however, could not disperse the lingering malaise of that "Read the newspapers". More than ever, it brought home to him that he would never belong in the world of *that kind of people*. At the *Convivio,* he had once again encountered the civil but reserved welcome, quickly replaced by dismissal, like he had no business being there. And he had to agree, he did *not* belong among them. Their conversation made that clear: not only *what* they talked about, but *the way* they talked about it. Pier was soon lost in their sea of words. He struggled to get the gist of their arguments, to understand what caused such intensity of emotions, but it made no sense to him. Later, all he remembered was a few names which conveyed nothing to him, though he vaguely remembered having heard or seen them somewhere before.

Now, several days later, the whole experience remained coloured for him by that snippy response, when he had innocently asked who Gobetti was, *"Legga i giornali."* Read the newspapers. Until that moment, he had accepted his disorientation as something Signora Agiati had warned him about, the discomfort of a newcomer joining an ongoing group. "At this stage," she'd told him, "you still lack the background information to make sense of these discussions, that's all. Over time, you will read what they read and then you will be able to follow." But for him that rebuff had transformed his newcomer's disorientation into a humiliating rejection, into an awareness of a shameful, personal flaw that branded him as an interloper. Under the stinging putdown, Pier shrivelled up, and the *Convivio* became the enemy. Even Signora *Agiati* became tainted: why had she exposed him to this humiliation? She must have known that he would make a fool of himself.

Legga i giornali. Read the newspapers: that simple sentence, carelessly thrown out in the heat of a passionate discussion, had cut Pier down at his knees. Now it haunted him day and night. Every time it came into his mind, he blushed, feeling anew the brush-off and his recoil into himself. The wound festered in his mind, until the very sight of a newspaper or a news kiosk brought on a physical nausea. And, perversely, newspapers began to crop up and taunt him everywhere he went. On trams and cafes, men stood or sat, immersed in their newspapers. News kiosks seemed to have sprouted on every corner of his usual routes. This morning, in Don Marco's study, he had been waylaid by the clutch of newspapers scattered all over the coffee table. One of them, folded open like its reader had just momentarily set it down, occupied the chair on which Don Marco motioned him to sit, and Pier had had to shift the paper off the chair and onto the stack of other papers on the coffee table before sitting down. He had lifted it *du bout des doigts* – barely touching it with his fingertips – the way one might deal with a rotting dead rat.

And at the Regio as well, when he went to Professor Rexel to work out the details of his new training program, he found the professor reading *La Stampa* and grumbling in German. Even his old friend, Paulin, huddled on his stool by the stage door, squinted at a folded newspaper he held at arm's length. "Pah!" he'd said with a disgusted slap at the paper, "all that fuss, last year, about this new *tubercolosi* insurance, and here it is..." again he slapped the newspaper, "this year alone there are fifty-nine thousand *new* cases. Their insurance hasn't stopped this epidemic, has it? What good is all their fancy medicine, eh, you tell me that. It didn't save my nephew. Twenty-six, Ricu was, when he died last June. Fat lot of good their new *Val Chison* sanatorium did him. Might as well have stayed home."

Pier escaped from his angry grief with a few awkward words of sympathy. But he was shaken. *Everyone* read the newspapers except him. It had never occurred to him to read them: how stupid could he be? It was his own fault that he didn't fit in.

That afternoon, on his way to the tram to Santa Rita's, Pier reluctantly stopped by a news kiosk. There he stood, staring at the bewildering array of publications, uncertain which paper to buy. By the cashier's window he saw two separate stacks of newspapers, one of *LA STAMPA,* the other of *IL CORRIERE DELLA SERA.* He read the front-page headlines of both: the same words, names, phrases appeared in both – *OMNI, Confindustria, Gran Consiglio, Battaglia del Grano, Farinacci:* and, of course, Mussolini, and *il Duce.* Pier had no idea what the headlines referred to. As he hovered in indecision, an arm pushed by past him –*"Scusi, permette?"*– pardon me – and grabbed a copy of *LA STAMPA.* Another man took advantage of Pier's stepping aside to snatch up a copy of each paper. That puzzled Pier: why read both, since they seemed to carry the same stories? Next to him, on the left side of the kiosk, two boys argued about the adventures of some character in one of the cartoon magazines; and a little girl squatted, bare knees peeking out from under her pleated skirt, lips moving laboriously, totally absorbed. Pier stepped closer to see what held her so spellbound: *IL CORRIERINO DEI PICCOLI,* he read, surprised – a magazine just for kids!? At *La Speransa,* the only printed things around had been prayer books, the occasional saints' lives Don Michel leant his Ma, and the old newspaper pages the general store tore off to wrap dry goods in.

Pier returned to the two stacks of newspapers by the cashier's window. *La STAMPA,* he remembered, was the paper he had removed from the chair in Don Marco's study. He decided for that.

He started to read it on the tram, standing up against a rear window, as usual, his paper folded lengthwise, the way he saw the other men hold theirs. He went through article after article, mystified by acronyms, wondering who the people discussed were. One of the titles, on the second page, it read, *Smobilizzazione degli Squadristi. That* he remembered hearing about. The excesses of the Fascist death squads had been on everyone's lips in his early days in Turin. Everybody had talked about the *squadristi's* involvement in the murder of a Senator called Matteotti. Surely, demobilising those squads was a good thing.

Another article caught his eye: Mussolini promised to spend a portion of the fifty million dollars loan he had just received from an American bank on incentives to agriculture. What did that mean, how would that work? Would money be given to farmers? Might his ma get any? No, even if money were given to farmers, it would go to his pa, and *she* wouldn't see any of it.

Other articles puzzled him even more: one of them said that the office of elected mayor was to be replaced with that of appointed *podestà.* Pier wondered what the point of the change was. Another article said they were changing the title of the Duce himself, from *Presidente del Consiglio* to *Capo di Stato.* Pier had always understood that *the king* was the head of the Italian state, but this article said that, as *Capo di Stato,* Mussolini would be reporting to the king. How would that work, Pier wondered, one head of the state reporting to the other? Who had the last word?

He turned the page and refolded his paper. A nightclub in the Turin hills had been raided, suspected of serving as a meeting place for *sovversivi; people* had been arrested. Pier read a list of names which meant nothing to him, but he read on, hoping to find out what *sovversivi* were. All he found was that they were enemies of the Fascist party, and therefore enemies of the state; and that people suspected of being subversives were stripped of all their rights and earthly goods, and exiled *al confino,* on a tiny volcanic island called Lipari.

When the tram ground to a stop at the end of its line, Pier folded his newspaper and slid it in his coat pocket. The oily smell of the paper suddenly hit him, and he felt nauseated, disgusted at the greasy residue on his fingers. He rubbed it off on Nina's carefully laundered handkerchief, feeling guilty at the greasy black smudges it left on it.

On Nina's doorstep he stopped: that last article haunted him. What made one a *sovversivo*? What put one at risk of being sent away to the island-prison, *al confino*? He needed to find out; he would go and ask Don Carlo to explain. But on the way to doing so at the Santa Rita's church, a new thought occurred to him: Don Carlo might *not want to* talk about this. Talking about it might somehow put him at risk, maybe even make him a *sovversivo sospetto*. Pier shuddered at the thought: he had no earthly goods that could be taken from him, but it would be intolerable to be sent away from Turin just now. Maybe it wouldn't be wise to ask about it. Maybe it would be better to just ask Don Carlo for some pointers on how to make sense of reading a newspaper.

Pier's news at *La Speransa*

On that last Saturday in November, free of FIAT and glowing with young love and the prospect of a life of music, Pier arrived at the gate of *La Speransa* in the black, long-nosed car. He had asked to be dropped off at around two o'clock, so it wouldn't look like he was coming home to scrounge a meal, even though he came bearing gifts. And by two o'clock his pa was likely to be gone, and it was his ma he wanted to talk to, his ma and Tilde.

It was getting on for half past two when Vigin-a, busy drying the midday washing-up by the window, glanced out over the farmyard. "Well," she cried, astounded, "an automobile!"

"*Ma va*," Tilde, her younger sister, scoffed, squeezing in at her side to peer out of the window – what nonsens: automobiles did not come to *La Speransa*.

"*Ma sí*, look, it's stopped at the gate."

"*Òmmi pòvra dòna!*" (Oh me, poor woman!) Maria cried out, hurrying to the window. Seeing the car at the gate, she rushed out with Vigin-a and Tilde on her heels. "*Còsa a l'é capitaje,*" she whimpered. (What has happened?) Taboj, on his chain, yelped and leaped about, wild with excitement, his bark broken by the strain the choke chain put on his throat. Then, the front passenger door opened, and Pier emerged, an anxious grin on his face, and waved to the women. before reaching into the rear passenger door and retrieving a small sack. He stopped a moment to talk to the driver, then stood aside while the car manoeuvered the difficult turn-around in the narrow and muddy lane, and trundled off carefully on the deep cart ruts.

Tilde flew to open the gate for her brother. Still in the middle of the yard, his ma called out to him, "You in trouble?"

Pier laughed, his heart sinking. "No, Ma, I'm *not* in trouble. I came to see you."

"But that automobile… I was sure there'd been an accident…"

Again, Pier laughed: his ma always expected the worst. "No," he said, "no accident." He squatted a moment to fondle old Taboj's head. "Don Marco doesn't want me to ride my bike in winter, so he sent the car."

"Well," Vigin-a scoffed, "aren't we precious these days!"

Pier ignored her, letting the dog's pink, wet tongue wash all over his face. She'd become even meaner since Nina had sent her back home from Santa Rita. He glanced at the homestead and asked, "Who's home?"

"Just us three," Tilde told him.

With a last pat to the dog's head, he stood up. Tilde gave him a hug and stretched up on tiptoes to kiss his cheek. "We haven't seen you forever."

"It has been a long time," Pier agreed, touched and embarrassed by Tilde's affectionate welcome.

Maria snapped at her daughters: "Well, don't just stand there like a pair of ninnies, you two. Get inside and get the stove going. We'll make coffee." She glanced at Pier and added, "You'll need warming up."

Inside, she steered Pier to the table, urged him to sit next to her place at the foot of the table, and sat on the edge of her chair, while Tilde and Vigin-a bustled about, executing her orders. After a long, awkward silence, she asked: "*Tuti bin?*" Everybody all right? She didn't add '*a cà'*, at home: the city was *not* home.

"*Tuti bin,*" Pier nodded, joining her in the customary catechism of obligatory inquiries and responses. He laid his sack of gifts on the table next to her.

"*E le cite?*" Maria continued. (And the little girls?)

"*A stan bin. As fan grande.*" (They are well. They are getting big.

"*E ti?*" (And you.)

"*E mi…*" Pier answered, sheepishly, "*Mi i l'hai 'd neuve.*" (I… I have news.)

"*Che neuve?*" (What news?) demanded Vigin-a, bending by him to pour out his cup of chicory coffee. She sat down across from him, elbows splayed on the table, not to miss any crumb of his news.

Unable to contain herself, Tilde tapped her big brother's arm, "*E daje, no, conta, conta!*" (Come on, tell us.) For a moment, an excited grin flickered across Pier's face, then his eyes turned to his ma and quickly sobered. She sat straight backed, rigid, hands clasped into a tight, white knuckled knot in front of her, waiting. Pier's excitement turned to anxiety.

"A lot has happened, Ma," he started, "since I was last here."

Vigin-a interrupted. "You got fired!"

Tilde scoffed at her sister, "They don't send you home in an automobile when you get fired. Shut up, silly, let him talk."

"No," Pier snapped at Vigin-a, "I wasn't *fired*. I quit!"

"*Òmmi pòvra dòna,*" his mother cried out, "you've left FIAT! How you going to earn your living now?"

Pier laid a reassuring hand on his mother's. "Ma, I won't have to earn my living anymore. At least, not at FIAT. That's what I came to tell you."

Three pairs of gimlet eyes now bored into him, frightened, eager, demanding explanation. "I'm to study music, Ma," Pier explained, "Full time. Don Marco and Professor Rexel have arranged it all for me. No more FIAT."

"But…but… Who's this, this…*professor*?" his mother queried, alarmed, bristling with mistrust. "And what kind of a name is that? It's not one of ours. Is he even a Christian?"

His mother's reaction came as no surprise to Pier. He did his best to explain despite his ma's frequent '*òmmi pòvra dòna*', and his sisters' constant interruptions, the alarming phenomenon of the duomo, the theatre and his new post at a boy's school. "You mean…*you* are going to be a teacher?" Vigin-a screeched in disbelief. "What have *you* got to teach*?"*

"Not a teacher, no. Just a teacher's assistant," he qualified.

"And they pay you for *that*!?"

"An opera house!" Tilde exclaimed, eyes sparkling. "In a theatre…"

Òmmi pòvra dòna, ommi pòvra dòna. I knew you'd go wrong *in Turin…*"

"But, Ma," Pier cried, "I haven't *gone wrong*! There's nothing wrong with what I'm doing. Don Marco himself put the plan together for me."

"*Giá, giá,*" Maria muttered, shaking her head with deep mistrust, *"*he and this… this…*Germa!*"

They sat silent for a while, then his ma refocused. "And Don Carlo?" she asked, "You're not doing anything for him anymore, are you? After all he's done for you!"

Pier sighed, his bleak expectations confirmed. "He doesn't mind, Ma," he said, "He is *happy* for me. We told him last Sunday."

Maria pounced on the pronoun, "W*e*? Who's we?"

"I went to *Benedission* with Nina and the girls. I tell you, he is very happy for me."

"Don't call her Nina," Maria corrected him. "Her name is Catlinin. But…in a theatre! How could you?"

He found himself starting all over, explaining, justifying, invoking Don Marco's authority, then the church's, to pacify his mother. "Do you really believe Don Marco would send me to the theatre," he said, "if it was a sin?"

The argument drew on and on, until his mother withdrew into a hurt silence, and they sat sipping at their cold chicory coffee, until Tilde asked with forced cheerfulness, "And that sack, what have you got in it?"

Gratefully, Pier drew the sack closer to him and opened it. "Just a few things for Christmas," he said, pulling out one by one a large *panettone,* a box of chocolates, a packet of menthol cough drops, hard candy bitters for his mother's digestive problems, and a tray of pastries. Then, solemnly, he presented his ma her special present, three hundred grams of the best fresh-roasted Arabian coffee beans in their sealed foil bag.

"*Òmmi pòvra dòna,*" Maria cried, reluctant hands clutching the gift. She undid the folded top and the rich aroma filled her room. "All this stuff… It must have cost a fortune. You'll run yourself into the poor house one of these days." But she opened the coffee bag and inhaled its penetrating aroma. For a moment her lips un-pinched into a rare smile. "What a wonderful smell!" Then she thrust the bag into Tilde's hands. "Quick," she said, "hide it away, don't tell Pa. We'll keep it for special occasions."

"But, MA! This *is* a special occasion," Tilde protested. But Maria waved her off. "We've already had our coffee," she scolded, dismissing the subject.

The mention of Pa had dimmed the afternoon. Now, across the misty fields, the faint voice of *San Dalmass'* tolled four times.

"I'll have to go soon," Pier said, regretfully. "I'm going to see Don Michel. The driver's waiting for me there." But he did not get up. With an anxious glance at his Ma, he started, "There is…something else I have to tell you…" She looked at him wearily. "I've met a girl…"

Maria's lips pinched. "At this…theatre?" she asked sharply.

"No, Ma," Pier told her, pleading, "She works at FIAT, in the station next to mine." He let that sink in, then added, "We've…been seeing each other since October."

"So," Maria said, "now that you've quit you won't see her anymore."

"Leaving FIAT has got nothing to do with it!" he cried, frustrated.

An awkward silence followed, then Maria asked, "Does she go to mass?"

"Of course, Ma! Every Sunday, with her mama. And she came to the duomo once, to hear me sing."

Maria sniffed and looked away. After another silence she resumed her questioning. "You've met her ma?"

"Yes, I have. We meet at their home in the evening, and her mama sits with us while we read together."

"Hmm," was Maria's only response. But Tilde leaned across the table. "Gosh, Pier," she said excitedly, "You've got *a girlfriend*! Is she nice? What does she look like? What's her name?"

Vigin-a cut in, "What does she do at FIAT? How much does she make?" Pier answered some questions and evaded others.

"Hmm…" his ma hummed, sceptical, "And her ma, you say, sits with you when you're together? Does she work at FIAT too?"

"No. She works in a *lavanderia,* just like Nina…"

"*NO,*" his mother cut him short sharply, "*not 'like Nina',*" she mimicked. "Catlinin *owns* her own business."

It was not a comfortable end to the visit. After a few minutes' silence, Maria sent her daughters out to look for fresh-laid eggs to send home to Catlinin. In the ensuing silence, Pier laid a small bundle of banknotes on the table, nudged it toward his mother's hand. "It's not as much as last summer," he apologised. "There aren't so many weddings this time of year." Maria fingered the thick wad, then secreted it into a pocket under her apron.

"You *are* a good son," she conceded. "But I worry about you, alone out there in that city." She shook her head, a mournful, worried look in her eyes. "And now this theatre thing…"

Pier struck out along the lane to San Dalmass', burdened by the familiar let down. He'd hoped, this time, his mother would be proud of him.

No, he hadn't, he had to admit to himself. He'd *wanted* her to be proud. He'd steeled himself to tell her his news, wanting to believe that *this time* she would be pleased. But deep down he'd known she wouldn't be.

He reached the church square in a dismal mood. The car sat waiting in front of the church. Urchins hung about it in awe, under the stern eye of the driver in the front seat, like flies around a prize steer. As Pier shuffled up to the small portico, the church door flew open and Don Michel, arms wide open, rushed out to meet him. "Pier!" he cried, "I heard! But this is too marvellous! I'm so proud of you! Come in; come tell me all about it!"

The welcome cheered Pier up and at the same time stabbed him deep: why couldn't his ma greet him like this? Why couldn't she ever see that he wasn't doing anything bad?

Pier returned Don Michel's warm embrace: "I owe it all to you," he said.

"No, no…" the priest demurred, "I wouldn't go as far as that."

"If it weren't for you, I'd still be working the woods for my pa," Pier laughed.

"A lot of water under that bridge," Don Michel said. "Come on in, it's so good to see you! And I want to hear all about it."

They sat down at the table in the small room at the back of the church, and Don Michel busied himself uncorking a grungy-looking bottle.

"*Barbaresco*," he said, displaying the bottle for Pier's inspection. "Ten years old. From my brother's vineyard at La Morra. Been saving it for a special occasion, and here you are: *Salute!"*

They raised their glasses, and Pier praised the wine's rich colour, its subtle fiz, the complex texture.

"Congratulations," Don Michel said, beaming. "And, God willing, every success!"

"Thank you, Don Michel, thank you! *Salute,"* he raised his glass to touch the old priest's.

Over the next hour Pier told his tale, prompted again and again by Don Michel to fill in more details. "Ah, those were the days," the old priest sighed when Pier's tale was done, "when I had you here with me every Thursday and Sunday! I knew it wouldn't last, but it was lovely. I knew you'd go far. But I never dreamed, when I sent you to Don Carlo… And then I heard you were moving on to the duomo and, well, I knew I'd been right. I wanted to come and hear you there, but… You know how it is: I'm alone here, can't get away on Sundays. And here *you* are! But I still miss you singing mass with me…"

"And you're not…disappointed," Pier queried shyly, "about the opera?"

Don Michel gaped. "About the opera?! Why on earth would I be? You're moving on, that's all. You found…new things in the city we out here knew nothing about, and you're taking them on. I'm glad for you, proud, yes, I'm *proud!*" Pier's eyes welled up with tears. He coughed to mask his emotion.

On an impulse, he proposed, "What if…next summer, I come out and sing a mass for you…" Touched, Don Michel shook his head.

"You've better things to do nowadays," he said with a rueful smile.

"No, but I mean it. *I'd like* to come," Pier urged. "Would you let me? We'd have to plan it ahead, of course, check with Don Marco. But I am sure he wouldn't mind."

Don Michel sat gazing at Pier with deep affection, his shaggy white head shaking, half declining the offer, half from a surfeit of joy.

"What if," Pier suggested, "we tried to plan on next *San Dalmass'* day?"

"Ah, Pier!" tears welled up in the rheumy old eyes, "That would be wonderful!"

They parted with a long hug on the church steps. Don Michel followed Pier down the few steps to the waiting car, then shook his hand one more time through the window, hanging on, reluctant to see him go. The driver slipped into first gear, and the car began to slowly roll forward with Don Michel taking a few steps alongside. He only stood back when the car began to gather speed. Still he waved and waved in its wake as the motorcar gradually faded in the November dusk.

In the back seat, Pier turned for a last look at his old pastor, watching him framed in the rear window, as the dark mass that was Don Michel kept waving and waving a long farewell. Then, suddenly, right across from the church. a small light came on above the tavern door. Its door swung open and a man lurched out: his pa.

Blushing furiously, Pier cast a furtive glance at the driver: the man, intent on managing the motorcar on the rutted dirt road, stared straight ahead straining to see the road's verges in the rising ground fog. Pier stared wildly through the windshield, that last image in the rear window seared in his eyes: the church square, Don Michel and his pa. Suddenly, his ma's voice rang clear in his head, an ominous echo. "God and the devil."

Chapter Eleven

First week of Advent

The following Sunday, after the duomo mass, on his way to have lunch with Lena and her mama, Pier stood, as usual, at the rear of the tram, dazed. The events of the past week continued to replay in his mind like a disjointed dream in which normal space and time dimensions alarmingly scrambled. Up to the previous week, his life had been pretty much what it had been for the past two years, shuttling between the brutish smell and din of the factory and the timeless aura of the church, while his heart and soul yearned for some other world at the door of which he'd been blindly scratching, sensing rather than knowing what lay beyond. And now, suddenly, with last week's meeting with Don Marco and Professor Rexel, that world seemed to have thrown its doors wide open to him, to invite him in. Yet, incongruously, here he was, still doing one last week's penance at FIAT.

Somehow, in his daydreaming, Lena seemed to be the linchpin between his two worlds. During this last week at FIAT, Pier had glanced a hundred times a day in her direction. There she was at her bench, his Lena, hands busy with her work, but still intensely aware of him, of his eyes on her, now and then answering them with her sweet smile. At the same time, he'd felt a difference in her presence: she was at once the same and, somehow, in herself, other, brighter, bigger, as though some inner light illumined and magnified the solid lines of her flesh. This new Lena so filled Pier's mind and senses that he saw her, radiant, even while his eyes were focused on his work at his screaming lathe. He'd glance back at the real girl, busy at her bench in the next work station, and saw her sweet beauty, saw it with pride and awe. Yet the thought of their future together sent through him a *frisson* that held a hint of fear.

Then last Friday, when he'd walked out of FIAT for the last time, his chest had opened up in a ravenous breath, as though suddenly relieved of a burden that

237

had oppressed him all his life. He'd felt ready to take on the world, for the first time free and *alive.*

To celebrate this new sense of freedom, perhaps to *hold on to* his sense of newfound power, he had invited Lena to a film at the Cinema Corso. And this afternoon, after their Sunday lunch with Gioana, they'd go to the premier movie house in the city, right in Via Roma. But yesterday's visit to his ma had deflated the buoyant mood he had enjoyed since Friday night. The warmth of Don Michel's welcome had somewhat restored him; and this morning Don Marco's enthusiastic response to Pier's wish to sing for Don Michel on the next San Dalmass' day had brought back that expansive state he had first tasted upon leaving FIAT for the last time.

Now he sensed something about himself he couldn't quite put into words. He sensed that, at some obscure level, he had feared that trusting himself to Don Marco's plans for him meant surrendering the right to choose his own life. This morning had cleared that fear away: Don Marco honoured what *Pier* wanted to do, what he wanted to be. He was helping him to achieve it.

Acknowledging his fears and his relief, be it without words for his feelings, Pier felt how foolish he'd been: Don Marco *loved* opera. And all that time Pier had felt he had to sneak about, hiding his visits to the Regio. "But why couldn't you tell me?" Don Marco had asked at their meeting. Why indeed. Looking back on the scene in Don Marco's office, the three of them, ten days ago, Pier laughed at himself. What he had put himself through, and all for nothing! Don Marco loved opera, and he wanted to share the excitement of Pier's progress, wanted to help him pursue his dream.

In front of the Cinema Lingotto, Pier got off the tram and made for Le Basse. The corner greengrocer was just shutting down, but gladly helped Pier to three luscious persimmons, soft and heavy, wrapped them up in the usual newspaper cone. "Give my greetings to Lena," he winked, handing Pier his purchase, "and to Gioana."

"I will," Pier said, surprised that the grocer knew where he was going.

A few minutes later, he knocked on Gioana's door. "Come in, come in," Gioana welcomed him, stepping aside to let him in, "take your things off, come and warm yourself up. There's quite a *bisa* out there today." Pier handed her his newspaper cone and held out his hands to warm them up by the heat of the stove. Gioana praised the gift, smiling, "*Che bej mòj.*" (A perfect dessert.) "Come sit down. Dinner will be on the table in a moment." Pier sat down at his now customary place at the table. "Lena will be right out," Gioana added.

And indeed, in less than a minute, Lena appeared in the bedroom doorway. "*Ciao, tesòr,*" she called out to Pier. He turned towards her and his mouth gaped open. Lena, wrapped in bright red, turned right then left, showing off her new winter coat. Pier stared speechless, shocked at the vivid red colour. It was beautiful and brought a sparkle to Lena's cheeks; but… At *La Speransa,* red was a suspect hue. It stood for sinful, forbidden things.

"Don't you like it," Lena asked her voice tremulous with disappointment. Pier closed his still gaping mouth, shook his head. "I…" he stammered, "I don't… know what to say… You just …took my breath away. You look… great. It's…stunning on you…"

Lena's chin quivered, "But you don't *like* it."

Pier heard the hurt in her voice, saw her face crumple like a child's on the verge of tears. "Oh, my sweet," he cried sincerely, "I do, I do! It's just that… You took my breath away, that's all!"

Lena's hurt gave way to joy, "I'm so glad!" she cried. "I was *so afraid* you wouldn't like it! I almost bought the grey *stòfa* because of it, but this was so-o-o beautiful, I just couldn't resist. I'm so glad you like it." Now reassured, Lena now strutted back and forth across the kitchen, displaying her coat the way she'd seen models do it in the films. "I'm so glad you like it," she repeated, "I so wanted a winter coat to go *a Turin* with you."

"It looks wonderful," Pier stuttered, "but you really didn't need to…"

"No, I know, but I wanted to, *i voria nèn fete fé bruta figura an centro.*" (I didn't want to embarrass you downtown.) At that moment, Gioana placed an earthenware croc-pot on the table saying, "Come eat your dinner before it gets cold." Lena ran back to the bedroom to hang up her new coat, and then sat down next to Pier. From the centre of the table, the dish of pasta shells exuded an enticing aroma, but Lena's mind was still on overcoats. "Next," she announced, "we're going to have one made up for my mama." She patted Gioana's hand on the table. "The blue wool, *neh, Mama*? That's the one she likes best." Gioana smiled and dished out a helping of pasta onto Pier's plate.

After their meal, the three left the courtyard together, Gioana to spend the afternoon with her friend Cichin-a, Pier and Lena, arm in arm, to go to the movies at the fancy Via Roma cinema.

As soon as Gioana disappeared into her friend's building, Lena wriggled closer to Pier, excited about the special treat Pier had planned to celebrate the changes in his life. She knew that the admission tickets at *Il Corso* were at least four times those at the local cinema, and it thrilled her to be taken there. She anticipated that the downtown cinema would be as different from her neighbourhood movie house as the cathedral was from the *Lingòt* church – simply in a different class. It was a different world, and she was being taken there to a show!

Once in the cinema, they both revelled in the luxury of the baroque décor, its plush velvet seats. They also felt somewhat intimidated. Lena, proud in her brandnew coat, scanned the audience and congratulated herself: she looked as smart as any of the girls in the *primi posti*, the expensive downstairs seats Pier had bought. The older ladies…well, that was different, they wore fur coats, or at least fur stoles over their overcoats. And most of them wore hats. All of them, as far as she could see, had on leather or chamois gloves. On one gloved wrist she caught a hint of fur peeking out.

During the intermission, Pier bought chocolates from the usherette's refreshments tray. Lena recalled her Sunday afternoons at the *Lingòt* cinema: Carlin had always brought his chocolates in with him, but here one didn't have to. Everything was so much finer here. Eventually, the lights dimmed, and the program started. Sitting close together, they watched the film arms and hands entwined.

Afterwards, they strolled up one side of Via Roma and down the other, window shopping and people-watching. It was the first week of Advent, and the stores' windows sparkled with Christmas decorations and elaborate nativity scenes, airy snowflakes floating down on invisible threads. And there was the endless fascination of the displayed goods themselves.

Pier walked along, happily following Lena's lead, looking forward to taking her to *ël Caval ëd Bronz* for hot chocolate and pastries, later on, to the café in Piazza San Carlo he had watched from the shadows on the night, months ago, when he'd first discovered the elegant heart of the city. Tonight, he would be *inside the café* with his beautiful Lena. They would sit at one of those tables and be waited on by a waiter in a white jacket. Meanwhile, strolling under the Via Roma arcades, Pier thrilled at the way men's eyes lingered on Lena, his chest swelling with pride: she was his. And she did look wonderful in her new red coat!

Suddenly, his mother's disapproval flashed through his mind, clouding his pleasure – Lena in a red coat, today's extravagance… He shrugged, refusing to let the momentary gloom spoil his day. On his arm, Lena stopped to gaze at the display in a *Pelletteria*. In its window, leather goods were exhibited with artful sparseness. "*Coccodrillo*," she stammered out the unfamiliar word printed on a small, gold-rimmed card next to a large travel bag. "What is that bumpy stuff?"

"That's crocodile," Pier told her.

"What's that?"

"It's…like a big lizard."

"And that? And that?" Lena's interest shifted from item to item, her catechism continuing and Pier doing his best to satisfy her questions, making up an answer by sheer invention for whatever he did not know.

Eventually, Lena moved on, then stopped again, this time by a jeweller's window, dazzled by the important jewellery displayed – tiaras, matching sets of necklace, earrings and bracelet, impressive rings with diamonds surrounding fabulous coloured stones.

"There are no prices," Lena noted.

"People who buy those things don't care about prices," Pier informed her.

"Hmmm, that must be nice…" Lena said with a wistful little laugh, and stepped away from the window, snuggling up tighter on Pier's arm. Together they weaved a leisurely course through the flow of elegant Sunday strollers. From time to time, they had to duck out of the arcade to get around knots of people - family groups, parties of young men, couples - that had congealed in the middle of the pavement, obstructing traffic.

Returning from one such detour, Lena drifted towards a furrier's window. She felt, so *a post* today, in her new red coat and with Pier at her side, so very right with the world. But furs… *they*, now, set the rich apart as a fascinating, unapproachable world. She moved up to the display as though drawn by a magnet: "*Ma che bele sté plisse… Che ròba bela…*" (What beautiful furs), she sighed, gazing longingly from fur to fur. "Such beautiful things. Look at that one," she cried, leaning in closer to the glass, "the one with the dark spots. What is it? I've never seen anything like that." Pier admired and speculated. "That one there," he pointed to a tawny coat glazed with long silver hair that reminded him of the tail of the foxes his pa shot in the woods. "That's fox."

They strolled on. Eventually they reached *ël Caval ëd Bronz*. The café's maitre, in striped trousers and cut-away coat, met them just inside the door, bowed, escorted them to a table in the middle of the room, then snapped his fingers at a waiter who swooped to their table in response to the summons. Pier ordered hot chocolate. "With whipped cream," he emphasised. The waiter bowed and left.

"I've never eaten whipped cream," Lena whispered with awed-happy anticipation.

Starry-eyed, she looked around. Her eyes travelled from the mirrors that covered the walls behind the bar's counter, to the gleaming brass sconces on the polished walnut panelling, to the coffered ceiling. "It's all so beautiful here," she sighed.

Pier sat, enjoying her awe, smiling with pride: even here, men's eyes lingered on Lena.

Movement in the café's centre aisle drew their attention: a waiter was escorting an elegant couple to a secluded table. Pier caught a whiff of fragrance and was reminded of the lady who had swept by him under the arches on that first night. This woman, too, was a lady. She, too, was swathed in furs.

As the couple passed, the man's eyes lingered on Lena. Pier smiled. And Lena was his.

He turned to her and whispered passionately in her ear: "I'd like to cover *you* in furs and jewels one day...."

Lena turned a grateful, blissful, adoring eye on Pier, gazing deep into his grey-green eyes

"Your hot chocolates, sir." The waiter said, setting his tray down on the table, delicately arranging the steaming cups in front of first Lena, then Pier. He bowed to each in turn, his eyes lingering a long moment on the girl in the red coat. Pier smiled, glowing.

That afternoon, Guido was strolling down Via Roma with a few friends when he caught sight of Lena. He blinked and looked again: Lena in a red coat! What was *she* doing, gazing into a jeweller's window?

He stopped short. It had been weeks since he'd laid eyes on her. Not since that Sunday at the *Lingòt* café, when he'd seen her with that farmer boy.

He hadn't been in *Lingòt* much lately, not since he had taken over the membership roster for the *Borg San Paul Fascio,* and moved to better rooms off *Cors Re Umbert* – a much better part of town, a more influential class of people. But Lena in a red coat... He sneered: a shawl was what he'd expect to see her in.

He shifted his eyes to her escort, expecting the Sella boy. But it wasn't he. Guido glowered, studying the new man. Who was this jerk?

The jerk was hovering over the bitch, pointing to something in the jeweller's window. What was he up to, promising a bauble? "A bauble for your charms, m'dear," he sneered to himself.

His pals had stopped in the middle of the arcade, hotly disputing the latest football match, obstructing pedestrian traffic. He rejoined their group, but hung out on its fringes so that he could continue to watch Lena and her new man: he was young, younger than the Sella boy. Town-bred, he'd say. Well, maybe. One didn't see that build or that carriage in the country, not even among the well-to-do. Farm work thickened you, made you stockier, taught you to move slowly.

Watching the other, Guido squared his own shoulders in their tailor-made overcoat, proud of his own figure. His own brothers looked what they were, farmer's sons. His hand surreptitiously patted his abs: his stretch of athletic youth leadership at the *Lingòt Fascio* had made his body hard and trim.

By the jeweller's window, Lena laughed, a happy, tinkling peal. Her companion gave her a sideways hug and a peck on her cheek, and she gazed up at him adoringly. Guido flushed with anger: the bitch was in love. He restrained the impulse to go and strike the jerk. "Must find out who he is," he growled to himself.

His friends were moving on, dragging him along with them. He glanced he had to keep a clear head about his own best interests. But this was not the time to make waves, not with his new post at the *Fascio*. Nor was it the time to draw attention to himself *over a girl*, not with Maria Cristina Follati in the wings.

He moved on with his group. He had his way to make in this city, and the Follati girl's dowry and connections fitted his plans very well. She wasn't Lena, but she wasn't bad looking. And her father's money and position would satisfy both his own ambitions and his parents' narrow mindedness. The girl was city-bred, like he wanted, and the Follati wine export business had its roots in their family's holdings in the Asti hills. Their vineyards did not adjoin *Colin-a Longa,* like his brother's wife's dowry, but their connections could bring him the influence he craved. "Besides," he sneered, casting one last look at the couple by the jeweller's window, "I prefer to deal with my…rivals on my own terms."

Pier visits Collegio Sacro Cuore

On the first day of the Christmas school holidays, Pier went to visit the *Collegio Sacro Cuore,* the boys' boarding school that was part of Don Marco's educational plan for him. Pier approached the impending interview with the college headmaster in a state of mind fraught with excitement and apprehension. He knew that it was an opportunity beyond his wildest dreams, but couldn't shake a fear that he would be seen through, judged not suitable for the job, even more, not suitable to live among the kind of people who taught at, or were sent to, private schools.

On the tram, leaning against a rear window as was his habit, he gazed at the unfamiliar area of town he was traveling through with mixed discomfort and mistrust. He couldn't quite specify how, but these buildings felt hostile. He found them intimidating, though he couldn't figure out what made them so. Then, during a tram stop, he caught sight of two caryatids supporting a second story balcony. He stared at them, noticing their faces, the muscular arms, the stone carvings around each window and door. Then his eyes rose to the elaborate wrought iron fretwork on the railing. By the time the tram moved on he had something to explain why the buildings felt so alien: they were very fancy. He began to focus on individual buildings the tram passed with a different eye, noticing differences, liking one better than its neighbour. He appreciated that, while this area was different, it reminded him of the upper stories along Via Roma. But then, on the very next block, the familiar fascist daubs, **VIVA IL DUCE - CREDERE, OBBEDIRE, COMBATTER -***,* **CHI SI FERMA È PERDUTO,** appeared on the walls of the elegant buildings. They offended him, just as they did in Via Roma and Piazza San Carlo.

By the time he rang the brass bell set in the frame of the boarding school's massive portals he was eager to see what *this* beautiful *palazzo* was like inside. After several minutes, a pass-through door, set in one panel of the portals, was opened to him by a young cleric, and he stepped into an impressive covered entryway, paved in polished-granite. At its far end Pier caught a glimpse of a cobbled courtyard, bathed in a pale wintry sun and, in its centre an ice-glazed fountain – a sculpture of a young boy with his dog. Midway inside the entryway, two broad flights of granite steps disappeared, right and left, into the upper regions.

"This way, please," his young guide said, leading him up a few steps to a corridor on the ground floor, "The headmaster is expecting you."

Pier followed him, his heart thumping hard. The young cleric stopped at an oak door and knocked. Inside, a firm voice called out, "enter."

The cleric pushed the door open and announced, "Pier Venturi, Father." The priest, busy at a vast desk, lifted one hand and waved Pier in. Pier stepped in and stopped just inside the door. Wintry daylight filtered into the room through two tall windows, their wrought iron grills casting shadowy scrolls onto the highly polished floor.

"Come sit down," the priest at the desk said, continuing to write on the notebook in front of him. "I'll be right with you."

Pier squared his shoulders and stepped forward, stopping in front of the vast desk. The master sat with his back to the window and the green-shaded desk lamp cast a bright cone of light on the papers he was working on, but left the man's head in shadow. Pier waited, silently taking deep breaths to steady himself.

"Have a seat," the headmaster repeated, still without looking up from his writing. Pier sat down in one of the two leather-covered visitors' chairs facing the desk. His hands found the wooden arms, unconsciously gripping them. Then he became aware that his palms had started to sweat. *Relax,* he scolded himself, and deliberately loosened his arms. Opposite him, the priest lay down his pen, closed his notebook, and, at last, looked up.

"So!" he said, folding his white hands in front of him. Pier noticed them, and quickly slipped his callused hands under his thighs.

"It seems you're going to join us for a while," the headmaster said, surveying Pier's face. "I hear a lot of good things about you. Don Luca will be glad of your assistance."

"I'll do my best, Father."

"And we'll do our best by you. Don Marco tells me that you want to catch up on your general education while you're with us. We'll put together a program for you, a list of classes you can sit in on, and work out who's going to follow your studies here. You mustn't mind that the boys here are much younger than you. You will not be identified as one of the students. You'll be the music master's assistant."

The rest of the interview did not take long. Within fifteen minutes, the headmaster pressed a bell, then handed Pier a fat manual, titled simply *Studi al Sacro Cuore.* "Take a look at that," he said. "It will tell you what to expect, *and* what the *collegio* expects of all its members." There was a discrete knock on the door, and a middle-aged priest entered.

"Ah, Don Luca," the headmaster said. "Here's your new assistant, Pier Venturi. I'll leave you to discuss how he's going to assist you, and to show him around." He returned his attention to his paperwork as Pier and his guide left the office.

The tour started with the chapel, set in its own cloistered courtyard. "Our weekday services," Don Luca explained, lingering in the choir section, "stick to Gregorian chants. I hear you're an old hand at them. For Sundays and Holy Days, we work up other kinds of scores. Of course, our students go home for Xmas and Easter, so we adjust our schedule of performances to their schedule. Right now, we are working on Palestrina. I believe Don Marco said you play the harmonium…"

"A bit."

"Good, good, that'll help with practice. Of course, I will tell you each week what I want you to work on with the boys. With your fourteen years' experience, you should have no difficulty."

"I'll do my best."

They moved on, crossing two more cloistered courtyards, Don Lucas explaining as they walked that the school offered the entire range of secondary education, so that there were three sets of boys, attending the *Scuola Media,* the *Ginnasio,* and the *Liceo.* "So, you see, our boys range from eleven to eighteen. In the choir you'll be working right away with all ages, but in the classroom, we will let you start with the younger boys."

Eighteen, Pier thought. *I was set to work on the farm at six, and at ten I was sent out to earn my living at Teit Piat.* He listened, nodding, keeping his thoughts to himself.

They passed into a different courtyard. "This quadrangle," Don Luca informed him, "is the *Scuola Media.* The layout is the same in all three school units – classrooms and offices on the main floor, day quarters and some master's offices on the second, dormitories on the third."

Pier followed his guide, listening, struggling to keep his bearings in the maze of information, courtyards, stairways and corridors. He kept thinking of his Volvera schoolhouse, two whitewashed rooms, one for boys and one for girls, all grades together. And even *that* cut short by winter snows and the big farm works. And by Pa's demand that he does his share of work on the farm.

Now Don Luca was climbing to an upper floor of the *Ginnasio* quadrangle. He pushed a door open and stood back, an invitation to Pier to enter. "This is your room," he said.

It was a small room, just enough space for a bed on one side of the single window, and a desk on its other side. A small wardrobe stood next to the entry door.

"I trust you'll find it comfortable."

Pier almost laughed: comfortable! He'd never even had a *bed* of his own. He looked out of the window, at the flagstone courtyard below. "It'll be perfect," he said, stepping back out into the corridor.

Don Luca closed the door behind them. "Our junior teachers serve as house proctors," he explained, "so their rooms are upstairs with the dormitories. But you won't have any overseeing duties after class and practice. You'll be able to come and go more freely from this floor. Any questions?"

Pier shook his spinning head. They headed back down.

"You'll soon get used to the tram lines to the cathedral and to the Regio," Don Luca assured him, unlatching and pulling open a side door to the street. "Neither is very far. There's a stop right there. See you on the seventh."

Pier crossed the avenue and stood at the tram stop opposite the door he'd just left. He gazed up at the *collegio,* overwhelmed: it took up a whole city block. He tried to figure out where, in the labirynth of floors, windows and courtyards, his room was located. On the second floor, he told himself, overlooking a courtyard. But he had no idea where.

My own room! he thought and laughed out loud. The thought took his breath away. No more blankets laid down under Nina's counter. He felt like breaking into a run, kicking up his heels and yodelling. But a well-dressed woman was approaching the tram stop, a little girl by the hand. And, across the avenue, the impressive dignity of the sober grey *palazzo* restrained him. He imagined Don Luca looking out of one of those windows and seeing his future assistant caper about for joy. He disguised his grin by casting his eyes down.

But he couldn't stand still. Under the staring eyes of the little girl, he glanced down the empty tramline, as though checking for an oncoming tram, then, with a shrug, he struck out briskly up the avenue towards the next stop.

Pier proposes

Pier's commitments at the duomo during the weeks leading up to Christmas became so all-consuming that he had no time for personal celebrations. He wanted to be with Lena, but during the morning hours, which were his only free ones, she was at FIAT. He worried that he would offend her if he did not spend Christmas with her, but he had to sing both at the midnight Christmas Eve mass and at the noon one on Christmas day, so he wouldn't be free until after two o'clock. He hesitated to broach the subject with her, but finally did on the last Sunday of Advent.

"I've been worrying that I won't be able to be with you over Christmas," he said.

"I've been worried too," Lena answered. "I don't want you to be hurt if we do not spend it together. I mean you and me especially. But…my mama and I always go to midnight mass with Cichin-a and her daughter. We also cook Christmas dinner together, at her place." She glanced at Pier to gauge his reaction, then went on, "My *mama* says to invite you to join us, but I wasn't sure you'd want to come. I mean, it's just us women."

Pier heaved a sigh of relief. "I wouldn't mind at all, I'd like to," he said, "but *our Messa Solenne* won't be over until well after one."

"Then just come when you can. Cichin-a said we'll keep your dinner warm for you. She always makes *agnolòt e capon.*"

"Well, if you're sure Cichin-a won't mind," Pier said, "I could be there around two thirty."

"I'm sure she won't mind. She said so."

"All right then. I'll bring the *panaton.*"

The Christmas problem solved, Pier was still not satisfied. He craved time alone with Lena, time for private talk, and that just couldn't happen at the Christmas dinner. So what he had to say would just have to wait. "But…" he started, taking Lena's hands in his, "let's have New Year's Eve together, just you and me."

Lena beamed. "Just you and me *alone*! That'll be so lovely!"

"Well, wherever we go, there'll be lots of other people. But it'll still be just you and me alone."

"Oh," she clapped her hand in excitement. "You're taking me somewhere! Where are we going?"

"The Regio is doing *Il Barbiere di Siviglia.* I'd like to take you to that."

"What's that, a new movie?" Lena asked, glowing at the memory of their outing to the Cinema Corso.

"No, it's an opera. They're playing it on New Year's Eve."

"But…at the Regio!" she cried, alarmed, movies images of ladies going to the theatre in evening gowns crowding her mind. "I don't have anything to wear!"

Pier shrugged. "What you wore to the Corso is just fine. You'll look lovely."

"But doesn't one wear evening dress to the opera?"

"The…toffs do, but they are in the boxes or downstairs in the *platea*. We'll be up in the top gallery. Your black skirt will do very nicely. And…" he rubbed his hands, "I have a little surprise for you, your Christmas present."

"A surprise! Oh, tell me what it is," she demanded, clapping her hands. Laughing, Pier caught them in his and kissed them.

"No. That would spoil the surprise."

So, on New Year's Eve they stood outside the Regio, arm in arm in the nipping December cold, inching forward in the long queue of gallery operagoers. One of the billboards announced the upcoming performance of Verdi's *Mefistofele*. "*Che brut!*" Lena laughed, pointing to Aurelio Pertile in his Mephisto costume. A little puff of white mist hovered in front of her mouth. "Do you know all these people?" she asked. Pier squirmed, always loathe to admit ignorance.

"I've read about them in *LA STAMPA*," he said.

"He looks like the devil," she observed. "What's the story?"

"He *is* the devil*,*" Pier answered, taking a guess, "if you like, I'll bring the libretto and we can read it together."

She snuggled up closer to him. "That'll be nice."

Little by little, the queue inched forward and eventually they got out of the bone-chilling cold. Once in their seats, perched up high in the top gallery, they sat, hands demurely interlaced on the armrest between them. Lena craned her neck to check out the surroundings: up here, she was satisfied that she looked right in her black wool skirt and fine knitted top, Pier's surprise Christmas gift. Her hand rose to finger the modest beaded border at its neckline, her glance drifting down, attracted by the muted whining in the orchestra pit, the string instruments being tweaked ready. Her eyes lingered on the downstairs audience, then up in the boxes. It was a very different world. Lavish gowns, furs, the sparkle of jewellery on bosoms, fingers, wrists and hair. She spotted the little crowns that had puzzled her in the Via Roma jeweller's window. And the men down there were just like the gentlemen in the movies, in evening suits with sparkling white fronts.

The house lights dimmed and there was silence. The conductor appeared, greeted by loud applause, from a side door, strode to the podium. Tingling with anticipation, Pier squeezed Lena's hand, leaned his head to hers and whispered, "That's *Maestro* Guy." Lena beamed at him.

She was still gazing around at the audience when the orchestra erupting into the overture startled her, drew her attention to the rising curtain and the stage set, the exterior of a stylised Spanish house in the grey light of dawn. She watched a band of musician stroll onto stage from the wings, strumming, then a gentleman step forward, gaze longingly at a second story window and sigh, before intoning the opening aria, *Ecco ridente in cielo, to* coax the sleeping Rosina out of bed. "That's Almaviva, the count," Pier whispered, close to Lena's ear, the libretto open on the armrest between them. They had read it together during the past weeks. Lena smiled at him. With a little shiver of excitement, her eyes returned to the stage, eager to see Rosina appear, even though she knew the girl wouldn't for quite a while.

The next couple of hours flew by in a merry riot of music, spectacle and intrigue. They left the theatre humming the opera's highlights together. "That was such fun!" Lena cried, emerging once again into the bitter cold. *"Io sono docile…"* she sang in a flat, off-key voice. Pier thrilled at his Lena's excitement: she had enjoyed her first opera! It would be a passion they could share. Lena skipped happily, snuggling closer to him. "It's the best New Year's Eve I've ever had!" Pier laughed, sneaking in a kiss to her neck.

"And it isn't over yet," he cried. She giggled and tucked her chin down into the red coat collar to evade his kiss, but didn't pull away. "We are going to toast the New Year in," Pier told her. "It's almost time. Come, let's hurry before the old crockery start flying out of windows."

Hand in hand, they ran down a side street, then down a flight of stairs to a basement club. "What's this?" Lena cried, trotting down the steps next to him, "We're going to a cellar?"

"Not just any old cellar. This's the famous *Tampa Lirica,"* Pier explained. "It's a singer's hang out. You'll see. Quick, get in before the clock strikes."

He pushed the club's door open onto a large, vaulted and very crowded, space. Inside, broad masonry arches rose all around a dance floor, creating a ring of alcoves, now packed with revellers. Between the alcoves and the dance floor, a ring of revellers, young and old, crowded together, swaying to the rhythm of one of the *Traviata* choruses, *Ah godiam… La tazza e il cantico La notte abbella e il riso; In questo paradiso Ne scopra il nuovo dí* – let's enjoy ourselves, wine, song and laughter make this a beautiful night; let daylight find us in the paradise. Then the ring of revellers formed into a line, hands on the hips of the person in front, still singing, moving forward in a dance step. Pier found a break in the snake and joined in, steering Lena in front of him. She twittered and blushed, but picked up the step, dancing joyously, eyes looking over her shoulder more often than not, seeking Pier's. Then the imperative rat-ta-tat of an invisible drum demanded attention as a portly gentleman in a red peaked hat stepped out from the musicians arch and into the centre of the room, gathering the revellers around him, calling out in a strong bass voice: *"Attenzione! Arriva l'ora fatal!"*

The snake formed a wavy circle around him, friends and strangers joined hands, while a steady drumbeat punctuated the passing of time, one stroke per second. Invisible in the background, strings sustained a muted hum. When the bass called out "TEN!" the throng of revellers picked up the call, loudly clapping out the countdown, pressing forward towards the central space: NINE! EIGHT! SEVEN… On the ONE, the drum rolled madly and the lights went out. A collective gasp died into a second of total silence before bright lights sprung back and the crowd roared, BUON ANNO! FELICE ANNO NUOVO! VIVA IL 1926! Streamers crossed the air, confetti fluttered down, lodging into hair, *décolletés,* on black evening suits, and the circle dissolved into clusters of friends and acquaintances, some drifting towards the tables in the recesses, others, on the centre floor, starting to dance to the strains of *The Blue Danube*, while waiters scuttled around with trays of sparkling wine. Pier gathered Lena's hand and launched into the waltz.

When the music came to an end, Pier drew Lena to a vacant settee in one of the alcoves. *"Buon Anno, tesoro!"* he said in Italian, gazing deep into her eyes. His stemmed glass clinked against hers.

Lena answered with another Italian formula of New Year's wishes, *"Felice Anno Nuovo!"* Then she switched to her familiar *Piemontèis.* "It *will* be a good new year, the best year of my life. You and me together! I'm so happy!" They hugged blissfully for a moment. Then Pier pulled his head back.

"Then I can ask you," he said, at once excited and scared, "Will you marry me, Lena?" He drew breath to elaborate, to explain what he'd been preparing for days to say: they'd have to wait – no money, no job even, right now, just dreams. But she stopped his words with kisses.

"I will! I will! Of course, I will! Pier, *mio caro,* I'm so very happy!"

"We'll have to wait, you know," he finally got out.

"I know, I know! But it doesn't matter, we're together!"

"I don't know *when* we'll be able to…"

"I know, and it doesn't matter. What matters is that *you want* to!"

"Oh, I do!" he cried. "I've been wanting to ask you for months, but I had nothing to offer you. Even now… I have no money. No job, even. Right now I can't even buy you a ring. "

Lena interrupted him, "You will when you can. And then we'll get married." Pier arched his back to hold her eyes while he said what he need to say. "And starting next week I'll be living at the *Sacro Cuore,"* he added all in a rush. "It's a *boys'* school. So, you see, we can't be together there. Don Marco has promised he'll put me onto as many weddings and functions as he can, but it may be *years* before I can make a living as a singer."

Lena was silent, serious for a moment, studying his face, then she shrugged. "So," she said, "we'll just wait. Meantime, *I* have a job and I can start saving for when we can."

Hours later, they left *La Tampa Lirica* closely entwined. They ambled slowly, ignoring the clatter of a distant tram, the last of the night. It would be a long walk home to *Lingòt*, but they didn't care. She walked with her head on his shoulder, he with his cheek against her hair, both oblivious to the cold. After a while, Pier placed a soft kiss on her hair. He was struck by its scent. His breath warm on her head, he murmured, "For now it might be better to keep our engagement secret. I'd like to take you to meet *mia mama* first," he added, adopting her town *Piemontèis* way of referring to one's mother. It came natural to speak *Piemontèis* with her. Somehow, speaking Italian set up an invisible distance between them, almost a barrier he didn't want.

Without lifting her head from his shoulder, she nodded. After a while she ventured, tentatively, "But… We could tell my mama, couldn't we?"

"Yes, of course, let's go tell her right now. But she'll have to keep it to herself."

Pier moves into *Collegio Sacro Cuore*

That year the feast of the Epiphany marked a new start in Pier's life. Moving out from Nina's *retro* and into the *Collegio Sacro Cuore,* he was leaving behind the world of struggle for bare survival and stepping into the world of middleclass culture in which the young went to school and were allowed to have dreams. At Santa Rita's, at the cathedral, and last year at the Regio, Pier had been scratching at the gate of that world. Now, with the Regio scholarship and the move into the *collegio* as a master's assistant, he felt admitted into that world's privileged enclosure. He felt the excitement of this shift in his very bones.

He spent the afternoon of the *Epifania* in Nina's *retro*, packing his brandnew suitcase. He did not want to arrive at the *collegio* with a bundle on his shoulder, the way he had arrived in Santa Rita's, three years earlier. His new suitcase lay open on the couch that had been his bed in his sister's kitchen, and Pier gazed at it with pride: it wasn't leather, but it was smart enough, its canvas sides bound by leather-trimmed seams and corners.

On top of his odds and ends of clothing, he carefully laid into the new suitcase the two suits he had acquired last summer under Signora Agiati's guidance. With a last smoothing stroke to the lapels, a caress really, he closed the lid and snapped the brass latches shut. He stood his packed suitcase by the *retro*'s courtyard door, next to the old leather briefcase Don Marco had passed on to him to carry his scores in. Pier looked at his two-piece luggage with satisfaction: he would arrive at *Sacro Cuore* in respectable style.

Behind him, the door squeaked open and Nina came in from the courtyard. "Oh," she said with a glance at the waiting luggage, "you're already packed. I was going to do it for you."

"No need," Pier said.

Nina stepped up to him and brushed at the shoulder of the old grey suit he was wearing. "Well, don't you go spend money on dry cleaning," she said. "You bring your suits and shirts to me, once a week. I can still look after them for you."

"Like you haven't enough to do," Pier said, gruff, but touched.

"No, but I mean it," Nina insisted. "And don't you go forgetting us…"

"Like I ever would!"

They stood facing each other by the door, tongue-tied. Then Pier said, "I'd better go. I'm supposed to be there before the evening meal."

"I'll walk you to the tram," Nina said, picking up his briefcase.

Bundled up against the January cold, they ambled shoulder to shoulder towards the terminal, Nina carrying the baby on her left hip and his briefcase in her right hand, little Anna trotting along on Pier's left, holding on to the handle of his suitcase, her smooth child's hand against his rough, labourer's one.

At the terminal, the waiting tram's open front door exhaled its stale breath. Pier set down his suitcase next to it. "Don't forget us now," Nina said again, eyes shiny.

"You're just like Ma," Pier tried to scold. "You'd think I was off to America. I'll be all of a half hour tram ride away."

Nina nodded, forcing a smile. A half hour's tram ride and a world away. She handed him his briefcase. He leaned forward to place one last kiss on the baby's cheek, then squatted down by Anna and held her tight in a long, long hug. Straightening up, he stood facing Nina for a long silent moment.

The tram driver, now at the controls, glared at them, a hand locked onto the door's lever, impatient to close his doors against the cold. Seeing them linger, he stamped on his bell pedal. Pier climbed aboard, suitcase and briefcase in hand. Behind him the door hissed shut with a clatter, and the tram ground into motion. Pier staggered his way along the lurching tram toward the rear window: on the sidewalk, Nina and Anna stood waving to him, while the baby gazed after the tram, a thumb in her mouth. Pier waved back, a lump in his throat, forcing a grin.

Half an hour later, still heavy with the sadness of the farewell and angry about his sadness, he stood by the side door of the *Sacro Cuore* which led directly into the *Ginnasio* quadrangle, where his room was located. Almost reluctantly, he rang the bell. A friendly young priest opened the door and led him up the stairs. Pier followed him in silence. On the second floor, his guide unlocked a door and reached in to switch on the light.

"With our headmaster's welcome," he said, handing Pier a key to the street door. The room key remained in the lock. "Supper is in forty-five minutes," he added. "I'll come get you, show you the way to the dining room."

Pier latched the door behind him, glad to see the other go. He needed to be alone, to dispel that last image of Nina and the children waving goodbye as the tram pulled away. An odd weight oppressed him, made him feel cheated and somehow guilty. He should be happy, excited to be here. He *was!* And yet he felt awful in these new surroundings, in the new conditions of his life, knowing that Nina and the children were stuck in his old world.

Trying to shake the mood off, he made a conscious effort to inspect *his room*. The small wardrobe by the door prompted him to heft his suitcase onto the bed, preparatory to unpacking. Under its weight, the bed gave a slight bounce. Surprised, Pier pressed down on it with one hand, then sat down, testing the soft-firm give: there must be *springs* underneath the mattress!

He glanced around the room. The desk under the window loomed aggressively bare under its large green blotter. Pier's old briefcase looked oddly out of place on the desk chair, quite forlorn.

With a sigh, Pier stood up and stepped over to the desk. Listlessly, he opened the briefcase and began to pull out his scores and his few books, stacked them in the small bookcase against the wall. He placed the volume of *La Fortuna dei Rougon* he was currently reading, on the night table, next to the bed.

And then he saw it. No, that wasn't correct, he'd seen it before, but it hadn't sunk in: a small, bedside lamp, on the night table. It had a switch on its base so you could turn it on and off without getting out of bed.

Pier sat down on the bed, and his hand tentatively reached for the switch. A circle of light defined by the white shade, spread half-way across the bed's width. Pier switched the lamp off, then leaning back against the pillows, he stretched out his legs, straddling the open suitcase at the foot of the bed, then switched the lamp on again, basking in its circle of light. He switched it off, then on again. He raised himself on one elbow, picked up his book and opened it: he could read in bed!

With an excited sigh of satisfaction, he closed the book, carefully laid it back on the night table. Then he sat up and inspected *his* room yet again. The wardrobe next to the door seemed to be inviting him to stow the contents of the suitcase on its shelves and hangers. The room no longer felt alien. It was up to him to make it his own.

He got up and started to unpack. He hung his suits and stacked his underwear, socks and few shirts neatly, each on a different shelf. At the bottom of his suitcase, under the heavy raw wool sweater he'd brought from the farm, lay *Studi al Sacro Cuore,* the school manual he had been given at his before-Christmas interview. He had been pouring over it for the past two weeks, but now he decided to refresh his memory while waiting for the dinner call. He laid it on the bed, closed and latched his suitcase, stowed it neatly atop of the wardrobe, surveying the room for a moment before settling down to read. It looked neat again, but now the stowed suitcase atop the wardrobe declared that the room belonged to someone. It belonged to him.

Pleased, Pier stretched out on the bed, turned on the bedside lamp, leaned back on his pillows, opened the manual and began to review the section on the *collegio*'s dining room etiquette.

The expected knock on the door startled Pier. He leapt off the bed and rushed to the door just as the clear tinkle of a bell rang out through the building.

"There it is," said the young priest with a friendly smile from the hallway, "the house bell. You'll get used to its calls, and by and by you'll figure out which you need to heed, and which are not for you. Are you ready?"

Pier cast a quick glance over the room, joined him in the hallway, latching his door behind them. "By the way," his guide said, "I'm Don Marcello. I joined *Sacro Cuore* last October. My first teaching post." He grimaced. "Scared stiff. But our boys are well behaved."

They headed down the stairs and along a series of corridors towards the first-floor dining room. Pier tried to memorise each turn, but was soon disoriented. "Tonight," Don Marcello explained, "the *collegio* is still empty. The boys will drift back tomorrow. Then you'll be able to follow the noise down," he grinned. "Here we are."

Across a handsome foyer, a steady stream of cassocks converged towards wide double doors, now flung open. Here and there a few sober suits mingled with the cassocks. Chatting, the schoolmasters entered the dining room, climbed onto a dais and found their seats at the head table or at one of two auxiliary ones that formed a U facing an array of some thirty pupils' refectory tables down the length of the hall. On the far side of the dais, an oak lectern held a large open book, a spotlight clipped to its wooden edge. At the far end of the room, the centre aisle ended in an ample stained-glass window, a Sacred Heart dripping blood through Christ's cradling fingers.

When most of the seats at the high table were occupied, Don Marcello led Pier in. "This is your seat, with us junior masters." He pulled out the next chair. "We can sit down while we wait for the headmaster."

Pier sat and looked around. Behind the head table, a vast crucified Christ hung upon the wall. Beneath it, the head table, facing the hall, had chairs only on the side facing the body of the hall. The two side tables had chairs on both sides. "Ah, Pier," a voice said behind him. Pier stood up and bowed to Don Luca, the *collegio's* music master. "Sit down, sit down," the music master said. "You got here all right. Had a chance to settle in?"

"Yes, Don Luca, thank you. Everything's very comfortable."

"Excellent. Tomorrow, come down to my office after breakfast and we'll go over your duties and your classes."

Don Luca moved on to his place at the high table and engaged in conversation with the elderly priest in the next chair. A few minutes later, a silvery bell tinkled, announcing the entrance of Don Cornelio, the headmaster. The buzz of conversation subsided, replaced by the scraping of chairs and the rustling of cassock standing up. The headmaster stood behind his chair, briefly surveyed the three tables, and signaled the stuff to sit down, before he addressed them.

"Only one brief announcement tonight," he said. "I ask you all to welcome the new member of our staff, Pier Venturi." Under the table, Don Marcello nudged Pier's knee, and he stood up, ears blazing, and sketched a bow to the high table, then to the two side tables. "Pier is here to assist Don Luca," the headmaster continued. "Young as he is, Pier comes to us with fourteen years of experience in sacred music, first at his home parish, then at Santa Rita's, and this past year at the cathedral, with Don Marco Veronese, who very kindly is lending him to us." Cassocks again rustled as bodies twisted on their chairs, and faces smiled at the newcomer. Don Cornelio continued, "Pier will be studying lyric opera with Professor Rexel at the Regio. Please introduce yourselves to him after supper and give him your assistance in settling in with us." He sat down.

One of the cassocks got up, went to the lectern and started to read aloud from the open book: "...and when they drew nigh onto Jerusalem..." The reader finished the text for the day and returned to his seat. There followed a few minutes of silence, heads bowed, then the headmaster tinkled his bell and the supper service began, delivered by a crew of lay brothers. The buzz of conversation resumed. At his table, Pier found himself the centre of interest through the first part of the meal. Then, the conversation shifted, and he discovered that the *collegio* put on two oratorios every year, one during Advent and the other, upcoming, a prelude to the Easter season, before the students went home from their spring break.

Throughout the meal, Pier's attention was divided between this chatter around him, and the stream of dishes that kept following each other. Along the centre of the table, three bowls, one of fruit, one of nuts and one of *bischeuit,* chestnuts first boiled, then dried up in the oven, an after-dinner delicacy. Pier's mouth kept watering in anticipation, even while he was enjoying the hearty stew.

After the meal, Don Marcello led Pier out of the dining room and drew his attention to a stand of cyclamen massed on a centre table. There they stood, admiring, their bodies angled to welcome anyone wishing to approach them. One by one, the teachers stopped by and introduced themselves and welcomed the newcomer. Soon, names, faces, and subjects of study swam in Pier's mind. He longed to run from this throng and to retreat to the seclusion of his room.

As the last cassock said good night and drifted towards a staircase, Pier looked around, uncertain which way to go.

"There you are," Don Marcello grinned at him, "officially welcomed. Going back to your room?" he asked, casually leading the way out of the foyer. "I'll walk with you as far as the parting of our ways. Tomorrow the boys will be here. You'll be able to follow their noise to your room – and at times you'll wish you couldn't," he added with a grin. "You'll have no trouble with the younger lot. The upperclassmen," he grimaced, "…they can be a handful. Most are all right, but there's always the odd snotty troublemaker."

At the foot of a staircase he stopped. "My room's that way," he said, "yours is up these stairs. Second floor and to the right. Good night. See you tomorrow."

Pier took the next flight of stairs at the decorous pace befitting a master's assistant. But once out of sight on the first landing, he cast a quick look at the now silent stairwell below, and scrambled up to his new room three steps at a time, eager to be there and alone. Once inside, he locked the door and leaned his back against it, heaving a huge breath, like a diver coming up for air. Still taut, he took in the room in front of him: *his* room. He began to relax. He strolled over to the window and looked out. Across the dark courtyard, a few windows glowed yellow on the second and third floors. He recalled now that the first two floors housed offices and classrooms, and the third sleeping quarters. Down below, all he could see was the vague paleness of snow.

He turned to his still virgin desk, switched on the reading lamp, sat down, and slid drawers open. He had nothing to put into them yet. Tomorrow he'd find out what he needed at his meeting with the music master.

He switched off the desk lamp and switched on the one on the nightstand. The light on his pillow brought a smile to his face.

He began to undress, carefully hanging up his jacket in the wardrobe. The sharp smell of soap drew his attention to his shaving kit, rolled up in one of

Nina's clean, white towels. He had started to slip off his suspenders, but now he stopped: he couldn't remember where the washroom was. Don Lucas had told him two weeks ago, but he couldn't remember. He considered doing without. He wouldn't want to get caught bumbling along the corridors. And he was used to holding on, both at *La Speransa* and in Nina's courtyard, to avoid the night cold on the way to the outhouse.

Then it occurred to him that, if he didn't find it tonight, he'd have to find it in the morning, and there might be more people about. He slipped his suspenders back onto his shoulders and set out on his quest, towel-wrapped soap under his arm.

Half an hour later, refreshed by his wash, he switched off the ceiling light and got into bed by the light of his bedside lamp. He basked in the unspeakable luxury of his soft, warm bed. The fresh, crisp sheets brought him a pleasant hint of familiarity – the smell of Nina's *lavanderia.* He lay there, enjoying the pattern of light and shadows the shade of his bedside lamp cast on ceiling and walls. His eyes rose to the ceiling where the lamp cast a small, bright circle of light, right above his head. *God's eye on me,* he thought, adapting one of his mother's sayings.

He lay there, looking at that eye for some time. From somewhere in the night, a bell tolled eleven. The bass voice went on and on with what struck Pier as censorious overtones: what was he doing, needlessly burning electric light? He stretched out his arm and switched off the lamp. The night chill nipped him his arm, and he quickly pulled it back into the warm cocoon of his covers.

But now he lay wide-awake. In the dark room, tomorrow loomed vaguely threatening. Working with the choir on Gregorian chants, did not worry him, but dealing with the students did. And the choir meant students. The *Liceo* students were only a couple of years younger than he. Would they accept him as their tutor? Fragments of old conversations in Santa Rita's dressing room echoed in his mind – school subjects, assignments, studying for exams, games, sports. He'd never been part of any of that. He'd never played sports. He had not been to school after the first few weeks of third grade. Lying warm and comfortable in his bed, he still felt the chill of exclusion. Would it be any different here? Would the boys take one look at him and *know?* What would happen if they refused to let him fulfil his duties, refused his leadership in choir practice? He stood to lose everything.

The thought kept him tossing and turning, haunted into an inchoate sense of doom. Throughout the night, the deep, censorious tones of the nearby church bell kept score of the passing hours, like a recording angel tracking bad deeds.

At last, in the pitch dark, a familiar noise broke the spell – the racket of the day's first tram. Relieved, Pier got out of bed and peered out of the window to find its friendly presence trundling down the tracks. Then he remembered: his window looked out on the courtyard, not out onto the street.

Still, the sound had broken the evil night spell. Pier shivered in the morning chill, but stood up straight, defiant: he would not make himself sick with bad thoughts. He must trust that Don Marco would not have sent him here to be pilloried. He squared his shoulders and raised his chin: it was up to him to inspire the boys' respect. "Confident," he said out loud to himself, echoes of Signora Agiati's voice blending with his own. "Masterful."

Reassured, if far from sure of himself, he slipped into his trousers, put on his raw wool cardigan, and, towel and shaving kit under his arm, sailed forth toward the washroom.

After breakfast, Pier found his way to the music master's office. Promptly at nine o'clock, he stood outside the wide-open door. Don Luca was already at his desk, writing. In the pool of light from the desk lamp, his long hands looked waxen. Pier hid his own gnarled and calloused labourer's hands behind his back, hesitating on the threshold. An involuntary throat clearing caught the master's attention and he looked up.

"Ah, Pier!" he called out, "You're here. Come in and shut the door."

Pier stepped in, closed the door, and quickly grasped his hands behind his back. Don Luca had risen from his desk and was heading for a trestle table placed by the office windows. He sat down at its head and motioned Pier to the chair next to him. Pier sat down, hands folded in his lap. Wintry sunlight came through the window and reflected on the polished dark wood. Don Luca leaned back in his chair, one white hand resting by the stack of books set out on the table.

"The students," the music master said, "are coming back today, but classes won't start until tomorrow. Choir practice starts next Monday. So, you have four days to get your bearings. Starting on Monday, you will sit in on my classes as my assistant. You won't have much to do to begin with, but it'll give you a chance to hear what the students are learning. Later this term I plan to introduce the choir to Monteverdi's Vespers. I believe you're familiar with it. During those classes, I will ask you to demonstrate certain passages. That will help establish your expertise with the students." He looked at Pier, gauging his response. Pier nodded, flushed, worried about all the things the students knew, and he didn't.

Don Luca resumed, "As you know, our *collegio* offers secondary education right through the *Liceo Classico*. We also offer a strong music concentration. We are one of the few schools in Turin that prepares students for *conservatorio* studies. Our music concentration is, of course, elective. But even for those who just do the regular *Liceo*, music is very much part of our culture. We train all our boys, right from the *prima media*, to read scores and sing in the choir. Those who choose to, can learn to play an instrument, and quite a few of our boys actually do. You will start working with the younger boys, eleven through fourteen. Later, I plan to have you work one on one with some of the older singers, on specific sections of scores we are rehearsing. How does this sound to you?"

"I think I can manage that," Pier answered.

"And sometimes I'll have you lead choir practices for our services. If you run into any difficulty, come talk to me and we'll discuss how to handle them." Pier nodded, eyes down. Don Luca studied him for a moment then said, "As my assistant, you are a member of our teaching staff. Students will ask you questions. We encourage our students to do that. It's a good way to learn. But at times students ask you about things outside your expertise. Don't try to answer. Just tell them their question is not in your field, and they'd better ask the master who teaches that subject. No need to be embarrassed. That's what we all do. But you need to learn who teaches what." Pier was still nodding thoughtfully, eye on in his lap. Don Luca resumed, "That way you can refer questions to the right person. This," he ended, handing Pier a roster of faculty names with their respective subject, "should help you."

"And now," Don Luca said, "let's talk about *your own* education. As you are aiming for a musical career, I will be the one to oversee your studies here. Your operatic training is in good hands with Professor Rexel; but you'll need to study other aspects of music. This term I want you to sit in on Don Marcello's class on music history, as well as on my elementary music theory class. Both of them are open to students from the *Ginnasio* and up. Both are in the morning, so they won't interfere with your other commitments. You will have to do all the class assignments, like any other student, but you won't turn your homework in during class. You'll bring it to me, or to Don Marcello, in our offices. Your role as a *Sacro Cuore* student is strictly between us. Publicly, you are a master's assistant. How does that feel?"

Pier answered with a crooked little smile of relief.

"You'll get on fine," Don Luca assured him, standing up. Pier followed suit. Don Luca laid an arm around his shoulders. "I'm glad you've come to us," he said walking him towards the office door. "I look forward to hearing your voice at some of our services."

The door closed softly behind Pier. Don Luca's parting comment stirred up an uncomfortable thought in him: should he have attended mass this morning? Had it been expected?

Decorously, he walked down the hallways, passing doors to masters' offices, many of them open. Through one of these, he caught a glimpse of a sunlit inner courtyard, clusters of older students streaming across it. Pier saw *himself* crossing that sunlit courtyard, almost one of them! A surge of joy made him feel like kicking up his heels and yodelling. A moment later, he again chafed with uncertainty: *almost* one of them, but not quite.

Suppressing his turmoil, he returned sedately to his room. He had to get ready. That afternoon he was to meet with Professor Rexel to lay down the plan for his training program at the Regio.

Chapter Twelve

Or like stout Cortez when with eagle eyes
He stared at the Pacific...
John Keats

La Tampa Lirica

It did not take Guido long to find out who Lena's new man was. He simply set one of his bulldogs from the Borgo San Paolo *Fascio* to follow them, and in the process, he found out that Lena now worked at FIAT.

"Damn her!" he cursed. Now that angle was gone. He'd have to turn his attention to the guy. It surprised him to find out that Lena had met him at FIAT, in the *Carrozzeria* department, working at a lathe in the station next to hers. The bloke looked a better class than that. "Bigger than his breeches," he muttered, displeased.

The thought festered in his mind. Of course, a word in the right ear could have the jerk thrown out on the street. Nowadays, the Party had clout at FIAT, and he, Guido Delloria, was not without influence with the party's watchdogs. But would that help? It would not get him any closer to Lena. He had to find out more about him.

A few days later he got a report that his man had followed the pair to the Regio and that they had stayed on for the show. What was an *operaio* doing at the opera, he wandered, confused. Surely, even gallery seats would make a nasty dent in his wages. True, on that Sunday, last month, in *Via Roma,* the bloke had looked better dressed than his FIAT wages. He'd have his man to make more inquiries, see whether the jerk was known at the theatre. And if another report came in that they were at the Regio, he'd go over and see for himself.

The next report came in the day he returned from his New Year's celebration at the *Saint Vincent* casino, a guest of the Follati family. The report did not please him: yes, the young man was known, he was a protégé of Professor Rexel. He

263

had got to the Regio from the duomo, where he was in training with Don Marco Veronese and sang at functions on a regular basis. Also, his man had followed the pair to the Regio on New Year's Eve. They had stayed for the opera and finished the night at the *Tampa Lirica.* "Very lovey-dovey," his man had smirked.

Guido received the intelligence with his best stone face. All he said was: "Find out more. About his job at FIAT, where he lives. I want to know what he does with every minute of his time." But as soon as he was alone, he struck a violent fist on his desk, sending the ink well flying. "Damn, damn, DAMN!" he cried out with a violent kick to the wall. It hurt his foot, and he hobbled back to his desk chair. He wasn't prepared to take on Turin's cathedral and the royal theatre at this time. But he *could* still make the jerk's life hell. His discrete informing for the Party's political watchdogs gave him the means, and he would do it, if he found the slightest hint of political doings. But for a purely personal reason… He'd have to tread lightly. He was courting Maria Cristina Follati. Any hint that his true reason for hounding the Venturi youngster was that he lusted after an *operaia* would ruin his chances with the heiress. And any rumour that the *operaia* had snubbed him would make him a laughingstock. And any such scandal would put an end to his plans with the Follati family.

His mouth pursed as a thought struck him: maybe he could *make it into* a political issue. The new *leggy fascistissime* made that easy. He'd begin with finding out whether Venturi was a registered Fascio member, and if he was not, he would look into his other affiliations: any connection with potentially subversive groups, however vague or innocent, would do the trick. He could use it to get the jerk away from Lena. He couldn't let her get away with humiliating him.

Pier's second visit to the *Convivio*

Every day since leaving FIAT, Pier had laboured his way through *La STAMPA*, spurred on by the need to not make a fool of himself again at the *Convivio.* He did not enjoy reading the newspaper, but he was beginning to get the drift of how the articles worked, never giving you a full story, but returning to a topic day after day, adding bits and pieces, referring back to earlier bits, often from months, even years ago. These references often baffled him, a painful reminder of his humiliating first visit to the *Convivio.* Then he discovered that the library kept past issues of newspapers, and he started to trace references back to earlier reports. The thought of that *Legga i giornali*, at that first *Convivio* meeting, still sent a flush through him.

The group had not met over the holidays but was scheduled to resume right after New Year. Pier wished he could get out of it, but knew Signora Agiati would be disappointed; so he planned to continue to attend the meetings, and was working hard to catch up on current events, comforting himself with the thought that, at any rate, he had now learned not to ask stupid questions.

On the night of the next *Convivio meeting*, he waited in the shadows of a doorway across the street from the *Trattoria delle Arti,* where the group met. When he saw Matilde Agiati approach, he crossed the road to meet her so as to go in with her. The moment they entered the private dining room where the group was meeting Pier sensed the tense atmosphere and the hair on the back of his neck stiffened. Most of the members were already there, standing in small groups, talking in agitated whispers, aperitif glasses forgotten in their hands. As soon as the last latecomer arrived, the group drifted to the table. Pier opened the Ginsberg play that was to be read that evening and looked around at the others.

"I hear Gobetti is still unconscious," said the reviewer from *LA STAMPA,* after a worried glance towards the closed door. This time Pier did not have to ask who Gobetti was. He had been reading the guarded reports about the Christmas Eve *pestaggio* that had left the young political writer a bleeding heap on a dark street corner. The articles had tiptoed around the fact that the brutal beating was an obvious retribution for the challenge Gobetti's magazine, *Rivoluzione Liberale,* had flung at the Mussolini regime. Now, outrage, anger and fear stormed about the *Convivio*, their literary pursuits overshadowed by political passion. Outraged and confused, Pier's eyes darted from speaker to speaker around the table, his heart in his throat, frightened by the violence of their passion. The appalling event had stirred up resonances of the violence Pier had suffered at home, suffusing the *pestaggio* with painful personal meanings. And he *was* confused: hadn't he read weeks ago that Mussolini had disbanded his death squads? Had he misunderstood? Who, then, had carried out this brutal assault?

A loud knock on the door abruptly silenced the *Convivio.* Startled, frightened faces stared at each other. A second knock. The group's senior member, university professor Rusconi, grabbed the play script in front of him and opened it at random, motioning to the others to do the same. Matilde Agiati's penetrating contralto suddenly pealed out a laugh and others around the table, at first startled, soon joined her with stilted laughter. Professor Rusconi quickly glanced that everybody had a book in his hands, then called out a firm, "Come in." Two waiters trundled in a trolley laden with their supper, and started to serve.

The rest of the evening remained constrained. While the waiters bustled about the room, the conversation focused on the recent Christmas season – the family visits, the shows in town, the new exhibit at the *Museo di Arte Egizia.* But as soon as the waiters withdrew, the anger and fear at the recent outrages burst forth again, be it at a restrained volume, the danger that criticism and intellectual debate entailed under the fascist regime vivid in everybody's mind. New laws, passed in the last few weeks, had frightening implications for all of them. All associations, all groups were now obliged, under severe penalties of law, to register their aims, structure and membership; public servants were obliged to swear allegiance to the Fascio, and those who refused to, faced dismissal or worse; newspapers hostile to the regime were to be shut down, or taken over by regime supporters.

"*La STAMPA* is a clear example of what this means," wailed that paper's book and art reviewer. "Since Agnelli took over last October, every review I write is being vetted and maimed. My article on the Ginsberg's production at the *Carignano* was thrown out altogether because her play is considered subversive."

"It isn't any better at the university," Professor Rusconi put in. "It's only a matter of time. The trend is clear: toe the line or end up like Gobetti. Or *al confine.*"

"What about our group?" Matilde Agiati asked anxiously. "Do *we* have to register?"

The question stopped the assembly cold. They stared at each other. "Well...we are not really a political group..." muttered Professor Rusconi, glancing uneasily from face to face. A storm of alarmed arguments broke out.

"We have no official structure, so we are not even, properly speaking, 'a group'."

"We're just a bunch of amateurs interested in the arts..."

"So is *la Ginsberg.* Nonetheless, she was censured off *La STAMPA* today. "

"So if we choose to discuss avant-garde authors, does that make us *sovversivi?* "

The anxious, outraged discussion went on until closing time. At one in the morning, the members of the non-group walked out into the street under the frigid January sky, and cautiously scattered in different directions. Pier escorted Signora Agiati to the nearest tram stop, saw her onto the last tram to her home in Via Madama Christina, and hurried across the street, hoping he had not missed his own last tram.

On the way home to *Sacro Cuore* in the clanking tram, he wondered what would happen next: would the *Convivio* stop meeting? If it didn't, should *he* stop going?

NO! His mind screamed out, not now! He had not enjoyed going to the group, and he would have stopped, but for Signora Agiati. But now he wouldn't be driven away; he would not let the arbitrary oppression stop him, any more that his father's beatings and mockery had stopped him at home. The recent events, the brutality of last month's attack on Gobetti, the summer murder of Senator Matteotti, all the other fascist abuses to which he had been oblivious until a couple of months ago, tonight took on for him an intolerable personal meaning; they became a violation of his own personal reality. He could not stop attending the *Convivio* now, any more than, two years ago, he could have begged his pa to stop his brutal beatings. He'd hated his pa then, and he hated the fascists now. He hated the senseless cruelty, the coercion, the high-handedness that brutalised the helpless around him. He *would* stand by the *Convivio* now, cost what it cost.

At that thought, a broken sob choked him, a noise he quickly disguised with a cough, a protective hand on his throat. "Not now," he silently pleaded, not *now* when he, at last, had something to lose – the Regio, the duomo, his room at the *Sacro Cuore*... He couldn't bear to have them snatched away now.

Maybe they'll dissolve, flashed through his mind. The thought knocked his breath out, hit him like a mule kick in the stomach. Did he want the *Convivio* to dissolve so that *he* would not have to stand up to the threat, stand up against the fascist outrages? He flushed with shame: he wanted *others* to take the coward's way out, to submit to the party's coercions, *so he wouldn't have to.*

It was not until the tram ground to a stop in front of the *collegio* that another thought hit him. Lena! Could they harm Lena if he got into trouble? And what about Nina, would his defiance bring trouble home to her as well? Crossing the *corso,* he glanced surreptitiously over his left shoulder. By the time he reached the *portone* he was out of breath, haunted by images of police squads searching Nina's retro. He fumbled the large iron key in the door lock and dropped it. He retrieved it with an oath, cursing himself for making noise, and hurriedly slipped in through the door, once more scanning the empty night street behind him while bringing the pass-through slowly to.

Inside the covered carriageway, he pressed his back against the solid door, holding his breath, the thumping of his heart, loud in his ears, the only sound in the semi-dark silence. It echoed in his mind like the familiar clip-clop-glup of the leaky faucet in Nina's *retro*.

He drew a deep breath and forced himself to relax, to breathe slow and deep until his heart stopped kicking at his ribs. Then, his back still pressed against the protecting door, he realised that his shirt was drenched and stiffening in the freezing night air. He stood away from the door and straightened his posture: he must not catch cold, must go change right away, to protect his voice, his ticket to the life he craved.

Pier and Rexel work out his program

Promptly at five to four Pier arrived at the Regio for his appointed meeting with Professor Rexel. In the foyer leading to the offices and rehearsal rooms, he was hailed by a buxom young woman with bobbed hair and a clinging, pencil-slim skirt.

"You Pierre Venturi?" she asked, pinching her 'r' in a pseudo-French manner. "Follow me." She scurried off on clacking high heels down a series of corridors, clutching a stack of scores to her chest. Pier followed her, fascinated by the pert round buttocks that leapt up and down with each step. With her chin pinning her load to her chest, she said, "In here." She reached out and shoved the door open. "The professor will be with you shortly." She flashed Pier a plump, lipstick smile, and clattered down the hall. Pier watched her go, buttocks leaping, until she disappeared into another door further down the hall; then he turned to the open door.

Accustomed to the austere order of clerical rooms, he stopped aghast on the threshold: the large room before him flaunted the look of a dishevelled stage set. On the far left, an ornate desk with cabriolet legs lay smothered under a mess of papers. A worn leather armchair hugged the end wall, a lamp next to it on a low side table. Opposite the door, two windows let in fading afternoon light onto a grand piano cluttered with open scores. On the far right, an odd cluster of sundry furniture faced the armchair at the opposite wall. Somewhere in mid-room, a *Recamier* sofa, carelessly trailing a silk shawl onto the floor, struck a somehow lewd note.

"Ah," said a Germanic voice behind him, "you're *hier. Gut.*" Startled, Pier swung around. Professor Rexel scurried past him into the room, hurried to his desk, throwing a command over his shoulder. "Bring up that chair, ve've got a lot to do." He dropped the scores he was carrying to the floor next to the desk and sank heavily into a swivel chair.

Pier hurried to fetch the indicated chair, hovering with it in front of the desk, uncertain where to set it down. The professor was absorbed in rummaging under the papers that cluttered his desk, scowling. Suddenly, a smile broke out on his freckled face. His hand re-emerged holding a biscuit tin with a Toulouse-Lautrec dancer on its hinged lid. "Sit down," he ordered with an impatient jerk of his chin toward the right. Pier set his chair down at the professor's elbow, as instructed, and sat down while the professor, eyes closed, chewed with meditative absorption. "Now," he said at last, munching, then swallowing. "Vhere do ve go from *hier, ja?*"

For the next fifteen minutes he quizzed Pier about his previous training, about his daily practice routines – breathing exercises, voice, diction and body techniques – scribbling furious notes on the back of an envelope perched on a corner of his crowded desk. Next he moved on to Pier's hygiene, diet and sleeping habits. "Eight hours every night," he decreed, "in bed by ten on weeknights. Gargling and stretches every morning and every night. Must keep your airvays clear, *ja*? And don't overdo it vith your girlfriends." Pier blushed furiously but kept nodding.

The professor grinned. He shoved aside some of the papers cluttering his desk to clear a space, brought out a score of *La Bohème,* and beckoned Pier to pull up closer. Pier obeyed, while the professor hand dipped into the biscuit tin again, shoved another *marron glacé* into his mouth, started to close the tin's lid again, then he stopped and reached the tin over toward Pier, who gingerly took one while the professor snatched one last *marron* and popped it into his mouth before stowing the tin away into a desk drawer.

"*So,* now vhat next: you vill continue your vork with Matilde Agiati *hier* at the theatre. You vork out your schedule with her. *And,"* he added, "you might start to…" his index finger tapped his forehead, "*think* in Italian, not *Piemontèis.* That will help you with the Italian rhythms. Of course, you vill sing at the duomo vhenever Don Marco vants you. *I* vill vork with you tvice a veek, reframing your voice for opera. Ve must make sure you're clear about vhat is right for church and vhat is right on stage, so you can do either vone at vill." He glanced at Pier, saw him overwhelmed, and smiled. "Meantime," he went on, "ve vill start you vorking on duets and scenes. In a couple of months, I vant you to haff a trial run at *La Tampa Lirica,* just vone duet. If that goes vell, ve'll start you vorking on your first recital. Any qvestions?"

Pier's mind was reeling with questions, but he shook his head, unable to disentangle his thoughts to form a coherent sentence.

"Gut," the professor went on, "ve start vith Puccini. You already know *Che gelida Manina.* Tonight I vant you to read the whole libretto. Get to know the story inside out, *all* the characters. Then study the score of your aria. Any spots that give you trouble, note them down and ve'll go over them together. Clear?"

Again, Pier nodded, utterly overwhelmed.

"*Gut.* Next veek you vill meet your Mimí. Vhat is your schedule at the *collegio?*"

For the next ten minutes they worked on coordinating Pier's duties at *Sacro Cuore* with his schedule at the Regio, until a rat-tat-tat sounded on the door and the buxom young woman bounced into the room. "Your five o'clock is here, *Herr Professor*," she announced. Rexel waved a dismissive hand at her without looking up from Pier's schedule. But, from under his unruly red mop, his eyes lingered appreciatively on the generous young bust and the leaping buttocks.

Pier's first class at *Sacro Cuore*

The next day, the Monday after the Epiphany, saw the start of Pier's life as a music master's assistant. He was already up and giving his serviceable grey suit one last brush-up when the first morning bell tinkled through the building. He had not slept well. Dreams had plagued him that he was lost in the *collegio's* maze of corridors and staircases and could not find his way to Don Luca's class. It had been a relief to wake up and find that he was, after all, safe in his warm bed. He had reached out and switched on his bedside lamp, a warm feeling pervading him as he basked in its soft glow. The January chill in the unheated room bit at his arm, and he'd pulled it back under his cosy covers with a pleasurable shudder. Now he heard a tram clatter by and glanced at his clock: six thirty. He slipped into his suit and carefully knotted his tie, pulling it straight in front of his shaving mirror. He was not due in class until 8:30, but he had decided to go down with the boys and attend the before-breakfast mass. It might be expected, and it would give him a feel for the *collegio's* daily routine.

When the second bell tinkled, he opened his door and listened for young voices and the boisterous tramp of feet down the stairs, then followed the herd to the chapel, trying to memorise the twists and turns of the route as they crossed two cloistered courtyards before reaching the chapel in the third. Pier filed in with the others, dipped his fingers in holy water and genuflected before settling into a rear pew. Soon the flow of stragglers, Don Marcello among them, stopped. A bell rang by the altar and mass started – everyday antiphons and responses in plainchant. Pier joined in, his voice clear and distinctive. The chapel was cold, but the service did not last long. Soon, the students shuffled out in a steady, whispering stream of blue-trimmed maroon school blazers, with here and there a monitoring black cassock. Out in the courtyard, a pale sun struggled with wind-driven clouds.

After a tramp to the refectory for a breakfast of bread and *caffelatte,* boys and masters dispersed to the first class. Pier had already scouted out the location of the classes he was to attend – music history, and Don Luca's theory class – so now he made his way through the corridors with a certain assurance, the two assigned textbooks tucked securely under his arm. He was the first to arrive at Don Marcello's class, as he thought appropriate for a master's assistant, and propped the door open to receive the *Quarta Ginnasio* class. As he waited, he took in the layout of the room: the master's desk on a podium, on its right the blackboard, on its left a spinet facing the student desks, and, next to the piano, a narrow, adult-sized table and chair. High on the wall behind the teacher's desk a crucifix and, side by side below it, two photographs, King Vittorio Emanuele III and *Il Duce.* The two *heads of state,* flashed through Pier's mind. On the sidewalls, pictures of musical instruments, and colourful scenes of people playing or listening to music.

At the sounds of juvenile voices approaching down the hall, Pier stepped back into the corridor and stood waiting at the side of the door. Don Marcello appeared around a corner, cassock flying. Instinctively, Pier squared his shoulders and straightened his spine. "Good Morning, Father," he greeted him.

The young priest stopped next to Pier by the open door. "You found your way, I see. Good," he said, his eye on the last straggler hurrying towards class along the corridor. A bell shrilled, and the boys broke into a run. "Walk, don't run," Don Marcello said sternly, ushering the laggard in and closing the door behind him.

The herd of fourteen-year olds swarmed to their desks, each homing in toward his previous quarter's assigned seat, chattering, stowing their books in the open hutch beneath the desktops. Pier stood by the teacher's platform, uncertain what to do. *At their age,* he thought, *I was fetching bricks for the old bastard.* For a moment, an image flickered, vivid, in his in mind – the leering, wizened face, and the long spew of tobacco juice the master mason liked to pursue him with, taunting him, tormenting him, until he had smashed the tormentor's skull with a half-brick.

Next to him, Don Marcello cleared his throat to catch Pier's attention, then motioned him to the assistant's table and chair beyond the piano. He waited until Pier was seated, then rapped his pointing stick on the desk. The noise subsided. "Good morning, boys," the young master said. "Welcome back."

"Good morning, Father," the class chanted back in dutiful unison.

"Here we are again. Ready for the new term, I trust."

"Yes, Father," the chorus answered.

"This term we have the benefit of a master's assistant. Let us welcome him: Signor Venturi."

The class rose and dutifully chanted, *"Benvenuto, Signor Venturi."*

Pier blinked, startled by that *Signor Venturi.* That was *him.* Nobody had ever called him Mister before. He half rose to his feet and nodded to the class.

"So," Don Marcello went on, "let us pick up where we left off last term, the music of the early middle ages. Can anyone remember what we found?"

Two hands shot up, then a third and a fourth. "Plainchant."

"Polyphony."

"Ave Maris Stella."

"Ars Antica." The class was off.

At his desk, Pier listened and watched: he caught the nudging elbows in the back rows, the stealthy hand retrieving something from a pocket and sneaking it into the mouth, the toe poking and poking at the buttocks in the seat in front, the quick, backward, half-playful half-angry slap to the nudging foot. But the class was engaged, orderly, twenty-odd boys of roughly the same age. *"Clot's age,"* Pier thought; but so different from his nasty younger brother.

The image of another classroom long ago arose in his mind — a bare, whitewashed room, witheringly cold, clustered with children grouped by size, first graders to almost full grown – the classroom of his brief schooling days in that one-room school in Volvera. He recalled the hours' tramp across the winter fields in wooden clogs and scratchy raw wool knits that were never warm enough.

He glanced outside the nearby window: the clouds had closed in, and now desultory snowflakes drifted past the glass panes. Don Marcello's voice broke through into his daydream.

"...so let us recap: last term we saw that art and music reflect the spirit of the times. The dark ages. Can anyone remember when that was?" Hands shot up. "Molino."

"Six hundred to a thousand *dopo Cristo.*"

"Precisely. And what marked those four hundred years?" His eyes queried the class here and there. Hands shot up.

Pier's attention drifted away. He hadn't seen Lena in three days. He missed having her constantly in his sight, sitting at her FIAT workbench; missed being able to meet her eyes whenever he raised his.

"*I barbari.*"

"*Gli Ostrogoti.*"

"*I Visigoti.*"

"*Barbarossa.*" Pier heard the juvenile voices responding, but his mind was miles away.

"*Bevi, Rosmunda, nel cranio di tuo padre.*" (Drink, Rosmund, from your father's skull.) The ghastly sentence brought Pier back to the here and now.

"Yes," Don Marcello was saying, "those were brutal times. And the only bastion against barbarity was... the church."

A hand shot up.

"Yes, Alfonsi, you have a question?"

"Yes, Father. What does it mean 'the spirit of the times'?"

The young master's eyes drifted to the floor. He paced back and forth below his desk, thinking. By and by, he stopped, faced the front centre desk, scanned his class, and said pointedly: "You remember Christ's words, 'Give onto Caesar...'" Here and there on the school desks heads nodded.

"That's one of the dilemmas of mankind: what is Caesar's and what is God's. We live in a temporal world, full of conflict and pain, and yet...we *long* for peace, for happiness, for the eternal bliss of heaven." He paused, scanning the attentive young faces before continuing.

"Christ," he went on, "recognised that we *must pay our dues* to the material world, but we must also preserve our soul for..." his eyes rose toward the ceiling, "for *that other world* we long for, the beyond, the world of spirit, which…" again, he paused, palms raised, facing the class, in an ecclesiastical gesture, "…*but for faith*, must forever remain a mystery to us."

He strolled to the window and back again, stood facing the class. "We try," he said with great intensity, "*always we try…*" quick flex of the knees to heighten the emphasis, "…to fathom that mystery, to get closer to God." He paced to the classroom door, then back again. "The Church helps us do that. But…" Once more, he paused and stared at the floor, searching for words fourteen-year olds might understand.

"You see," he went on, "what happens in our world inevitably shapes our view of human existence, of human destiny – both temporal and eternal. And when daily life is *so grim* that people feel in constant danger, they tend to stay close to home. They don't venture out, don't try new things. Trying new things feels dangerous, *sinful.* Then life, death and suffering, are simply accepted. Only the hereafter holds any promise, any hope."

He stopped speaking and paced to the window and back again. "That's what the dark ages were like – very dark indeed. So people huddled around what safety they knew, our spiritual home, the church. They flocked into abbeys and monasteries – which, incidentally, had good strong walls that might protect them from the Barbarians' assaults."

He stood, silent for a moment, in front of the centre desk, facing the class. "Imagine," he resumed, knees dipping, "what *it must have felt like* – to live under such conditions." He stepped up the aisle between two rows of desks, fourteen-year-old heads and shoulders twisting on desk seats in wrapped silence to follow his progress.

At the back of the class he turned and stood a moment before he scanned out his next sentence. "The conditions – of our lives – *inevitably* – shape – the way – we see the world."

Slowly, he strolled back toward to the podium, and there he stood, back to his master's desk, silent for several seconds before a breath-holding class.

"In the dark ages," he resumed, "nothing could remove that constant threat to daily life, but…*in the hereafter*…the church promised to save their souls. It promised happiness, *eternal bliss*. So, with so little to be hoped for in *this* world, all hope turned towards Heaven. The *spirit of the middle ages* reflects that everyday experience."

Pier listened, enthralled, eyes fixed on the speaker, his mind scurrying back and forth between the words he heard and images of his life at *La Speransa*. He saw his ma's tight lips, her grey, pinched face, her tired Sunday shape huddled in her pew, shoulders hunched forward, forehead pressed on hands clasped tight in prayer. He thought of her mistrust, her hostility to the city, where everything, she felt – and especially *the theatre* – was the work of the devil.

Don Marcello was saying: "The music of the dark ages shows this very clearly: it was *written for God alone*, to praise him. In so far as it was written *for people*, it was so that faith might sustain them with its promise of the bliss to come. Peoples' minds turned to Heaven as a refuge from the pain of this world.

"*Then* …the first thousand years after Christ drew to a close. People believed that the year 1000 marked the end of the world…"

Giggles rippled here and there among the desks.

"They believed Judgment Day was at hand…

"So it made good sense to invest all one's hopes in the Hereafter.

"But then… the new millennium came, and… *the world did not end*!"

Again, twitters rippled among the desks, excited boys shifted in their seats, leather-soled shoes scrabbled against the raised wood desks platforms.

"Instead," Don Marcello went on, "with time, things began to get better. And, as a result, the spirit of the high middle ages began to get lighter. Man dared to venture out from his walled enclosures. New *tools* were invented: instead of scratching out a living from the earth with a stick and a hoe, as men had done for thousands of years, *the plow* was invented. Horses were brought into Europe from the Arabian world. And soon the plow became *horse-drawn*."

The teacher paused, giving the class time to absorb the significance of these changes. He paced calmly back and forth, then went on: "Can you *imagine* the difference in the ease of growing food? Windmills were invented, canals were dug, rivers diverted to irrigate the fields… Human work became easier and more productive, food more plentiful…"

As Don Marcello spoke, familiar images arose in Pier's mind: the hours spent under the scorching sun in the outlying fields where the *La Speransa* irrigation ditches did not reach, drawing water, bucket after heavy bucket pulled up at the end of a rope from deep, hand-dug wells; long days labouring in the fields, then the twilight chores in Ma's kitchen gardens, stiff backs bent and sore, watering, weeding, tending young plants that had wilted in the day's heat.

"…and more crops meant *more trade*," the teacher's voice rose to a lighter pitch, increased in tempo. "Artisans produced more goods, cities grew bigger. The improved everyday conditions *freed the spirit to soar*…

"The first universities were born."

Again, Don Marcello waited for the impact of the images he had evoked to take hold. Then he went on:

"In gratitude, mankind built splendid cathedrals to the greater glory of God, wonderful, awe-inspiring places where a man could worship, could *breathe in* a whiff of the bliss to come.

"And then …over time… people began to take a look around: *everyday life* had now become something to celebrate, no longer only the glory of God. So…

"Lighter expressions of the human spirit began to emerge: poets began to sing of *human* stories, of man's hopes and dreads; of his dreams, and of his loves, the way men had done eons ago, in ancient times – *before* the dark ages had set in – since the very dawn of time.

"*Vernacular literature*," the teacher scanned out the new word, wrote it on the blackboard, "was born. Stories and poems began to be told, no longer just in Latin, but in the language people spoke every day. Think of the *Troubadours* in France, of the *Dolce Stil Novo* in Italy…"

Don Marcello went on, increasing his pace, building on the excitement he had infused in his class: "Music expanded. *Ars Antiqua*…" – he wrote the two words out on the blackboard – "celebrated God. Now a new form of art, *Ars Nova…*" again, he wrote the new words on the board – "celebrated *this*, world *human life itself*, with songs and dances." He bent over the piano and sketched out a couple of isorhythmic phrases.

"That, boys, is *Ars Nova,*" he said, facing his class. "The New Art. This term, *Ars Nova,* is what we will explore this term; this new, *man-centred*, art."

Again, he paused to let his words sink in, to give the class a chance to ask questions. He almost smiled at the eager, expectant faces. He went on. "You are all familiar with plainchant, from last term." He scanned the class, then, satisfied with the youthful, nodding faces, he continued: "Next class, I'll play you a motet by Machaud, *Quant en moy,* circa 1350. There you will hear the difference in the spirit of the times."

A bell shrilled in the corridors outside – the end of the class. Books slammed shut, feet shuffled. To be heard above the clamour Don Marcello raised his voice. "Read the first five pages of your textbook for next Thursday. Class dismissed."

The polite attention of the past hour dissolved into a hubbub of young voices in the hallway, it erupted into the boisterous rumpus of boys scrambling to the momentary release between classes.

Stunned by this first encounter with middleclass education, Pier sat at his assistant's table, craving for more – craving to learn, to know, to read; abashed by all he did not know, all he had not read, not learned all those past years.

A discreet cough broke in on his brown study: next to him, Don Marcello stood waiting. Pier scrambled to his feet, head shaking hurriedly collecting his belongings. "I am a tadpole," he muttered, cowed by the depth of the other's knowledge, "...from some backwater pool." He glanced up and met Don Marcello's kind eyes. He coughed, embarrassed. "I'm so glad I am here," he added, as his own eyes fell to the floor.

Don Marcello smiled. The lad's rapt attention during the class, his mind obviously scuttling between what he heard and powerful mental images of his own, had flattered the teacher. For the eleven years of his Jesuit training, his role had been to hang on the words of his masters. Today, for the first time, he had felt himself the master, and one with an eager, grown-up disciple, not just young children. Time and again, he had found Pier's eyes riveted to his face, had recognised behind those eyes, a mind scurrying back and forth between present words and past images, and then, maybe, on to novel thoughts and possibilities; still struggling to put two and two together and finding, perhaps for the first time, that it all made some kind of sense.

"*I* am glad you're," he answered, smiling.

"But I feel...all...topsy-turvy. Like I've been fished out of my muddy pool and thrown into a fast stream."

"Well," Don Marcello answered seriously, "now that you have found the mainstream, I'm sure you'll soon get along swimmingly with the current." He turned and headed for the classroom door. Pier hastened to join him.

"If," Don Marcello said, cautiously, "you'd like to talk, sometime, just come over to the Junior Masters' common room. I'll be glad of a chat." He stopped in the classroom door and, unconsciously reproducing the gesture of his seminary mentor, laid an arm around Pier's shoulders and shepherded him into the hallway, adding, "But now we must vacate this room: its needed for the next class in a few minutes."

Guido investigates the *Convivio*

Determined to find something he could use against Lena's new man, Guido continued to deploy his bulldogs to sniff around for something questionable in Pier's activities. In the next few days, he found out that Pier now lived at the *Sacro Cuore.* That was an unwelcome and puzzling bit of news. What was the jerk doing in a boys' school?

Next he found out that Pier had again been followed to the *Trattoria delle Arti,* where he had attended a long-standing group that called itself *Convivio Litterario.* With a few unsubtle references to what could happen to restaurants and clubs that served *sovversivi sospetti* since the passing of the recent *Leggi fascistissime,* his sleuths, now working in pairs, had quickly extracted from the alarmed *trattoria* owner the names of the group's regular attendees.

Guido poured over the list of names: apparently the Venturi kid was a newcomer, first appeared last November. Hmm, he mused, that was enough. As to the group's activities, according to the two waiters serving at their gatherings, they spent their evenings reading aloud and discussing – poetry, plays, sometimes just stories. Guido scoffed: a bunch of milksops wasting their time on trivial pursuits. He threw the report aside.

Except... it could be a blind. He picked up the report again. He had better make sure, get a clearer idea of who these people were. He examined the list of names: *Professor* Enrico Rusconi, *Universitá di Torino.* Hmm...an intellectual. Professor of what, what was his subject? He put a question mark in the right margin. Next was a *Professor* Alberto Felice, *Liceo Classico Giuseppe Giacosa.* What did he teach? He put a question mark in the right margin. He read down the list, entering checks or question marks next to each name: *Professoressa* Maria Luisa Buscaglia, *Liceo Classico Giacosa. Signor* Roberto Scagliosi, *La STAMPA.* Guido put in a double check mark in the margin: a journalist was always worth investigating. *Sig.* Meo Bonfiglioli, *Teatro Nuovo. Sigra.* Renata Filiberti, *Teatro Nuovo.* This new theatre put on *avant-garde* stuff. There might be something there; so, question marks next to the two names. *Sigra.* Matilde Agiati, Teatro Regio, check. *Sig.* Alberto Ferrucci, attorney, check. He stopped, backtracked, thinking: the Agiati woman was from the Regio, she might be the link to Venturi. He'd have to find out what kind of link.

It went on: *Dott.* Eraldo Banfi, with no further notation. What was he, a medical man? Check. He scanned down the list: Don Giacomo Gioberti, *La Gran Madre.* Hmm, a priest. He'd have to find out what his position was at the basilica.

He put his question mark next to that name and next to the two ones that followed, identified simply as 'students'. He lingered on the last name: *Sig.* Pasquale Lombardi, *Teatro Carignano.* That was *la Ginsberg*'s house. Her latest play had raised party eyebrows, had been censured off the stage.

He continued to ponder the list: three professors, a doctor and a priest. He'd need to tread lightly. But he *would* find out what *really* brought them together. With a bit of luck, he might find that their *Convivio Letterario* was a cover. He'd send his men back out to find out more about these people, but carefully, not to stir up any unnecessary hornets' nest. The Agiati woman, now…He tapped her name on the list: she was the link to Venturi, he was sure. He would start with her, while he waited for more information. As a likely link to Venturi, he would tackle her himself.

Piers meets Melina Cortesi

Horst Rexel sat at the piano in his more than usually dishevelled lair. A score open in front of him, his freckled hands skipped across the keyboard, sketching snatches from the end of the first act of *La Traviata.*

"Good afternoon, Professor," Pier called out, stopping on the open threshold.

"Ah, Pier! Come in, come in. I've been thinking about Alfredo *e* Violetta for your venture at *La Tampa Lirica.* Vhat do you think, eh? The last scene of Act I?" He stood up, gathered the score from the piano and trotted over to show it to Pier, his finger directing his attention to a section of the open page.

"That's fine," Pier answered.

"From '*o qual pallor'…ja?* Ve'll cut out Gastone and the crowd. Just you and Violetta. Vhat do you say: can you make passionate love?" Pier shrugged, blushing.

Rexel hurried back to the piano and sat down. "Here,'" he said, "let me hear you declare your love." Pier followed him and peered at the score over the professor's shoulder. The professor looked up at him and flirted in a high falsetto, *"Da molto e' che mi amate?"* Pier sang, *"Ah si, da un anno…e da quel dì, tremante, vissi d'ignoto amor…"*

"More feeling!" the Germanic voice demanded, "more intensity: you're crazy in lof!"

Pier nodded and sang on, "*…quell'amor che'e' palpito, Dell'universo, dell'universo intero, Misterioso, altero, Croce e delizia al cor…"*

From the room's threshold, an assured soprano echoed, "*Croce e delizia al cor.*" Melina Cortesi had arrived.

"My dear…" Horst Rexel purred at her, leaning back on his piano stool to receive her perfunctory kiss on his cheek, "you've come… 'something something upon the hour.' Come meet your Alfredo." Melina turned to meet Pier, hand extended in greeting, an open smile upon her face. "*Piacere,*" she said. Pier bowed slightly, shook her hand with a discrete click of his heels. "*Na ja, gut,*" Rexel noted with a private grin. "Melina here," he told Pier, "is as 'blessed' (his hands sketched quotations marks in the air) as you are. Her voice, like yours, spans an amazing range. She sings both soprano and mezzosoprano roles. And," he twinkled, "she has *other* amazing talents as well." He turned back to the keyboard. "Come *hier*, Melina," his head summoned her to stand next to Pier. "Together now," he ordered. "Take it from *Gli è vero…*" His hands rippled over the keyboard, playing the lead notes and they started their duet.

"*…Da molto è che mi amate?*	Is it long that you love me?
Ah, sí, da un anno	Ah, yes, over a year.
Un dì felice, eterea,	One happy day, ethereal,
Mi balenaste innante	you appeared before me
E da quel dì tremante	And from that day, trembling,
Vissi d'ignoto amor…"	I lived of secret love…

Chortling, Rexel played on: no problem now with Pier's credibility. He'd known that's how it would be. Melina Cortesi was no beauty, but she simply *oozed 'It'*. On stage, their voices and their chemistry would sweep audiences like wildfire. He watched them sideways over his shoulder and chortled again. How long, he thought, would his choirboy's innocence survive the storm?

Pier bent toward the score, an eager finger tracing their next phrase. Excited, Melina drew closer, caught Pier's eye and twinkled.

Na ja, Rexel thought again, *how long?*

Guido intimidates Matilde

Guido started with having Matilde followed. His instructions were to let her see the man following her, so she would get the wind up. Next he would have her brought to the San Paolo *Fascio*.

Early one evening, she was accosted at her tram stop by two thugs in wide-brimmed hats and long overcoats. None of the people waiting with her at the tram stop reacted when a car with blinded windows screeched to a halt on the tram track in front of them, and the two thugs manhandled Matilde into the back seat, piled in after her, and threw a blanket over her head while the car sped off again with a loud squeal of tires.

Pushed down on the car floor under the stifling blanket, Matilde struggled for breath. The car travelled for a long time. At one point, Matilde felt the engine labour up a steep incline, wheels screaming on sharp turns, then it sped downhill.

Then, at last, it stopped and she was dragged out of the car, still unsteady from terror and motion sickness, into a cobbled courtyard, the blanket slipping off her head so that, for a moment, she saw a scattering of lighted windows dotting three-storied walls typical of a *Torino* courtyard. Then the blanket was thrown back over her head and she was marched, blind and stumbling, up a staircase and down long corridors into an interior room, where she was forced into a hard chair, the blanket snatched off her head and a fierce spotlight trained full into her eyes. She tried to avert her face, but rough hands forced it into the light again. Pinned to her chair, she tried to turn her head enough to look at her captors, but rough hands shoved her face forward into the blinding light again. Time went by in silence. The only sound in the room was an adenoidal breathing right behind her.

After an eternity, there was a squeal of hinges, then a door slammed shut. Slow, heavy footsteps echoed at the far end of the room; metal clattered, as of a chair picked up and slammed down on marble. She twisted her head and squinted to see past the blinding light. A rough hand forced her face straight back into the spotlight.

Again, the silence lengthened, punctuated now by one foot tapping, slowly, on the floor. Then a harsh voice barked out: "Matilde Agiati!" Matilde jumped in her seat, heart pounding, throat parched.

"Answer!"

"Yes, yes, that's my name."

"What is your connection with Alberto Scagliosi?"

"We… both attend…" She stopped abruptly: the *Convivio* had ignored the recent *Leggi fascistissime*'s injunction to register, giving the names of all the group's members, as well as its structure and purpose.

"Answer!" the harsh voice roared.

"We…sometimes get together to…read a bit of literature," she stammered out, terrified.

"Where? When? Who are the others?"

Matilde hesitated. A hand gripped her shoulder tighter. Talon-like fingers digged into her flesh.

"We…we meet at the *Trattoria delle Arti.*"

"When do you meet?"

"At the beginning of each month."

"Which day? Who are the others?"

"Just… people with an interest in literature…"

"Which day? Names!"

Another raucous voice bellowed right next to her ear, "Names!" It shocked her and she started to cry. Ashamed, she tried to stifle her panic-stricken sobs.

"THEIR NAMES, bitch!"

Whimpering with shame and terror Matilde named names.

"What's your connection with Pier Venturi?"

Matilde's sob came out as a howl.

"PIER VENTURI!" bellowed the voice next to her right ear. Cruel hands grabbed the top of her head, ground it into her neck.

"Pier Venturi!" the voice from the far end of the room repeated, heavy with threat. "Answer the question!"

"He is…my student…At the Regio. *"* She heard the fear and pleading in her own voice, and her shame deepened. But she couldn't control her terror.

"He's been seen at the *Convivio.* What's he doing there? What's his function? Is he one of the conspirators? Whom does he work for?"

"No! No! Nobody!" Matilde screamed desperately. "There *is* no conspiracy! We don't work for anybody! We just study literature. I brought Pier there to improve his accent. He's a talented tenor, but he's from the country and has a strong *Piemontèis* accent."

"And what's wrong with a *Piemontèis* accent*,"* Guido snarled in his broadest *Astigiano* dialect.

"Nothing! There's nothing wrong!" Matilde cried. Suddenly she became aware of snot flowing down into her mouth and her shame became intolerable.

At the far end of the room, the heavy footsteps paced back and forth in an ominous rhythm. Minutes later, the voice across the room boomed, slow, impersonal, in a menacing *staccato:* "From *which* country?" Matilde didn't understand the question. She squirmed in her chair, trying to elude the glaring light, to see the speaker. He head was yanked back into the blinding light.

"WHO IS HE SPYING FOR?" the voice bellowed.

"Nobody!" Matilde cried. To her horror, she found herself howling. "Nobody is *spying*," she bawled. A boot kicked the back of her chair, sending it forward a couple of feet, knocking sideways onto the floor.

"Take her away!" the impersonal voice ordered from the door, sounding bored. A latch squealed, a door groaned open and slammed shut. Outside the room, heavy footsteps died away, leaving a deafening silence. Harsh hands righted her chair back onto its feet, bit into her shoulders, the light again full in her face.

For a moment, Matilde half-lost consciousness. Then she felt herself hefted out of her chair and dragged, feet scrabbling, across the room, along a corridor, and down several flights of stairs.

Cold air hit her face, bringing her back to herself. But her eyes, still dazed from the brutal light, could see nothing. She sensed she was back in the courtyard, being shoved into a car, a blanket again thrown over her head. The car took off, travelled for what felt like hours, but this time she sensed no hills. Then, suddenly, the car screeched to a half-stop, its door swung open, and she was thrown out onto tram tracks, and the car sped away.

There she lay, breathless, unable to move. Time went by. By and by, she began to recover her wits, saw people at a tram stop, staring down at her from the sidewalk. A tram clanked irritably, coming closer. She felt a cold rail against a cheek. With a supreme effort, she crawled towards the curb, out of the oncoming tram's way, glanced at it, caught sight of its number: it was a # 7, her line. She rose onto her knees, stood, still dazed, and stepped onto the sidewalk. The people at the stop took a step back, away from her. She waved frantically at the tram,; it ground to a stop. She scrambled on. No one else moved.

Unsteady on her feet, she fumbled for her fare. Suspicious, the conductor stared at her. The few, late-hour passengers scattered in the seats, stared, censorious, at her torn clothes, her dishevelled hair, their expressions, guessing and disapproving: a whore? A lush?

She stumbled towards the rear, past the staring hostile eyes, ineffectually trying to smooth her soiled and tousled hair. She suddenly realized she had lost her hat. She collapsed into the last seat. Her eyes landed on the tram's clock: ten past eleven. They had held her for over four hours. She sat there, staring at the clock, in a state of shock, oblivious to the tram's progress.

Then, suddenly, a corner building registered in her brain: Corso Vittorio Emanuele II. She had just missed her stop. She straggled to the rear exit, rang for the next stop.

For the next five days Matilde was unable to leave her bed. The bruises on her arms and shoulders were beginning to turn yellow and hardly hurt anymore. But she continued in a shocked state, panic shimmering underneath her skin. Any sound, the phone ringing, a door clicking shut, a clatter in the kitchen, drenched her with cold sweat. She pleaded the flu and kept to her bed. She'd been fortunate, the night she'd stumbled into her front door after her ordeal, that her husband and her sister were already fast asleep in their beds. She had retreated to the guest room and stayed there. Even now she wrestled with recurring images from those ghastly four hours. She had not mentioned what had happened to her to anyone. She simply had the flu.

But she was wracked with guilt: she had given the others away. If at least she could warn them – but how? She'd read about the Political Police's wiretapping. If the *Convivio* was now considered a subversive group, her phone – all their phones – might well be bugged. And why else would they have abducted and questioned her? The phrase, *sovversivi sospetti,* throbbed in her mind, sending shivers down her spine.

On the fifth day she recalled that Professor Rusconi usually stopped for his nightly *aperitiv* at *Café Baratti,* on his way home from the university. Could she arrange an 'accidental' meeting there? She glanced at her watch: five forty-five. If she was to catch him, she'd have to be there before seven, and she hadn't washed in five days. She threw off the covers and stumbled to the bathroom.

By six forty-eight, she was riding to Piazza Castello in a taxi she had summoned from her home. She couldn't quite face tram stops yet. And during the ride she kept glancing back through the rear window, dreading to see a car tailing her taxi.

At five past seven she pushed open the café's glass door and scanned the bar counter for the familiar grey-haired figure: he was not there. She ordered *vermouth* and settled down at a table close to the door, hoping to catch him, if he came in. Self-conscious about the dark bruises on her neck, she pulled her silk scarf up to her chin. There was nothing she could do about the dark circles under her eyes, about the haunted strain she felt on her face. She wished she had worn a hat with a veil, but she hadn't. She pulled her hat's brim down to her brows. Time and again she glanced out of the café window, scanning the arcade and the square outside, hoping to see the professor approach, dreading to see long overcoats and wide-brimmed hats.

At twenty past she finally caught sight of Professor Rusconi hurrying across Piazza Castello, making for Baratti's door. She perched on the edge of her chair, she let him enter, waited until he'd reached the bar's counter and ordered his usual *vermouth,* checked that no one followed him, that no one hung around outside, keeping watch. She waited still, until he'd got his drink. Then she rose from her seat and, the glass in hand, approached him.

"Professor," she said behind him, her throat still hurting. She heard the fear in her voice and swallowed, to relax her throat. As the professor turned, surprised at the unexpected greeting, she forced a bright smile.

"Signora Agiati, che piacere..." the professor said, looking startled rather than pleased.

She smiled and drew up close to him, her back to the room. *"Due parole, per favore, professore,"* she said lowering her voice and tipping her head away from the crowded bar.

Professor Rusconi followed her, alarmed. *"Ma che c'è?"* he queried, "Did something happened?"

She managed a coquettish tilt of her head and a flirtatious laugh as she led the way toward a vacant booth in a quieter corner room of the café. "Did something happen," he inquired again, anxiously, in her wake. She looked back at him over her shoulder, vaguely flirtatious and let her famous contralto laugh ripple through the room as she threaded herself into the booth. Alarmed, the professor leaned closer. *"Mi dica, mi dica,"* he whispered, sidling in next to her – tell me what happened. Matilde raised her handkerchief to her face. His concerned question threatened to loosen the floodgates again. With an effort, she pulled herself together, sipped at her *vermouth.*

"I can't stay long," she whispered, "but had to warn you..." she swallowed hard. "I've had a ... visit," she said, holding his eyes with a meaningful look, "a *four-hour* visit."

"Una visita? Ma che cosa..." the professor whispered, confused. Then he caught on, and his hand flew to his mouth. He leaned even closer.

Matilde thought, *We do look like conspirators.* Hurriedly, she straightened her posture, gave a *risqué* little laugh and laid a flirtatious hand on his lapel, drawing him closer. "Our *Convivio…*" she said in a whisper that might have been intimate, "I…won't be coming for a while…" She let her sentence trail.

His face turned gray, his mouth contracted into a soundless "NO!" Now he noticed her strained look, the dark circles under her eyes.

"*Le hanno fatto male?*" he asked in a cautious whisper. (Did they hurt you?) She shook her head. "Nothing serious," she said turning away. "I can't talk about it."

She gathered purse and gloves, stood up and said in a clear public voice, *"Le mie scuse alla famiglia…"* (My apologies to your family) "…ma proprio non posso."

She left. Professor Rusconi, on his feet for the polite goodbyes, sat back down, stunned. He felt something wet running down his leg and looked down in alarm at his trouser's leg, flooded with shame. Then realised he had spilled his *vermouth.* Thank goodness. He mopped at his leg with his handkerchief and waved a waiter over, ordered a double *cognac.*

When it came, he slugged half of it down in one gulp. Feeling somewhat steadier, he scanned the room for any alarming presence. Reassured, he took the next, modest sip. What should he do? The others had to be warned. But would it be wise to use the telephone? He had to think. And the regular meeting was only a few days away. He had to act fast.

The roots of Guido's malice

The phone call came just as he was undoing his tie and slipping his suspenders off to go to bed. He glanced at his clock: eleven forty-five. At this hour, the call had to be for him. His landlady did not take kindly to phone rings disturbing her first sleep. He flipped the suspenders back onto his shoulders and ran down the stair to the front hall.

"Guido," his brother's voice said at the other of the line, "*Barba Guido* has had a stroke. He's dead. Our Mother wants you here."

Guido bristled. He was done with being told what to do. And he didn't give a fig about *Barba Guido,* he'd never liked him. He recalled with disgust the wet kisses his mother's brother insisted on smacking right on the corner of Guido's mouth. "When's the funeral?" he asked.

"No, no, she wants you here *now*," his brother stressed. "We'll pick you up at the 5:45." The phone clicked dead.

Stock still, Guido stood staring, unseeing, at the wall phone: she was still giving him orders! He slammed the receiver down on its crutch and stormed upstairs. "Quiet!" bellowed an irate male voice from the landlady's quarters.

"Go to hell!" Guido snarled between his teeth. Five fort-five, he fumed: he'd have to catch the four fifteen to make it, and it was now past midnight. He slammed his overnight case shut and threw it on the floor by the door, set his alarm clock, switched off the light and threw himself into bed. "And all for bloody *Barba Guido,*" he cursed.

The train hadn't quite stopped when he caught sight of the *Colin-a Longa* carriage, waiting outside the station. He scanned the platform for his brother, and saw Tomàs, his father's groom, standing on the platform, cap in hands. They had sent a servant, hadn't even bothered to have a member of the family come to meet him.

"Bad news," the man said, assuming a grieved air, "*Monsú Guido*, he is dead. *Madama*'s waiting for you to get under way to *Fontan-a Freida*."

Glowering, Guido shoved past him without bothering to answer: *why did the cretin think he was here*? He stalked to the carriage and threw his case onto the seat. If they were driving right away to *Fontan-a Freida*, he might as well have stayed on the train until *Cheiràs,* saved himself the carriage's jostling on the muddy road. He hated horse-drawn carriages.

At *Colin-a Longa* he found the family assembled in the parlour in dutiful black, waiting for him to start the trek to *Barba Guido's* estate. His mother stood up, coat and hat already on. "Do you want a *caffelàit* before we go?" she asked, discouraging it.

"I could do with something hot," Guido answered. His mother's lips pinched. She led the way to the kitchen and stood, handbag in hand, while the cook rustled him up a bowl of milky coffee and a chunk of farm bread, which Guido broke into his *cafelàit* in bite-sized chunks. His mother stood, watching him eat. "You were always his favourite nephew," she said while he chewed.

Some two hours later, they all stood by *Barba Guido's* open bier in *Fontan-a Freida*'s vast, stone-flagged parlour. It reeked of forced flowers and hot wax. The two daughters of the house, Angelin-a and Carlòta, sat in mournful black by the window. Against the wall, a long trestle table was smothered with floral tributes. More wreaths and swags leaned against the walls, awaiting removal to the hearse. Brother Michelin, in his seminarian cassock, swooped to the bereaved sisters and seized their hands in turn in consolatory grasps. Neighbours tiptoed in, carrying more flowers, lingered a moment by the open casket, then moved aside to whisper in clusters.

"Go on," his mother nudged Guido's back toward the open bier. Reluctantly, Guido stepped up to the dead. The corpse lay in a dark suit and tie. For a moment, Guido was taken aback: absurdly, he had expected his uncle to be in his hunter's greens. His mother poked him again, "Go on, kiss him."

Guido stiffened. The death smell hit him, a blend of corpse, hot wax and unseasonable flowers. The network of livid blood vessels on the corpse's nose and cheeks repelled him, as did full lips, not quite closed. *Even now,* he thought, *his lips are wet.*

His mother poked him harder. "Kiss him!" Guido stormed out. His mother sent Giacu to bring him back.

The next day Guido and his brothers were detailed with the pallbearers. They walked the coffin down the steps and across the front yard to the waiting hearse. Wreaths were hung around the black and silver frames of its glass windows, swags and cushions covered the coffin, filling the air with their flowers' nauseating smell.

The casket installed, the men of the family took their place directly behind the hearse. By his mother's doing, Guido found himself in the centre of the first row, with his father and Giacu on either side, and Michelin and Carlòta's husband as his wingmen. There were no other men in the family. Behind them came the women. The dead man's daughters and their five female cousins, walked in the wake of the men; the aunts, including Guido's mother and one grandmother, rode in two carriages. The dead man's wife was long dead.

Guido's mother, in the first carriage, kept dabbing and dabbing at her eyes with her handkerchief. It was a close, dank day. The road oozed mud. On its verges, last year's poplar leaves, long buried by the winter's snow, now leaked out yellow-brown corruption in the thaw. The leaden March sky hung low, trapping smells, intensifying them. The hearse horses steamed under their funereal silver-edged, black quilts. Their smell, and the smell of the carriage horses behind them, blended with the repulsive scent of death, with the suffocating reek of hyacinths and *tuberosas*, nauseating Guido. The road, five miles from *Fontan-a Freida* to the cemetery where the family vault awaited *Barba Guido*'s remains, crawled up and down the Astigiano hills among regimented vineyards, just beginning to burgeon. With each step, Guido sank deeper and deeper into nausea, and, with it, deeper and deeper into anger, in fact, into *hate:* why were they – why was his mother – putting him through this?

A childhood echo of his mother's cajoling voice answered him, *Your Uncle likes you. You be nice to him.* He knew the rest, the recurring refrain from his childhood seared indelibly in his memory: *You're his favourite nephew. Barba Guido has got no children of his own. One day you'll be the master of Fontan-a Freida.* Those words of his mother's were vividly present to him now, and *her hands*, her cajoling, blandishing hands on his face, on his arms, caressing him, *coercing* him to go where he loathed being, with his uncle, the old hands, old lips straying and touching and stroking where he did not want to be touched.

The ordeal came to an end, at last, with *Barba Guido* safely stowed in the family vault. The Delloria family piled back into the *Colin-a Longa* carriage and headed for home. With each stride, the horses' smell deepened Guido's nausea. His mother's voice...*no children of his own*...kept pounding in his mind with the clip-clop of the horses' hooves.

Well, Guido countered angrily, *now he has two, two daughters.*

In the jolting carriage, the long-buried echo of his mother's voice argued. *But you are the only male. You might still inherit.* Even yesterday, on the ride to *Fontan-a Freida,* she had still clung on to that forlorn hope. Guido leaned over the carriage side and vomited.

That night at *Colin-a Longa,* his mother saw him to bed with a hot water bottle and a steaming chamomile. He refused to touch either. He fell into a dead sleep from which he woke in the pre-dawn dark with a wide-eyed stare: he'd remembered.

He'd remembered the long rides in *Barba Guido's* two-horse curricle, those dreaded rides he had begged his mother not to force him to take. Years of dreaded drives. Long years of pleading and pestering, and finally of storming, until his father, at last, had sent him away to a *collegio* as incorrigible. He remembered the lonely beech grove on *Fontan-a Freida*'s domain, where *Barba Guido* claimed the horses needed to rest. He remembered the plaid wool horse-rug spread out on dank green moss, in the grove's deepest shade. He remembered the repulsive wet lips on his cheeks, on his lips; he remembered the fondling hands, the smell of moss and horse sweat, and the sour reek of wine and tobacco on old skin. He remembered the *taste,* the foul taste of stale sweat and sex, *Barba Guido*'s sex, spurting in his mouth, gagging him, dribbling down his chin.

With a strangled roar, Guido sprung out of bed in the dark, his fists battered the rose-papered walls, furious kicks gutted the antique *armoire* that had come from *Fontan-a Freida* with his mother on her wedding, until he at last collapsed, cursing, nursing a broken toe.

Hobbling, he stormed out into the moonlit night and howled.

Chapter Thirteen

And lead us not into temptation…
The Lord's Prayer

Pier at La Tampa Lirica

Pier's eagerly awaited appearance at *La Tampa Lirica* finally came in late February. At their first meeting, last January, the professor had decided that he and Melina Cortesi were to work together and present the last scene of *La Traviata*'s first act. He had instructed them to work through the whole opera on their own, in one of the *Regio*'s downstairs rehearsal rooms, '…as a vay of soaking up its emotional atmosphere,' he had said.

They had. Week after week, scene after scene, they examined and discussed the motives and reactions of all the characters, reading the lines of the other roles and singing their own. Then, after a couple of weeks of this preliminary work, *Herr Rexel,* as Melina called the professor, had worked intensively with them on their duet, 'cleaning up their singing', as he put it, and deepening their emotional connection until, at last, Pier had become Alfredo, desperately in love with Violetta.

For weeks, Pier had been looking forward to 'taking the stage' (as Melina put it) at *La Tampa Lirica,* but tonight the eagerness left him. He felt wooden, his passion frozen. Week after week, he had shared with Lena his excitement about this night, about his duet with Violetta, about this first step towards an operatic career; and about Melina Cortesi, about her beautiful voice and her acting talent. He had pleaded with Lena to be there with him on that night, despite her reluctance, her fear that she would be out of place.

"But you will be there *with me,*" he had urged.

Of course, she had given in, and tonight she would be there to witness his triumph. For he had had no doubt that it would be a triumph, he had felt sure of it, had read it in Melina's eyes, in her smile. Signora Agiati had known it too, and she had encouraged him to believe it. Even *Herr Professor* had reluctantly concurred. *"Na ja,"* he had said, "it's just a try-out, but you're ready. Don't you fret and mess it up. And don't let it go to your head."

But this morning Pier had woken up in a blue funk. He'd had to drag himself out of bed and through his classes. And this evening, when he boarded the tram to go fetch Lena, he found that, after all, he didn't want her there, not tonight. As the tram ground to a stop in front of Cinema Lingotto, he caught sight of her in her bright red coat, eagerly waiting for him and, with a catch in his breath, he felt a sudden revulsion. Hate almost. He was tempted to squat down among the seats, to hide in the tram; to leave her there, at the tram stop.

He'd suppressed the guilty impulse, of course. And now, riding together in the tram toward the club, he struggled to hide his black mood. But Lena sensed it. "Nervous about tonight?" she asked shyly, "I know *I*'d be scared to death," she added.

"Just as well it isn't you, then," he snapped at her. "You wouldn't know what you're doing."

Lena recoiled as from a slap. Instantly guilt-stricken, Pier pleaded, "Ach, don't mind me. It's just first night jitters. It's normal." But they rode the rest of the way in silence.

They were the first to arrive at Professor Rexel's reserved table, large enough to accommodate the two singers and all their well-wishers. *La Tampa Lirica* was already full and noisy, the spotlighted dance floor empty, waiting for the show to start. Pier took Lena's coat to hang it on a peg on the wall, all the while scanning the room over his shoulder for his group. "Do I look all right?" Lena asked anxiously, hands smoothing her black skirt.

"You're fine," he answered, still searching the crowd over her head. He pulled out a chair for her at the table. "Look," he said, "I've got to go warm up. You sit here. The others will be here shortly. I'll be back in fifteen minutes." He vanished through a curtained doorway at the back of the hall.

Alone at the empty table, Lena felt totally *dëspaisà,* utterly lost. She had envisioned the place the way she remembered it from New Years' Eve, with Pier, loving, at her side. Now she was alone, and the place felt strange, somehow disreputable, a dangerous den. Her eyes blurred: Pier wasn't himself tonight. What was wrong?

"Good evening," said a cultured woman's voice behind her. "Are you with the Rexel party?"

Lena felt caught in a place where she had no right to be, and stammered defensively, "I'm…I'm…with Pier Venturi."

"Oh, I see…" The woman's look of surprised enlightenment stabbed Lena. But then the woman smiled. "I'm Matilde Agiati," she said, stretching out her hand in a friendly greeting. "Pier did say he would be bringing a friend." She sat down next to Lena, looked at her encouragingly. Lena relaxed somewhat.

"You are… Signora Agiati," she said, breathlessly. "Pier speaks about you all the time. About his work with you, I mean."

She drifted into silence and stared down at her hands in her lap. Silently, she rehearsed the little speech Pier had helped her to labouriously prepare. Suddenly she spoke up again, "Just this week Pier said to me, 'Lena, if it were not for Signora Agiati, I would not be at the Regio now.' We are ever so grateful to you."

Matilde smiled graciously at the nervous girl. *So*, she thought, noting that the girl had not introduced herself, *her name is Lena, and it's 'we'. Her accent is appalling.* Aloud she said with a deprecatory smile, "It's true, I helped open the first door for Pier, but the rest is entirely due to his own merit."

Behind them a Germanic voice boomed above the din: "*So!* Matilde!" Horst Rexel had arrived. He dragged a chair back from the table and plunked himself down next to Matilde, handing his hat and coat to the buxom young girl who had come in with him, for her to hang them on the wall. "And who is this delicious creature?" he added, straining towards Lena.

"This is Pier's friend," Matilde answered, "Lena." She turned to Lena and added: "My dear, meet Professor Rexel, Pier's mentor at the Regio."

"*So…*" Rexel crooned, holding Lena's hand longer than necessary and peering deep into her eyes across Matilde's lap. Lena blushed and looked down. Matilde tried to distract the German, to defuse the girl's obvious discomfort. "Frau Rexel won't be with us tonight?" she asked, glancing around. "I trust she is well?"

"*Ja ja,* she's fine," Rexel dismissed *Frau Rexel*, his eyes firmly on Lena. He got up, walked around Matilde, and sat in the chair next to Lena. "Ah, beauty!" he cooed, prying her hand from her lap, "It is a joy forever!"

"Good evening, *Herr Rexel*," called out a well-focused voice behind him: "Is Venturi here yet?" The newcomer stood, scanning the room. Lena turned to look at the speaker, her mouth falling open, her hand flying up to cover it. *She's like a film star,* she thought, her eyes devouring the silver screen vision in front of her: flowing champagne silk under an open, soft-coloured fur. A lavish russet collar matched the vision's shingled hair. Dazzled, Lena caught a shimmer of soft moss-green among the champagne folds. *Her dress matches her eyes,* she noticed dreamily.

Eyes still on Lena, Rexel snapped, "*Ja, ja,* Melina, relax, he's here, varming up. You go do the same. Ve're on in tventy minutes." With a quick glance at her over his shoulder, he waved her away toward the curtained doorway beyond which Pier had disappeared. *"Raus,"* he ordered her, "go." Then he noticed she was still in her fur coat, not moving. "You give your things to Cora," he told her. "She'll hang them up."

The table was beginning to fill. Lena was surprised to see a priest stroll towards it, draw out a chair and sit down across from her. Then it dawned on her: of course, Don Marco! Pier had said how much the duomo's music master loved opera.

The petulant tinkle of a silver bell claimed the room's attention. The lights flickered, then dimmed to a subdued glow while the room's hubbub subsided to a muted rumble. From the musician's alcove, a piano struck a ripple of notes. A spotlight picked up a man in striped trousers and cut-away jacket in the centre of the show floor. "Ladies and Gentlemen," he announced, "…for your pleasure, tonight," he scanned the audience, "please, welcome…" An arm opened up, focussing the audience attention on a portly young man suddenly picked up by the spotlight, "Arnoldo Billieri, *basso*, here to delight you with…Rossini's Bartolo!"

The evening's first singer advanced rapidly, bowing right and left on his way to the stage. The announcer withdrew, and the piano played a few introductory phrases, then a strong bass boomed:

> *"A un dottor della mia sorte*
> *Queste scuse, signorina?*
> *Vi consiglio, mia carina,*
> *Un pó' meglio a imposturar…"*

Lena listened absently, twisting in her seat to scan the room for Pier. The Rossini *aria* was drawing to a close when she, at last, spotted him dodging among the tables, tiptoeing his way to their party.

Next to her, Matilde followed the direction of her eyes, saw them brighten into a smile at the sight of Pier. *The child is badly in love,* she thought. *Poor thing.* She changed chair so Pier could sit next to Lena. She caught the strained look on him, and laid one hand on his arm to draw his attention. With a reassuring smile, she brought her other hand to her diaphragm, discretely miming 'deep breathe'. Pier took her prompt and sat down next to Lena, taking slow, deep breaths. Lena gazed apprehensively, adoringly into his face. Next to Matilde, Rexel stage-whispered in her ear, "Ah, young love! How it brings beauty to life!"

The smirk that accompanied his ambiguous statement irritated Matilde. On the stage, the bass sang, "*E Rosi…na…inno..cen..ti-i…na.. Scon…so…la-a…ta, di..spe..ra-a.…ta..*" From the curtained back doorway, Melina hurried to rejoin their table. The bass sang on: "*…in sua camera serra-a-a-ta-a… Fin ch'io voglio star dovrà! … Signorina, un'altra vo-o-o-lta…A un dottor della mia so-o-rte…*"

His performance came to an end and the audience rewarded the singer with generous applause. He bowed centre, right and left, then hastened to his table in one of the alcoves amidst the renewed hubbub of people enjoying themselves – snatches of laughter, clinking of glasses, waiters scurrying back and forth with laden trays, the noise soon deafening.

Don Marco rose from his seat and made his way around the table to rest a hand on Pier's shoulder. He bent down close to be heard over the uproar. "I look forward to your performance," he said, "It's the first time I'll hear you outside the duomo. I'm excited." Pier looked up at him over his shoulder, deeply grateful.

The bell tinkled, the lights flickered thrice, the piano rippled its warning. The noise died down. "Ladies and Gentlemen," roared the announcer in the spotlight. Melina nudged Pier. The spotlight swung over the throng to pick them up at their table, prompted them to rise, and followed them as, side by side, they made their way to the stage. Lena watched them go then, suddenly, her eyes narrowed: she had caught *La Cortesi* (as Pier referred to Melina in his nightly accounts of their Regio practices) taking Pier's hand as she walked by his side.

The piano rippled a few introductory phrases. On the stage, the spotlight held the two performers as though in a separate, magical world. *La Cortesi* took a couple of steps away from Pier and stopped, eyes focussed, vaguely, in the space above the seated crowd.

Lena watched *La Cortesi,* puzzled at her gazing, apparently lost, somewhere in mid-air, above the audience's head. Then Pier sang out, *"Oh qual pal...lor!"* At the edge of the spotlight, *La Cortesi* turned slowly, apparently startled to find Pier behind her. Lena scoffed: the minx knew perfectly well that *he* was there: they'd walked on stage together.

La Cortesi sang, *"Voi qui!"* And Pier, solicitous, hurried to her, answering, *"Ce..ssa-a...ta è l'an...si-a... Che vi tur..bó?"* The performance was underway. Discrete shuffling in the alcoves: people began to stand up, some shifting about for a better view. Lena's eyes softened as she thought, *Pier looks so distinguished in his blue suit.* On stage, Violetta broke into flirtatious laughter, tinged with bitterness, *"Gli è ve...ro! Si gran...de amo-o-or...dime...ti-ca...to ave-e-e-a..."* And Alfredo, looking hurt, responding, *"Ride-e...te! ...e in vo-o..i v'ha un co-o...re?"* Yes, Lena agreed, the woman was a heartless minx. How could Pier *like* her?

Yet she was enthralled. The minx's shimmering gown fizzed down her body like *spumante.* A dropped waist hugged her slender hips while ethereal silk gathered softly above a bugle-beaded waistband and the low-cut back revealed hints of skin under a chiffon glazing. Sinuous arms glinted inside slit sleeves. A scarf flowed behind her from bugled *epaulettes,* and a beaded headband scattered flakes of gold on the russet shingle of her hair. In the spotlight, Violetta turned to face Pier as he sang his lines, and Lena saw her full-faced for first time. *She is* not *beautiful,* she thought, partially relieved. Minutely, she inspected the illuminated face; she took in the curious triangle of the lips, the high, wide cheekbones, the planes of the cheeks that met at the pointed little chin. *Even her eyes look...pointed,* she gloated, *like a two of diamonds on playing cards. How can Pier like such a face? I'm far more beautiful than her!*

In the spotlights, Pier sang, *"Oh amore misterio-o-o-so-o, Misterio-o-oso-o, al-te-e-ro-o, Croce e deli-i-i-zia al co-o-or."*

The duet came to an end in an uproar of applause. At the tables, people on their feet, cheered *"Bravo! Brava! Bravi! Bravissimi!"* On their way off the stage, Pier and Melina were mobbed, their hands grabbed and shaken, Pier's shoulders slapped, Melina was hugged and kissed, then so was Pier. The crowd herded them here and there among the tables into more welcoming arms and flushed, congratulatory faces, while their teachers trailed, beaming, behind them, bumped and jostled by the ecstatic crowd. "Vat did I tell you?" Rexel cried excitedly at Don Marco's elbow. He chortled, delighted: "I knew our *bube v*ould be a smash, he and Melina!" Bushy red mop and slender black cassock disappeared in Pier's wake, with Matilde sidling her way behind them.

Alone at the Rexel table, Lena watched Pier getting swarmed by the crowd with a sinking feeling: he wasn't coming back to her. Her face crumpled. In a momentary gap in the press around the triumphant singers, Matilde caught sight of Lena alone at the Rexel table. She looked forlorn, a child on the verge of tears. *Poor child,* Matilde thought, *She's feeling out of place, I dare say.* Dëspais, she added in the descriptive *piemontèis word.* The childlike sorrow on the lovely face touched her heart with a mixture of sympathy and irritation. She began to work her way back towards their table, to join her.

"Isn't this splendid!" she cried in the din, sitting down on a chair near Lena. Lena nodded, eyes down on the hands in her lap. Matilde was touched by the youthful sorrow. "Come," she said, reaching across the table for an open bottle of wine, "Let's drink to Pier's triumph." She poured out two glasses and handed one to Lena, asking, "What did you think of it?"

"It's just like…" Lena mumbled without looking up, the glass unsteady in her hand. She stopped. She had almost said "like the movies", but then she finished, "…like in a real theatre." The glass in her hand wobbled, and she hurriedly set it on the table to avoid spilling.

"Oh, you've seen *La Traviata* on stage?" Matilde said with an encouraging smile. There was a long pause. Then Lena shook her head and murmured, "Pier took me to the Regio last New Year's Eve."

She risked picking up her glass again and taking a tiny sip. She twisted in her seat, eyes scouring the crowd behind her, looking for Pier. Matilde suppressed a sigh: this beautiful child was hopeless.

Again and again, she tried to engage Lena in conversation, to distract her from her misery. At one point, the crush in one of the alcoves parted for a moment and Pier came into view, Melina next to him, her arm around his waist. From their table, Lena and Matilde watched him laugh, head thrown back, then draw Melina close in a sideways hug, give her a quick peck on the cheek.

She's rich! Lena thought with a pang. A desolate mood weighed her down.

The crowd shifted again, the gap closed, and the pair disappeared from sight. Next to Matilde, Lena stared, open-mouthed, at the tablecloth. Matilde tried again.

"How long have you known Pier?" she asked, staying with the only subject that seemed to engage the child.

"Since last September, when I got the FIAT job. My station was right next to his."

"Your station..." Matilde echoed, puzzled. Then she caught on. "Oh, I see... So, you two were in each other's sight all day long. It must be hard for you now. You must miss him a lot, now." Eyes down, Lena nodded. Matilde thought she caught the glint of a tear falling on the folded hands in the girl's lap. She heard her sniff.

From the musicians' alcove came the first strands of a Viennese Waltz. Couples drifted from the tables toward the now empty dance floor, beginning to dance after the scheduled floorshow.

"Who is she?" Lena's question surprised Matilde who was now watching the dancers.

"Who?"

"The girl. Violetta."

"Oh! I see..." Matilde read the quivering chin, the intense, questioning eyes. She also caught the edge in the *Piemontèis* voice. She thought, *This poor child is burning with jealousy,* Aloud she answered, "Melina Cortesi is one of the professor's advanced students." Lena stared in silence, and Matilde began to feel impatient of her obstinate sorrow.

Privately, Lena thought, *Advanced student! Fast, that's what she is!*

A chair dragged back from the table interrupted her thoughts. "Vell, Vell! That vasn't so bad, vas it, Matilde, my dear, for ze first time! Our boy did all right," he said. Then he turned to Lena. "And vhat is this beautiful creature doing, sitting here all by herself?" he demanded. He winked at Matilde and grabbed Lena's hand. "Come!" he ordered, all but yanking her to her feet, "ve must dance, celebrate. I bet you can do the polka." He scuttled off to the dance floor, drawing Lena, half resisting, along behind him.

Soon, the two disappeared in the swirl of couples. The next time Matilde caught sight of them, Rexel was hefting Lena into a series of vigorous leaps, and she was laughing excitedly. They again disappeared among the couples while Matilde caught sight of Melina sidling between abandoned chairs toward their table, Don Marco a few steps behind her. As she reached their table, the duomo's music master caught up with her.

"Well done, Signorina Cortesi," he said, taking the young singer's hands in his in a congratulatory grasp, "Very well done indeed. Your voice is so…perfectly assured."

He slid a chair back from the table for Melina to sit down, then turned to Matilde. "They work very well together, don't they," he said, sitting down and turning back to Melina. "I'm looking forward to your recital this fall," he said. "Do you know already when it is going to be?"

"Oh, Professor Rexel told you about that?" Melina said eagerly. The priest nodded. "He's very excited about you two, and with good reason. We all expect great things." Melina flushed with pleasure. She glanced towards the dance floor and caught sight of Rexel leading Lena back towards their table. Three pairs of eyes followed the odd couple's approach.

"This beautiful creature is an absolutely *marvellous* dancer," Rexel announced, joining the three at the table and drawing back a chair for Lena to sit next to him. "*Aber jetzt,*" he then cried, panting, "I am in need of *sustenance!*" He beckoned a passing waiter over. "*Pasticceria, bitte!*" he shouted, "Lots of it!" He reached for an open bottle on the table and poured out two glasses of wine, passing one to Lena. "And vhere is our Pier?" he then asked, glancing around. "Ve'll break out the champagne ven he comes."

At the question Lena's laughing face crumpled: yes, where *was* he? Was he with *her?* She craned her neck to scour the room, searching for the pair, unaware that Melina was sitting all of three chairs from her.

At last, her anxious eyes landed on Pier, still surrounded by enthusiastic admirers in one of the alcoves. One middle-aged, richly gowned lady reached up on her toes and planted a kiss on the corner of his mouth. Rexel heard Lena's sharp breath intake, saw panic spread on her face and yanked her back to her feet. "Come on," he ordered, "ve can't miss this glorious tango." He swept her away to the dance floor, and soon the other dancers cleared a space around the odd couple deeply absorbed in spectacular Argentine gyrations.

Matilde watched, surprised: they were actually very good, though they made a peculiar spectacle – she young and beautiful, innocently absorbed in her provocative dance; he portly, middle-aged, holding her a shade too tight, a gnome with an unruly red mop struggling to contain a leer, his masked eyes devouring her.

Matilde squirmed: the pair remind her of the lewd postcards she'd seen last summer in the Ōtzthal on the racks of news agents and souvenir shops – a rubicund rustic in grey *Loden* or *Lether Hosen,* smirking as he ogled a buxom child in pigtails, rear end up in the air, white bloomers glowing in the sun over firm round buttocks innocently exposed under a wind-blown Austrian folk dress.

Suddenly uncomfortable, Matilde looked away: across the table, she caught sight of Don Marco intently watching the couple on the dance floor, an ironic half-smile twitching the left corner of his mouth.

After the triumph

The performance at *La Tampa Lirica* stirred up in Pier a maelstrom of emotions. That night, after the show, riding to Le Basse in the back of Don Marco's chauffeured automobile with Lena, he'd felt exultant one moment, then piqued at her moodiness, then, the next moment, brutally let down by it, then wallowing in guilt. His mind had been so full of the evening's intoxicating moments – Alfredo and Violetta's lovemaking in the spotlight, the glowing Melina next to him, holding his hand as she bowed her thanks to their enthusiastic audience. And all the while Lena sat rigidly silent, turned away from him, refusing contact, staring unseeing out of the car window.

Even now, their audience's congratulatory phrases rang in his mind, in the exact speakers' voices, just as he'd heard them, the flattering comparisons to cherished opera stars, eager inquiries as to where and when, *he, Pier,* or he and Melina, would perform again. That awful night ride, too, kept coming back into his mind, vivid and jumbled, like broken revenants from a lost dream – Lena, morose, next to him in the car; himself still revelling in his moment of glory, fragments of *croce e delizia*...echoing in his mind. Melina's soft hand in his, the startling sensation of her arm briefly around his waist, the shiver it had sent down his spine. And Melina taking his hand as they walked up to the stage. That simple gesture, her hand seeking his as they walked side by side to the stage, had taken him by surprise. In fact, for a swift moment, it had startled him, so that he had recoiled from it.

But *then*... That seeking hand in his, there, in the public eye, had become a declaration, an endorsement that legitimised his taking his place among *'cola gent lì'.* There had been such a trusting feel in that hand reaching for his that, for an instant, he had experienced Melina as a little girl seeking the reassurance of her big brother. Then Melina, striding next to him assured and confident, had glanced up at him and that glance had established between them a different kind of intimacy: camaraderie, inclusiveness – the bond of trusted partners on an exciting adventure. It had declared that he and she were one, that *he belonged.* That simple gesture of hers assumed for Pier a kind of 'us against them', a 'two for the road' significance. His own assurance had surged, his jitters vanished, as though, with that public touch of her hand, Melina had anointed him, established *his right* to be part of her world.

That night, during their ride to Le basse, Pier, in a kind of glow, when he reached toward Lena, but found her withdrawn, shut off from him in her corner of the car, apart and rejecting, his anger flared up. He felt her gloom, her pain, her withdrawal, and resented her. He'd wanted her at the recital to share his triumph with her, and here she was, crouching in that corner like a beaten spaniel, ruining it all!

Her crumpled form deflated him, overwhelmed him with guilt. He had got so caught up in the thrill of his first public appearance that he had ignored her, left her alone among people who, to her, were intimidating strangers. In the shifting light and darkness of the fast-moving car, he cringed with guilt. He sought her hand to comfort her, to make amends, to reaffirm their closeness… and found it cold and limp, unresponsive in her lap. In her corner of the car, she sat obstinately facing outwards, refusing contact. Pier's anger flared hotter: why couldn't she understand? Why couldn't she forgive him?

The rest of the ride passed in rigid silence.

Pier's deflation persisted all through that night and through several days following. On the Monday morning he dragged himself through his *collegio* duties, a spent force. After the Music Theory class, Don Lucas approached him and enquired if he was feeling poorly. Pier muttered that he was fine. Don Luca laid an arm around his shoulders and said, "I hear great things about your first night. Don Marcello told us your performance caused an enthusiastic near riot. Do you need a rest?"

Surprised, Pier declined the rest: he had not known anyone from the *Collegio* had been there. He had not noticed Don Marcello or his friends.

Later that morning, in the literature class he now attended regularly, the teacher's words reached him as though through a dense cocoon. After class, the teacher approached him with congratulations about his debut, then frowned and asked if Pier was feeling all right. Buoyed and embarrassed by the masters' praise and concern, Pier was mostly annoyed that he had let his state of mind show, so he made a concerted effort to keep his moods to himself, despite his persisting *malaise.*

On Tuesday, still in the same insulated state, he caught the tram to his Regio sessions. Waiting for the professor in his practice room, he sat down at the piano, wanton fingers mindlessly picking out on the keyboard snatches *La Traviata's 'Lungi da lei per me non v'ha diletto'*, absently humming familiar phrases, until, suddenly, he caught himself: his mind was hovering around Melina. He jumped up and, blushing, turned away from the piano in confusion, Lena's sad face a painful reproach. Just then the *Herr Professor* entered the room.

"Ah, *gut*, Pier, you're *hier*," Rexel yelled gleefully, trotting to his desk at his usual bustling gait, beckoning to Pier to join him, waving the bundle of envelopes in his hand. "See, ve've got fan mail already," He cried, scrambling the clutter on his desk in his search for his letter opener. "*Hier,*" he said, handing the paper cutter to Pier, "ve open them together, *ja*?" His hand vanished under the papers again, and this time emerged with his biscuit tin. He sat down, savouring a first bite of a *marron glacé*. Pier started to slit envelopes open, smoothing out their contents into a neat stack on a corner of the crowded desk.

"*Ach schade!*" the professor unexpectedly lamented, munching, gazing fondly at a half-eaten *marron*, delicately held between middle finger and thumb. "The last of these beauties, I'm told. No more to be had until next season."

He switched his attention to Pier, "Vell then, vhat have ve got?"

Pier handed him the stack of opened mail. On top, was a newspaper cutting from *La STAMPA,* from Alberto Scagliosi's regular column, *Echi d'Opera*. He had not noticed the journalist from the *Convivio* in the *Tampa Lirica* crowd, and he certainly had not expected his first performance to be reviewed in the prestigious column. Still munching, Rexel wiped his sticky fingers on his trousers, before reaching for the cutting. "*So!* You've made the news. Not bad, not bad at all." He read on and chuckled: "*Na ja!* ... compares you favourably to Tito Schipa and Lauri-Volpe. Not bad company for a rank beginner, *nicht?*" He licked his index and picked up the next sheet.

"*Gut. Gut,*" he commented, pleased.

They had almost finished the stack of letters when Rexel rumbled, "*Tonner Wetter!*" Pier looked up, alarmed, but the professor kept reading. Pier waited anxiously, while the professor hummed several times before speaking. "It's from your kind patroness, the Contessa Vergani della Rovere. She congratulates you, and she vonders vhether you vould consent to sing at a *soirée* at her *salon,* next month. It's the last of her spring season. Naturally, you vill consent. Ve'll ask her vhat she vants to hear. But then," he added, "no more appearances until next fall."

"But what about…" Pier stammered. Rexel held up a repressive hand, "No more," he decreed, "your voice needs a rest."

"But I…" Pier argued timidly, "I have four more weddings scheduled…"

"Vell, *ja-a-a,* those are your bread *und butter.* You vill do those. And you vill sing at the duomo vhenever Don Marco asks you. But…no other engagements. Ve must start vork on your fall recital. October vill be here before ve know it. You and Melina, of course. *La Traviata* again *und Carmen.* How's your French coming?"

"I'm only taking first trimester French."

"*Ja*…but your pronunciation?"

"That's not hard. It's very close to *Piemontèis.*"

"*Na ja,* that could be a problem. Ve'll have Mademoiselle Chantal check your diction. *So*, now ve have a lot of vork to do." He grabbed an old envelope from the mess on his desk and started to scribble on it. "Your *croce e delizia* duet took eleven minutes. For a recital ve need about one and a half hour. I'm thinking two duets and two arias, one for each of you. Then ve'll also prepare something else for encores, in case ve need it."

The session moved on to the piano. Professor Rexel put Pier through a couple of selections from Carmen, working on his phrasing in some of the challenging sections – now and then clicking his tongue at his pronunciation. The hour flew by. Pier was gathering his scores to leave, when the professor abruptly changed the subject.

"Your Lena," he said, eyeing Pier from under his red bush. "She is a qvite a beauty. Where did you find her?"

"She works…where I worked," Pier edged, not liking to mention that he had worked at FIAT.

"*Na ja*, at FIAT," Rexel spelled out. "Vas she, too, making cars?"

Pier bristled at the teasing tone.

The professor twinkled. "No matter," he went on, teasing. "She is a beauty. And she dances…" he kissed the tips of his fingers in a mock-Italian gesture, "vith…*such passion.* You'd better guard her vell, my boy, guard her very very vell…"

Pier left, thoroughly disturbed by the unexpected ending of his session. Maybe it had been a mistake to bring Lena to *La Tampa Lirica.*

Guilt, doubt and love

The conflict of love, doubt and guilt plagued Pier for days. It was Lena he loved, with all his heart. Yet the image of Melina Cortesi kept intruding. And he kept getting angry with Lena, kept hurting her. Their night ride from *La Tampa Lirica* to Le Basse, after his performance, was still painfully vivid in his mind. It evoked that other awful day, the day of his black despair after the Regio audition, when he had believed that *Herr Rexel had* mocked his efforts, shattered his hopes. Pier shuddered, remembering that black moment, the way he had shut down, recoiled into himself, like a snail snapping back into its shell from a rough touch. This time, not misery but exultation had come between him and Lena made him lose sight of her and, once again, he had hurt her, as though he did not care.

But he did care! He had *wanted her there* to share his hopes, his triumph. She should have seen that it was *her triumph* as well! And instead…she had turned away from him. She just couldn't grasp how much that night had meant to him. And yet he was sure she loved him. Around and around his thoughts went, circling this hurt like buzzards, until they dissipated like water into sand, leaving his mind blank, his heart arid. And in that blank… uncalled, a *mirage* arose – the image of Melina; *of the two of them, bowing* to delirious audience, holding hands. *At one.*

That image, Melina next to him, bowing and smiling, shook him: he loved Lena. *She* was the one he wanted to marry. But Melina… An electric jolt ran through his frame. With her in the *La Tampa* spotlight he'd felt…well, *whole*, *real*, at one with their world.

And now a startling new view of himself emerged as through a fog: he saw himself somehow split into two disconnected selves, one loving Lena, fervently, and looking forward to a life with her; the other – a stranger he didn't trust – sniffing offensively around Melina.

On Wednesday morning Pier woke up to yet another bittersweet image: himself and Lena, reading side by side at the kitchen table and, across from them, by her stove, her mother quietly listening, her knitting needles a discrete accompaniment to their lessons. For months now he had *homed* to Le Basse and Gioana's kitchen like a pigeon returning to his coop. Day after day he had flown there to recoup from his day in the world. And now he'd been staying away.

He squirmed: he had not been to see Lena since the night of their ride from *La Tampa Lirica. I must go see her,* he scolded himself, but did not commit to when.

Irritably, he got up and gathered his books for the day's classes – French and Literature, after assisting in the Music History class. Today he was to sing Machaud's motet – his tenor to Don Marcello's falsetto. He thought of their rehearsing *Quant en moy,* this past week, of the strange intimacy of close work together. He struggled to shake his listless, irritable mood, but his mind kept drifting back to his confusion.

Now, as Don Marcello lectured to his fourteen-year olds, Pier heard words and dates drift through him as though from outer space – The Babylonian Captivity, 1305…the Great Schism, 1470…the Black Plague, 1347–1350…The Hundred Years War, 1338… Events and dates passed through him – body and mind – without registering, as through a sieve. Then among the students' desks, a hand shot up.

"Yes, Molino," he heard Don Marcello call out, "you have a question?"

"Yes, Father. I don't understand…what's 'a crisis of faith'?"

Pier was vaguely aware of having heard that phrase drift by him in the course of the lecture. Now the youngster's question focussed his attention: what could the plague and the hundred years war have to do with faith? His eyes turned to the teacher for his answer.

"Hmmm…" Don Marcello answered, starting to pace to and fro in front of his class. In the past few months, Pier had got used to that interval of reflection before the teacher responded to a question with an explanation. When he stopped, as he always did, square by the centre row of student desks, Don Marcello rephrased the pupil's question.

"Yes, indeed, what do earthly events have to do with faith?" His glance scanned the upturned faces, inviting tentative answers. When no hand shot up, he continued, "We must look at this the way a medieval person might have seen it. What was the medieval view of the world?" Again, he paused, scanning the class for answers. Finding none, he went on.

"Their world was so very small*, self-contained.* The Earth was the centre of the universe. The whole universe revolved around it. Everything they saw had been created by God. The world-order was a long chain, each kind of being a link in the chain. The Church was the first ring in that chain, the link between

God and Man. All creatures below man had been created for man's benefit, everything that happened, happened by God's will, or as an act of Providence. "

He paused, assessing his audience. Heads were nodding, the image he had created comfortably familiar to these fourteen-year olds.

"Now, think for a moment," Don Marcello continued, "of all the disasters that plagued the medieval world. How it could be for the benefit of mankind that war and pestilence happened, destroyed whole cities, and nobody could stop them?"

Frowns appeared on the young faces, and Don Marcello went on. "Until then, for the last few centuries, the worst 'plague' to hit the human world had been the hordes of Barbarians, ruthless warriors who were *not Christian,* seen almost as demons in human form." In their desks, young heads were nodding, remembering their medieval history lessons. The teacher continued.

"Throughout all their invasions, the fortified walls of abbeys and monasteries had been the one bastion against the invaders, providing what security there could be on earth, while faith in God promised a better life in the hereafter. But what was happening now? *Walls could not keep the plague out*." Don Marcello stopped, paced, let that last thought sink in.

"What's more, there now were *two* centres of Christianity, one in Rome, the other in Avignon…"

Again he walked to the window and back, "…*Two popes…Two contenders* to Saint Peter's throne!

"But how could that be, if God indeed spoke *through the church* and named Saint Peter' successor?

"Can you see *why* the Schism rocked the certainty of the faithful?"

Again the teacher paused, taking in the tense upturned faces. "You can see, can't you," he went on, "that such a situation put a lot in question. The splendour of the Roman Church had been cherished when it had embodied the glory of God. But if there were *two* popes…? If the throne of Saint Peter could be usurped by greed and ambition? Well then…the clergy might be no better than the feudal lords who oppressed the peasants."

He paced to the window and back then continued, "Remember, the Hundred Years War had been the rebellion of *the peasants* against *the lords*, a fight against exploitation, against poverty and oppression. Now, on the land people were starving, while *two papal courts* lived in the lap of luxury in Rome *and* in

Avignon. It's understandable, don't you think, that, under such conditions, people gave way to the temptation of doubt..."

Again he paced twice back and forth, then with strong emphasis, he said *"And ...doubt once stirred up...* people began to ask all kinds of questions...

"The good thing was that, as a result of that crisis of faith, people stopped depending on providence alone, and began to use their own ingenuity to try and solve the problems of everyday life.

"Once that started, it was only a matter of time before lots of other beliefs were put in question. A mere a hundred and fifty years later people like Galileo began to rely on *experiments* to establish the nature of the material universe. Who knows Galileo's dates?"

Hands that shot up throughout the class, and the teacher listened to his pupils response before continuing.

"That new way of asking questions – the experimental method – revolutionised Man's whole notion of the world order. Human science was born and, over time, began to compete with faith as *a path to a knowledge* of the *material* world. The church reacted to that challenge to its authority and as a result confusion arose as to...what was of Caesar's and what was God's. That is, what is *of this world* and what is *of the next*. This confusion was at the root of the church's efforts to stamp out what was then considered heresy, and many scholars suffered for it. Remember Galileo's, *'eppur si muove'?"* Heads nodded vigorously. The teacher resumed his explanation.

"Eventually the confusion began to clear up, and science was allowed to claim its role in the world: the universe *does not* revolve around the earth. The earth revolves around the sun, which is but a speck among far bigger stars! Can you see how that could lead to a complete change of perspective?

"In a way, this revolution, 14th century the crisis of faith, both freed Man and demoted him. Perhaps he could no longer see himself as, God's first born on earth, just one step down from the angels; but now, instead of waiting for bliss in Heaven, he could use his own ingenuity to make life better here on earth. So people began appreciate *human creations* as well, not just God's. That was how secular art and literature came into being, for the very first time.

"You've heard about this in your history and literature classes. Just think of the new merchant city states, of the poets you are reading now the *Dolce Stil Novo*, of Cavalcanti, Dante, Petrarca. All that began to happen less than a hundred years after this crisis of faith," Don Marcello concluded, surveying his class. He saw alarm on some of the adolescent faces, on others dawning comprehension.

"And that," the teacher went on, "leads us straight to what happened in music at that time, to our topic for today, to *Ars Nova,* to the New Art." He stepped to the piano and rippled a few notes. "Listen to Machaud's motet, circa 1350. It is *not* a hymn, not a prayer. It is a… *love song.*"

He sat down and sang, "*Quant en moy vint premièrement…*" (When love first came to me.) Along his *falsetto*'s eighty beat rhythm, Pier sang a second, distinct isorhythm in forty beats: "*Amour et beauté parfaite…*" (Love and perfect beauty.) The piano accompanied the two voices with a sustained plainchant.

The end-of-class bell drowned the last few notes. Don Marcello closed the keyboard, his voice raised above the din. "The plainchant," he explained loudly, "is the voice of sacred devotion. You will notice it is still there, but now it underlies the love song. We'll discuss this next time."

The boys filed out of the room with the usual contained rumpus. At his master's assistant's desk, Pier sat on, deep in thought. One of Don Marcello's phrases had struck him: 'the temptation of doubt'. It had never occurred to him to put faith and daily life together. Religion, the church, they were…well, Sunday affairs. Everyday life was just that, all the other days of the week, most of life. Don Marcello had brought the two together in that strange combination of doubt and temptation.

"Coming, Pier?" the young Jesuit called from the doorway.

Of course, the next class. Pier hurriedly gathered his things and rushed to join him. They walked out side by side until each entered his next class. But all day long that phrase, 'the temptation of doubt', kept nibbling at Pier's mind. He had never given much thought to religion and faith. Going to church had just been one of the facts of life, like feeding the chicken or drawing water from the well. His ma's life, he knew, revolved around her prayer book and her perennial, irritating "*se dio voel*" (God willing.) He had gone to church because everybody went and his ma had sent him. And later because Don Michel liked his singing. The matter of belief had never been big much of a concern for him. He believed what he was told to believe until it no longer made sense to him. Now he thought back to the time Don Marco had first proposed sending him to a seminary and Pier had thought he was being asked to become a priest. His mind had run to Lena. To Lena, and to what would happen to his singing if he refused to go. He had given no thought to what it meant to be a priest, or to the questions of faith and vocation.

The temptation of doubt. All through the day those words kept hounding him. Perhaps that was what had been troubling him since *La Tampa Lirica.* He had been plagued by guilt, anger and confusion, since that night. Did guilt and doubt have anything to do with one another? He felt guilty about the muddle of his feelings; about loving Lena and always being angry with her; and about being drawn to Melina. The words of a Dante sonnet from his literature class rose in his mind: *Tanto gentile e tanto onesta pare la donna mia quand'ella altrui saluta* (My woman looks so gentle and so honest when she greets other people.) Lena *was* gentle and sweet and honest, he had no doubt of that. What he doubted, what puzzled him was…well, it was … himself, his anger, the muddle in his mind.

Late that afternoon, still muddled, he left the *collegio* for his session with Professor Rexel, and that evening he returned for supper with that '*temptation of doubt*' still rattling in his head. Exasperated, he considered raising the question with Don Marcello, but then, embarrassed and annoyed with himself, he dismissed the thought. He sat in silence through a restless supper. But later on he sought out the young Jesuit in the Junior Masters' common room, found him sitting by the fire, immersed in a book. "Excuse me," Pier all but whispered, "could I… have a word?"

Don Marcello set his book down in his lap and shifted on the sofa to make room for the other. Pier sat down with a wary glance over his shoulder at the mostly empty room.

"It's…" he started, "that phrase from this morning in class, 'the temptation of doubt'. I haven't been able to get it out of my head all day…"

"Ah, yes, Molino's question about the crisis of faith. What troubles you?"

"Well…it's just…those words. Did you mean that the devil tempts us to doubt?"

Don Marcello smiled. "Sometimes doubt certainly feels like the work of the devil. Are you troubled by doubts?"

An involuntary sideways grin twisted Pier's face. "The work of the devil," he said. "My mother's very words. That's what she thinks of the theatre." No, I…I don't know about the devil. What's bothering me is…well…it's doubt itself, doubting oneself.

"You doubt your faith?"

Pier squirmed in his seat. "No, not quite what I mean. Oh, I can't explain!" He started to get up. "I shouldn't have bothered you," he said.

"No bother," Don Marcello said encouragingly. Pier sat back down. Don Marcello felt like he was in the confessional. "If you're troubled…" he said, letting the sentence dangle.

"Thing is…" Pier struggled to put his thoughts into words. "I don't… I don't want to …doubt what I feel. But I do! I do all the time. I am…" his hands fluttered above his head "…all confused. All the time!"

"It's easy to get confused, especially if something matters a lot. In the absence of certainty, the temptation of doubt is always there. If one has faith, one *chooses* to set doubt aside."

"You mean… it is a… matter of choice!?"

"In a way… Yes, it is. It's a choice that has to be made each day." Don Marcello said. Then he added with a slight grin, "Or at least whenever 'temptation' crops up."

"And if one can't?"

Don Marcello raised a tolerant, young shoulder. "Anyone can have moments of doubt. Of weakness, of confusion. Then," he added lightly, "*the Enemy* can wriggle his way in, and doubt…" he wiggled his fingers at Pier, "…worms its way in. Doubt," he added after a brief pause, very serious now, "can really shake us up, makes us…afraid. Even Christ… You remember, the Night of Gethsemane… 'Father, do not forsake me…' We all dread being forsaken…" He was silent for a moment before adding, "That's why *we choose* not to forsake." He raised his eyes and saw the other's fierce blush.

"But then…" Pier said in confusion.

"Yes, faith itself, is a leap of faith," the young Jesuit answered, still carried by his previous train of thought. "We all need to make that leap of faith."

Suddenly he felt something had gone awry. His mind flashed back to Saturday night at *La Tampa Lirica;* to the beautiful girl alone at Rexel's table, restless, on the verge to tears. He recalled the other woman, the soprano on stage, smiling, bowing, blissful in the spotlight with Pier. His mind did a summersault. Trying to rectify his misdirection, he redirected his words. "You see," he said very gently, "hope, trust, *love* even, all our deep emotions, require a leap of faith. One must trust, *to trust oneself.*"

He stopped, wondering: was he any closer to where Pier needed to be?

310

"That," he added in the continuing silence, "can be extremely difficult when one's confused. In the absence of clarity, doubt naturally creeps in…"

He waited, hoping Pier might take up the reference to love and trust; almost sure he was on the right track now.

But before Pier could respond, a senior master who had been reading and taking notes at table by the windows closed his notebook, stood up and approached. "Excuse me, Don Marcello," he said, "may I ask…"

Pier jumped up and left the room with a hasty good night, his mind wrestling with thoughts of Lena, of love, hate, reparations to be made, resentments, and of persistent guilt: why did he always feel that he was in the wrong, even when he'd done his best and was doing well? Why did it all *always* have to be spoiled? And then, in his mind, his own voice answered him. It sang '…*croce … croce e delizia, delizia al cor*'.

Guido investigates *Sacro Cuore*

One morning, shortly after Easter, two men wearing the notorious plain-clothes uniform of the fascist political police – long overcoats and wide-brimmed, soft hats – battered the studded portals of *Collegio Sacro Cuore,* deliberately ignoring its prominent electric doorbell on the right jamb. When the doors failed to open instantly, the battering resumed louder, this time with the knob of a stout walking stick.

In due time, the pass-through door in the portals inched open enough to let a startled fresh face atop a slim black cassock peer out through the crack.

"Open up," barked the long coat with the walking stick. "We have a search order."

The young porter blinked in disbelief, "A search order for the *collegio?"*

In answer, a shoulder was thrust into the panel and the door flew open, sending the young porter staggering backwards. "You can't do that," the young brother protested, "you can't come in without permission!"

"And *you*'re going to stop us?" snarled the second thug with a rough shove to the boy's chest, his face inches from the other's.

"Is there a problem, Brother Arnaldo?" asked a mild middle-aged voice from atop a six-step flight of stairs: the *Sacro Cuore* registrar had appeared from one of the nearby offices and now stood watching, hands folded inside his sleeves.

"We have a search order," barked the man with the stout cane.

Calmly, the master walked down the steps, "A search order, you say. Let me see it." The long-coats took a couple of steps forward, waving the official-looking document about. "Well," the master demanded, unimpressed, "bring it to me."

Truculently, the lead long-coat climbed the few steps and shoved the sheet of paper into the other's face. The master drew himself up with obvious distaste, but stood his ground. Without haste, took the paper with his fingertips and looked at it, holding it at arm's length.

Other priests, among them Don Marcello, then crossing the courtyard, noticed the disturbance and approached. "Any problem, Father," one asked. The college registrar, Don Antonio, unhurriedly came down the steps and handed the paper to him. "Pier Venturi!" Don Marcello cried out, reading over his senior colleague's shoulder. "But why?"

"None of your business," snapped the long-coat with the cane. "Give us access now, or there'll be…"

Don Antonio spoke firmly, matching the other's glare, "No need for threats. We'll proceed in due order." Sideways, he spoke to the young porter. "Kindly inform the headmaster of this request."

"This is no 'request'," the lead thugs snarled. He and his sidekick thrust forward, shoulder to shoulder, as though to break through the thin line of cassocks. Don Antonio raised a barring hand. "WE WILL…" he announced in his resonant pulpit voice, "…proceed with proper order."

The shouting attracted the notice of other priests then crossing the courtyard, and they converged on the problem group. The registrar continued, "If you can behave in a civilised manner, you can wait for the headmaster in my waiting room. Or you can stand where you are until we get word."

By now a double phalanx of black cassocks had formed behind him. A staring match ensued between the priest and Guido's bulldogs, fifteen, thirty seconds, but at length the lead long coat backed down. "We wait here," he growled, shaking his cane about. In the back row, two cassocks whispered urgently, then the younger one scuttled off along the cloister. "And don't anybody leave," the lead thug snarled inanely after them.

The tense wait dragged on; some twenty minutes passed. Then, at the far end of the courtyard cloister a door squeaked, revealing Don Lucas, flanked by two austere colleagues. They approached, hands tucked into folded sleeves, at a sedate clerical pace. The phalanx of cassocks parted, Red Sea-like, into two wings, a narrow path between them. "You are to come with us," Don Lucas stated in an authoritative tone, then turned on his heels and retraced his steps without looking back, followed by his two companions.

The long-coats hesitated. They glared at the stern walls of black cassocks for a long moment, still swaggering but reluctant to trust themselves into the narrow path between them.

Don Antonio and Don Marcello had fallen into step directly behind them and, in their wake, came the whole black phalanx, their soft-shod feet making an unearthly marching sound under the cloister's arcade.

Once in the headmaster's office, the two bulldogs were left stranded six feet from the massive desk, half a dozen senior masters ranged behind them just inside door, the rest of their escort standing guard outside. Don Lucas stepped forward to hand the search order to the headmaster, seated behind his impressive desk. The head of *Sacro Cuore* took his time inspecting the suspect document, but eventually laid it down in front of him, and raised his eyes.

"Of what crime is Pier Venturi accused?" he demanded.

"We're...not at liberty to say," the head long-coat growled aggressively.

"The signature on this order is not legible. On whose authority are you here?"

"We are here from the *Fascio*. The *Leggi fascistissime* authorise search and seizure on suspicion."

"Suspicion of what? From which branch of the *Fascio?* Who authorised *this* search? Show me your party credentials."

This time the long-coats squirmed.

"Well?" the headmaster insisted. "Your party identifications, please."

The two bulldogs threw their cards onto the polished desk, they slithered on the polished wood and snagged on the edge of leather-bound blotter. Without haste, the headmaster picked them up, one at a time, and examined them at length. "You are from Borgo San Paolo," he observed. "I am not aware of any connection of the Borgo San Paolo branch with any part of the political police. Who is in charge there? Whose scrawl is this?"

"We receive our orders at roll call," the senior thug mumbled, "We don't know who signs them."

The headmaster stood up, a tall, black figure towering over them, and handed their party cards back to them, like marching orders. "The *Collegio Sacro Cuore*," he stated, "will comply with official orders submitted under proper authority. Meantime, I have noted the particulars of *your* membership cards. I shall make inquiries." He nodded to the six masters standing by the door. They came forward and marched the interlopers out.

Over the next few hours, the *Collegio* buzzed with activity. The headmaster placed calls to his bishop and to the dioceses' cardinal. Don Lucas contacted Don Marco at the Cathedral, and Professor Rexel at the Regio. From theatre and cathedral calls went out to various influential people around the city. By mid-afternoon, the newly appointed *podestá* was besieged with phone calls. His henchmen descended on the San Paolo *Fascio* with angry inquiries as to who had signed the search order against *Collegio Sacro Cuore*. Nothing was found out.

The next few weeks were anxious ones for Guido Delloria. The storm of inquiries about the *Sacro Cuore* search order, and the efforts of frightened party officials to shift the blame for this mysterious intrusion on the church's privileged authority, created enough confusion for Guido to hope that his role in the affair might remain undetected. The two thugs he had send to *Sacro Cuore* he tried to cow with threats, then bought off with bribes. Scared, he slunk about his *Fascio* duties, doing his best to pass unnoticed. The huge fuss convinced him that he had better keep his nose clean for a while. For now, he decided, he'd better lay off Pier Venturi. Later, when things had calmed down, he'd find a way to get his own back – from Pier or from Lena.

Meantime, his own personal affairs dragged on at low ebb. Cristina Follati, having received her degree in *Economia e Commercio* from the University of Turin, announced, with an unheard show of independence, that she intended to handle the fortune she'd inherited from her maternal grandmother on her own. Meantime, her father, Vittorio Follati, was getting impatient with the lack of clarity around Guido's claim to his uncle's estate, *Fontan-a Frèida*. Was he or was he not the heir? This mattered, if Guido was indeed to be regarded as a serious suitor for Cristina's hand. He also started pressing Guido for a commitment with regards to the wine exports from *Colin-a Longa*. So far, Guido had been able to put him off with evasions – his father's health, prior contractual commitments, his uncle's will snarled up in legal red tape.

Guido knew perfectly well that he had no claim to his uncle's property, and not the slightest influence on his father's business decisions. By this time there was no doubt that the dead man's daughters were to inherit. His brother Giacu had made a point of calling him up to pass his mother's reaction to this outcome: she would never forgive Guido for not inheriting. Since his childhood, she had set her heart on seeing him master of *Fontan-a Frèida,* her pined-for childhood home. Guido had let her down. He would no longer be welcome at *Colin-a Longa.*

His mother's blind, absurd attitude did not surprise Guido, but it left him mired in impotent rage, torn between guilt and disgust. Yet, the same time, he revelled in private gloating: she'd done it all for nothing. *He had escaped.*

Rehearsing Carmen

Professor Rexel had scheduled Pier and Melina's first joint Carmen run-through for that afternoon. The previous week the two had been told to study the opera together on their own. Now they were to join the professor in his workroom to listen to a recorded performance of the opera, with a view to selecting the program of their October recital. For the second half of their recital, Herr Rexel had chosen the Carmen-Don José duet at the end of Act II, and the last duet of the opera, Don José's stabbing of his taunting love. What remained to be planned was the way in which the Carmen part of the recital was to be integrated into a single unit, so as to infuse it with the full dramatic impact of the opera.

Now, waiting for the arrival of his star pupils, Horst Rexel sat at the piano in his workroom, chuckling and rubbing excited hands together. Leaning forward, he laid his fingers on the keyboard, eagerly peering at a passage on the open score, flipped some pages, then quickly ran his eyes and fingers through a second and a third section. Again, he chuckled excitedly: this was going to be great!

There was a knock on the door and Pier walked in.

"Pier!" *der Herr Professor* called out, beckoning. "Come listen to this." His fingers ran through the selections he had been working on, an arrangement juxtaposing Carmen's *Habanera* to the theme of Don José's '*Doux souvenirs du pays',* from his Act I duet with Michaela. Throughout the piece faint strands of Carmen's Fate theme rumbled behind the two major themes, a subtle omen of approaching storm.

"This will introduce your first duet," Rexel said, "the seduction scene from Act III. We'll take it from your song Pier, *Dragon d'Alcalá.* The piano will fill in where the other voices are cut out.*"

Pier studied the arrangement, fascinated. He'd worried about doing two disconnected scenes from the same opera. Now he saw what *der Herr Professor* had in mind: between the two duets, a second piano arrangement restated the prelude, added the *Toreador* theme and intensified the rumbles of Fate that hounded Carmen. The whole thing was highly dramatic, quite electrifying.

A perfunctory knock on the door interrupted them, and a strange, dark beauty in a clinging red dress slinked seductively into the room. Pier blinked twice, breathless: who *was* she?

"*Guten Tag, mein Herr Professor,*" Melina Cortesi called out, striding assuredly towards the piano. On her way, she carelessly flung aside her fringed black shawl. It caught on a corner of the *Recamier* sofa and slithered suggestively toward the floor. "Good afternoon, Pier," she added. "Am I late?"

"*Nein, nein,* not at all," *Herr Rexel chimed* cheerfully, eyes taking in appreciatively her role-inspired transformation. He stood up and scuttled to the nearby phonograph. "Today ve shall listen to the opera to get the feel of its climate and action. As ve listen, you will *act* your way through the scenes you hear. No singing. You can hum along if it helps you get into your parts. After that, ve'll run through your first scene." He pointed to the stage setup at the near end of his workroom, "That's Pastia's tavern," he said, "set up for the third act seduction." He lowered the needle into the first groove. The opera's prelude engulfed the room, evoking the gay commotion of *Plaza de Toro* on *corrida* day. Melina, on her feet, strolled about the stage to the rhythm of the music. *Herr Rexel* stepped up to her with the exaggerated courtesy of a stage *gallant* and offered her his arm. Melina curtseyed to him with a coquettish flutter of eyelids and slid her arm through his with an enticing smile. Thus linked, they promenaded across 'the stage', elegantly flirting, right and left, with the imaginary crowd.

Pier watched astounded: he was having trouble recognising Melina under the thick, black wig, she looked so different. Carmen became real to him for the first time: she was *there* before him, real flesh and blood: sinuous in her red dress, her eyes flashing, teasing, over the edge of her lacy black fan. He blinked, confused: Melina's eyes were a hazel green. And there was no fan in her hand, yet the suggestion was strong, powerfully convincing.

The record came to an end and Rexel replaced it with the next and the next until Carmen's song rang out, "*L'amour est un oiseau rebelle que nul ne peut apprivoiser…*" (Love is a wild bird no one can tame.)
Melina, on her feet, began to sway to the rhythm of the song. Soon her swaying became a dance at one with taunting rhythm of the *Habanera*. She danced absorbed, eyes closed, moist lips sensuously parted. On the record, the soprano

sang, "*L'un parle bien, l'autre se tait: et c'est l'autre que je préfère...*" (One speaks well, the other shuts up: and it is the other I prefer.) Melina danced up to Pier, still sitting next the Rexel. Her hand snatched her non-existent fan from her face, tucked it behind her back. She stood in front of him, hips swaying, eyes flashing, taunting him, one finger beckoning, challenging him to join her in the dance. Pier squirmed. *Temptation,* flashed through his mind, *the snake in paradise.* Her eyes snapped open, as though in response to his thought, and her green gaze pinned him to his chair. Next to him, *Herr Professor* chuckled out loud in sheer delight. From the record, the soprano sang, "*Il n'a rien dit, mais il me plaît.*"

A furious blush swept over Pier, overwhelmingly hot. Melina flicked her pointed chin into the air and twirled away with a taunting laugh, glancing over her shoulder, her challenging eyes still calling Pier out to the dance.

Pier sat through the rest of the session fascinated and deeply disturbed: until now he had not recognised the quality of the passion in the recordings. Now there was no mistaking it. Melina embodied it. Melina in her black wig, her swaying hips in the clinging red dress, her absent fan.

His mother's voice suddenly echoed in Pier's stunned mind: *Red dress...devil's work.* It merged with Don José's line: "*Qui sait de quel démon j'allais être la proie!*" (Who knows to what devil I was to be prey.) Pier felt suddenly endangered: the world he loved, *opera,* the theatre, all of it, now gaped at him like the very maws of hell. Temptation was hot upon him. He sat hunched up in defensive opposition, arms clutched tight around crossed knees, right foot twined around left shin.

The record ended. Professor Rexel switched it for the next. Melina came to the chair next to Pier and sat down. Pier shrank tighter into himself. "*Na ja,*" Professor Rexel chuckled, coming back to sit on Pier's other side while the gramophone started the next record. "It makes a difference," he said, patting Pier's knee, "seeing the action live."

The records succeeded one another until they came to Don José's song in Act III, "*Halte lá! Qui va lá? Dragon d'Alcalá...!*" Sitting on Pier's left, *Herr Rexel* nudged him, his twirling wrist urging him to his feet, "Go on, then, up you get. *Be* Don José."

Reluctantly, Pier got up and took a few awkward steps about the stage set, his back to the Rexel and Melina, sitting watching him from their seats. After a moment, the Germanic voice boomed behind him, "Put your heart in it! You're a bony lad, *Dragon d'Alcalá*! You're young and strong and full of…*feuer*! So go on, show us your fire!"

Stiff as a board, his back to the watchers, Pier, took a couple of steps upstage, sneaking a shamed glance at his crotch, to check whether his fly gave him away, then quickly buttoned up his jacket. For good measure, he thrust a fist deep into his pocket. Then he faced his audience and sang with the tenor on the record, "*Óu t'en vas-tu par lá, Dragon d'Alcalá?* – *where are you going, Dragon d'Alcala?*" The sound of his own voice reassured him. His panic was over. He straightened his spine and continued, "*…Moi, je m'en vais faire, mordre la poussière á mon adversaire…*" (I am going to make my adversary bite the dust.) From his chair, Rexel shouted, "No singing! Just act!" Pier shifted to humming along with the recorded tenor.

Melina got up and strolled seductively around Pier. On the record the soprano sang, "*Enfin c'est toi,*" (At last it's you.) Carmen, black wig and red dress, swayed in front of Pier, taunting, half-scornful, half-inviting, infinitely tantalising. Pier and Melina went through the rest of the scenes until tenor and soprano on the record sang out their *adieux,* the duet came to an end and Rexel gave them their assignment for the next rehearsal.

That day, Pier left the theatre in a blur. He felt that, somehow, he now existed on two separate planes, at once, in two distinct worlds. In the one world he was totally absorbed in what he had just lived 'on stage', he *was* Don José, torn between love, duty, honour, and a lingering allegiance to those *doux souvenirs du pays,* to the world of innocence, of mother and Michaela. In that world he writhed with passion and shame.

At the same time, in the everyday world, he felt shattered by what he had just discovered about himself. The thrill of Melina's dance continued to send electric charges down his spine long after he left the Regio. He walked down the street in a daze, all kinds of neutral sights triggering a physical recall of her presence, of her lure. The sparks from trams' overhead cables, the cars' turn signal arrows, erecting to announce a turn, somehow evoked the feel of her, triggering that shooting sensation along his spine and deep into his loins. On the tram back to the *collegio*, Carmen/Melina approached him, seductively swaying her way down the trams' centre aisle, until an innocuous middle-aged woman, encumbered with string bags full of groceries, plunked herself and her shopping down into two empty seats. At the same time, his brain reeled with an unrelated, irrepressible tune that kept running through it. *Se amore vuol dir gelosia…*

Jealousy. *What did jealousy have to do with all this,* he mentally snapped at himself.

Or love, for that matter. He loved *Lena.* Melina was just… Melina had just… Well, Melina was Carmen. She was temptation. *There is no doubt,* he told himself, with the first clear thought he managed since leaving the theatre, *this is temptation.* No need to spell out what the temptations was. Words reordered themselves in his mind, and he recalled his after-supper conversation with Don Marcello, its drift, towards the end, from faith to love. Pier now added *lust.* He recalled Don Marcello's phrase *'the temptation to doubt'.* And suddenly he wondered if Don Marcello had known all along what was troubling him, Pier; whether the young Jesuit had known, before he himself had recognised it, the source of his confusion: the pull between Lena and Melina.

That's nonsense, he snapped at himself. *It is Lena I love. Melina is not even a possibility.* He got off his tram and strode decisively up to the *Sacro Cuore* portals. But his assurance was all bluff: inside he was as troubled as ever.

Chapter Fourteen

... but deliver us, from evil ...
The Lord's Prayer

The long reach of fear

Once in the *Ginnasio* wing, Pier sprung up the stairs three steps at a time, craving the seclusion of his room. But on his third bound he was stopped by someone calling out his name from the entrance hallway below. Pier stopped and looked back: the young porter was trotting up the stairs after him, a sealed envelope in his hand. Standing on the ninth step, Pier examined the envelope: addressed to him: the *collegio's* logo and nothing else; no further marks. Puzzled, he raised inquiring eyes, but the porter had already withdrawn into his glassed-in lair and closed his door behind him. Fretting, Pier set his briefcase down by his feet and tore into the envelope: Don Lucas asked him to come to his office as soon as he got in. Pier picked up his briefcase and hurried across the cloistered courtyard to answer the summons.

"Ah, Pier," Don Luca greeted him from behind his desk. "Sit down."

Pier instantly heard the edge in the Music Master's voice. Formality had eased into comfort over the months of daily work together, but right now Pier felt its presence in full force. Anxiously, he sat on the edge of his chair. What was this about? Had he done something to displease? Did this have to do with his conversations with Don Marcello? It could not possibly have anything to do with what had just happened to him today at the Regio. Not yet, anyway.

"We've had an unwelcome visit today." Don Luca said, his eyes boring into Pier's. "From some...fascist...officials. They came asking for you. Do you know of any reason for this to happen?"

Nonplussed, Pier raised his shoulders and shook his head, dumfounded.

The master persisted: "No reason for them to take an interest in you?"

"In me? The *Fascio*? No, Father, I know of no reason."

"Are you a member of the party?"

"Well…no, Father. I'm not. I've never… "

"Have you attended some rally, maybe, or lecture…or any event of a political character?"

Pier kept shaking his head. "I haven't, Father,"

"Perhaps while you were at FIAT; some worker's meeting there, maybe?"

"Can't say I have. I had no interest. And with my sessions at the duomo and the Regio I had no time for meetings."

Don Luca nodded thoughtfully, then added, "Some chance encounter at the Regio, perhaps?" Once again, Pier shook his head, thinking. "Whom have you met there? Professor Rexel, and…who else?"

"Well," Pier passed in review his contacts at the theatre, "Paulin, the stage-door keeper. Signora Agiati – she prepared me for the audition last fall. Then Signorina Cora, Professor Rexel's assistant. This term I started to work on my French diction with Mademoiselle Chantal. Oh, yes, and Melina Cortesi, of course. And her parents, at La Contessa's recital."

"Hmmm…" chin in hand, Don Luca pondered: Horst Rexel was too deft an opportunist to get himself tangled up in political complications. Melina Cortesi couldn't be it. Her father was a member of *Confindustria*. Matilde Agiati he only knew by reputation.

"Did Signora Agiati," he asked, "hold meetings at her apartment?"

"Not that I know of. When I was there, it was always just her and me. And her sister, of course," he hurried to add. "And once or twice her husband, in the apartment; never in the practice room. But no one else."

Don Luca pondered, then asked, "Have you ever had occasion to discuss politics in public, maybe in some café?"

"No, Father, I can't say I have."

"No gatherings at all?"

Pier started to shake his head again then abruptly stopped. "Last fall, before I came here, Signora Agiati had me go to a literary group with her. For my accent, you see. I wasn't hearing enough proper Italian…"

"What group was that?" Don Luca asked, bit by bit worming out the group's details: who, where, when; what they'd read, what they'd talked about. It all sounded innocent enough. But it would be as well to check with Matilde Agiati. He dismissed Pier and obtained her phone number from the Regio.

Pier went off in a puzzled state. What was this all about? What had he done to stir up trouble? *Not now,* he pleaded fervently to himself, *not now, not when he, at last, was getting close…*

That night he woke up with a start: he had been dreaming of his initial introduction to the *Convivio Letterario,* that first dinner conversation. His whole dream seemed frozen around that *'Legga i giornali',* that shameful indictment of his ignorance, the shocked, scornful faces around the table glaring at him – he did not read the newspapers! Then Alberto Scagliosi laughed; then *Signora Agiati* joined the scornful laughter, then all the others, laughing and laughing, mocking his shameful ignorance.

Pier sat up in bed in a cold sweat. The context that had led to that painful snub now replayed itself in excruciating detail in his mind: his naïve question, "*Chi è Gobetti?* Who is Gobetti?"

True, the snub had led him to reading *La Stampa,* and he had soon found out that he shared the *Convivio*'s outrage about the Christmas Eve battering of the young socialist. And, at that last meeting, early this past January, he had shared their dismay at the outrageous *Leggi fascistissime.*

Pier's mind froze in its tracks. That had been their last meeting. Later on, sometime last February, Signora Agiati had told him there would be no more *Convivio* meetings for a while, and he had not asked why, glad to be relieved of the obligation to attend, or the need to make a difficult choice.

Now he recalled his own reaction at that last meeting, his outrage and defiance against the abuse of power by the enforcers of those repressive new laws. He had quite forgotten that he had felt, viscerally, that he could not leave the group now that it was forbidden. He had never enjoyed the *Convivio* gatherings because he always felt badly out-leagued there; and he had no real interest in politics. But he had reacted to the new laws' prescribing what he could and could not do. He was glad that Signora Agiati had introduced him to the group because it had led him to discover literature, of which now he could not get enough, Zola, Verga, Flaubert, Leopardi, Balzac, they had all become revered companions to him. And now he had the *collegio*'s literature classes. He enjoyed that far more than the heated discussions at the *Convivio*. But what if…? What if the 'unwelcome visit' Don Luca had told him about had something to do with *that*, with those early discussions at the *Convivio*?

Suddenly, Pier shuddered in the warmth of his bed, staring in the dark, hardly daring to breathe: what if Signora Agiati was in trouble as well? He ducked deeper under his covers and, feeling endangered, pulled his pillow over his head.

But it was not a cold night, and under the covers he could not breathe. His heart kept racing. He jumped out of bed and rushed to throw the window open, snapping the drapes aside, and gulped in big, hungry breaths of cold night air. Gradually, it calmed him down. But the sense of endangerment still weighed heavy upon him. What about the others? Were they getting 'unwelcome visits' as well? Signor Scagliosi, anyway, was all right, he thought, recalling the *La Stampa* review of Pier's appearance at *La Tampa Lirica.* Or at least he *had been* all right when he had written it, a short while ago.

Then he wondered: *Did his review have anything to do with yesterday's 'unwelcome visit' to the Collegio?* He recalled the journalist saying that some of his reviews had been censored, that La Ginsberg's plays had been banned.

Badly frightened, Pier made an effort to pull himself together. There was nothing he could do in the middle of the night. Tomorrow he would tell Don Luca what he'd remembered. He'd try to catch him before the first class, tell him about the *Convivio*'s last conversations.

He returned to his bed and tried to fall asleep. Three hours later, the shrill noise of his alarm clock woke him up. A nippy breeze swelled the curtain in the window he had left wide open. Somewhere in the snowy courtyard a bird chirped insistently.

Still dazed, he sat up in bed, suddenly stabbed by an urgent need to see Lena, to be with her. And with Gioana. In their safe, warm Le Basse kitchen. He had a fleeting image of last spring's field, half-seen through their back window, the tender green wheat growing tall, flowing in liquid waves in the crisp April breeze. Tears blurred his eyes and a lump grabbed him by the throat, startling him: he had *never seen* those fields in April. He'd only met Lena last fall. Confused, he got up, threw on an old pair of pants and yesterday's shirt, and went to shave in the washroom at the end of the corridor.

As he peered into the mirror, scraping at the spare, blond stubble on his chin, an image of Nina came vividly into his mind: last January, just three months ago, when he had left her *lavanderia* for the *Collegio* – she and her two little daughters, standing at the tram terminal, waving goodbye. His life at Santa Rita, his makeshift bed in Nina's *retro,* and, later, under her *lavanderia* counter, already felt foreign to him now, like they had never really been part of his life, like he'd always been *here*, where he belonged. FIAT, *La Speransa,* the winter copsing for his pa, they all remained vivid in his mind, but they now seemed like scenes from someone else's life, or remembered from some novel read. Or, maybe, disturbing fragments from odd nightmares he could not quite recall.

And now this new *home* of his, his safety, his hopes, his prospects, were all at risk because of…something that meant nothing to him, that was actually no concern of his.

And Nina – the thought stopped his razor in mid-stroke. Would they hound her too? Was *she* in danger because of him? Again, he felt panic stirring in his stomach, rising to his throat, his heart kicking at his ribs.

"Good morning!" a cheerful voice called out, entering the washroom. The young porter bustled in. "Running late… Overslept…" His adolescent face peered into the mirror next to Pier's, searching for the sparse hair strands on his chin. "Guess I can skip the shave this morning. It's not too bad."

Pier regrouped. He wiped the soap off his chin and stowed his razor. Alone, there was nothing he could do. He'd go talk to Don Luca, ask his advice. Maybe he should call Signora Agiati, warn her. And the others, of course. But he barely remembered their names. And he had no idea where they lived.

Then another worrying thought intervened: would it be safe to contact them, even if he could get hold of their phone numbers?

He made for Don Luca's office before breakfast. "Father, may I come in?" he asked with a soft rap on the open door.

"Pier. Come in, come in. You remembered something else?"

"Perhaps I have, Father. I'm not sure it's useful."

Don Luca listened, peering at him over his gold *pince-nez*. It all sounded pretty innocent, but these days one never knew. He had left a message for Matilde Agiati last night, but she was out of town, visiting a sister in Florence. She should be back today.

"What shall I do, Father?" Pier asked.

Don Luca stood up, carefully stowing his glasses into a fold of his sash. "For now do nothing," he answered. "Just go about your normal routine, as usual. *We*'ll make some inquiries and let you know if there's anything we need from you."

As an afterthought, he added: "And avoid getting caught up in any crowds."

Pier went about his day, as instructed, at *Sacro Cuore* and later at the theatre, but he remained unsettled. From time to time, he found himself casting a surreptitious look over his shoulder. Time and again, in class, on the tram, at the theatre, that sharp yearning to be with Lena stabbed him, an actual physical ache; and the confusion about that spring wheat-field he's never seen. At times the yearning for that cosy Le Basse kitchen, where, for the first time, he had come to feel safe *and loved*, became nearly overwhelming. Throughout the day, he chafed at the fact that Lena was not there – *would not* be there until after work – and he needed to see her *now*. He'd go wait for her at home, he thought. No, he would go, pick her up at FIAT, when she came out.

Then he remembered the crush of homing workers, and Don Luca's warning not to get caught up in any crowds. He'd better go back to *Sacro Cuore,* find out if there was anything new. He could go to Lena after supper, when there would be no crush of workers on the streets.

That afternoon, at the Regio, Mademoiselle Chantal, working with him on his French diction in Don José's lines, scolded him for inattention, her sharpness in painful contrast to his memories of his early sessions in Signora Agiati's home.

He hoped *she* was not in trouble. Then it suddenly occurred to him that he had not seen her since their last session, on Thursday of last week. Fear stabbed him. He ran to the porter's booth.

"Is Signora Agiati in today?" he asked, breathless.

"Haven't seen her," the man answered, nonchalant. "She's out of town. Not expected back till tomorrow."

Tomorrow: he'd have to wait until tomorrow. Pier ran back to the rehearsals area for his session with Professor Rexel, to work out the program for his upcoming command performance at Contessa Vergani's *soirée,* at Villa della Rovere.

Waiting for the professor in his practice room, he ran through in his mind one of the Verdi arias that had been mentioned as a possibility for the recital, '*di quella pira l'orrendo foco*', from *Il Trovatore.* On the line '*madre infelice, corro a salvarti...*' his mind stopped cold: could this business bring trouble at *La Speranza?*

The image of black-shirted thugs swarming the farmyard and bullying his mother rose vivid in his mind, including poor old Taboj strangling himself on his chain to protect their ma.

Pier froze, desperately blocking out the thought. For several minutes he struggled to keep his mind blank, focused only on breathing slow and deep.

The day finally came to an end, and Pier made his way to the tram stop to the *Collegio:* he would find out if there was any new information. Then, if things were quiet, he'd go to Lena after supper. But, within two stops, his resolve dissolved: he couldn't wait. He hopped off the still-moving tram and ran the three blocks back to the nearest stop where he could catch a tram for Lingotto and Strada delle Basse.

Reconciliation

The instant he got off the tram in front of the main FIAT gate, the smell of machine oil, paint chemicals, sawdust and exhaust hit him like a physical blow. A grubby, bicycle-wheeling herd stampeding to Via Nizza and the ride home, clogged the gates and swamped the sidewalk. It engulfed and jostled Pier as he fought his way against the onslaught to go and wait for Lena at their usual spot, the acrid smell of tired bodies now mingling with machine smells, nauseating.

But, at last, Pier reached the gate's plastered pillar. Flush against it, he craned his neck to scan for Lena above the turbulent stream. Interminable minutes went by; well know faces from his FIAT days passed him without recognition: he no longer looked or smelled like one of them.

Then a broad, sneering *Piemontèis* voice called out, "Well, if it isn't *nòst pistin al cafelàit*," – our fussy milksop: Tony, Pier's former station mate, and his usual mocking epiteth. Tony had been the first to spot Lena on the day of her arrival at FIAT. He'd stopped dead in his tracks, bike at his side. Behind him the human flood snarled, rumbled, split around him, and surged on. "Quite the toff these days, aren't we?" he taunted. "What you doing here, slumming it?"

Still scanning over the other's head, Pier answered, curtly enough, "Hello, Tony. I'm waiting for Lena."

"She ain't here. Haven't seen her pretty face all week. You two still an item? No fancy *Turinèisa* for you yet?"

Pier was in no mood for banter. He sidled past Tony and shouldered his way deeper through the crowd. He had spotted one of Lena's station mates. "Ciot," he called out weaving his way towards her, "is Lena still inside?"

"She ain't here," Ciot answered, without stopping, "ain't been all week. Word is she's sick." She dashed past Pier to catch an oncoming tram.

Pier was stunned: Lena sick! All week. That meant since last Saturday, since the night at *La Tampa Lirica*. Guilt stricken, Pier fought his way out of the snarl of bodies and bicycles that had formed around him, and ran down Via Nizza, making for Lena's home. It was *his* fault: Lena was never ill. He'd made her ill with grief, leaving her alone all night among strangers because he was carried away by the excitement of success.

At the Le Basse courtyard he stopped, out of breath, a painful stitch in his side. He bent over to catch his breath, hands braced on his knees. From inside one of the courtyard's open doors came the sharp sound of a slap, then a child's howl. Somewhere nearby, a dog barked and barked. Gioana's door was conspicuously closed.

Pier stood up, wiped the sweat off his face, tugged his jacket straight, and rushed across the courtyard to knock on the closed door. Gioana's distraught face appeared behind the half glass, next to the hastily withdrawn curtain.

"Pier!" she cried, stepping back to open the door and let him. "She won't tell me anything! She just cries and cries and won't eat. What's happened between you two?"

He stood frozen on the doorstep. Gioana laid a hand on his arm, her face crumpled with concern. "Come in, tell me what's happened." Pier stepped over the threshold.

"It's all my fault, Gioana. Where's Lena?"

"She's in bed. She hadn't got up since Sunday morning. What happened Saturday night?"

"Nothing happened, Ma!" the last word slipped out unnoticed. "I mean, not between us, nothing! But…" his voice cracked and he swallowed a sob.

It was some minutes before Pier could tell Gioana his story – the intensity before the performance, the intoxicating response of the audience, the praise, the fuss… He'd got caught up in all the giddy excitement… He'd wanted Lena there to share it all with her, *and then*…he'd left her alone all night. It was his fault, all his fault. He had forsaken her among strangers. His fist actually beat his breast over and over again in the clerical act of contrition, *mea culpa, mea culpa, mea culpa,* until Gioana took him by the hand and made him sit down by the table.

"You sit down here. Catch your breath," she told him, pouring out a glass of lemonade for him. "I'll be back in a minute." She disappeared into the bedroom next door. At the table, Pier sat with his head in his hands.

It was a good ten minutes before the bedroom door reopened and Gioana reappeared, a wry-compassionate smile on her lips. "You two young things," she said, drawing a reluctant Lena along by the hand, "have a lot to talk about." She coaxed Lena towards Pier, "so I'll leave you to it."

"No, Mama, don't leave," Lena cried, clutching her hand.

"Please stay," Pier added, sensing Gioana's sympathy, feeling in need of a buffer. "You already know *all* I have to say."

He still hadn't been able to look Lena in the face. He did so now, a shy, tentative glance, and was shocked: all of Lena seemed somehow diminished. Dark circles swallowed her eyes, her lovely features collapsed into a preview of grieving old age.

"Oh, *mè tesòr*!" Pier cried out, grief-stricken. "What have I done to you? Forgive me; I beg of you, forgive me!" He seized her hands and covered them with hungry, desperate kisses.

Lena howled: he had never before called her his treasure! He did not usually speak endearments. She raised his hands to her cheek, then kissed them, again and again. "Do you still love me, then?" she asked, her voice quivering on the edge of tears, "I haven't … lost you?"

"Never!" Pier drew her hands to his lips and kissed them over and over again. "Never! I don't know what I'd do if I lost *you!* But…" he gazed at her with tears in his eyes, "I *am* a brute! I get so…so…Well, so *caught up*… You know how much this all means to me – *to us,* really. Last Saturday…my first public appearance… It was…well, you know, the first step to… all my dreams. Don't you see? The audience…the way they reacted. It was proof that *I've got a chance*! That I … Well, that *maybe* I can ... succeed, have a career in opera! All those people swarming over me afterward our performance! All those requests… Lena: they *want* to see more of me, don't you see? It all just…went to my head. And so I abandoned you."

"But," Lena whimpered, "you're sure you still want me?"

"I'm sure!?" Pier exclaimed. "As soon as we can, my love! And, Lena, in a few weeks, I am to perform at Villa della Rovere! Contessa Vergani's soirée. *For money*, Lena! Don't you see?! We'll be able to get married!"

They flew into each other's arms. Pier fumbled in his pocket for his handkerchief, dabbed gently at her cheeks. "Don't cry my love," he pleaded, holding her close. "It's all going to happen, you'll see..."

Behind them, Gioana sighed: now perhaps her silly girl would take some nourrishment. She walked to her larder, returned with two beakers of the *zabaglione* she'd made two days ago, Lena's favourite custard, to tempt her appetite, to keep her strength up. Lena hadn't even looked at it. Now Gioana watched with a somewhat wry smile as Pier fed the still-shaky Lena her first spoonful.

Anticipation: Villa della Rovere

The night of Pier's command performance at Contessa Vergani's villa was approaching fast. At her request, the recital's program was designed to give scope to the impressive range of his voice and dramatic resources. Professor Rexel, who was to accompany him at the piano, had crafted the program to show off his protegé's remarkable range of talents. It juxtaposed different moods, weightier arias interspersed with lighter, even comic ones, including two baritone arias among the predominantly tenor ones. The recital was to begin with Mozart – baffled, love-smitten Cherubino's *'Non so più cosa son, cosa faccio'*, followed by Figaro's scolding, taunting *'Non più andrai'*. The rest of the program included arias from Italian operas – Puccini's *La Bohème,* Verdi's *Il Trovatore, Rigoletto* and *Aida*, Mascagni's *Cavalleria Rusticana,* and Donizzetti's *L'Elisir d'Amore.* The recital was to conclude with, Cherubino's plea to the ladies to enlighten him about the mystery of love, the aria *'Voi che sapete'.*

Pier's anticipation of the evening was likewise compounded of conflicting moods and emotions. He was excited about his first paid operatic engagement, flattered that his patroness, the countess, wanted him to sing at her renowned *salon.* He felt secure about his program, familiar selections he had sung many times before and had worked up exhaustively with Professor Rexel to extract every last nuance of drama from each phrase.

At the same time, he fretted about his first exposure to Turin's high society. He remembered all too vividly his *gaffe* at his first *Convivio*. He feared he would be even more out of place in the aristocratic *salon*. Memories of the snubs suffered in Santa Rita's changing room still hounded him. He'd come a long way since those days, he kept telling himself, but that was less than two years ago. To comfort himself, he kept reminding himself that, this time, his musical friends would be there to support him, graciously invited to the *salon.* But, for all that, he could not stop dreading that he would somehow manage to disgrace himself.

And then there was Lena. He agonised over what to do about Lena. He loved her dearly and wanted her with him in all his endeavours. But the disaster at *La Tampa Lirica* gave him pause. He knew that, much as he loved his Lena, on the night of the recital his mind would not be on her, but on his performance in a utterly new and intimidating setting, the countess' *salon*, where he was worried he'd make some unforgivable gaffe. To add to his worries, Professor Rexel had informed him that the dress code was white tie, an attire he had never worn before and wasn't sure how to handle.

All this had Pier deeply alarmed. He discussed it with Matilde Agiati, who gave him an etiquette book to study, and the address of a tailor from whom he could rent his *frac*. She also coached him on how to handle himself in high society. But Pier found the very idea of appearing in a *frac* daunting: what did one do with those coat tails when one had to sit down?

Finally, he had shared his apprehensions with Melina, and she had gone with him to the tailor to see that his frac fitted him properly, then helped him practice managing his tails. It was a comfort to Pier to know that she would be at Villa della Rovere for the recital – be it together with her parents, who were regular guests at the countess' *salons.*

But Lena remained a problem. Pier agonised about hurting her again, no matter whether or not he invited her to the recital. With her there, he'd feel he had to take care of her, and he didn't feel up to doing that, what with everything else on his mind. And then there was the dress code: how would Lena feel among all those ladies in evening gowns? But if he *didn't* ask her… She'd feel even more slighted.

Tormented by these dilemmas, Pier could not bring himself to broach the subject of the recital with her. In fact, he carefully avoided talking about it to her. He stopped telling her about the intensive work the professor put him through. He did not mention the dress code. And, especially, he avoided any mention of Melina, or of their visit to the tailor.

In the end, it was Lena who broached the subject. She, too, had been dreading the evening, and worrying about telling Pier that she didn't want to be there. Since the night of their reconciliation after the *La Tampa* disaster, the date of the Villa della Rovere recital had burned in her mind like a hot coal. She knew that she would feel even more *dëspaisà* at the countess' aristocratic *salon,* than she'd felt at *La Tampa Lirica,* even more out of place. Pier would again be wrapped up in his performance, and she'd be alone, lost in the intimidating crowd. She couldn't bare the thought of another night like that. She'd much rather be spared, be allowed to wait out his special evening at home. She'd enjoy his success later, in the stories about the evening. *Then* she'd feel like she'd been there with him, like in a film, or in a fairy tale.

And she also suspected '*that Violetta*' would be there. Remembering the cloud of golden-green silk, the pale furs that matched the sunset hair, Lena was afraid: how could a working girl from Le Basse compete with a lady like that? Lena shrank from the thought. She must just hope, *trust,* that Pier loved her best; enough to come back to her after the show. After all, he had, hadn't he, come back to her, after the night at *La Tampa Lirica.*

In the end, Lena forced herself to broach the subject on the night before the recital.

"I believe," she said, an anxious eye on his reaction, "that tomorrow is…your big night." She had planned to say "your recital at the Contessa's *salon",* but, when it came to it, she felt ridiculous saying those forbidding words.

Pier felt cornered, caught unprepared, somehow guilty. His cheeks flush red with anger and embarrassment. His ears burned. Lena saw him shrink back into his shell, and she, too, shrank back into herself, eyes on her hands, clenched in her lap. Several minutes went by in silence before she found the courage to try again. "You know…" she started, and again got stuck, staring at her hands. After a while she pleaded, "Please don't be angry with me. It's just that…"

"I'm not angry with you," Pier snapped.

"No, I know. But… it's just… Well, I feel so out of place with your posh friends. They are all very *nice* to me, I know, but…" She got stuck again. "It's just that…what does one do or say with *cola gent lí?"*

There it was, glaring, the old problem: *cola gent lí* – that kind of people, a problem all too familiar to Pier. He took her hands and kissed them. "I feel that way too…much of the time," he confessed.

"Yes, but it's different for you. You are…" She gave up trying to explain and, instead, raised his hands, still holding hers, and cuddled them to her cheek. "I can't, Pier. I just can't! Please understand." Unexpectedly, the birthday party at Carlin's big farm came into her mind: it had been big and fancy, but she had not felt uncomfortable or shy at all; at least not after the first few minutes. She tried again, "It's that…posh people… They make me feel …scared."

They fell silent. Long minutes went by. Then, tentatively, searching Pier's face, she asked: "Would you mind terribly if I just…well, waited for you at home? It's not that I don't want to hear you sing," she hurriedly added, "I *love* hearing you. I *will* go to all your shows in the theatre, but *up there,* in the top gallery, among people like us…"

There it was again – *people like us*. A painful lump filled Pier's throat, made it impossible for him to speak. But he was relieved. He kissed her hands, grateful that she had taken the burden of decision off his shoulders. In silence, he wrestled with that 'people like us': he didn't know any more what 'like us' meant. Nor whether he wanted to fit in with Lena's 'like us'. The night, a few weeks ago, when he had gone to look for Lena by the FIAT gate had brought him face to face with that question: the swarming factory workers had not recognised him. The one person who had, Tony, had mocked him for looking like 'a toff'. Now Pier confronted the fact that he no longer wanted to be one of Lena's 'people like us', not if he could possibly help it. But where did that leave him and Lena? Somehow, he almost loved her more dearly, because she also struggled with this same dilemma. Maybe she could move up with him, out of her working-class habits, and into better, middleclass ways.

Suddenly, a disturbing thought flashed through his mind: was it love or guilt? Pier had no answer but felt deeply ashamed. It was not fair to Lena. Maybe he wanted something from her that she did not have to give.

The previous day, Professor Rexel had put Pier through one final rehearsal of his whole program. "Not quite a dress rehearsal," the professor had joked, "since you are not *in frac*. By the way, how did you make out with the tailor?" Pier assured him the *frac* fitted him very well. "And," the professor teased him, "have you got the hang of your tails?"

"I think so," Pier said unwarily. "Melina showed me."

Rexel chuckled: "She did, eh? *Na ja.*" Then he added, "And whom shall you bring as your guest tomorrow night? You're invited to bring a friend, you remember."

Pier stared at the floor, resenting the implications of the question. "I've asked Don Marcello," he muttered.

Rexel's eyes scoured Pier's shutdown countenance. "*Gut,* that's fine," he muttered after a moment, and strolled over to the window. Pier shoved his scores into his briefcase, suddenly eager to be out of there. But before he could get out, Rexel spoke again, vaguely gazing out of the window, "Your beautiful friend at *La Tampa Lirica...*" He did not complete the sentence. Pier closed his briefcase. Rexel continued without turning around, "So beautiful... I wondered if you'd invite *her*—"

"Lena," Pier snapped, angrily.

"Yes, Lena…" the professor echoed, letting her name linger on his breath, savouring its music. "As lovely a sound as she is herself. But you'd better… not get *too fond* of her. Vith your talent, you vill go far. Poor little Lena…" he shook his head pityingly, "She vouldn't be happy. And," he continued after a moment, "vhat you need is someone of *good family*, with ze connections to help you on your vay up."

Pier latched his briefcase close with an angry snap of its locks. *He's got no business…*he thought, furious, leaving his thought unfinished.

The professor turned to face him. "You think about it," he said, still shaking his head, pitying, censorious. "Your beautiful Lena, she can't make you ze *right kind* of vife. Not for you. …"

Pier snarled, "How do you know?! And what has it got to do with you? It's *my* business whom I love!"

"Love, love, love…" The professor waved dismissive hands at love. "You must be practical. Your Lena is…delectable, but she von't help your career. She's ignorant, socially awkward."

"She hasn't had much schooling, that's true," Pier protested, "but she can learn."

"But can she? That's vhat I doubt very much."

"Two years ago, I was just as ignorant as she is. But now I'm learning…"

"You, my boy, haf talent and brains. You've got passion, ambition…"

"She's got her dreams too…"

Rexel shrugged: "She's maudling. That's *not* ze same as passion." Unexpectedly, the feel of Lena dancing in his arms flashed through him.

If there is any passion in ze girl, he thought, *it spends itself on ze dance floor, vithout giving her focus.*

"How do you know?" Pier shouted, outraged.

Rexel's tongue gave a sympathetic click. "She *is* delectable, I know. I danced vith her at *La Tampa*… So…if you must haf her, keep her as your mistress, just don't marry her. Get yourself ze right kind of vife, with background, money, family connections that vill open doors for you."

"How dare you!" Pier screamed, shaking with hatred of the redheaded gnome in front of him. "I LOVE *Lena*! She is a *good,* loving girl. And I *don't want* a mistress!" He stormed out in a fury, made a headlong run for the river: the gall of the bloody German! Lena as a mistress! His ma was right after all, theatre people! They *were* corrupt, work of the devil…temptation…den of sin…

But when he reached the Po, he calmed down. Walking along its sluggish current he had to admit that what fanned his anger was more than just the insult to Lena. What he'd heard behind the professor's words was the old refrain, 'those kind of people', Lena's '*gent coma noi*'; and his own '*cola gent lí*'. He was angry and frightened because he no longer knew what kind of people *he* was, or with whom he *wanted to belong.* He no longer felt part of Lena's 'people like us', was no longer comfortable in a blue-collar life. But his agonising over the *Contessa's* recital, his anxiety about disgracing himself in polite society, reminded him that he also did not fit in with the affluent and cultured set. Already at the *Convivio,* he had felt out of place. At the *collegio,* the priests protected him, nurtured his talents as in a greenhouse, coached him past his mistakes, never shaming him for what he didn't know. But how would he fare in an unprotected environment?

An unsought thought deflated him: "At *Sacro Cuore,* I'm one of the kids." It was a sobering reflection: what he needed was to be brought up all over again, to be taught how to *be fit* for a decent place in this world. His voice had opened doors for him. Now it was up to him to see to it that he did not spoil his chances. He had to get himself the upbringing he needed in order to belong in the world he craved.

Matilde on Lena

Chastened but determined, Pier returned to the Regio for his scheduled session with Signora Agiati. He found her anxiously looking out for him in the corridor of the rehearsal wing. "Pier!" she called out, "I was afraid I'd missed you." She led the way to her own room and closed the door behind them. "I'm afraid I couldn't help but overhear," she said, referring to his row with Professor Rexel. "I'm so sorry."

"How can he talk like that about Lena?" Pier erupted, his outrage flaring up again. "She's good, loving girl."

"I know," Matilde said gently, "and very much in love with you. Unfortunately, she is almost *too* lovely, and beauty can be…well, a liability," she added with deep compassion for his hurt.

"What do you mean?"

"Men will hound her, Pier. And women…they will hate her for it."

"But that's awful!"

"Yes, it is. I'm so sorry."

"*He* said she's…dumb," Pier returned to his grievance. "How would *he* know? He doesn't know her." Matilde sat in silence, giving Pier time to calm down. "Do you think he is right?" he asked after a while, his eyes pleading for reassurance.

"I wouldn't know."

"But you know her as much as he does. You sat with her at *La Tampa Lirica,* and you talked to her. What do you think?"

"I could see she's very much in love with you," Matilde temporised. To herself, she said, *She is the clingy type; she'll smother him and he'll end up hating her.* Pier's eyes stayed on her face, pleading for a verdict. Matilde recalled the forlorn little figure at Rexel's table. She also recalled Pier's panic last spring, when he faced the prospect of a summer without opera, his eagerness, during the summer, to learn, to become part of the enthralling world of the theatre. Then she recalled the clatter, last June, of hobnailed boots down her building's marble stairs. The contrast to his supple grace now brought on an affectionate smile: he had learned a lot this past year, and not just about opera. He had become housebroken.

And Lena? For a moment Matilde recalled Lena's dismay at the fuss made of Pier by the *La Tampa* crowd, her rancorous gaze pinned on Melina Cortesi, then her thoughts returned to Pier: he *wanted* to break out of the harsh, narrow world to which he was born. His marvellous voice gave him a chance and he had driven himself hard to make it work for him. She recalled his bewildered enthusiasm, last January, after his first week at *Sacro Cuore,* when he talked to her about his first day in the music history class. He had described himself as a tadpole suddenly snatched out of a backwater pool and thrown into a fast mainstream.

Well, that tadpole, off-balance and disoriented at first, had soon managed to get used to the fast current, eager to learn despite the struggle. Now he'd found his stride and was making headway. He wanted to fit his new role so badly, he worked at it with a desperate tenacity. The question was, did *Lena* have any wish to leave her world? Matilde had seen Lena's alarm when he had been swept up in the audience's enthusiasm. Did the girl have the potential, the determination, to follow him where he was heading? Out loud, she said, "Poor Lena felt so…*dëspaisà* at *La Tampa* I couldn't really get much of an impression of her when she is…at ease, in her own world. The question is, are *you* still comfortable in her world?"

Pier recoiled from her. "What do you mean?" he cried, refusing to understand. In fact, he understood her only too well: she'd put into words the very doubts that had been gnawing at him. Matilde scrambled for a tactful way to explain.

"Do you recall," she started, "last January, when you first moved into *Sacro Cuore?* You told me then that you felt like a tadpole tossed into a fast current. Well, at *La Tampa*, that night, Lena struck me a bit like that, like a charming young frog, bewildered by a stream too fast for her. Might she not prefer to sit on her log and bask in the sun? Perhaps she does not have...*your drive* to leave the pond."

Pier glared at Matilde, bristling with anger. After a pause, she went on, "She is no fool, and I am sure she loves you dearly. But... the question is, can she face the struggle of learning how to fit into the world you're moving into? Might not her ambitions be...more modest, perhaps only to find a better log from which to flick her tongue at passing bugs? But Pier, I know her so little, I'm probably not doing her justice."

Pier now stared at his clasped hands, shocked into silence, haunted by the image of that predatory tongue. For a moment, he saw himself as the gnat snagged by that flicking tongue and swallowed. He roused himself with an effort and changed the subject.

"The professor," he said, "asked me if I've got the hang of the coat tails. Melina Cortesi showed me how to handle them, but...would you mind checking me out?" Matilde smiled.

"Stop by here when you've picked up your *frac*," she said. "I'll be here until six."

Recital at Villa della Rovere

The following evening found Pier struggling with a lamentable case of the jitters, not about the recital itself, but about his first appearance in polite society. At supper, in the *Sacro Cuore* refectory, his throat was so dry and tight he could not swallow anything solid. Instead, he drank glass after glass of water. Then it occurred to him that all that water would make him need a toilet at *Villa della Rovere,* so he stopped drinking. Next to him, Don Marcello tried to reassure him. "No need to be nervous," he said. "You know you will do well. You are well prepared." But Pier could not settle down. They were due at the *Contessa's* at eight o'clock. It was now almost seven. He fretted to be back to his room and get

336

into his first *frac*, now hanging in his wardrobe in its shroud of tissue paper. He had already washed and shaved before supper, but his hand kept rising to his chin, checking for stubbles. At long last, the headmaster released the assembly and Pier ran upstairs to dress.

An hour later, exactly as arranged, a light knock on his door. Don Marcello, in his most formal Jesuit habit, had come to fetch him for the drive to the villa in the *collegio*'s automobile. "Impressive," he said, inspecting Pier's trim form, "very elegant indeed."

They drove the fifteen minutes to the villa in silence. Outside its gate, the tree-lined four-laned corso was already bustling with automobile and carriage traffic, some arriving to deliver guests to the villa, invisible in its lush spring grounds. Two liveried footmen directed the arriving vehicles up the curving drive onto the property, while two more assisted chauffeurs needing to park along the *controviale*. At the villa's front door two more footmen ushered in the guests. One of them, recognising the *Sacro Cuore* automobile, hurried down the steps to guide Don Marcello to a reserved parking spot near the house. Pier waited for his return on the gravelled drive, inhaling the garden's night scents, marvelling at the multitude of Chinese lanterns glowing among the trees in bloom.

Inside, a butler announced each new arrival in a resonant baritone. In a second-story gallery at the top of the wide staircase, the count and countess Vergani della Rovere welcomed the incoming guests. The countess stepped forward to greet Pier and his escort. "Don Marcello," she greeted the young Jesuit first, as protocol demanded, "so glad you could come. I trust your dear parents are well?" Then she turned to Pier, "My dear Signor Venturi, so kind of you to consent to perform for us this evening. We and our guests have been looking forward to this treat."

A footman appeared at Pier's elbow and the countess continued, "Professor Rexel is already in the rehearsal room."

Pier followed his escort. They were crossing a first reception room – clusters of chatting guests, catering staff circulating with trays of champagne and *canapés* – when a familiar voice called out, "Pier! You're here!" Melina Cortesi, in a shimmering golden green gown. She stretched on tiptoes and planted a kiss on Pier's cheek. "Come meet my parents. They're dying to meet you," she said. She took Pier's hand and led him towards a cluster of *fracs* and gowns, the escorting footman a few discreet steps behind them.

"*Mammá, Papá,*" Melina said, laying a hand on her father's arm and glancing at the other guests to include them in her introduction, "meet tonight's artist, Pier Venturi, my colleague and special friend at the Regio."

Pier bowed all around. Signor Cortesi sketched an interested bow. "Our daughter," he said, "can't stop singing your praises. We are eager to hear you for ourselves."

"Yes, indeed," added Signora Cortesi, stepping forward and taking Pier's hand in both of hers. "We were so sorry that we were in London at the time of your evening at *La Tampa Lirica*. We read your review, of course. Most impressive. So tonight... I simply can't wait."

"Come, *Mammà,*" Melina cut in, "let him go. Pier has to warm up." She accompanied him to the rehearsal room and, as they walked, she whispered discreetly, "You look splendid! Join us later, will you, at least for a little while."

In a daze, Pier joined *Herr* Rexel in the rehearsal room and went through his warm-up, the stiff, unfamiliar, collar of his boiled shirt an irritant to his neck. Signora Agiati popped in for a brief well-wishing visit. She saw his jitters and mimed her usual signal to deep-breathe.

"He'll do fine," Horst Rexell assured her over the keyboard. "Don't fuss."

Pier knew he was right: he'd do fine, but he had to settle his nerves. He deepened his breathing, trying his best not to feel outlandish in his *frac*. From the ballroom, where the recital was to take place, came the clear peal of a silver bell – the signal for the guests to take their seats. Signora Agiati blew him a kiss and bustled off. A few minutes later, the professor and Pier filed in to the grand piano, bowed to their hosts, then to the expectant guests. At the piano Rexel ran through a few introductory phrases, then Pier sang, *"Non so piú cosa son, cosa faccio..."*(I no longer know what I am, what I'm doing: First I'm afire, then I'm like ice, every woman makes me change colour...) The clear, young voice fluttered with convincing bewilderment, his face and his lithe male body aquiver with juvenile confusion. *"Ogni donna mi fa palpitar..."* (Every women sends me into a flutter.)

The audience smiled, charmed, amused as the aria reached its humorous end, '...and if there's no one to listen to me I talk about love to myself.'

At the aria's end, the audience burst into generous applause. Pier bowed his thanks. The piano introduced his first baritone aria, then Pier's voice rose forth deep, assured, ironic, plotting mischief for Rossini's frolicking count. *"Se vuol ballare, Signor Contino, Il Chitarrino Le suoneró."* (If you want to dance, my little count, *I* will play your tune.) Whereas Cherubino had been all a-quiver with baffling emotions, Figaro's ironic voice and eyes proclaimed his cool determination. Again, there was warm applause.

And so the recital continued with increasing success through courting, swagger, revenge, longing and despair, and back to amorous dalliance, until it ended with Cherubino's final appeal to the wisdom of the fair sex: *"...Voi che sapete che cosa è amor, donne, vedete, s'io l'ho nel cor"*(You who know, ladies, what love is, look see if I have it in my heart.)

The genteel audience rose to its feet, applauded enthusiastically, cheering and laughing, formality forgotten in sheer delight. The *Contessa* came forward, both hands outstretched to grasp Pier's, to thank and congratulate him. The usually reserved count, wreathed with smiles, joined her with his thanks. Soon Pier was mobbed by the enthusiastic audience. Among the throng of *fracs* and gowns, two cassocks approached. "Well done, my boy," a delighted Don Marco yelled, to be heard above the hubbub. "That was truly delightful. And moving, most moving."

At the praise Pier's eyes welled up: it was almost too much. He laughed, and shook hands with his duomo mentor: next to whom Horst Rexel chuckled, *"Na ja,* vhat did I tell you?"

. "Pier!" Now Melina was next to him. She stretched to her toes to kiss his cheek, hugged him warmly. "That was wonderful, truly marvellous! Come join us when you can. We're over there." She withdrew, making room for others to close in and chat with the new discovery.

For Pier, the rest of the evening went by in a blur. It was well past midnight when, sitting in the car with Don Marcello at the wheel, he began to come back to earth. "I think I'm drunk," he observed, surprised.

"You didn't drink that much, did you?" his companion said. "Hardly had time."

"Two glasses" Pier answered, thinking of his brief time with the Cortesi, before he'd been stolen away by other eager admirers. "I think,"

"Two glasses on an empty stomach," Don Marcello grinned. "You ate nothing at supper. Success," he teased, "far more intoxicating than alcohol."

"It has been a success, hasn't it?" Pier prompted. He did not think he had made any *gaffes*. He had remembered his tails. He threw his head against the back of his seat with a sharp sigh of release. Of triumph. Of longing. Don Marcello cast him a wry sideways glance but did not speak again.

Chapter Fifteen

"Don't marry for money, but be sure
to fall in love where money is."

Melina's invitation

A couple of days after the *Contessa's* recital, Melina invited Pier for a celebratory drink at Baratti's. They had just finished yet another rehearsal of their Carmen program in Rexel's practice room. Crossing Piazza Castello on the way to the café, Melina threaded her arm through Pier's, walked very close to him. The swing of her hip against his thigh alarmed him. It was confusing. Melina was his partner, his colleague. He did not want to think of her as…as Carmen, he concluded not quite accurately.

Walking arm in arm, Melina chatted volubly, seemingly quite oblivious to his discomfort. She rattled on about the evening at the *Contessa's,* about their work together for next season's program, about the summer practice they needed for their fall concert tour.

Pier made perfunctory answers, distracted by the rustle of her silks at his side, by her warmth against his thigh. Confused and angry with himself, he hovered between wanting to shake off her disturbing closeness, and wanting to draw her closer. At the café's entrance, he disengaged himself from her, ostensibly to open its door for her. Melina entered, still talking over her shoulder, and headed for an inner room where an upholstered bench ran along the back wall, allowing patrons to sit side by side. She slid in behind the table and sat down, drawing Pier in after her – much too close for his comfort. Their drinks came, and she, once again, toasted his recent success, before returning to the issue of their practice schedule over the summer months. They were expected to work on their own, as *Herr Rexel* was to be away over the whole summer, and Matilde Agiati over most of July and August.

"We'll have to practice at least three times each week," she said, "But…in mid-June, my family goes down to *Cinque Terre,* before the Riviera gets too hot and crowded. Then in July, we move up to the mountains. That means that, to get our practice in, I'll have to spend a lot of time going back and forth."

"Maybe," Pier suggested, "we could rehearse on three consecutive days, then it would only be one trip a week."

"Yeah…but that's not ideal. Alternate days are better, with rests in between. But…what if…" she glanced at Pier over her glass, she stopped, a new thought giving her pause. "What about *Sacro Cuore,* when does it close for the summer?" she asked.

"Well," Pier answered, "the *collegio* never really closes; but the students are gone by second week of June."

"What about you, do you have any duties there during the summer?"

"Not a lot. Don Luca might have me help him with the textbooks for next year."

"Then you might be able to get away for some of the time?"

"Maybe," Pier said, thinking. Once the weather got stable, he might ride his bike out to see his mother, whom he'd not seen in a long time. And he'd like to spend some time with Nina and her girls. He might also ride out to Niclin and Candieul, to see his brother Minòt and Uncle Giachin. But none of that required overnights away.

"Great," Melina clapped her hands, "then there's no reason you shouldn't join us at *Cinque Terre* and *Valtournanche.* We can practice just as well there, and it would save me hours on the road."

He drew away from her, sputtering, "Oh, but I couldn't possibly."

"Why not?" Melina demanded. "We've plenty of room, and my parents would love to have you."

"But what about…our sets?"

Melina waved the stage sets aside. "We can easily put something up there. Besides," she added, "it will be fun. We could swim and hike in our breaks. It would be good for you. You know what they say about 'all work and no play'." She laid her hand on his arm. Under the table, her leg was warm against his. "Do come, it'll be such fun."

Blushing furiously, Pier tried to shift clear of the disturbing contact. "Well, I don't know…" he stammered.

"Well, do think about it," she said draining her glass. "No," she added, "don't think about it: just say yes."

"No, but I can't!" Pier cried out.

"But why not?" Melina argued, "It makes a lot of sense. If you don't, I'll just have to track back up here every week over those dusty mountain roads. Or spend hours on the train and get here covered in soot. Why can't you come?"

"I just can't."

"Why on earth not?"

"Because... I have ...other commitments."

"What commitments? More important than our practice? Can't you work around them? At least for a few weeks at a time?"

"No, I can't."

"But why not?"

"Because... Because I'm engaged to be married."

"Married! To whom? When?"

Pier flushed, angry at what he had blurted out. Yes, of course he'd marry Lena, but they never yet talked about when. All he had said to Lena was, "When I can." Why had he made that ridiculous statement? What was he afraid of? All Melina had proposed was a stay at her family's vacation homes so they could practice for their fall recital. But he knew why he'd lied, and shuddered. *It's yourself you're running away from,* he thought. He was the one who sweated and shivered whenever Carmen... He corrected himself, whenever Melina touched him.

For several minutes Melina sat, miffed and shocked, next to him. Then she sighed and asked, "Who is the girl?" Pier sat in mulish silence. "Is it the beautiful girl with you at *La Tampa?*" Pier nodded despite himself. "You never spoke of her. I didn't know. When?"

Pier stared into his *aperitiv.* "End of August," he finally muttered.

Melina leaned back on the bench, silent for long moments, recovering from the news. Then she sat up straight. "Well, then..." she said, "But we still have to rehearse. Come out with us in June and ...take the train back whenever you need to."

"But that wouldn't be right," Pier said, at the same time cursing himself for a fool. It made sense, and a part of him longed to see that other side of Melina's world. But how could he accept now that he had told that stupid lie? He was *not* getting married in August.

And then he thought of Lena. She wouldn't like it if he went away with Melina for weeks at a time. As it was, she was bitterly jealous of Melina already.

Then he thought, *She is jealous of everything in my life that takes me away from her.*

Next to him, Melina was saying, "Well, if you can't, you can't. We'll just have to make some other plan."

They parted, both subdued, Pier to catch his tram to the *collegio,* Melina to retrieve her car and drive back to her parent's home in the Turin hills.

A bad rehearsal

The encounter at *Caffé Baratti* left them both deflated and off stride. Their deflation became palpable the following day, during their practice session. Professor Rexel, slouched in his old armchair at the far end of the room, watched Carmen's dance in front of Pastia's tavern.

"*Nein, nein, nein!*" he yelled, his fist thumping the chair's arm. "Vhat is the matter vith you two today? Melina, you dance like you're constipated! And you, Pier, your voice has no fire. Haf you two had a qvarrel? You vere doing fine last Tuesday. Take it again. From '*je vais danser pour toi'*. Put some passion into it!"

They took it again, and again the professor was dissatisfied. "*Ach, nein!* It's no good. Ve'll take a break and try again in half an hour. Come on, I need *ein Bier.*"

It was sipping cool drinks at an outdoor café that Melina blurted out, "Pier's getting married." Rexel choked on his beer, slammed his glass on the table sputtered, "*Was?! Was ist das?* You're *getting married*!? And you didn't think to tell me?! Vhen?"

"August," Melina muttered. Pier mumbled something without looking up.

"And vhen, pray, vere you going to take the trouble to let me know!?" roared *der Herr Professor.* "Ve don't need this distraction vhile ve're vorking on your stage debut. You see vhat it's doing to your work: you're just *not there!* No, ve must postpone this nonsense to after…if you must marry *her* at all."

Pier flushed, ears blazing, strangling the glass in his hand. That stressed '*her*' rankled as much as the intrusion itself.

"You *must* postpone!" Rexel commanded, slamming his glass on the table. An oppressive silence settled on the trio. Rexel's hand swiped at his mouth as though to wipe away something disgusting. "*Na ja,*" he continued, struggling to contain himself, "you must reconsider… You can't…*not at this stage.* A vife…" he shook his head, "that vould be a serious handicap…even if it vere Melina, here," he added maliciously. "You just haf to postpone."

"I can't," Pier snarled.

"Vhy not?" Rexel insisted, "Is she pregnant?"

"No!" Pier screamed at the offensive inference. The glass he was holding shattered in his hand and blood spurted across the café table, splattering Melina's cheek, who jerked back with a muffled cry. From across the table, Rexel grabbed the bleeding hand. "See vhat you've gone and done now, you *bube!"* He clamped his handkerchief onto Pier's cut. "Vaiter!" he roared. A waiter came running. Rexel snatched the serviette hanging on his arm and wrapped it around Pier's hand. "This'll need stitches, you *dumkopf."* He snarled at the waiter, "Vhere is the nearest doctor?"

The three darted off in a taxi. Half an hour later, the emergency repair done, the doctor was bandaging the wound. "You nicked a tendon," he said, "your middle finger may never regain its full range of motion. We'll have to wait and see. Meantime, keep your hand up in a sling for a couple of weeks."

They left. Rexel insisted on riding back to the *collegio* with Pier, dismissing Melina with an impatient wave of the hand. In the taxi, he picked up the earlier scolding. "And your bride-to-be? Who's she?"

Pier did not answer. He sat staring out the window, his bandaged hand resting against his left shoulder. Next to him, Rexell huffed and puffed. "Is it…that luscious titbit, Lena?" he queried suddenly. "*Ach, nein,* Pier!" he harrumphed. "She *is* gorgeous, but she vill never do!"

Pier lashed out, "How would *you* know!? And what business was it of yours?"

"Vhat do you mean, vhat business is it of mine? When you came to the Regio you put yourself in my hands. You *made* your career *my* business!"

"My career, yes," Pier shouted, "but *not* whom I choose to marry! Stay out of it!"

Pier's vehemence startled *der Herr Professor* into silence, but he went on muttering angrily to himself.

A few minutes later, the taxi pulled up in front of the *collegio*. Rexel got out, insisted on personally passing the care of the wounded on to the *collegio's* infirmary brother, before he went up to see Pier settled in his room. When he, at last, took his leave, he still hovered by Pier's door, half-wheedling, half laying down the law. "Look here, Pier," he said, "be sensible. *You can go far.* Don't wreck it for yourself." Then, already in the hallway, he turned back to add, "Ve really *must talk* about your Lena." He gave a determined nod and left.

Lena at La Speranza

Having blurted out that he was getting married in August, Pier now felt an obligation to take Lena to meet his mother, but at the same time he looked upon the prospect with dread. He could not fool himself that his mother would be pleased with his choice of a city-bred fiancée. He hoped against hope that his ma would see, behind Lena's striking beauty, her sweet and modest nature. He also suspected that Lena's good looks would be another strike against her with his mother. Tilde, he was sure, would like her; but he could count on Vigin-a being spiteful.

Another problem was when to go and how to get there. Next week was already May. He had three weddings during the month, besides his Ascension Day commitments at the duomo. He wouldn't be able to get away before the end of the month. By then the big farm works would be under way with the first hay cut, so everybody would be exhausted and be on edge. At the very least he had to let his mother know that they were coming. But there was no telephone in San Dalmass, so the only way to get word to her would be to ride out to the farm on his bike. But Don Marco frowned on long bike rides, and Pier's hand was still in a sling.

Thinking of riding out to the farm brought up the other difficulty: Lena had never ridden a bike. He considered organising a car and driver, but his mother would see that as an extravagance and blame Lena for it. As it was, Pier expected that the announcement of his engagement would come as a bad blow to his mother: that was not how things were done in the country. Parents still arranged, or at least supervised, all matchmaking. In the end, he decided to consult his sister, Nina.

"No," Nina agreed in her Santa Rita *retro,* "it won't do to arrive in an automobile. And you'd better not surprise her with *this* news. She'll be upset enough that you're marrying a town girl. You know how she was when I brought Lorèns home." They were silent for a while, each thinking his own thoughts. Then she said, "Do you think Lena could learn to ride? You could borrow my bike. I hardly ever use." They sat on debating the problem and eventually decided to ask Don Carlo if he could help break the news to Maria through Don Michel at San Dalmass'.

"Hmmm, yes," Don Carlo pondered their request, remembering last summer's hot bike ride to the country parish. "There's no phone at San Dalmass," he said. "When are you planning to take your girl to meet your mother?"

In the end, it was agreed that he would write a note and Pier would get it to the *L'Asia* man who brought produce to Turin's general markets every morning. He could give it to Don Michel.

So now, on the last Sunday in May, Pier and Lena pedalled along in the dappled shade of plane trees of the broad carriage road that led from town to the royal hunting pavilion of Stupinigi. Pier's injured hand was newly out of its sling, but still bandaged, and Lena was still a bit tentative on Nina's bike. Their progress stirred the May air into a gentle breeze that wafted spring scents around them. Right and left, wide swatches of hay fields were already cut and drying, fragrant, in the sun. Here and there, fields of winter wheat rippled in the sun like rivers of pale gold, almost ready to be harvested, in the next couple of weeks. Next to Pier, Lena pedalled, wide eyed, enjoying her first bike ride in the countryside. Pier, anxious about their reception at *La Speransa,* glanced over to her, resenting her simple pleasure. So like Lena, he thought irritably. For three weeks now, since he had first suggested the visit to the farm, she had pestered him for reassurance he could not give her without lying. And now here she was, breezing along happy as a lark.

Suddenly she sniffed and exclaimed, "Ah, what's that lovely smell?"

"*Gasía,*" Pier answered, pointing to a row of acacia trees in bloom between two fields, "Those trees, down there."

"I never knew *la campagna* is so wonderful.*"* Pier looked at her beaming face, still lifted to the scent. The sun and breeze made an aura of her recently bobbed brown curls. Suddenly, he was intensely happy, his resentment dissolved into a smile. He hoped against hope that his ma would take to his Lena.

They got to *La Speranza* just after the midday meal. As they wheeled their bikes through the farm gate, Pier saw the wagon in the shed: *they* were home, not out in the fields, haying.

Taboj's frantic barking brought his mother to the screened kitchen window. Squatted down and scratching the dog's head, Pier waved to her. He couldn't hear her words, but he saw her mouth move and recognised her usual, *"Oh mi, pòvra dòna."* (Oh, me, poor woman.) Despite his apprehension, he smiled at her typical reaction. The door jerked open and Tilde ran out, yelling, "They are here, Ma! They are here!"

So, Pier thought, his ma had got word. He stood up and walked towards the house with Lena at his side, each leading a bike.

"What did you do to your hand?" Tilde asked, hovering at Pier's elbow and looking at his bandage. "It's nothing. Just cut it on a broken glass."

Moments later, his ma appeared in the doorway, hands smoothing down her apron. Behind her Vigin-a and Clot filed out, leery, inquisitive. Pier loosened the package he had brought for his mother from the bike's carrier. "I wrote you not to come," she said, "until the big works are over."

Pier felt the rebuff but did not respond. After the big works wouldn't have worked, as they lasted all summer, and he had said he was getting married in August.

Aloud he said, "I never got your letter. Where did you send it?"

"To Don Carlo, at Santa Rita's," she said, in a tone that stated the obvious.

"Must still be there, then, Ma," he said. "I haven't lived in Santa Rita since last January." He handed his gifts to his mother, who passed it on to Vigin-a without looking at it. Pier went on, "Better write to me at the *Collegio Sacro Cuore.*" He had given his mother the address and phone number of the *collegio* when he had first moved. They stood awkwardly in the yard, all eyes examining Lena, Taboj still excitedly straining at his chain and giving brief sporadic barks.

"Ma," Pier said, nudging Lena forwards, "This is my *morosa,* Lena." Lena took a timid step forward, hands tight on her handlebar, smiling tensely, uncertain whether to curtsy or shake hands.

Maria glared at the girl. "Surely," she grumbled, "this could have waited till after *Feragost.*" She turned on her heels and walked back into her kitchen.

Clot sidled up and took Lena's bike from her. Tilde took charge of Pier's, so he took hold of Lena's hand and gave it an encouraging squeeze. In awkward silence, they all filed into the kitchen, the two lovers first, the other three close behind them.

Inside, Maria was scratching at the stove's grate. She heard the door click shut and ordered over her shoulder. "Get some fresh water for coffee'." Tilde picked up a bucket and went to the pump by the kitchen door. Vigin-a laid Pier's gift on the table, near Maria's seat, then set out the coffee cups. Clot, one shoulder against a wall, gawked at Lena, who lowered her eyes. Tilde came in with the fresh water, placed the bucket on its stand between the stone sink and the stove. Behind them, Vigin-a was unwrapping Pier's gift on the table. Tilde went over to check on its contents. "Why," she exclaimed, "you brought coffee again! Look, Ma, Pier brought you coffee beans." She ran across to her mother with the coffee bag. "It smell: it's wonderful!"

"Hmm," Maria answered grudgingly. "Might as well grind us some, then," she said. She filled the kettle and put it on the stove. "And he brought us *paste* as well," Tilde added, unwrapping Pier's tray of *patisserie.*

The mention *of paste* drew Clot to the table, eyeing the tray. He cast a surreptitious glance at his mother, busy at the stove, then snuck a macaroon into his mouth, palming two more, before he went back to the wall and to staring at Lena.

"We've got to be back out to the fields," Maria said, pouring hot water over the coffee grounds. "The hay needs turning and time is getting on."

Heavy steps lumbered over their heads then down the stairs: their Pa, coming down from his Sunday *siesta.* "So you're here," Maté muttered at Pier through a yawn, scratching his armpit. "I thought your Ma wrote you not to come." He ambled towards his chair by the table and added, "Suppose I'm not to expect any help with the hay."

"I can help for a bit, before we go back," Pier answered. "But, Pa, this is my *morosa.*" Maté's mouth stretched into another, , wider yawn.

"Morosa, eh*?"* he said sleepily, glancing perfunctorily in Lena's direction, then, with a double blink, stared at her, this time fully awake. Clot hovered close by his pa, gawking at Pier's town girl. Lena blushed and looked down, uncomfortable, drew a bit closer to Pier. He took her hand and held it tight, hiding his gesture between them.

"She's going to walk the fields in them heels?" Maté sneered, lowering himself into his chair at the head of the table. Then he spotted the tray of pastries, reached for it and stuffed one in his mouth, gathering two more before settling back in his seat, angling his chair out so he could keep his eyes on Pier's *turinèisa.* Then the aroma of fresh-brewed coffee reached him, and he sniffed the air. "You making *coffee,"* he observed, disapproving.

"Pier brought it to Ma," Tilde cut in.

Pier led Lena to a seat near his mother's end of the table. Maria brought the coffee pot and started to pour. Vigin-a passed the filled cups along, nudging Tilde to pass the pastries. Tilde offered the tray to her ma, and Maria grudgingly took one *amaretto* and set it down by her cup. Fragrant steam hovered over each cups, wafting the coffee aroma around the room.

"So," Maria said, sitting down, "why couldn't this wait till August?"

"We want to get married, Ma," Pier said.

Clot guffawed, eyes riveted onto Lena's bosom, prominent under her red cardigan. Under the table Vigin-a gave him a sharp kick. All eyes were on Lena – Maté's with a leer, Vigin-a's assessing, envious, vaguely hostile, Tilde's friendly, admiring.

Maria lifted her cup to her lips, blew daintily over the steaming brew, and took a careful sip, refusing to look at Lena at all. She set her cup down and nibbled at her *amaretto,* before she lifted her eyes to the stranger, inspecting her. She watched her draw a bit closer to Pier, as though to take cover behind him. She took in the bobbed hair, the red lipstick, the patterned silk blouse with its airy *jabot* flouncing on the girl's remarkable chest. Between the flaps of her unbuttoned *red* cardigan. "Hmmm," she mumbled. Silence fell on the room and Maria let it lengthen. After a significant pause she spoke to Pier. "Are you still going to sing for Don Michel on San Dalmass' feast?"

"Of course, Ma."

"Just as well," she said. "You'll break his heart if you let him down. He's announced it in church over and over."

"Won't let us forget it," Vigin-a mumbled.

"I won't let him down, Ma. It's all arranged."

"Hmmm, let's hope you won't."

She picked up her *amaretto,* inspected it with mistrust, then bit off another small piece. Across the fields, came the faint sound of San Dalmass' bell, struck three times. Maté scraped his chair back and left the room without a word. Clot followed him, eyes still lingering on Lena as he walked out. Vigin-a and Tilde bustled around the table, gathering up the cups. Maria got up and walked to her sink.

"Three o'clock," she said. "Better get back to the hay, if it's going to be turned before nightfall. You two," she said to her daughters, "go along. I'll finish here."

Dismayed, Lena sought Pier's eyes. He squeezed her hand and said, "We'll go with the others and lend a hand."

"Not in that get up," his mother muttered without looking around, clattering the cups and saucers in her chipped enamel basin.

Pier held Lena's hand tight and led her outside. Taboj was straining towards him on his chain, tail wagging. Pier squatted down by the dog and drew Lena down next to him. "Well, anyway," he tried to joke, nuzzling the shaggy old head. "*He* likes us."

From the kitchen window his mother's voice called out, "You'll get fleas." In the shed, the mule snorted and pawed. Clot snarled, "Hold still, you stupid bitch." Maté climbed onto the wagon, still cluttered with haying tools they'd used that morning. Tilde and Vigin-a hopped onto its back, legs dangling over the edge. "Want to ride with us?" Tilde called out to the two standing by their bicycles. "They've got their bikes," Vigin-a answered her, repressive.

Lena shook her head and straddled her bike. Clot walked the farm gate closed behind the departing wagon, then ran a few steps to catch up with it and scrambled up onto the front seat with his pa. The whip cracked, the mule strained and picked up a reluctant trot. Outside the farm gate, Pier and Lena stood side by side, astride their bikes, watching them leave.

Pier cast a sideways glance at Lena. "Don't mind them," he said lamely. He reached over and patted her hand tight on the handlebar

"They don't like me," she whimpered.

"No," he lied, trying to comfort. "It's just their way. And Tilde likes you. My ma will come around, in time." But would she, he wondered. His ma could hold a grudge a very long time.

They rode slowly after the wagon, in silence. Away from the farmyard, their mood eased somewhat. They got to the hayfield. Maté unhitched the mule and tethered her to a sapling, where it could graze on the verge. He returned to the wagon, reached into a stack of sacks under the driver's seat and took a long swig at a gourd stashed there, corked it and put it it back. Then, grabbing a pitchfork, and headed for an unturned row.

Further out in the field, Vigin-a and Clot were back to work where they had stopped in the morning, tossing pitchfork-fulls of hay in the air to speed up the drying. Behind them, swallows darted around, snatching insects out of the air. At the start of a nearby row, Tilde stated to turn her row, pitching hay into the air.

"Get a move on," Maté barked at her as he walked by. She let him walk by without responding, then ran back to the wagon and pulled down the folded horse rug folded on the driver's seat.

"You may want to sit on this," she said, handing it to Lena, who smiled, grateful for the friendly gesture. Tilde rushed back to her row, checking that their Pa hadn't turned around to see.

Pier spread the rug out in the shade of a mulberry tree and Lena sat down, pulling her skirt over her out-stretched legs. A butterfly fluttered across the rug and came to rest on Lena's delicately coloured blouse, opening and closing fragile wings in a leisurely, hypnotic rhythm. Tilde saw it from her row and called back, "See, she likes you! That means you're chosen!" Lena glanced up at Tilde and smiled, then returned her gaze to the opening and closing wings.

Relieved, Pier stood up. "Will you be all right, here, by yourself? I'd like to help for a while. I'll just be over there. You can see me." Lena nodded, enthralled by her winged guest.

They had been in the field for a couple of hours when Maria arrived, bringing fresh water. She stowed her gourds in the shade and sat down on the verge, at some distance from Lena, her shoulders resting against a mulberry trunk. By and by the workers made their way back for a drink and a rest. Pier took one of the flasks to Lena, some ten feet away, exchanged a few words with her, then went to sit by his ma, who simply looked away. Neither spoke. From time to time, Lena cast a timid glance over her shoulder, seeking Pier. He smiled back at her, a discreet nod towards his mother promising that he would talk her around. Next to him, his mother's eyes remained steadily on the rows of drying hay, refusing any contact with the town girl. Lena's chin dropped to her chest, and her face crumpled.

Pained, Pier asked, "Why don't you like her, Ma?"

Maria sniffed, glancing with some satisfaction at the bowed head and drooping shoulders: the girl was cowed. "If you need to ask..." she said repressively.

They sat in silence, their eyes on Lena's back. Minutes went by. From time to time, Lena glanced briefly over her shoulder, and Pier tried to smile at her, but his wistful little smiles failed to reassure her.

"She's a good girl, Ma," he urged. "Really, Ma, she is." Maria stared at the distance. "She can't help where she was born," Pier pleaded. "She and her mama are good people, I promise you. Hardworking. God-fearing," he added in the hostile silence. "And loving, Ma, both of them. They love me. Please, Ma, give her a chance."

His mother rose to her feet, started to gather the now empty water gourds she had brought, stowed them in her basket. She glanced at the field to make sure that Maté and Clot were out of earshot, then turned to Pier.

"When?" she asked.

"Haven't decided," Pier answered. "But soon."

"When what?" Vigin-a called back. She had been lingering some way down her row, eavesdropping.

Nobody answered her. Maria turned and walked away, her basket on her arm, heading for home.

Pier stood up, joined Lena. "Let's go," he said sharply, reaching down for her hand to help her to her feet. They wheeled their bikes through the stubble.

"Goodbye, goodbye…" Tilde called out from deep in the field, waving to them. Pier waved back without turning.

They reached the narrow footpath along the ditch, mounted and pedalled away in single file. For a long time, they rode in silence, as though distance were needed before they could bear to speak. When, at last, they were pedalling on the smooth surface of Corso Stupinigi, the stag on the roof of the royal hunting pavilion bold against the sky behind them, Lena whimpered, "But why didn't they like me?" She was hurt and confused. People always did like her.

"Tilde liked you," Pier said.

"Your *mama* didn't… And your *papá*… And Clot…" She did not complete her sentence. She could not mention the creepy feeling she had had as those two kept ogling her.

"Ach, Lena, it's just their way," Pier said lamely, unable to comfort because he knew Lena was right.

They pedalled along in silence. Lena's hurt lay heavy on Pier, oppressed as he was by his own anger, and by an inchoate sadness compounding the pain of rejection with an amorphous sense of loss. He was angry at his mother, at Rexel, at Signora Agiati. *Why is everybody against Lena?* he thought, angry and hurt.

Some minutes later, desperate to break through Lena's silence, he blurted out, "What about *Feragost?*"

"*Feragost?*" she answered, pedalling, "what about *Feragost?*"

"Us getting married. You have two weeks off for *Feragost.*" *And the big farm works would be over*, he thought, automatically deferring to his mother's farm-cantered time. It had been a mistake taking Lena to the farm now. His ma was always sharper during the big works, when Pa was around: she stiffened

352

against him, and that made her hard on everybody else. He should have waited. But he had blurted out at the Regio that he was getting married in August so he couldn't wait.

"You mean…*this Feragost?*"

"Yeah, why not? You want to, don't you?" he added, suddenly anxious.

"'Course I want to. It's just…" Lena let her sentence die into silence. Pier did not speak again. In the plane trees of the corso, sparrows chirped and fussed; and wallowed swooped about them.

They were now on the edge of town. Clusters of two or three houses began to appear between intervals of farmland, lonely outposts of the city ahead. On the *corso,* traffic began to thicken – occasional motorcars returning from a Sunday outing in the country; wagons bringing the newly harvested hay home to outlying farms before nightfall; bicycles, single, in pairs and in groups; and now and then a motorbike. Borgo Santa Rita, where they were to return Nina's borrowed bike, was only a few minutes away.

Don Marco's advice

Like a stone cast into a pond, Lena's appearance at *La Speranza* caused ripples that reached far and wide into Pier's life in the city. Within two weeks of the visit – just time enough for his mother to pour out her woes to Don Michel, and for Don Michel to write a letter, bike to Volvera to mail it, and for it to travel to Turin – a message from the duomo arrived at the *collegio,* informing Pier that Don Marco wanted to see him right away. That same afternoon, Pier and the duomo's music master sat in the latter's office facing each other across the desk.

"Don Carlo received this letter from San Dalmass' and passed it on to me," Don Marco begun, holding the letter in his hand. "I hear you plan to get married…"

Taken by surprise, Pier's shut down. An angry flush darkened his face. He wasn't ready for another argument. Surely, getting married, and to whom, was his own affair.

"I hear your choice – a FIAT girl, I believe," Don Marco continued, "has distressed your mother quite a bit."

"Why is everybody against her?" Pier broke in. "She is a *good* girl. Why does everyone hate her?"

"I doubt very much that anybody hates her, Pier," Don Marco corrected him. "As for me, it's not who you marry that disturbs me, but that you're thinking of getting married *at this time. And* that you didn't see fit to confide in me."

"I knew you'd try to talk me out of it."

"You're quite right: I think it's a mistake. But *not* because of the girl. I don't know her."

"You've met her, that night, at *La Tampa Lirica."*

Don Marco's chin went up, his lips rounded in sudden enlightenment. "That lovely young girl at Rexel's table!"

"Yes, Lena."

Don Marco said, "She seemed sweet and modest enough. No, Pier, your Lena is not the issue here."

"Well, everybody else is against her. Signora Agiati says that she's a liability because she is too beautiful. She thinks the life I am trying to make for myself won't suit her. And Professor Rexel…" Pier stopped, blushing furiously.

"What did the professor have to say?"

"He told me to keep her as my mistress!"

Don Marco disguised his guffaw as shocked disapproval. *Trust the old lecher,* he thought. Aloud, and with a very straight face, he said, "That piece of advice I urge you to decline." He paused, thinking back to the girl's anxious scanning of *La Tampa*'s crowd. "She did seem quite distressed when the audience detained you," he recalled. "Might she be a bit…possessive? But no, what worries me is that you're thinking of marrying *now.* Are you aware of how that will affect your development, your career?"

At that question, Pier hunkered down in his chair, shut in tight as a clam, a reaction that brought back to Don Marco the Pier of his early days at the duomo. It brought back to his mind the scene last Fall, when Pier felt cornered between the two music masters, the duomo's and the theatre's, his penchant for opera unexpectedly revealed. Now he noticed Pier's scarlet ears, vivid against the straight blond hair. Pier had come a long way in the past year. He had acquired a veneer of poise and grace; but underneath he was still very much a frightened colt at bay. He got up and strolled over to the side table, poured out two glasses of *marsala.*

"I quite see that this is a difficult juncture for you," he said, casually handing Pier a glass, who took it daintily by the stem. "You're in love," Don Marco continued. "At least, I assume you are in love with your Lena?" He waited for Pier's answer.

"Yes," Pier muttered, sulking, "I love her very much."

Don Marco took in the humped form in the chair and wondered just how sure Pier was of that, how much he had been pushed into his absurd stand by the opposition he had encountered. He regrouped and adjusted his approach.

"At difficult junctures," he resumed, strolling about his office, glass in hand, "the important thing is *not to rush*; to take time to consider, to examine the problem from all angles. Have you given some thought to how getting married at this point might change your situation?"

Pier's eyes flew to his, questioning. Don Marco raised his glass to Pier with an encouraging gesture. "Here's to *not* leaping before one looks," he said with a thin smile, taking a sip at his wine. Pier did the same, the morose stiffness still obvious in his neck. Don Marco sat down on the couch between the windows and gestured to Pier to sit down across from him. He set his glass down on the coffee table at his elbow. "You've been at *Sacro Cuore* almost six months now," he continued. "I hear you've done well there. Has it suited you?"

"It's been great!" Pier answered, glad to steer the conversation away from Lena and marriage.

"What's made it great?"

"Oh," Pier gave an overwhelmed shrug, "everything...the classes, time to read, people to talk to about what I'm learning; the library; the choir; working with the boys; learning so much..."

"*My own room,*" he almost said, but was embarrassed to mention it.

Don Marco listened, nodding. He took another sip of wine. "Yes," he said, "Don Luca tells me you took to it all like a duck to water. You're now a valued asset to their music program. And I hear your Italian, too, is improving." Pier blushed, a mixture of pleasure and shame at the implications of the praise. "Oh, yes," Don Marco went on. "And at the Regio... Professor Rexel can't stop bragging about you and Melina Cortesi. His best students in years, he says. And I can see why. And Villa della Rovere... You made us both very proud."

He stopped and sipped, letting the image of Pier's triumphal evening at the countess' recital come to vivid life in the youngster's mind. He waited to see the recollection reflected in Pier's expression before he continued, "Have you considered how all that might change, if you marry now?"

"But why should it change?" Pier protested, setting his glass down on the coffee table. "I'd still do everything I'm doing now," he cried.

"Ah! But would that be possible? You could continue here at the duomo, of course. But I don't know how getting married at this time would be viewed by your Regio sponsors. And you'd have a wife to support."

"Lena's not a problem. She earns her keep."

"Ah, yes," Don Marco said, "at FIAT, like *you* did, until...recently. Have you discussed this with her?"

"Not yet."

"I suggest you do. She needs to understand what marrying now would entail for you. For one thing, where do you plan to live once you're married?"

"Why... I...thought I would continue at *Sacro Cuore.*"

"Your bride can't move in there, it's *a boys'* school."

"No, but I mean... Lena lives with her *mama.*"

"Oh, I see, you mean you'd live together at her mother's?"

"Well, no..."

"Lena doesn't have her own room, perhaps?"

Pier blushed. "I would like stay on at the *collegio* and continue my work, just like now. We could be together..."

"...in your spare time?" Don Marco inserted. "Yes, I see. How would that suit your bride? What if there are children?"

This time, Pier glared at him, scared. He'd given no thought to that obvious possibility.

"You'd have to get a place of your own. That would entail a significant expense." He let that sink in before he continued. "And... I wonder, what do you and Lena speak to each other, *Piemontèis?*"

Pier looked down, crestfallen.

"Yes, of course." The music master let the uncomfortable silence lengthen. "But that's a bit of a problem, isn't it?" he resumed. "Besides, a new wife has a right to expect a bit more from her husband than his spare time. Can you see the problem?"

Pier's chin sank to his chest. Another tense silence followed. Then Don Marco went on, "You're now at a point in your development where it is *critical* for you to stay to the course without distractions. You need to consolidate the gains you've made this past year. Two or three more years at *Sacro Cuore* and you will be able to hold your own in any drawing room. Besides, Professor Rexel needs the next couple of years to establish your name in the opera world."

"A couple of years!" Pier cried.

"It's a long time, I know. But…" he paused, then added, "That might also give your mother a chance to…shall we say come to terms with…a town-bread daughter in law?"

Recognising the sense in the cantor's arguments, Pier retreated further into his shell.

"You think about it," Don Marco concluded. "Today, all I ask of you is that you promise me not to rush into anything."

As Pier did not respond, he pursued, "Will you promise me that much?"

Pier refused to look up.

Don Marco accepted temporary defeat. "All right, then," he said. "Come see me next Thursday, when you've had a chance to think things over. We'll talk more about it then. Three o'clock all right?"

Pier's muddle

Pier ran down the duomo steps in a state of overwrought confusion. He knew he was angry, very angry, and depressed; but he wasn't sure *what* exactly he was angry about. Unlike Professor Rexel and Signora Agiati – unlike his mother, he thought with bitter hurt – Don Marco had not made out that Lena wasn't good enough. Or had he? He certainly was against Pier's marrying, at any rate against his marrying now, but he'd said it was because of his career, not because of Lena. Pier had to admit he had a point: even if the *collegio* allowed him to keep his room, he couldn't bring Lena to live there. And there was Don Marco's remark, early in the interview, "A bit possessive, perhaps…" The thought hovered over Pier like a cloud. Well, perhaps Lena was. She certainly was jealous of his time with Melina. She pouted if he failed to go see her after supper, so his continuing at *Sacro Cuore* after they were married would not sit well with her. She'd expect them to be together all the time. He hadn't thought about those things, but now…

On the tram on his way back to the *collegio,* Pier revisited now another part of his interview with his mentor: Don Marco miffed that Pier hadn't talked to him first… Lena modest and sweet… Don Marco's reaction to the professor's advice. Pier's mind snagged on that point, his anger at Professor Rexel flaring up again – Lena a mistress! And Don Marco's reaction: "That piece of advice I urge you to decline." *He* had seen the absurdity of the suggestion.

"I urge you to decline," Pier repeated out loud, capturing Don Marco's exact tone, the rhythm of his refined Italian. The beginning of a grin quivered on the corners of his lips. That was how he learned, listening and emulating; making what he heard his own. That was how he got into the skin of a character.

"That piece of advice I urge you to decline," he repeated again, vaguely amused. And then it happened, just like it did in rehearsals: having caught the exact tone and rhythm of the words, he also caught the corresponding emotion. The left corner of his mouth twitched up in wry amusement.

The twitch at the corner of his mouth jolted him upright: Don Marco was laughing at him! Pier flushed, angry and hurt. Don Marco had laughed at him! He had trusted the priest, believed that he was looking out for him, and all along the man was laughing in his face!

Angry and confused, Pier felt unable to stand still. He stormed to the tram's exit door, pounded on the stop bell, jumped off the still-moving carriage, jostling the crowd waiting to board the tram. "Watch where you're going, young man!" protested an elderly gentleman, steadying the lady on his arm. The scolding recalled Pier to the present. He stopped, faced the outraged gentleman and sketched an apologetic little bow, before turning on his heels and storming off.

All of a sudden, a thought flared in his mind. "I'm scared!"

The realisation shocked him. The *Sacro Cuore* and his education, his Regio scholarship, his dream of an operatic career – he was risking it all; he stood to lose it all! *That* was why he was so angry, he was afraid he'd lose everything he had fought so hard for. It all could be snatched away from him in an instant if he crossed his sponsors and married against their advice. He thought of his evening at Villa della Rovere, the countess' delight, Melina and her parents, everybody fussing about him. He couldn't lose all that now, when his *real* life was just beginning.

Suddenly, he was angry with Lena. No, not with Lena, he checked himself: he *couldn't* be angry with Lena – he loved her, how could he be angry with her? He was angry with himself *because of* Lena. He so often *was*, angry with himself. And snappy with her. Why did she have to be so…? *Possessive* Don Marco's voice said in his head. Yes, she *was* possessive. And "limited," Signora Agiati had said. "She doesn't have the imagination to follow you," she'd said. Signora Agiati was right.

Suddenly Pier knew what he had refused to admit to himself. He got angry with others because he did not want to admit the real difficulty to himself. How could he be so confused, and so...*critical of Lena* when he loved her so much? The image of Lena now rose up in his mind, Lena in all her loveliness, with her shy, childlike eyes, her charming, playful giggle, her *"ma va là, mi si che sai"* that made light of her own ignorance, dismissing any expectation that she learn better ways; rejecting the invitation to grow.

Then, a counterpoint to that image, another image arose: Melina – Violetta, Carmen – her straight, teasing gaze, her spunky, ironic mouth. Melina, assured, elegant, challenging and accepting life's challenges...

Pier stopped in his tracks. Was he in love with Melina Cortesi? The thought was absurd. He loved *Lena!* And Melina was way out of his league. She belonged to the Turin of *la gente bene,* the proper society. How could he even compare them, Lena and Melina? It was not fair.

Yet that was where his thoughts kept going: Lena and Melina. In frustration, he threw himself down on a bench, seeking relief from the late afternoon sun in the shade of the *corso's* plane trees. Trams sparked their way to and fro; on the centre tarmac, automobiles and trucks rolled by; in the two *controviali,* horse drawn cabs trotted by, plying their trade. On the gravel promenade under the trees, people strolled by in the cool of the shade, nannies pushing strollers, elderly men walking with heads down, hands clasped behind their backs, two middle-aged ladies, arm in arm, a spaniel on the leash.

Pier gazed unseeing at the scene. Lena was...he sought for the right word. She was 'home'. She and her *mama* were 'home'. He was comfortable in the quiet Le Basse kitchen. Oh, it was not what he wanted; it was not where his life was going, but he was comfortable there. And Lena loved him, he was the world to her, she needed him, to guide her, to... His thoughts dissolved like an early summer mist. He knew she loved *him*, he concluded irritably, that was all. Loved him and needed him. Whereas Melina...

He saw himself back in the tailor's workshop, being fitted for his first *frac,* the week before the recital at the contessa's *salon,* Melina, sitting at her ease in the tailor's visitor's chair, long legs crossed like she owned the place, scrutinising Pier's reflection in the three-sided mirror, giving the tailor instructions: "Nip in the waist a bit more, lengthen the sleeves a tad..." She had taken over the whole fitting, and the tailor had acquiesced without argument. No, Melina did not need him. Melina was born to take charge.

In the midst of this confusion of admiration and resentment, a pleasing after-thought sneaked in: she seemed to enjoy his company. He liked her company too, though she often made him uncomfortable. Whenever he was with her, he would often come over all pins and needles, like his skin had suddenly shrunk, when she got too tight for him. It was a tantalising, vaguely unpleasant sensation. On the other hand, he liked that they could talk opera, performing, and stagecraft. And he liked that she made it easy to get into character. She was so good at becoming her part. *That is the secret,* he told himself, *always becoming one's part.*

An afterthought emerged clear in his mind: on stage and off, in one's own life, one had to become the character one needed to be. In Melina's world, he would always *be playing a part.*

But what, he argued with himself, if one wasn't sure *what* one needed to be? What if he didn't know what role he wanted to play? What was his part now, in his own life? Who, what was he supposed to be? He had a different role in each of the worlds he straddled: one thing in Lena's world, another at *Sacro Cuore,* another at *La Speransa,* another at the theatre. "The clown with a thousand masks," he muttered bitterly. But what about a face of his own? Did he even have one?

He stood up and walked on restlessly, vaguely heading toward the *collegio.*

Don Marcello becomes a friend

That evening, waiting for supper, Pier hung back from the clusters of teachers and students gathering in the refectory anteroom, taking refuge in the relative solitude of the cloistered courtyard.

Entering the anteroom, Don Marcello saw him strolling around the central fountain and called out. "A lovely evening to be outside." He had been watching Pier for some time from an upstairs window, had seen him pace restlessly about, avoiding contact. Pier did not answer his greeting but stopped and waited for Don Marcello to join him. Over the two quarters of close work together in class and at choir practice, the young Jesuit had found in Pier a startled curiosity, an eagerness, a kind of hunger to learn, almost, that he found endearing, in fact, exciting. As a result, a degree of cautious intimacy had grown between the two young men, with, on Don Marcello's part, a stirring of affection for this unusual master's assistant. Recently, Pier's increasing up-tightness had not escaped him, and this evening, watching him pace restlessly in the courtyard below, he had felt an irresistible impulse to go to him.

"Too nice an evening to waste it indoors," Don Marcello said, stopping by Pier. "How about a stroll down the *corso,* after supper?" Just then the refectory bell rang for supper and the two young men walked in side by side. "Why not?" Pier answered with a shrug. He really should go to see Lena, but he wasn't feeling up to it.

A couple of hours later, they were strolling along Corso Re Umberto in the evening dusk, cassock and suit, shoulder to shoulder, hands clasped behind their backs. under the horse chestnut trees still in bloom. Around them, other strollers enjoyed the early summer evening in pairs, in small groups, or in solitary musings. After several minutes Don Marcello broke the silence.

"One week to go," he said. It was the end of the spring term and next week, right after the exam results were posted, the students would be leaving the *collegio* for their summer holidays. "Any summer plans?" he asked casually. Pier only shook his head. They walked on in silence.

A few minutes later, Don Marcello reflected out loud, "I've really enjoyed your company these past six months. It's made teaching…more rewarding, somehow." His comment was met with silence. "Maybe," the young priest went on in the lengthening pause, "it's having someone close to my own age to work with."

At last Pier mumbled, "It's been good for me, too."

They lapsed into silence. Ahead of them, the monumental fountain of Piazza Solferino splashed and twinkled in its night lighting. In the deepening dusk, Don Marcello steered their walk towards a bench in the deeper shadow under a horse-chestnuts tree. He sat down at one end, silently inviting Pier to join him. Another long silence. Then Don Marcello said quietly, "You've seemed…somewhat *distrait,* these last few weeks." There was no answer. "Year-end blues?" Don Marcello enquired lightly. A deep sigh reached him from the shadows next to him. "Something troubling you?" he asked. Persistent silence. After a while he added, "I don't want to pry, but…at times talking can help one…see things more clearly." Next to him Pier moaned.

"I sure could use seeing things clearly."

"What's the problem?"

"Ach!" Pier groaned with deep self-disgust. "I'm so muddled…!"

"Oh? What about?"

"I'm a coward," Pier groaned, falling back into silence.

Don Marcello waited. After a while, he spoke softly, as though to himself. "Heavy burden indeed," he said. "But…could it be that you're a bit hard on yourself? It might help you if you talked about it."

Pier sat on, silent, for a long time. Don Marcello was pondering how to reach him, when Pier's strangled voice wailed out: "I should be with Lena now!"

"Lena?" Don Marcello echoed, surprised. "A girlfriend?" He sensed rather then saw the nod next to him and scoured his mind for any reference to a Lena. He failed to find any. Pier had never mentioned girls to him. In fact, he had never spoken of any aspect of his life beyond the *collegio,* the duomo and the Regio. Then he recalled the lovely, unhappy-looking young girl at Professor Rexel's table on the night of Pier's and Melina Cortesi appearance at *La Tampa Lirica.* He remembered the girl dancing with the professor, laughing, full of life. "Is Lena," he asked, "the girl at Rexel's table at *La Tampa Lirica*?" Again, he felt the sullen nod on the bench next to him. "Are you…having problems with her?"

"Everybody's against her!" Pier moaned.

Don Marcello heard the tremor of tears in the pained words. "Surely not! Such a lovely young woman! What makes you think so?"

Pier now leaned forward, elbows on his knees, head buried in his hands, deep in shame. Don Marcello sensed that he was silently crying. The dam had broken, the flood could now pour out, relieve the pent-up pain. He waited.

Moments later, Pier's anger and grief began to gush forth, unstoppable: the opposition, the objections, his mother's hostility, his own confusion, loving Lena and being angry with her all the time. And *Melina…* Her disturbing attraction, and she was way out of reach. And Rexel hinting, prodding, and pushing him toward her. "The thing is," he concluded, "I'm all muddled up. I'm not sure of anything anymore. I don't know what I want… I don't know what I *feel*, or what I *should* want. And there is so much at stake…" His voice broke on a sob he quickly suppressed before adding, "…all my dreams…"

"You have every right to dream," Don Marcello encouraged him softly in the night.

"But Melina…" Pier wailed, and stopped, his voice trembling.

In the silence that followed, Pier heard a deep sigh next to him. "You might assume," said Don Marcello's disembodied voice, very soft in the dark, "that because I'm a priest I can't understand, but *I do…* Only too well. Taking orders does not stop one being a man. Doubt, confusion, they can plague anyone."

There was a long silence. Face still hidden behind clasped hands, Pier glanced sideways at the shadowy figure next to him, hoping and dreading that Don Marcello really *did* understand, wanting the voice to go on, but unable to ask. Then the voice, barely audible, spoke again, "When we first met, last January, I told you that this is my first teaching post, that I only started at *Sacro Cuore* last fall. That is true, but... I actually finished my seminary training five years ago. I just couldn't decide what I wanted to do. Celibacy doesn't come easy to a young man. I won't bother you with details, but yes, it has been a struggle. And yes, there were girls, *two* girls, in fact. At times I even doubted the very things I love – music, philosophy, literature, the life of the mind... I doubted whether any of it made any sense at all."

"So...how?" Pier asked almost inaudibly. It was Don Marcello's turn to sign in the dark.

"Doubt, confusion... They make cowards of us all," he said slowly. "It's the paradox of moral courage..." Pier listened, breathlessly. "...The problem of how to choose under conditions of uncertainty." Pier frowned, not understanding, but needing to hear more. But the silence grew longer.

"I don't understand," he pleaded at last.

"It comes down to one's courage to make a choice," Don Marcello seemed to be talking to himself. "That sounds so simple, doesn't it? But it can be very hard. One can be pulled every which way. Deep-rooted beliefs, family expectations, religious teachings, one's own flesh, one's loves, one's dreams – they can all be at odds with one another." He dropped into silence again, and Pier frowned, more confused than ever.

"What moral courage comes down to," the voice next to him resumed, "is...well, it's the refusal to retreat before that confusion, to be paralysed by it. It comes down to refusing to *not choose*...out of fear of choosing wrong. You say you are muddled... In difficult situations, *we all* long for someone or *something* to tell us what the right thing to do is. We tell ourselves that, if only we knew that, *then* we could choose, no matter how hard, and *then* we could act."

Pier felt the other turn eagerly toward him. "But that's too easy," Don Marcello's voice hissed in the dark, "that's black and white mentality, reality is a symphony of greys." He now spoke with great intensity, "Situations can be wildly complex. In the midst of a storm of emotions, when faced with conflicting claims, with the claims of one' own dreams...and...and *desires*, the best of moral codes can't tell us what the right choice is..." He drifted into silence with a heavy sigh. After some thought he resumed, "Certainty, *clarity* is what we all crave. But *that* is something we all have to wrestle toward, each in our own lonely way."

Pier sat, mute on their dark bench, struggling to make sense of the other's words, sensing the pain behind them, wanting to comfort his friend, and wrestling to connect those confusing words to his own present dilemmas.

Then, suddenly, a fragment of his own thought hit him: *His friend.*

The unfamiliar notion startled him, grabbed him by the throat, chocked him with emotion. He sat up on the bench, his eyes scouring the vague paleness next to him, the Jesuit's face. *My friend,* he thought, surprised, struggling to comprehend the notion. He sensed the other's nod in the dark next to him.

"That's right," Don Marcello said softly, almost thinking out loud, "it comes down to the courage to live with our own uncertainties, to survive them, and do our best with them. When we do and survive it, clarity *may*...one day...come...when we've learned to trust ourselves. It comes *from inside,* you see?"

The quiet voice stopped, and they sat next to each other in companionable silence. After some time, Pier leaned forward again, calmer now, forearms on his knees, absently picking at cuticles he could feel but not see. "So," he said after a while, "Lena...and ...Melina..."

"Melina Cortesi," Don Marcello said thoughtfully, "is...an intensely sensuous woman. Very sexy. It's not surprising she stirs your senses. I feel her attraction as well."

Pier sat up and searched the dark for his friend's face. "That's right," Don Marcello gave a crooked grin, "of course I do. I am celibate now, but still a man! One chooses not to act upon the attraction, that's all."

Pier pondered a long time, then admitted, "It's more than just her attraction... She's so...well, so different. She's...oh, I can't put it into words. She's like...a creature from another world, one I barely dreamed existed before I met her. A world I could only look in on from the outside. When I'm with her I feel like I...you know, like *I belong!*"

"It's your dream world," Don Marcello said very gently, nodding understanding. He sensed rather than saw the nod next to him. He shook his head. "But don't kid yourself," he said, "society, is a very *real* world, make not any mistake about that. For all its polish, it can be ruthless, brutal."

Pier listened, pondering, for a while, then spoke again, starting from where his own train of thought had taken him. "She's invited me to join her for the summer; you know, at her family's places on the Riviera and in the Alps. We have to keep rehearsing for October, you see, and next week she goes off for the summer with her family. It would make sense for me to join her, so she doesn't have to spend hours on the road every week, going back and forth for our practice. But I couldn't accept. Because of Lena. But now I think it's…because I'm *scared* of her." Then he added, "And Lena would mind a lot."

"Ah yes, Lena," Don Marcello mused. "She's very beautiful. That night, seeing her dancing… I had a fleeting image of her as a young Venus newly risen from the sea." He kept the rest of his image to himself: the young Venus was dancing with a satyr. "So very lovely and fresh. Innocent as a child…"

"She *is* very innocent," Pier agreed, shutting out the image of Rexel dancing with her. "And she loves me so much,"

"And you?"

"Oh, I love her, too. A lot. I want to marry her. But…you see, I…well, I keep getting angry with her. She's so… My recital at Villa della Rovere, she just wouldn't come to it. She says she feels out of place in places like that, and that worries me."

Again, he fell silent, thinking. When he resumed, he spoke bitterly, "Signora Agiati says she is like a young frog that wants to bask in the sun but doesn't want to leave her home pond."

"And *you* long for wider waters."

Pier nodded. "If I can."

"And Melina beckons?"

"Oh, no," Pier sat back decisively. "Melina," he said, "well, I like her a lot…she sets me on fire. But, well…she scares me. I feel she'd just devour me."

"On stage, you two make a dynamite couple. That chemistry is irresistible."

Pier smiled, wistfully. "A stage couple, yes…but in everyday life?"

There was another pause before Pier went on: "One of the things that anger me about Lena is that she always talks about '*gent coma noi*', you know, people like us. She means…" Pier searched for a way to put her meaning into words. "It's like, well,,, If her 'people like us' go to the opera, they go up to the third gallery. I am happy watching opera from anywhere, but I also want to join in for the champagne party afterwards."

He stopped, nursing his grievance. Then, after a thoughtful pause, he sighed and said: "I know what she means. *I* often think of that other world, the world of Melina Cortesi, as *cola gent lì* – the rich and cultured people who send their children to *Sacro Cuore*. The kind of people who sit in boxes at the opera seem like, well, a different species. I can *see* the difference between them and our kind of people – I mean…people who have to work hard to make a living, but I *admire* their difference, I *long* to be like them. I feel that, in their atmosphere, I could…well, really live, s*oar!"* He stopped, as though enjoying that imaginary flight. After a while, he admitted, "I only hate them, when they shut me out, when I feel I can't join them. Oh, I want…I so want…"

"You want to join that kind of people."

"And why not!" Pier challenged fervently. "If I can!"

"Well, my dear friend, you have every right to dream. And your voice gives you a fair chance. But to succeed, to turn your dream into reality, you must make the most of every opportunity that comes your way. And when it comes to marriage, *it is wise* to consider that aspect. *And* it is important to consider whether the person one wants to marry can be comfortable in the kind of life one wants to live, the life one is working to make for oneself. Anything else is…well, it's romantic self-delusion. It can only make for disaster."

"But Lena and I…we've been together for over a year. I owe her…"

"You don't owe her to be miserable. You'd only make her miserable, too."

In the deep shadow under their tree, Don Marcello sensed Pier's hand rising to his mouth, teeth gnawing at nails.

"Are you sure," he asked gently, "that you…don't…want to marry Lena for…well, for safety's sake?"

Pier stopped gnawing and stared at his friend. He caught Don Marcello's hands gesturing 'quotation marks' in the dark. Don Marcello explained: "You know, labelled '*reserved*'? Marriage, like holy orders, says 'hands off' loud and clear. 'Not available'. Is that what you need Lena for, a wife to protect you? But protect you from what, Pier? From Melina? That won't work, you know, not if the temptation is coming from within you."

They sat on companionably on the bench. From the tree canopy came the cry of a nightjar. In the centre of its gravelled expanse, the fountain plashed and murmured. The flow of strollers had thinned. The traffic noise around the ring of trees had dwindled to an intermittent swish of tires on tarmac, the clip-clop of hoofs from an occasional horse-drawn cab, the clatter of a late tram on its iron rails. From somewhere beyond the trees a church bell tolled eleven times.

On the bench, Pier stretched out his legs with a groan of release.

"Shouldn't we be heading back?" he said, his voice now calm. Don Marcello got up and stretched tall.

"Yes, we'd better," he agreed. Pier rose as well and, side by side, the two young men strolled their leisurely way back to the *collegio*.

Chapter Sixteen

...Still by himself abused or disabused...
Alexander Pope

Pier's discovery

Pier was startled awake in the pre-dawn gloom by an unfamiliar thought: *he had friends.* He found himself batting his eyes in disbelief. Friends. Like last night, in the shadow of the trees, the unfamiliar notion again choked him with emotion and he almost cried out. The clanking of an early tram reached him from the streets outside. It calmed him down. "I have *friends*," he repeated, this time out loud with a curious stirring of excitement.

Moments later, a second thought coalesced in his mind: he must have had friends for quite some time now. He just hadn't known it. Still sleep-fuzzy, his mind fell to cataloguing the friends he had not known he had. Signora Agiati. His mind lingered on her many kindnesses, from that very first cup of hot chocolate in the Via Verdi café, the day of his black despair because the opera season was coming to an end. Lying in his comfortable bed in the early morning light, he found himself smiling at that despair. And then there were her coaching sessions, all through last summer, and her introducing him to Professor Rexel, the audition...

His mind now ranged further afield. Before Signora Agiati, he considered, there had been Don Marco. Pier counted the ways in which the duomo's music master had befriended him. He had taken him under his wing, paved his way to where he was now. He'd got him out from under his pa's thumb; got him out of FIAT, found him this place at *Sacro Cuore.*

He snuggled deeper into his comfortable bed. Yes, he *had* had friends all along. At *Santa Rita's* as well: Don Carlo had made sure he got to the duomo.

Again, Pier smiled, thinking of his first ride into the heart of Turin, his discovery of *Via Roma*, the theatre-going party drinking champagne in the *Caval 'd Bronz* windows, their cab ride that had led to his discovery of the Regio.

And before them, Pier's catalogue continued, at San Dalmass' there had been Don Michel. Dear Don Michel: he, too, had been a good friend. He, too, had taken him under his wing, looked out for his wellbeing. Pier thought back to the years of Thursday afternoons spent with the old priest in the bone-bare church, the way the old parson had nurtured his child's voice into a fitting vehicle for Gregorian chants.

Unexpectedly, Pier found his eyes welling with tears, a tide of sudden, painful affection for the old priest in his rusty old cassock, its front spangled with crumbs when they sat together after practice, eating bread and nuts. Yes, Pier thought, dear old Don Michel. He had fed him faithfully after every session, before sending him home across the fields, making sure he got enough to eat.

Yes, he thought, *affection.* The word surprised him: until now he had not known that feeling, had not known that he loved the old man. His mind went back to his visits to *La Speransa:* winter before last, when he'd gone to tell his mother that he was to sing at the duomo; and last Advent, when he'd told her about *Sacro Cuore* and the Regio. He sighed, still oppressed by his mother's leery disapproval. It was so hard to love anyone or anything at *La Speranza.* But afterwards he had gone to see Don Michel and *he* had been thrilled at his news, revelled in Pier's success. *He* had cheered him on. Pier saw it all again in his mind's eye, his shabby old form framed in the rear window of Don Marco's departing car, frantically waving a last goodbye from the steps of his poor church. The recollection softened Pier's face. But then that other figure had appeared behind Don Michel. His pa, lurching down the steps of the tavern across the square from the church. Pier sighed. At *La Speransa* everything was tainted, caused alarm, disapproval, suspicion, anger, even the duomo's automobile. There was no pleasing his ma. Her recurring motifs rippled through his mind now, stirring up bitterness: *Òmmi pòvra dòna... Work of the devil... Den of sin.*

Pier dragged his mind away from these painful thoughts, turned it to the fascination the theatre held for him. Soon he was back in Don Marco's office, the afternoon he'd walked in and found Professor Rexel there – the duomo and the theatre masters in the same room! He had had the fright of his life. He smiled, remembering his shock, thinking his cheating had been found out. He'd expected the wrath of God to fall upon him right there and then!

His smile lingered. But there was sadness in that smile as well. *The bitter pain of ignorance,* he thought. All that fear, all that guilt, all that sneaking about, when he'd done nothing wrong. And then he'd discovered that *Don Marco loved opera* as well! That the priest and the Herr Professor worked together to ensure that he, Pier, would get his chance.

Abruptly, Rexel's insult to Lena erupted in his mind – "If you can't give her up, keep her as your mistress." A rush of hot anger crushed any stirrings of affection for the Teutonic brute. The heat of outrage spread up Pier's face, the top of his ears burned: Lena a mistress! He *loved* her. She was the first person who had ever made him feel loved. She and her *mama*. He thought of the three of them together in the warm Le Basse kitchen, reading; of the quiet comfort he had found there. Pier's resentment against the professor flared hotter.

And yet, and yet… Pier struggled with his conflicting emotions: Rexel, too, had gone out of his way to make things possible for Pier. Melina had helped him see that.

Melina… Pier squirmed, threw his sheet aside and sat up. What about Melina? What did he feel for *her*? Suddenly restless, he jumped out of bed and went to perch on the sill of the open window, seeking the solace of the cool morning air. In the courtyard below, the small fountain splashed, serene, birds chirped under the eaves, swooped down to drink and bathe in the fountain's spray.

Melina was a friend. That much he was sure of. But there was a lot more than that. Last night, Don Marcello had helped him come to terms with those other feelings. Now he had to figure out how to deal with those feelings, decide what to choose, what to do.

That evening stroll with Don Marcello had led Pier to realise that he had supportive friends, but hadn't dispelled Pier's muddle. It did, however, deprive it of its paralysing effects. That morning, getting ready for the day, Pier found himself pondering his recent urgency to marry Lena by summer's end. He now recognised that it had been a panic reaction to feeling attracted to Melina. He reviewed the many practical reasons Don Marco had pointed out not to rush into marriage, not least among them his chance of an education at *Sacro Cuore* and his Regio scholarship. He had to take care not to antagonise his sponsors by dismissing their advice. They were his friends.

This last thought stopped him. He struggled to realise the meaning of that key word, *friends*. He felt the *magic* in it. Discovering he had a friend, no, that he had *friends,* had changed everything. It had transformed his world from malevolent to benign. Or at least…manageable – *à la mésure de l'homme."*

Quiet voices went by outside his door and once again he found himself smiling. *Friends*. He lingered on the word, savouring the unfamiliar notion: he had friends.

His mind returned to the moment of discovery, last night in Piazza Solferino – Don Marcello's presence on the bench next to him, sensed rather than seen in the shadow of the horse chestnut that sheltered them from the lights of the fountain in the square's centre. He now looked forward to his meeting with Don Marco the following Thursday: he would sort things out with him, tell him he had reconsidered, and recognised it was best to postpone the wedding until his career was a bit more established. As to *Herr Rexel...* He would say the same thing to him, despite his hurt at the professor's insult to Lena. And tonight, he would go to Lena and work out with her when they could reasonably get married.

The little phrase, *Herr Rexel,* Melina's way of addressing the professor, had snuck into his mind unbid. It brought a smile to Pier's face: it was all right now; Melina was his friend, his colleague. It was up to him to manage their relationship.

That evening Pier waited for Lena by the FIAT gate. "Have you given any thought to our getting married?" he asked once they were clear of the noisy crowd.

"I have…" she said tentatively, afraid of offending him. "But…well, *Feragost...* I'm not ready. I mean, my hope-chest isn't complete yet*.*"

"I'm not marrying you for your hope-chest," Pier rebutted, before he could take himself in hand. "But…if you'd rather wait, well, that would probably be better. It'll be a couple of years before I can support us."

"Oh, that doesn't matter," she said, "I have a good job."

"I know, but…" He stopped: he hadn't come here to argue. "So," he started again, "when do you think we should do it?"

"I don't know, a year, two, maybe?" Lena said tentatively. "Is that too long?"

"It sounds like forever, but…To be practical, that sounds just about right. By then. I'll have next year's tour behind me, a better chance at making a living from my singing. Meantime, I'd like to know that we are properly engaged."

"Why, aren't we?" she asked.

Pier shrugged. "I haven't given you a ring yet."

"A ring!" Lena cried, "I'd like that," she said, and suddenly, she giggled: "I've been dying to say *'mè fiancé'*," she giggled, "like in the movies, not just *mè moros*." (My fiancé, not just my boyfriend.)

"Maybe I can get you one by the fall," he said tentatively, "except…first I have to buy a *frac* for the concert tour."

"That must come first," Lena agreed.

"And," Pier started hesitantly, then paused before rattling off, "I'll have to be gone for weeks at a time."

"I know," Lena nodded, accepting. "You'll be…touring the provinces…"

"No, before that. The next few months there'll be a lot of rehearsing." He glanced at her, checking her reaction before slurring out, "with la Cortesi."

Lena's eyes dropped to her hands. After a brief silence, Pier continued, "May have to be away some of the time. Next month, she goes in *villeggiatura* with her family, but we have to keep rehearsing. So, some of the time, I will have to go to them, otherwise she'll have to do all the going back and forth."

"I know," Lena nodded, head still down, "it wouldn't be fair. You have to do your share. I won't be silly anymore, I promise."

"Even if I have to go be gone for… weeks at a time?"

"Why, where are they going?"

"To the seaside for the next five weeks, and then to the mountains." Lena stared at her hands for some moments. Pier watched her in anxious silence. He knew she was thinking *cola gent lì*. He felt sad for her.

"So how are you going to practice?" Lena asked in a small voice.

"They've asked me to stay with them for part of the time, so Melina isn't on the road too much. Her mother is afraid she'll have a wreck on those mountain roads."

"And…are you thinking of going?" Lena asked, trying not to sound jealous.

"To be fair," Pier said, "I have to split the travelling with her. We have to practice at least four times a week."

There was a long, uncomfortable silence, then Lena asked. "But how will *you* get there?"

"There's a train…"

"But that'll cost a lot, won't it?"

"Yes, the train is expensive."

"And you'd sleep?"

"At her parents' house."

Another stiff silence followed, then Lena sighed, crestfallen and murmured, "But…what about us, if you go?"

"That won't change anything: Melina knows we are engaged."

"She does!"

"Yes of course. They all know about us."

"Well then…" she sighed, resigned, and patted the hand holding hers. "But I'll miss you ever so much."

Pier heaved a sigh of relief. "And I'll miss you. I will write to you, every day. You can read my hand quite well now."

"Yes, I can," she said, pleased with herself, "can't I? Every day," she added eagerly.

"Everyday. I'll write you what I've done each day, then I'll mail it once a week, so you get it for Sunday."

"For Saturday. There's no post on Sunday."

Pier laughed, "For Saturday, then."

"You will? And you'll tell me all about the sea and the mountains?"

"And about our practice, and all the people I meet there. Do you think you could put up with that?"

"For your sake, my treasure, I can put up with anything. You are going because it's necessary to make our dream come true, so go! Become famous. Then we'll get married, and be together forever and ever."

Attempted rape

All day an oppressive heat hung over Turin, trapped under a heavy blanket of sooty haze that hid the towering Alps at the city's northern and western horizons. By early afternoon, muffled thunder began to rumble above the low, sulphurous ceiling, intimating violent storms above. Then, a couple of hours ago, a sudden flash of lightening rent the sky, instantly followed by a crash of thunder that stunned the Lingotto. Daylight dimmed to an untimely dusk. Inside the buildings, the familiar noises of living and working were drowned by the racket of a torrential downpour. Hail battered windows and roofs.

At FIAT, the six o'clock whistle blew, bringing the workday to an end, triggering the daily exodus. An eerie light hung in a sky, darker than a winter dusk. Then, suddenly, a ray of sun split the lurid, roiling clouds to reveal a narrow wedge of blue. Outside the gates, Lena headed homeward at a run, bare feet in open-toed summer clogs skipping along the glistening sidewalk to avoid the fast rivulets that gushed from perimeter wall to curb, and then pall-mall into the gutter along the tram tracks. Still running, she reached Strada delle Basse, now a turbulent stream, and broke into the kitchen with a shrug, kicking her wet clogs against the wall.

"Oh, good," Gioana greeted her, stepping over from the stove for the usual welcome home kiss, "you made it home dry." She leaned out the door to glance up at the sky. "Do you think it might still hold off a while? We're quite out of salt. Meant to get it on my way home but went and forgot."

Lena stepped back into her clogs and grabbed her reticule from its peg in the wall. "I'll just run out and get it," she said.

"Take the umbrella," Gioana urged. "And," she added, "you might as well get a kilo of coarse salt and a litre of vinegar. We're running low on those as well. Here," she dropped some coins into Lena's hand. Lena stepped out and glanced at the sky: the sun was gone, a tumult of wind-driven clouds scuttled overhead, what little daylight was left hung low and sulphurous, the pungent smell of cold rain on hot dust and tarmac still strong. And there was a new nip to the air.

She ran across the yard, her reticule flapping from her wrist in the tearing wind, and leapt across the headlong torrent the alley had become. Courtyards and streets were deserted, the usual end-of-day loungers chased indoors by the storm.

A five-minute run saw her at the tobacconist, right before the cinema. Another two minutes, and she was out again, her half kilo pack of fine salt and kilo of coarse salt heavy in her reticule. She cast a quick glance at the sky: the rain was still holding off. No need to run. Around the corner, she stopped at the grocer for the vinegar.

Across the street, Guido stood inside the corner café, glaring out over the café's half-curtains, a cognac glass in a white-knuckled hand. The last few weeks had been hell. Cristina Follati's father, the rich city girl he needed to foster his ambitions, had backed him into a corner, demanding that Guido make good on the promised export deal with his father's winery. That was a promise Guido had known he would never keep, as he had no influence on his father's affairs. Frustrated, Follati had then challenged Guido's other claim – that he was heir to *Fontan-a Freida,* his uncle's extensive vineyards in the Asti hills. The predictable outcome had followed their row: any engagement to Cristina was now out of the question.

And then, this evening had come the other blow. He'd left his FIAT lab for a long-overdue visit to his office at the Lingotto *Fascio,* where he was nominally still head of the neighbourhood youth programs. He hadn't actually put in any time there in several months, not since his appointment to the Membership Committee of Borgo San Paolo, a far more influential, middleclass neighbourhood. Today he'd strolled up the stairs of the Lingotto *Fascio* only to find the hallway to his office obstructed by a large, unfamiliar desk. Annoyed, he sidled past it, wondering who'd had the nerve to leave it there, and found his door wide open and, inside his office, two party lackeys busily dumping the contents of his desk into two cartons, open on the floor.

"What's going on here?" he demanded arrogantly, stepping inside.

"Orders," snapped the older lackey, continuing his ransacking.

"Whose orders?" Guido snarled back.

"Mine," barked a harsh voice behind him. Guido swung around to face the challenger. He scowled at the plebeian figure – paunchy, short legs wide apart – blocking the office entrance. What was this nobody doing, swaggering in his office? The man might have risen through the ranks by *services to the party*, but he was a nobody, a middle-aged *operai* without education or social standing.

"What's going on, here?" he snarled, matching the other's aggression, glaring down at the intruder from the height of his five-foot-ten, contempt clearly stamped in his face. "This is *my* desk."

"Wrong!" rebutted the stranger with equal arrogance, "this is *my office* now."

Guido sputtered, "You have *no right* to—"

"I have *every right*," the other barked. "I've taken over this office because *you* haven't been doing your job in months! Now *I'm* the boss here and you'd better toe the line, or I'll report you. The Party demands discipline from the *lower ranks*…" The heavy stress of that *'lower ranks'* made Guido see red.

The dispute had raged for several minutes, edging close to physical violence, the two minions watching it, Guido's papers still in their hands, until Guido had stormed out in impotent rage to irrupt, minutes later, into the corner café in a towering temper, screaming for a double cognac.

And now he stood by the door, glaring out above the café curtains. He could not risk trouble with the party at this stage. He had to play it cool if he wanted to work his way up in its hierarchy, gain the influence he craved. But still…

He ordered a second double cognac and downed it, forcing himself to calm down. Time, he told himself, was on his side. He'd get back at the *old bastard,* but he'd do it in his own good time. He, Guido Delloria, was not one to be trifled with. And he never forgot an insult. His time would come.

He kept glaring out at the wet, wind-blown street. "Another double cognac," he snarled over his shoulder, and the waitress scurried to bring him his drink.

Just then, Guido spotted Lena across the street, trotting towards Via Nizza, reticule flapping behind her in the wind. His eyes narrowed: the fool had forgotten something and was running out to buy it before the storm let loose again. A thought flashed through his mind, *this might be my chance*. He watched her disappear around the corner, slugged back his third double cognac, slammed the empty glass down on the nearest table, and forged out into the wind. The glass door crashed shut behind him, setting the bar glasses tinkling on their shelves.

With a quick glance at the angry sky, Lena turned the corner onto Via Passo Buole. Thunder was again rumbling ominously above the tumbling clouds. If it held off a few minutes more, she'd make it home dry. Her feet were now cold in their soggy, open-toed clogs. She glanced over her shoulder for non-existent traffic before running across the street, then ran close to the walls for some shelter from the tearing wind. As she ran by the last *portone,* a gust of wind blew her hair over her face. Her free hand shot up to brush it back and…struck a hand trying to clamp down onto her mouth. She cried out but was dragged into the dark passageway and knocked to the ground, the weight of a man heavy on her. Terrified, she struggled, kicking and trying to scratch her assailer. A hand now clamped tight onto her mouth, while the other was tearing away at her blouse. Writhing desperately under the weight, she felt the edge of his hand against her teeth, and bit down hard.

"Damn bitch!" her attacker cursed, striking a hard blow to her chin. The covered passageway reeled around her for a moment, then all went black. When she next regained some sense, she felt the man's hands ripping away at her knickers. She wanted to fight, to scream, to run, but could not move under his oppressive weight. She heard her underwear rip and felt a hot, hard touch between her thighs, brutal knees forcing them apart. She screamed just as a flash of lightening split the sky, instantly followed by a vicious clap of thunder. Rough fingers forced her privates apart, fumbling for a thrust. With a groan, she grasped her reticule, still wrapped around her wrist, and swung hard. The vinegar bottle met the man's skull with a sickening thud, the table salt package splitting on impact.

"'*Orca Madòna!*'" the man swore, furious, knocked half-way off Lena, "You foul bitch!"

Lena recognised the voice: the fresh *fieul from* the corner café. The one who'd fixed her shoe at the Niclic fête. She felt him fumble, trying to mount her again. She swung her reticule at his head again, over and over. Now soaked with vinegar, the table-salt package scattered its contents. Salt spread into her attacker's eyes. She heard his strangled curse as he jerked back, instinctively protecting his eyes.

Just then, a male voice echoed down the dark stairwell from the invisible upper regions. Heavy footsteps stomped hither and thither on an upper landing, then started down the stairs. "Oi there!" a man's voice called out, "What's going on down there?" Guido scrambled to his feet, struggling to do up his trousers, and ran. "Oi," the inquisitive voice from above called again, "is anybody there?"

Lena froze. She couldn't let anyone find her like this. She couldn't let anyone know what had happened to her. She suppressed a whimper. Supporting herself against the wall, still clutching her reticule, she dragged herself to knees, then to her feet, holding her breath lest she be heard. Up above, the heavy footsteps on the stairs stomped down a few more steps then stopped. Lena waited, not breathing, until she heard them retreat upstairs again, heard a door slam shut.

Still she waited. Minutes went by. Skirting the wall and clutching her string bag to her chest, she crept, cautiously, to the foot of the stairs, squinted up, listening for footsteps, for noises, for anything that told someone might still be there to see her. There was nothing but silence and fading rumbles of thunder.

She stood up, whimpering now, her free hand trying to smooth her rumpled skirt over her torn knickers. She tucked any ripped, dangling strands up into the elastic of her waistband, hiding any tell-tale sign, trying to look decent. Then she crept to the *portone*'s entrance, still hugging the wall, and peaked out, right then left, in the renewed downpour. In the empty street, she crawled out onto the sidewalk and down the alley towards home.

The clatter and thump at the kitchen door announced Lena's return. A startled Gioana swung around from her stove when the door crashed open against the wall. One look at Lena, and she knew something dreadful had happened. Lena's contorted stance, her torn and dishevelled clothes, brought the worst to Gioana's mind: Lena had been run over, like poor Teresina's daughter. She rushed to help her in, kicking the door shut behind her against the wind-driven rain. "*Mia pòvra cita, còsa a l'é capitate?*" (My poor child, what has happened to you?) One arm around her waist, she supported the distraught Lena in, settled her down on a chair at the set table, stroking and stroking the hand that clutched at hers.

Soaking wet, Lena sat whimpering, shaking, breathless between dry sobs. Gioana reached for the towel warming on the stove's rack, wrapped it around Lena's shoulders. She saw blood running down her arms. "*Mia pòvra cita,*" Giaona coaxed, nursing her cuts, patting the shaking shoulders dry, "did a car hit you? Ach, you're so cold!" She ran to the bedroom for a woollen shawl, wrapped it around Lena. "What happened, *mè tesòr*?" Lena's sobs deepened, but still there were no tears.

Gioana fetched a glass of their sparingly used *Marsala,* held it to Lena's trembling lips, coaxed her to drink. Lena took tiny, obedient sips, barely wetting her lips. Patiently, Gioana held the glass to her mouth, tipping it up by small degrees, to match Lena's ability to absorb the wine. On the floor near the door, under the abandoned reticule, a small cone of fine table salt was growing larger. The rock salt bag lay, spattered with vinegar but undamaged, among shards of green glass.

By and by, Lena's tears began to flow. Gioana sighed with relief: she would be all right. She dared to ask again, "What happened child, tell your mama?"

Lena crumpled forward, hid her face in her folded arms, sobbing.

"Child, child..." Gioana murmured, stroking the rumpled hair, the shaking shoulders, "you are *alive*, that's all that matters! It can't be as bad as all that."

Lena howled louder. Gioana sighed: it was too soon. She must let Lena take her time. She was alive, and that truly *was* all that mattered. She stroked her child's hand, felt it ice cold. Quickly, she fetched the brick they used as a doorstop, put it in the stove to heat it, then ran into the bedroom for yet another shawl, stroking Lena's shoulders as she passed by her, coming and going. Back by the table, she wrapped the now warm brick in a corner of the shawl and slid it under Lena's feet, winding the free bight of the shawl around Lena's legs. Her hand felt a torn bit from Lena's knickers. "Oh, my God," she groaned, aghast, "my poor child!"

For what felt like eternity, Gioana crouched by Lena's chair, rocking her gently, stroking her hair, her cheeks, her shoulders, while Lena sobbed and sobbed. Now and then, Gioana's loving hand tucked a dishevelled bit of hair behind an ear. But at last, Lena lifted her head, then sat up in her chair with a sob. Her eyes landed on Gioana, and she broke out into a desolate wail: "Mama!"

"Yes, my child."

"Don't be mad at me!" she pleaded.

"I'm not, child, I'm not. I'm not mad. But *tell me*: what happened?"

It was slow in coming, but eventually, in broken pieces, the story was told – the walk back with the bits of shopping, the empty streets, the noise of the wind, crossing the street, as usual, one building before the Le Basse corner, the assault, the voice from upstairs, the shame, the fear that she'd been found out.

"Is it a sin, Mama?" Lena asked, when at last all had been told. "Do I have to confess it?"

"No child, it is not *your* sin. The sin and the shame are all his."

"But what if people find out? They'll talk."

"We'll think about that, and we'll decide what to do," Gioana said firmly. She again offered the glass of *marsala*, encouraging her daughter to finish it. Lena took it and sipped at it.

"Am I still a good girl, Mama?" she asked, tremulous.

"My sweet child!" Gioana cried, "Of course! You can bear no blame for what you did not choose."

"But Mama… What about Pier? Will he still want me when he finds out?"

Gioana now grasped the full depth of her daughter's distress: she feared she'd lost her beloved. Reality, people's judgments, had little regard for right and wrong, for choice or coercion. One was a virgin or one was not. And if one was not, one was damaged goods, fair game – a whore.

"He will," she affirmed, "if he is a good man, and we know he is that, don't we? But…" she went on gently, "tell me *exactly* what the man did to you."

Lena's chin dropped to her chest and cleaved there. Gioana waited, stroking her daughter's hand, encouraging. She waited for long, anxious minutes.

"*A l'ha butame doi dij ën t'la pisarina,*" the barely audible answer came at last (He put his fingers in my pipi hole.)

"But…did it hurt you? Did it…make you bleed?"

Lena nodded, chin down, then shook her head. After a moment's silence, her mama repeated the critical question in a near-whisper, "Did he make you bleed?" Lena shook her head, eyes down.

Gioana heaved a sigh of relief. "My darling," she said, reassuring, "he has hurt you, but he has not damaged you. You will be all right. You are still a good girl."

"Am I, Mama? And will Pier still *want* me?"

"There's no reason why he shouldn't."

"But…do I have to tell him, Mama? What will he *do*?"

Gioana thought long and hard, stroking her child. She had seen Pier's alarming black moods. She had seen the fierce flush of anger redden up his neck and face, but she'd never seen him violent. Still, he was a man… Slowly, thoughtfully, she shook her head, "No, child, you don't. We'll not tell him anything. It is better that way. You bare no fault and no shame. You don't have to tell *anybody anything*."

"Not even Don Paolo?" Lena whimpered.

"No, child. You have nothing to confess. We just wait. When you're calmer, we'll decide what's best to do." Lena stretched out her arms for her mama to hold her, and Gioana folded her child in a long, protective embrace.

In the raging storm, Guido ran helter-skelter down Strada delle Basse, to get away from any angry, pursuing crowd: to lose himself in the empty fields beyond the edge of the city. For hours he ran across the fields along verges, covered of trees and shrubs. For the first time since he'd come to Turin from his father's estate in the Astigiano, he was afraid of the city, afraid of people, afraid to be seen. He had committed a crime – at least, what *some* people would condemn as a crime, if ever they stopped laughing at him. He could tolerate the thought of neither the punishment nor the humiliation. So, he ran and hid, deep in the countryside, while the storm raged on throughout the night, lashing the world around him. Eventually, sometime in the depth of night, he came across a decrepit lean-to at the edge of a wood, possibly a hunter's blind, and took refuge inside it, while the rain continued to pelt down on what remained of its reeds roof. Until, from sheer exhaustion, he fell asleep.

He woke up to a brilliant sun, just clearing the eastern hills in a sky as crisp as a new-laundered sheet. It took him a moment to grasp where he was, what he had done, then horror seized him, disbelief contending with shame and guilt, guilt and shame about his failures: he, Guido Delloria, had been driven insane by repeated vicious blows to his life plan, to his image of who he was. He'd been found out, humiliated, expelled, just like he'd been by his own family. Expelled by the Follati, by the boor at the Lingotto *Dopolavoro,* by that stupid bitch, that negligible *operaia* he had stooped to notice, would even have helped, had she but let him… "Small wonder," he growled, grovelling in self-contempt. Small wonder he had lost control, last night, and let himself down.

Now he was hungry. Even more, he was thirsty. And he was deep in the middle of nowhere, in the countryside, in the hated *campagna.* He squared his shoulders and ran his fingers through his hair, trying to restore some scrap of his battered dignity. He brushed off debris of the wet straw he had slept in that still clung to his clothes. He straightened his jacket, stuck his chin up, and looked around: was that a dirt road, down there, beyond those trees? He struck out across the fields towards that faint vestige of civilisation.

By mid-morning, Guido was back at the outskirts of Turin. Still leery, he avoided Lingotto, and entered the city by the Moncalieri bridge, then along the right bank of the Po. Just before the Corso Dante bridge, he came across a café just opening for the day. He downed a cognac, then stayed for some breakfast. Feeling somewhat restored, he ambled slowly across the bridge, absorbed in his own thoughts, drifting to a stop in mid-span. Corso Dante lay just ahead of him, the location of his first FIAT job, that momentous start of his life in Turin, before the company had even acquired its permanent name, when it was just a messy little outfit at the back of someone's workshop. And now known all over the world, the new *stabilimenti* taking up most of Via Nizza, right by the railroad's shunting yards. He glanced over the parapet at the turbulent water roaring along. And his place there, his own work bench in the development lab, the fulfilment of so many boyhood dreams. His gaze drifted absently down-river. Now his *other* dream, to return triumphant to his dismissive family, would never be fulfilled.

He tore his thoughts away from *Colin-a Longa:* he had no taste for the life of a grape-grower, he told himself for the nth time, almost believing it was true, that *that* had been the issue. He stared down at the waters tumbling past under the bridge, swollen by yesterday's storm. In the brilliant sunshine, myriad little diamonds leapt about on the surface of the turbulent current. His eyes drifted downriver to an eight-man crew battling the flood towards the bridge to the rhythmic call of the coach in the bow. He had never made it to one of those prestigious Right Bank clubs. A profound sense of loss hit him below the belt: he had betrayed himself. Fatigue, humiliation, *rage* – last night they'd had the better of him, and he had committed a crime. A *stupid*, humiliating crime against that stupid Lena. All because Cristina Follati had turned him down, because her father had seen through his spurious claims, and had called him on them. Because he *had made* those stupid claims, and laid himself open to exposure and ridicule! There in mid-bridge, in full daylight with a Val Salice tram trundling by, he writhed in an agony of shame and despair. No point carrying on now, *he'd let himself down,* and now he'd be caught, exposed. He laid his hands on the parapet, his eyes on the flood below, knees crouched for the spring. But then his pride rebelled, and he hesitated: but *NOT* at the hand of those fools.

"OI, THERE!" someone cried, then a hand clutched Guido's arm, light but strong. "Lost something?" said a concerned voice. A black cassock, not even a prelate, just a plain priest, hardly out of seminary by the looks of him. Guido smirked at the irony of such humble interference, but he stopped in mid-spring, shook himself, dog-like, pulled himself together, even managed a bitter, crooked grin.

"You might say so," he muttered. Then, as the young priest kept looking at him with an alarmed face, he added, with a few brisk swipes at his coat sleeves as though to brush off some disgusting dirt, "Myself perhaps... But now I'm...found again."

The young priest stared, shook his head, uncomprehending. "That's all right...*Father,"* Guido laughed, stressing that ludicrous 'father'. But then he added, "Really, I'm all right now. Truly. You've done me a good turn." And away he strode the rest of the way across the bridge to the familiar left bank, leaving his Good Samaritan perplexed in mid-bridge.

He *was* alright now. His moment of dread and despair had passed. Now he would take stock of what could still be salvaged, and what he might be able to rebuild from that. As long as nobody knew what had happened, he still had his beloved lab, his appointment on the party's membership committee and his digs in prestigious Borgo San Paolo.

"And Lena," he said out loud, "will still be there. I'll wait for *my right time* to come."

Epilogue

With the success of their tour of the provincial opera houses, Pier and Melina returned to Turin at the end of their first professional year, fully ready for their eagerly awaited début at the Regio, with their trusted warhorse, *La Traviata,* scheduled for the end of April. Professor Rexel had already secured an agent for their second year, and they could look forward to engagements at several major Italian opera houses, the success of their *Carmen* and *La Traviata* in the provinces having been favourably reviewed in the national press.

But, important as that was to both of them, the year's tour and, perhaps even more critical, the few months that had followed his momentous evening walk with Don Marcello, had opened up for Pier a whole new horizon he had never before suspected, let alone hoped for: *he had friends!* So simple and yet so...*dear.* He had friends, and knowing that, had allowed him to discover new depths to his feelings for Melina, once he'd stopped being afraid of her sensuous allure.

The attraction was still very much there, and he knew it. But the months spent together on the road, the days and nights of close work rehearsing and performing, of being lofted, soaring and breathless, on those golden wings of success, the months of exhausted after-performance, *tête-à-tête* in one bedroom or the other, had created between them a new and different kind of intimacy, a much deeper bond of friendship and – yes – of *love*. But, he'd told himself, not the kind of love he'd ever need to blush for before Lena. Or before his mother.

Whenever he was in Turin, during breaks from their provincial tour, Pier again lived at the *collegio,* now no longer a master's assistant, but as a much-fêted young artist-in-residence of whom great things were expected. And there, too, his friendships deepened, his heart expanded in the gentle climate of camaraderie. And after each tour Don Marcello, that unlikely mentor in the art of being human, was there to greet him, to cheer him on, to cherish his friendship, to value their young-males bond, in an utterly unexpected way.

Their second year on the stage brought Pier and Melina no disappointment. Their Italian tour having included Naples' *Teatro San Carlo,* and, toward the end of the season, *La Fenice* in Venice, they were now being groomed for their first European tour, the following year.

Pier particularly cherished their engagement at *La Fenice.* On a brief rest period in Turin before leaving for Venice, he and Don Marcello had discussed the myth of the iconic bird with its myriad reincarnations. On the way to Venice, Pier had whiled away some of the tedious train journey reading about it, and discussing with Melina. Once in Venice, Pier insisted on relaxing between engagements by taking long, moonlight gondola rides with Melina. The first, exciting one took place the night before their first performance. It was later repeated, whenever possible, between rehearsals and the endless promotional engagements scheduled by their agent.

During a particularly intimate one of these rides, Pier had told her about his despair after his first audition with *Herr Rexel.* Gliding silently in the deep night, he had revisited that traumatic event with ironic detachment. Close together on the gondola cushions, they had laughed and cried at his youthful panic, at his Werther-like despair. Then Melina had mentioned the name of the opera house they were then performing at and cried, *"La Fenice,* how very fitting! That's you, my friend, rising from your own ashes!"

Another time, he had spoken to her about moving from his sister's *Lavanderia* in Borgo Santa Rita to the *Collegio Sacro Cuore,* about his breathless excitement on that first day in Don Marcello's class, when, for the first time ever, he'd begun to grasp the vast scope of the world, the culture, he had missed, and she had joked, "From tadpole to Phoenix in two years! Not half bad. In fact, not bad at all!"

"No," Pier had agreed, "not bad at all. But I nearly crashed and burned before I ever got started!"

But despite their success, and despite his growing intimacy with Melina, those two years were not easy ones for Pier. He missed Lena badly. As he had promised, he wrote to her faithfully every week, long letters, a bit added each night, telling her the happenings of each day. In return, each Thursday, he received from her a few scratchy lines, written with obvious effort, in which she did her best to tell him, in the clumsy Italian of the habitual *Piemontèis* speaker, what she and her mama had done that week, repetitive accounts of the narrow circle of their lives, lived between work, home, church and the Cinema Lingotto, each letter ending with worn-out formulas of undying devotion which Pier soon began to find flat and unsatisfying. He did his best to not fault her for the crudeness of her writing, but these letters scared him: was he making a mistake? But how could he back out on Lena now. He loved her, didn't he? His doubts added to the growing urgency he felt to get back to her, to shore up their commitment to each other, to save his love. Meantime, Melina was constantly at his side, vibrant, exciting, a dear friend, a colleague, a partner in a wonderful adventure…and a persistent temptation.

But despite their growing intimacy, Pier chose to stay true to Lena, recalling Don Marcello's words on the night of their walk under the Piazza Solferino horse chestnut trees. He'd said, "It comes down to the courage to live with our uncertainties. The courage to make one's choice. One simply chooses not to act upon the attraction, that's all." Those words had long become a mantra for Pier, a beacon and a guide he called upon whenever temptation became too insistent. So, Pier had choosen: he would stay true to Lena.

Melina, on her part, though at times teasing and mischievous, and despite her strong attraction to Pier, had chosen as well: she'd honour Pier's decision. Her ever-deepening affection for him made her respect his choice to 'go unsullied to his wedding night', as he'd put it. However, she'd struggled not to smile at his quaint expression, which she recognised as a citified echo of his country upbringing. Besides, she'd come to recognise that, after all, she had to agree with her much-worried *mammà*: Pier was a superb artist, a generous stage partner, *and* a beloved and rewarding friend, but he was a very questionable marriage prospect.

For Lena, those two years had truly been hellish ones. She pined for Pier and constantly worried that she would lose him to Melina. However, she carefully kept her anxiety to herself, afraid that her jealousy would scare Pier away. She comforted herself by always wearing his engagement ring, a thin gold band framing a small garnet. She wore it to work as well, despite the risk of damaging it. To some extent, that ring shielded her against undesired male attentions and, more important, it lessened her ever-present anxiety and self-doubt. Pier had given it to her at the end of his provincial tour with Melina, and she still cherished the words with which he had slipped it on her finger, "One day this will be a priceless ruby. But for now…will this do? Small as it is, let it tell you that I'll always love you." For Lena that had been more than enough: the ring declared their engagement to her world. That being the case, she could wait, be it breathlessly, for their separation to come to an end.

And, finally, it had. Pier and Melina had come back at the close of their second opera season tour, excited by the prospect of their European tour the following year, with the prospect of a possible engagement at *La Scala.*

But for Lena the end of the separation from Pier was not as blissful as she had hoped, it was not the end of her anxieties. Pier had changed. He now found it difficult to readjust to the world he'd once shared with Lena. So much had changed for him in the past two years. Even his beloved *Sacro Cuore* now felt limited, constricting, despite his continuing pleasure in the company of Don Marcello and of his other friends there. He now yearned for that *Greater World* he'd recently discovered in working on Gounod's version of the *Faust* myth – a possible project for the following season.

As for Le Basse, that dingy alley of run-down farmhouses, crowded as it was with the city's dregs, now struck him as unbearably squalid. It hurt him to see his Lena still living there – Lena and Gioana. He wanted to take *them both* out of that squalor as soon as possible. But he also doubted that Gioana would ever consent to leave the neighbourhood where all her friends were. And Lena would never leave her *mama.* Every time he broached the subject of marriage she squirmed, both eager and anxious, always pleading for more time.

In the end she had agreed to fix their wedding date – on their old target date, 15th of August, *Ferragosto,* the start of her annual two weeks paid vacation, so she would not lose any part of her earnings.

Pier hated having their wedding date determined by any association with FIAT. He wanted nothing more to do with the place. His singing income was now just about enough to support a wife, but he could well understand her fears: to be jobless and poor meant to be helpless. Pier knew only too well how that felt. So, in the end, he reluctantly accepted her chosen date, privately promising himself that, after the wedding, he would prove to her that they could make hands meet on his earnings alone. Then he would *insist* that Lena left FIAT forever.

So, on the 15th of August, the wedding duly took place at Lena's parish church. It caused quite a stir in working-class Lingotto where wedding parties followed the bride and groom to the church on foot, in their Sunday bests. For, Pier's wedding guests arrived early, in a convoy of three long-nosed motorcars that stopped in front of the modest church, jamming up busy Via Nizza, and holding up three trams.

The next surprise was the flock of black cassocks that solemnly escorted the groom, resplendent in a pale grey suit, a gardenia in his buttonhole, into the church.

Minutes later, a fourth motorcar stopped by the church, and the bride appeared in an ivory *silk suit,* rather than in the expected serviceable frock. Her mother busied herself explaining the anomaly: Lena had chosen to be married in a travelling outfit because the couple was leaving right after the ceremony for a two-week honeymoon on Lago Maggiore.

Gioana's explanation only stirred up more excitement: a two-week honeymoon! And on Lago Maggiore! Nobody went that far, or for that long, on a honeymoon!

Inside the church the wedding continued to disconcert. The guests on the groom's side were in sharp contrast to the guests on the bride's side. On the bride's side, things were as expected, a bevy of local girls in their Sunday outfits, with Cichin-a's daughter as maid of honour.

On the groom's side the pews were sparsely attended, as many of Pier's friends and admirers were still away on *villeggiatura,* and only his close friends and supporters from the *collegio,* the duomo and the theatre had been invited, or had chosen to cut their *ferie* short to attend his wedding. So, the pews sported lots of cassocks, interspersed with smartly tailored dark blue or grey suits and a profusion of silk gowns speaking in refined Italian voices.

What confused the onlookers even more were the two working-class women among the silk robes in the first row, whispering together in *Piemontèis.* The bride's friends hasten to explained: the groom's sister and sister-in-law, the wife of his best man.

*And then…*who d'you think stood up with the groom as his best man? Why, a thick *operaio* in his Sunday clothes! Again, the brides' friends whispered explanations: that was the groom's brother, a mechanic who lived in Niclin. But the groom sang at the duomo and lived in a boys' school run by priests.

The music, too, came as a shock. Instead of the usual harmonium (now shoved out of the way against a side wall) and maybe a soprano singing the *Ave Maria,* there was an ensemble of strings, wood winds, and brass. Mendelssohn's wedding march accompanied the bride up the aisle. Then the glorious sound of a (much reduced) duomo's choir filled the small church in the magical aura of a Palestrina mass.

Outside the church, bride and groom, showered with rose petals as they emerged from the church, were crowded about and cheered by one and all, and soon carried off in a long-nosed car to Porta Nuova for their train to Pallanza, where, it was excitedly rumoured, a countess had put her villa at their disposal, a secluded love nest on a private headland on Lago Maggiore.

But for Pier the day was not so sunny. The chauffeur tapped Pier's arm and whispered they had to leave now to catch their train, and he, still waylaid by well-wishers for a last hand shake, a last kiss to a powdered cheek, was about to join Lena in the car, when, over its roof, he caught sight of a pair of baleful eyes across the street, staring at him with such malice that the hair stiffened on Pier's neck. The intensity of the hate in the stranger's eyes froze Pier's blood in his veins: who was the man? Did he know him, should he recognise him? Such malevolent intensity implied prior acquaintance, but Pier could think of none.

For a second, a gargoyle countenance from another life, from another *world*, long ago, flashed through his mind: the old brute that had tormented him during his brief apprenticeship as a bricklayer's. But no, *this man* was young, thirty, thirty-five, at most. And he was no labourer.

The chauffeur's hand on his back urged Pier into the car and he stepped in, still looking across the street, through the side window, past Lena. Then the car door slammed closed and the car inched forward. Deeply disturbed, Pier asked Lena, "Do you know that guy?"

"What guy?" Lena said, smoothing a wrinkle on her silk skirt.

"That guy, over there," Pier pointed, "across the street." She glanced briefly at the sidewalk across the street, but just then a tram came trundling by.

"I don't see anyone I know," she said, her attention back on her skirt. "Shoot," she added, frowning, "There's a spot on my silk skirt."

Knuckles rapped on the car's windows, well-wishers waved and shouted one last cheer to the new couple as the car gained speed and merged with the traffic for the short run to Porta Nuova.

Once on the train, the happy couple sagged, their rejoicing dissolving into melancholy reflections: no one from *La Speransa* had attended the wedding. The single solace from San Dalmass' on their wedding day had been hand-delivered by Don Carlo – an affectionate, congratulatory, well-wishing letter from dear, old Don Michel.

THE END